RED STONE SECURITY SERIES

BOX SET VOLUME 5

KATIE REUS

Cover Art by Sweet 'N Spicy Designs
Editors: JuliaEdits.com, JRT Editing, AKA Editorial Services
Digital Formatting by Author E.M.S.

Red Stone Security Series Box Set Volume 5/Katie Reus.—1st ed.

ISBN-10: 1-63556-012-8
ISBN-13: 978-1-63556-012-1

For my wonderful, wonderful readers.

PRAISE FOR THE NOVELS OF KATIE REUS

"Sexy military romantic suspense!" —USA Today

"...a wild hot ride for readers. The story grabs you and doesn't let go." —*New York Times* bestselling author, Cynthia Eden

"Has all the right ingredients: a hot couple, evil villains, and a killer action-filled plot. . . . [The] Moon Shifter series is what I call Grade-A entertainment!" —Joyfully Reviewed

"I could not put this book down. . . . Let me be clear that I am not saying that this was a good book *for* a paranormal genre; it was an excellent romance read, *period*." —All About Romance

"Reus strikes just the right balance of steamy sexual tension and nail-biting action....This romantic thriller reliably hits every note that fans of the genre will expect." —*Publishers Weekly*

"Prepare yourself for the start of a great new series! . . . I'm excited about reading more about this great group of characters." —Fresh Fiction

"Wow! This powerful, passionate hero sizzles with sheer deliciousness. I loved every sexy twist of this fun & exhilarating tale. Katie Reus delivers!" —Carolyn Crane, RITA award winning author

"You'll fall in love with Katie's heroes." —*New York Times* bestselling author, Kaylea Cross

"A sexy, well-crafted paranormal romance that succeeds with smart characters and creative world building." —Kirkus Reviews

"*Mating Instinct*'s romance is taut and passionate . . . Katie Reus's newest installment in her Moon Shifter series will leave readers breathless!" —Stephanie Tyler, *New York Times* bestselling author

"Reus has definitely hit a home run with this series. . . . This book has mystery, suspense, and a heart-pounding romance that will leave you wanting more." —Nocturne Romance Reads

"Katie Reus pulls the reader into a story line of second chances, betrayal, and the truth about forgotten lives and hidden pasts."
—The Reading Café

"If you are looking for a really good, new military romance series, pick up *Targeted*! The new Deadly Ops series stands to be a passionate and action-riddled read."
—That's What I'm Talking About

"Sexy suspense at its finest." —Laura Wright, *New York Times* bestselling author of *Branded*

"...a captivating, heated, romantic suspense that will pull you in from the beginning and won't let you go until the very last page."
—Amy, So Many Reads

CONTENTS

LOVE THY ENEMY

PROLOGUE

Six years ago

"Mom!" Dominique called out as she shut the front door of the crappy two-bedroom duplex they lived in behind her. She hated this place, hated that they'd had to move here after her dad's gambling debts had taken everything from them. Thanks to nonexistent insulation, she was pretty sure their new neighbors were dealing drugs too.

Everything was surprisingly quiet now, but it was noon. She figured the jerks next door were probably sleeping off a bender.

Her mom hadn't been answering any of Dominique's texts, though. And that wasn't like her. Not to mention her mom had missed work yesterday, according to the owner of the restaurant she waited tables at. When he hadn't been able to get a hold of her mom, he'd called Dominique, worried. The older man had taken both of them under his wing and had been trying to find them a better place to live.

Since she'd just graduated high school yesterday Dominique had celebrated by staying over at her best friend's house last night instead of coming home. The thought of coming back here had been too depressing and her mom had been okay with it. She'd said she was headed to work and that Dominique should have fun. For the first time in a long time she'd actually seemed happy.

They'd even talked about moving out of this place soon.

Dominique had been saving from her part-time afterschool job and her mom had picked up extra shifts at work so they finally had enough to find somewhere safer.

"Mom!" she called again as she reached the living room. An empty bottle of cheap red wine was on the coffee table along with an empty bottle of pills. Xanax.

Panic punched through her as she raced down the hallway to her mom's room. Her mom had struggled with depression over the last six months. Understandably.

But Dominique had thought things were different now. Her mom had seemed so freaking happy yesterday… She stopped in her tracks outside her mom's open bathroom door.

The water in the tub was…dark. Red. Her mom's head was laid back against the wall, her eyes closed, her face unnaturally gray and one arm draped over the side of the tub. Dried crimson streaks trickled down the outside of the tub and stained the square black and white tiles.

Bile rose in her throat as terror streaked through her. She tried to force her legs to move, but couldn't cross the threshold into the bathroom.

"Mom?" The word just slipped out even though she knew her mom couldn't hear her.

She wasn't stupid. She knew her mom was dead. She wasn't breathing and that blood was from slit wrists. Stepping back, Dominique lost it, all the contents of her breakfast coming back up and onto the floor until she was on her hands and knees, sobbing and dry heaving.

When she eventually found the energy she crawled away from the doorway opening and collapsed back against the wall. With trembling fingers she managed to dial her older cousin Quinn. He'd been a cop and now worked for some big deal security company. She wanted him to help, not some random strangers, and she knew he'd call the police.

Her mom had cut that side of the family out of their lives because she'd been ashamed of how 'far we've fallen,' as she'd put it. It was stupid and Dominique didn't care about any of that right now. She needed help. She needed family.

She needed her mom not to be dead.

When Quinn answered the phone she lost it and started sobbing again.

She'd thought her dad dying was the worst thing that could have happened, but this was way worse. Her mom had *chosen* to take her own life, leaving Dominique all alone in the world.

CHAPTER ONE

Viktor Ivanov could barely hear what his acquaintance was saying as he stared at the tall blonde beauty he'd seen talking to various employees of Red Stone Security. She had a body made for pleasure and right now all he could envision was burying his face between her thighs, listening to the sounds she made as he made her come over and over.

He'd never had such a visceral reaction to anyone before—and he'd been with his share of beautiful women. Lately not so much, as even sex had started to become more of the same. That was what happened, he supposed, since he only employed escorts for sex anyway.

He managed to get in a few grunts of acknowledgement until Abram, his business partner/half-brother, subtly stepped on his foot.

Blinking, he turned back to Shane Hollis—the man who'd been bothering him the last ten minutes with inane conversation about an investment opportunity. The truth was, he didn't give a shit what this guy said. He wasn't going to do business with Hollis. He'd already bought some of the man's restaurants a year ago because Hollis couldn't manage his money. The trust-fund baby liked drugs too much, something Hollis didn't think Viktor knew.

Tonight Viktor had simply been trying to be civil because that's what normal people did. They behaved in certain ways because it was socially acceptable.

He hated it the majority of the time but he was a businessman. It didn't matter that he couldn't stand most people. He could put on an act. Most of the time anyway.

Tonight he couldn't stop staring at the curvy woman with legs that seemed to go on for miles. He wondered if she worked for Red Stone. Or maybe she was just friendly with the wives of the brothers who ran the company because he'd seen her talking to Elizabeth Martinez Caldwell a lot. Lizzy, as her friends called her, came from a very wealthy, influential family and she'd married one of the Caldwell brothers a couple years ago. They'd just had a kid not long ago too, something he remembered seeing in his files—because he kept files on anyone in the city who was important.

"She is not for you," Abram murmured next to him.

He blinked and realized he'd been staring again and that he and Abram were alone once more. Hollis must have left, thank fuck. If Viktor hadn't just invested in a new restaurant—that had a big display here tonight—he wouldn't even be here at the Celebration of Chefs. "Who?"

"Don't pretend. You and half the men here tonight are watching her. She works for Red Stone, I hear. She's not for you." Abram shook his head. "That kind of woman...she wouldn't look twice at men like us."

Viktor just grunted, dismissing his brother's words. The owners of Red Stone were fucking Boy Scouts and the people they hired were the same. That didn't mean he couldn't *speak* to the woman. Talking was harmless.

Mesmerized, he drank in the sweet lines of her body as she waved at a friend and said goodbye to the people she was talking to. When he saw her headed to speak to a couple he knew—the man, anyway—he straightened.

In her heels she was over six feet tall, a virtual goddess. Most women with that much height would choose to wear shorter heels, but she clearly owned who she was. He could see it in every confident step she took. Those curves were enough to make a man want to lock a woman down for a marathon of sex. And a woman who looked like that—he didn't think any sane man would want to let her go.

If she truly worked for Red Stone, it was...annoying. Maybe she was a former spook like the founder and one of his sons. She was young though, under thirty. Maybe even closer to twenty-five. It was difficult to tell.

When Rhys Maxwell, one of the people she'd been talking to, broke away from her and another woman, Viktor headed in Rhys's direction. He stopped next to the British businessman at a display of champagne glasses.

"Maxwell," he murmured, nodding politely.

The other man smiled, nodded. "Ivanov. Surprised you're here. Thought you hated stuff like this."

"Just bought a restaurant."

"Ah, that makes sense." Maxwell's gaze turned back to the two women, his interest in the shorter brunette clear. Unfortunately for Maxwell, Viktor was fairly certain the woman didn't plan on sleeping with him. He was good at reading people and her body language screamed she wasn't interested.

"Is that the same woman you brought to the last event?"

Maxwell turned to look at him, his expression turning slightly possessive. "Yes."

"Who is her friend?" The words came out harsher than he'd intended, but he wanted to know.

Maxwell blinked, seemed to relax at the question. "Ah, one of Raegan's friends. They work together." He tilted his head in their direction. "I'll introduce you."

A burst of anticipation hummed through him as they headed over, but as they started walking, the blonde darted away and into the crowd, moving with clear purpose. He was surprised by the disappointment that slid through his veins.

As they reached the brunette, he said, "Who is your friend?" The question came out demanding and he had to remind himself about those stupid social niceties, to act normal.

Maxwell cleared his throat, looked slightly annoyed at him. "Ah, Viktor, this is Raegan. She works for Red Stone Security. I believe you have some acquaintances in common."

He turned to look fully at the woman. She had an innocent quality to her and he could see he frightened her. Or at least made her nervous. He did that a lot to people without meaning to. It was his size. He was six foot five and big all over. He hid most of his tattoos, but some still peeked out and he couldn't do anything about the ones on the backs of his hands. Not that he gave a shit what people thought of him. Hell, most of the time he used his size and appearance to his advantage, especially in business. But he didn't want to frighten random women.

"It's nice to meet you." He smiled politely, held out a hand and was careful to shake her smaller hand gently.

"It's nice to meet you too." There was a wariness in her gaze as she eyed him before she dropped his hand and turned to her date. "Will you give me a few minutes?" she murmured to Maxwell.

Viktor's business acquaintance gave her a soft smile. "Of course."

Once she'd disappeared into the crowd as well, he turned back to Maxwell. "She doesn't seem like your type." Much too innocent and soft. And if the rumors were true, Maxwell had a darker side to him, liked rougher sex.

"She's just a friend," Maxwell said through gritted teeth.

Ah, so she was definitely not sleeping with him.

"She's Keith Caldwell's niece," Maxwell added.

Well that was interesting. He made a note to find out more about her. Anyone related to the Caldwells would be important enough to keep on his radar. Especially since Harrison Caldwell owed Viktor a favor. One he'd been sitting on for many years. Frowning, he wondered if she was the woman Porter Caldwell had contacted him about—the one who'd been drugged at one of Viktor's clubs. He dismissed the thought for now. He'd see when he reviewed the video footage.

"Who is the blonde she was talking to?" There was no point in pretending he didn't want to know. Not when he was certain Maxwell had figured out the only reason he'd approached the Brit was for an introduction. Even if they had mutual acquaintances, they weren't friends and didn't move in the same social circles.

"Name's Dominique. Works for Red Stone, but I'm not sure what she does." He lifted a shoulder, clearly not interested in the woman.

Which soothed something jagged and unexpected inside Viktor. His half-brother was right—she wasn't for him. He slept with paid escorts for a reason. It kept things simple, uncomplicated. The women he used went through an agency run only by women, and all the escorts worked there willingly and were paid well. It was illegal, sure, but he'd done a lot of illegal things in his life. As the son of a dead mobster, he'd learned young that the world operated in shades of gray. He couldn't remember the last time he'd used the escort agency, though. Over a year ago, at least.

A loud shout drew his attention to one of the restaurant displays. There were twelve celebrity chefs on site and anyone who was anyone in Miami was here. For the most part. The event was mostly outdoors in a park-type area. Twinkly lights and a huge gauzy canopy were high above everyone, strung between two buildings: an art center and a convention center.

He turned to see Grant Caldwell race toward the convention center, shoving a waiter out of his way as he ran. His two brothers, father and one of his brothers' wives were all behind him, moving at a rapid speed.

Maxwell murmured something next to him before hurrying in that direction. Viktor was mildly curious about what was going on, but the majority of his focus was on finding the woman again.

"We need to go," Abram said quietly, appearing at Viktor's side out of nowhere. Like a ghost.

Because that was what Abram did. He moved with an impressive stealth. Which was good for getting into places he didn't belong. "Why?" he asked, scanning the area, still looking for the blonde. *Dominique.* He wanted to say her name out loud, to feel it on his tongue.

He wanted to feel *her* against his tongue.

Annoyed with himself, he rolled his shoulders once.

"You have a meeting and I don't like whatever that just was." His brother frowned in the direction the Caldwell brothers had gone.

"Let's go. The display tonight..." He trailed off, feeling a little guilt that he hadn't paid much attention to their newest investment. The restaurant he'd just taken over had an exhibit here tonight—the whole reason he'd even come. And he'd been by only once to speak to the chef.

Abram nodded. "Good. Everything is good. Lucy has everything under control."

Viktor held back a snort. Lucia—who insisted they call her Lucy—was the new assistant they'd recently hired and he knew his brother had it bad for her. He looked at his watch. "Stay until the end of the event. One of us needs to be here and I want to make sure Lucy has an escort to her vehicle." The last part was true.

He could tell his brother wanted to argue, probably because he didn't want to be around Lucy even though he was attracted to her, but Abram would watch out for her because he cared for her and because they looked out for their employees. In the past more so than now, Viktor and Abram had engaged in...more than one illegal activity. They'd made enemies, so all of their employees could be potential targets. Especially one who worked so closely with them. They never forgot that.

Abram straightened stiffly. "I'll make sure she gets home safely."

Viktor nodded once and headed out. Going into business with Abram two years ago had been one of the best decisions he'd ever made. He hadn't even *known* he had a half-brother until three years ago.

He texted his driver as he headed toward the art center and away from whatever commotion had just happened. It was fairly late for a meeting, but there was a piece of property he'd had his eye on and the real estate agent couldn't show it until tonight.

The art center was silent as he stepped inside, his shoes almost completely noiseless as he headed down a long hallway that would exit onto a quiet side street. Instead of parking in the main garage attached to the convention center he'd had his driver drop him off. It made things easier when he wanted to leave. No traffic to deal with.

There were a few staff from the Celebration of Chefs and probably from the art center itself along the hallway, acting as 'security' so people wouldn't wander into closed display areas they weren't allowed in. But everyone was silent as he passed, simply smiling politely and nodding.

When he pushed open one of the glass double doors at the end of the long hallway, the salt-tinged, slightly humid Miami night air rolled over him. The heat of summer could be sweltering during the day but at night it was more than bearable, especially with the breezes.

Not that he cared about any of that when he spotted the tall, sexy Dominique talking quietly to a man around her height. At least with her heels they were the same height. They were standing near a built-in bench along the sidewalk next to a cluster of palm trees. Even though it was evening there were enough lights around the center, including one nestled in the palm trees, to illuminate her perfectly.

When she shifted her feet he realized there was another woman next to the man. A petite brunette with Mediterranean coloring who was tucked up against him, her arm wrapped around his waist. They were all murmuring quietly.

The goddess had her back to him, showing off the sweet curve of her ass and her toned calves. It was like she'd walked out of his fantasies. Her long, blonde hair cascaded down her back in big waves and he wondered what it would be like to run his fingers through them. To wrap his fingers around a thick section and hold her head back, nibble along her neck and jaw before he claimed her mouth.

What the fuck is wrong with me?

Beautiful women in Miami were a dime a dozen, but she was…stunning. There was no other word for her. Something about her poise and confidence called to him. The way she walked and moved was like…a goddess. Like she didn't give a fuck what anyone thought about her.

As if she sensed him watching, she turned around. Her dark eyes widened, then just as quickly narrowed in clear anger.

At *him*.

He stilled, watching her carefully. Her reaction to him was

unexpected. They'd never met. That much he was sure of. He didn't date. And she was someone he'd never be able to forget.

Her jaw clenched as she watched him for a long moment, the anger there so clear, so potent, he felt it like a body blow.

She broke eye contact first, turning away from him, her body language changing in an instant. Her back was ramrod straight and he could practically feel the tension rolling off her.

Frowning, he headed in the other direction to where he knew his driver was waiting, but he kept her in his peripheral vision.

Only once he was inside the back of the armored vehicle did he text his half-brother. *Find out who the blonde is. Her name is Dominique. I want everything you can dig up.*

He wanted to do the checking himself but Abram was a genius with computers and getting into places he didn't belong. While Viktor could eventually find out what he wanted, Abram would do it in a quarter of the time.

Right now he wasn't feeling patient where she was concerned. He wanted to know what the hell he could have done to warrant such a reaction from a stranger.

Consider it done.

His brother's responding text soothed a fraction of the tension surging through him. But he wouldn't be satisfied until he found out exactly who she was. And until he met her in person.

CHAPTER TWO

"You don't have to stay and help. I'm fine getting out of here by myself."

Abram watched as Lucy slid the clean champagne glasses into the storage container. She was so methodical in everything she did, so damn organized. She was the best thing that had ever happened to him and his brother. Business-wise.

Because if his brother had ever looked at her in a sexual manner, Abram would have lost his mind. Which was stupid, because she was just an employee.

He placed a hand over hers, even though he knew he shouldn't. Touching her was dangerous to him. To her as well. He had no business wanting her, for too many reasons. The least of which was that she worked for him and his brother. But mainly because she was too good for him. He'd told Viktor that the blonde from earlier wasn't for him and he hadn't been kidding. He knew he should take his own damn advice, but... "And you don't *need* to even be here anymore. The restaurant staff should be cleaning up." He ground out the last couple words, beyond annoyed that she was still here. She worked too hard as it was.

He glared at one of the waitstaff of the fusion restaurant he and his brother had just acquired. They were getting paid double overtime for this event tonight. He'd had to take a phone call and when he'd come back he'd found Lucy helping with the breakdown of the tables, moving around like the Energizer bunny.

"Hey, I tried to tell her she shouldn't be helping. *Three* times." The employee whose name eluded Abram held up his hands in mock defense before he went back to stacking the tea light candles. "Maybe she'll listen to you," he tacked on.

Abram nearly snorted. Doubtful. She never seemed to stop, no matter what task she took on. She was a dark-haired little pixie. Her espresso-colored hair fell in a sharp bob around her face. Usually she kept it stick straight but tonight there were soft waves in it and she had some sort of sparkly headband on. It should have looked ridiculous but it just made her look like a fucking princess.

Another reminder he had no business wanting her. She was too sweet and innocent for him.

She pulled her hand away from his, frowned up at him. Even in her four-inch heels she was only five feet four inches. "The faster we get this done, the faster everyone gets out of here."

"It's not your responsibility. They're getting paid handsomely for tonight. Now let's go. Viktor made me promise to get you home safely." Using his brother as an excuse usually worked.

Her expression softened then. "That man is so sweet. Fine. Let me grab my bag."

Abram gritted his teeth as she turned away, the fluffy skirt of her blue strapless dress twirling out as she moved. There were little sparkles in the skirt too. His brother wasn't sweet, but Lucy seemed to think he was a big teddy bear. It was ridiculous. With him? She usually just seemed frustrated. He didn't understand why.

She pulled a big black bag she called a purse out from behind one of the folded-up tables. It was her 'work bag' and he'd rarely seen her without it. The thing was so big he was surprised she didn't topple over with it. On instinct, he plucked it from her hands.

She let it go with a sigh and he was glad she didn't argue. By now she probably knew it was pointless.

He grunted, hoisting it onto his shoulder. "What do you have in this thing?"

"I can carry it for you if it's too heavy," she murmured, giving him a mischievous look.

God, what he wouldn't give for a taste of her. Just one. "I think I can manage."

"If you say so."

He found himself grinning at her slightly sarcastic tone. At least she didn't seem annoyed with him anymore. The woman made him crazy. "Did you get enough to eat tonight?" He knew she usually skipped lunch and basically seemed to exist on caffeine.

She snorted. "I didn't get anything. I meant to, but got too busy. Hey, why are we going this way? My car's in the parking garage."

"I had one of the guys take it back to the office for you." It was a company vehicle so they all had keys to it. "Viktor wanted to make sure you got home safely tonight. My driver will take you."

"Oh...thanks." There was an odd note in her voice, one he couldn't define.

"Besides, I heard you say you wanted to see the Sanchez exhibit. I asked one of the staff from the art center if we could check out the display and they're allowing us in before we leave," he said as he opened the door to the art center. But he would make sure she got something to eat on the way home.

Sanchez was an up-and-coming photorealist artist in Miami. Abram didn't give a shit about art but he could appreciate the man's talent. The images were all of places in Miami or Florida and had soul.

Lucy blinked up at him, paused in the open doorway. "That's very nice." Did she have to sound so surprised by that?

He lifted a shoulder, uncomfortable with the way she was watching him.

She gave him a soft half-smile he felt all the way to his core. "Thank you."

It took a moment for his legs to catch up to his brain. He fell in step with her in two strides then had to slow down because of their height difference.

After walking through the exhibit—which she seemed to thoroughly enjoy—they finally left the art center. His current driver, Kir, was waiting by the curb, just like he'd instructed.

He held open the door for Lucy before Kir could get out and do it. When he slid into the backseat after her, she looked almost surprised. Maybe she hadn't realized he was coming with her. He didn't care that Viktor had just said to make sure she got to her car safely. He was making sure she got *home* safely. There wasn't even a threat against them at the moment, but he still wanted to take care of her. *Because she is a good employee,* he told himself. That was it.

"Does he know my address?" she murmured, strapping herself in.

He nodded, strapping in as well before telling Kir to head out.

"Did you have fun tonight?" she asked, her dark gaze on him.

"It was fine." The bright city lights played over her delicate features as they drove toward downtown.

Her mouth quirked up. "That's not really an answer."

"It was…business. Not for fun." Fun would be stripping her naked, making her come, seeing her lose control. He didn't do relationships. He'd never had time, but lately he found himself thinking he'd make an exception for Lucy. Which, again, was stupid since she was an employee.

Now she shrugged. "So? You can still have fun at events."

He'd seen her talking to a multitude of people tonight, some clearly for business, but others he knew she was friends with. Because everyone seemed to adore Lucy. It was hard not to. "It was fine," he said, repeating his earlier statement. He felt stupid and tongue-tied around her. Always.

She gave him one of those frustrated looks and started to respond when her phone dinged from her giant bag, indicating an incoming text. Instantly she reached for it.

"You don't have to worry about work anymore. It's okay to go off the clock." He worried that she might burn out. Maybe they were working her too hard?

She laughed as she responded to the text. "When you and Viktor slow down, I'll slow down."

He swallowed hard, looked out the window. It was doubtful he and Viktor would slow their pace anytime soon. Money gave him security and some days he couldn't seem to make enough. Abram had grown up poor, unlike Viktor. But it didn't matter. Viktor'd had it bad too. Abram was glad he'd only had limited contact with their father when he was young. After he'd turned eight he'd cut off all contact with the bastard, told his mom he didn't want to see him again. Thankfully his mom had been more than happy to, even though it had meant cutting off any support from the sperm donor.

He'd assumed Viktor was just like that monster but he'd found out differently when he'd started to dig into him more. Only then had he approached him and had been surprised Viktor had no clue about his existence. It had taken time, but they'd eventually become friends.

Best friends. The first one he'd ever had. Abram didn't trust many people. Just some of the guys he'd served with from his Marine Corps days. And his brother. No one else.

When he realized Lucy was still texting, he plucked the phone from her hands.

Letting out a soft gasp, she stared at him. "What are you doing?"

"You're done for the night."

"Damn it, Mr. Ivanov—"

"Abram. My name is Abram," he gritted out. She called his brother by his first name. But she'd never called him by his first name. She either completely avoided using his name, or when she was annoyed called him Mr. Ivanov. It was ridiculous and made him insane.

She let out a frustrated growl. "I know that. Please give me my phone. I just need to respond to one thing and then I'm done for the night. Promise."

"Say my name and you get your phone."

She blinked at him, her cheeks flushing pink. "What?"

"My first name. Say it." He knew he was pushing her, should probably stop. But he didn't care. He felt practically possessed right now with the need to hear her say his damn name. He was also aware of Kir watching him in the rearview mirror curiously.

"Fine, Abram. Can I have my phone now?" She held out her palm, her hand slightly trembling.

He frowned, wondering if he'd frightened her, but...he didn't think so. Her eyes were slightly dilated and her cheeks were still flushed. She almost looked aroused, but that couldn't be possible. The woman couldn't seem to stand him some days. He gave her the phone. "Don't call me Mr. Ivanov anymore. If you do I'll start calling you Lucia."

She simply gave him a dark look as she took the phone and didn't respond one way or another. For some reason she didn't like her given name, but he thought it was beautiful. It fit her.

As she continued to text, he looked out the window at the passing lights and traffic. He should have just walked her to her damn car. Not given her a ride home. Being around her always put him on edge, made him feel awkward. Maybe he should limit his contact with her even more. Normally he just emailed or texted her with instructions about work but sometimes working with her directly was unavoidable.

The truth was, though, he looked forward to the time they did spend together. Even if she seemed perpetually annoyed with him. Or aloof, which was even worse.

When he saw the number on screen he answered the phone after three rings, forcing himself to remain patient. "Yes?"

"Abram has definitely taken an interest in the new assistant. He followed her around all night." The man snorted in amusement.

"Are you in a secure place?"

"Of course. I'm at a park. No chance of anyone overhearing."

"Good... What else do you have?" Because that wasn't enough. He'd seen that himself over the last couple months. And Abram wasn't the one he hated. It was Viktor, with his smugness, the way he looked down on him. The man thought he was better than him. Which was ridiculous. Viktor's father had been a common criminal, a thug.

"That's it for now. You wanted me to call with updates on them." His contact sounded annoyed.

"What about Viktor?" He couldn't keep the disgust out of his voice.

"What about him? He never brings women around."

He knew that. Viktor seemed to prefer paying whores, which was no use to him. He needed to find the man's weakness and a woman would be the best one there was. Men became stupid over women. He didn't let his disappointment show. "This is good. Thank you for the update." Even though it wasn't what he wanted, he liked to keep his contact happy because he never knew when he might get something useful.

"I'll be in touch when I have anything else."

He ended the call. There was no need to talk any longer. He'd approached the man he'd been using for information because he knew of the man's secret addiction to strip clubs. Pathetic, really. Spending all that money for nothing except some grinding and maybe a blow job in a back room.

But the man was risking a lot by crossing the Ivanov brothers. They'd been careful though. No one would ever figure out he was getting information on them, building up a reserve of information he might be able to use.

Because Viktor would pay for taking from him.

CHAPTER THREE

Dominique glanced up as her boss, Porter, stepped out of his office. He'd been here earlier than her this morning, which was pretty unusual, especially for a Monday.

Their two offices were connected by a big door and they both had huge windows overlooking the city. The elevators opened right up into her office space where she was the basic 'guard' for Porter. Not that he really needed one. He oversaw one of their security divisions so the only people who ever came to see him were employees directly under his purview. Or potential new clients, but he usually met with them in one of the conference rooms down the hall.

"You don't have any meetings until ten," she reminded him. It didn't matter that she updated his online calendar—and had synced it to his email account and phone so he got hourly alerts—he still sometimes forgot stuff. He'd once told her it was because he was getting old, which was ridiculous since she was pretty sure he was only thirty-four. She had a feeling his forgetfulness had more to do with his one-year-old son who hadn't been sleeping through the night lately.

"I know. I forgot to tell you I've got someone coming in. It has to do with what happened to Raegan. Would you get some coffee and refreshments for us?"

"Of course," she said, automatically standing. "Do you have news about who drugged her?" Her friend had been drugged on Friday night. And Raegan was Porter's cousin so of course he'd be involved in finding out what happened to her.

Too much had happened over the weekend. Raegan had been drugged—and almost taken by some random guy at a club—but thankfully someone had been there for her. A 'sexy cop,' as Raegan liked to call him. Dominique had no idea what was going on with those two but she had a feeling she'd find out all the details soon enough. She was just glad Raegan was okay.

"No, but I'm hoping to get something this morning," Porter answered.

"Any news about what happened Saturday?" Raegan had been almost attacked at the Celebration of Chefs, as well. Dominique had missed most of the commotion because she'd been out front talking to her cousin.

He shook his head, his expression grim.

"Do you think...the two things are related? Raegan didn't say, but I thought maybe, I don't know. It seems like a coincidence that two bad things like that happened to her so close together."

"I...don't know. We're looking at the events as if they might be connected. The cops are doing what they can, but we've got better resources. The guy who's meeting me has a video of Friday night. I want to go over it. You were there too so if you wouldn't mind looking at it, I'd appreciate it."

"Of course. Anything I can do to help. I'll go grab those refreshments and be back in a few minutes. What time—" She stopped talking as the elevator doors whooshed open and Viktor Ivanov stepped out.

Seeing him made a sharp burst of anger pop inside her, but she shoved it back down. She was a professional and she'd worked very hard to get a job like this. She wasn't going to ruin that because she couldn't control her temper. Even if she did want to punch Ivanov right in his perfect, chiseled face. This must be the meeting Porter had been talking about.

Of course. Ivanov was the owner of the club Raegan had been drugged at. It made sense he would be here. But he looked more like a thug than anything else. The no doubt custom-made suit he had on didn't hide the fact that he might as well be a street brawler. His dark hair was more or less a buzz cut, cropped close to his head, and his blue eyes were icy. She could see a few tattoos peeking out under the cuffs of his jacket and the ones on his knuckles were always visible. She'd heard the rumors that he'd once been part of his father's criminal organization in Miami. When his father had died he'd supposedly gone legit, but she didn't buy it.

She pasted on her best smile and hoped it didn't look too fake. "I'll grab the coffee," she murmured to Porter as she nodded politely at Ivanov—who was staring intently at her—and left her office. Her heels clicked against the tile as she headed down the hallway to the community kitchen they shared with the other offices on this floor. Red Stone owned the entire building and they didn't rent out offices to anyone else so everyone here was a vetted Red Stone Security employee.

When she stepped into the kitchen she was glad it was empty. Right now she didn't feel like exerting any energy to make polite small talk. After starting a fresh pot of coffee, she pulled out the tray of muffins, cookies and scones they kept on hand for impromptu meetings. Everything was fresh, replaced daily. Once she had the refreshments set up on the rolling tray she headed back to her office and tried to ignore the nausea churning in her stomach.

Seeing Viktor Ivanov just reminded her of everything his family had taken from hers. From what she'd heard, he was just as bad as his dead, gangster father. She couldn't believe Porter was meeting with the man, but to get video of the club where his cousin had been attacked…yeah, she would meet with the devil too if it would help her friend.

When she rolled the cart into Porter's office, she found both men sitting in front of Porter's laptop. Porter paused the video as she entered and both men stood.

It annoyed her that Ivanov was being polite and standing for her—and still watching her with those intense blue eyes. She ignored him and smiled at her boss. "If you want I can set up the projector in the conference room for the video. You'll be able to see everything more clearly."

He nodded once, his expression still tight. "That'd be great, thanks."

Leaving the refreshment tray, she exited the office, able to breathe again now that she was out of Ivanov's presence. She usually towered over most people, or was at least the same height as most men in her heels, but not him. She hated that.

It was rare that someone made her feel off her game, but he did. After what his family had done to hers, what his father had done to her mother… She swallowed hard, shoved all those thoughts aside as she focused on her job. She could get through this morning then he'd be gone and she'd never have to see him again.

Unfortunately, an hour later she found that not to be true. Porter and Ivanov walked back into her office as she was getting off a phone call.

"Dominique, if you can spare the time, would you mind walking Mr. Ivanov out? He has some questions about Red Stone and I told him you're the best person to answer anything." He smiled, a genuine one as he turned back to the big thug. "I don't know what I'd do without her."

Ivanov half-smiled. "I have an assistant like that as well. She keeps me in line." There was just a hint of an accent in his voice.

She knew he'd been born in the States, was an American, but his father and she was pretty sure his mother had both been born in Russia. It explained his slight accent.

Even though she wanted to say no, there was no way she ever would. No matter her feelings for this man, she would do her job. Porter had placed a lot of faith in her the last few months and she'd already gotten one raise. She wasn't going to screw this job up. Smiling, she stood from her desk.

"Of course. Don't forget, ten o'clock."

Porter blinked once, letting her know he actually had forgotten, then nodded. "Right. I've got everything ready to go."

He'd been part of the security team for so long that she guessed transferring to a more admin position had been an adjustment for the former Marine.

Keeping her fake smile in place she nodded at Ivanov and motioned toward the elevators. "So what would you like to know about Red Stone?" *Ugh.* She hoped he wasn't looking to hire the company. Though she wasn't sure they'd even take him on. Porter's dad, the founder, had an intense vetting process, even for their clients. He didn't take on known criminals, no matter how much money they had.

"How long have you worked for them?"

She cleared her throat as she stepped through the open elevator doors. "About five months."

"You were with Porter's cousin on Friday night." It wasn't a question and no doubt he'd seen her on the video.

She cringed at the thought of her boss seeing her out dancing on that video. She hadn't been drunk or doing anything stupid, but still, it felt a little weird. If she'd known that Ivanov had owned the club she'd gone to with her friends, she'd have never gone. At least he'd been willing to give Porter the video feed in an effort to find out who'd tried to take Raegan.

"Yes." The elevator started moving moments after the doors closed. She stood next to him, trying to ignore his presence. It was hard, considering what a giant the male was. He was crowding into her space without even trying. His cologne was light and she hated that he smelled good. If he was anyone else she might have even...checked him out. Which just annoyed her even more.

"I'm sorry your friend was drugged. I've already fired the security staff from that night."

Surprised ricocheted through her at his words and for the first time since getting in the elevator she looked over at him. "Seriously?"

He frowned, his gaze flickering to her mouth. "Why are you surprised?"

She lifted a shoulder, not liking what she saw in his icy blue eyes. She'd been on the receiving end of lust from males since she was fourteen. She could tell he liked what he saw when he looked at her and it pissed her off. When the elevator doors opened on the bottom floor she pushed out a sigh of relief, belatedly realizing her reaction was a little too obvious as they stepped out of it. "Did you have any questions about Red Stone?" Because she didn't want to talk about herself or Friday night.

"Have we met before?" he asked. She could practically hear the frown in his voice, but didn't meet his gaze as they crossed the main lobby.

Smiling, she nodded at two of the security men behind the huge circular reception area. She knew they were both armed to the teeth. "No."

"Then what have I done to offend you?" he demanded softly.

Surprised by the bluntness of his question, she looked at him. He'd stopped walking so she did the same. "Why would you say that?" She wrapped her arms around herself.

His expression was hard, the angles of his face sharp and defined. He looked every inch the ruthless businessman everyone said he was. "Because of the way you looked at me Saturday night."

Damn it. She was hoping he hadn't remembered or even noticed her. She'd been unable to rein in her reaction to him though. She took a steadying breath. "If you do business with my boss it won't be a problem. I'm a professional." She didn't want to be on Viktor Ivanov's radar in any way, shape or form, but...

Staring into icy blue eyes so similar to his father's, she was close to losing it. When she looked at Viktor, she saw blood and death, her lifeless mother in her tub. And it made her want to cry.

"Your family disgusts me," she gritted out before turning on her heel. She couldn't be around him any longer, couldn't fake being polite. Though clearly she hadn't done a good job of that anyway.

Viktor scrubbed a hand over his face as he read over the file his brother had given to him. It was very thorough. He couldn't get rid of the image of Dominique's almost scared expression when she'd looked at him. He was used to people being afraid of him.

But he'd hated that she'd looked at him like that. Which was stupid, since he didn't even know her. Maybe it was because, more than fear, he'd seen raw pain in her gaze.

Now he knew why.

He closed his eyes. "Fuck," he muttered.

"You had nothing to do with it." Abram's voice was whiplash sharp. As always when he was annoyed.

"My family—our family—owes her a debt." He looked up, sat back in his desk chair.

Abram was half sitting on the front of his desk, his arms crossed over his chest. "Bullshit. Her father had gambling debts. No one held a gun to his head and made him go to Ilya for that loan."

Even now Abram wouldn't say 'my father' or 'our father.' It was always Ilya. "When her father died the debt should have been settled with the life insurance and the house." He looked down at the files again, saw how much the life insurance and house—which was on the beach and was prime real estate—had been worth. It hadn't been quite enough to cover the debt because Dominique's father had racked up an obscene amount. "I think Ilya took the rest of the debt from Dominique's mother. Probably through sex."

Abram shifted uncomfortably on the desk before shoving to his feet. "We can't know that."

No, but Viktor could read between the lines. His father, gangster that he'd been, had kept impeccable records. "Even after her father died the debt was paid down in credits." He tapped a finger against the old file even though Abram already knew what it said. He was the one who'd discovered that Dominique's father had been in deep to their own father. "Not money. You know what that means. Then her mother kills herself six months later?" It was clear why. His father had been a monster, had probably driven Dominique's mother to suicide with his sick demands she'd been forced to fulfill.

"I wish he was alive so I could kill him," Abram muttered, clearly referring to Ilya. He went to the big window that overlooked downtown, and was silent as he stared out of it.

Viktor didn't respond, just flipped over the current page and stared at Dominique's mother. She had Mediterranean coloring as well as dark hair, and according to the file she'd been five feet five inches. It was clear Dominique favored her father in height and hair color, but she'd gotten some of her mother's traits as well, including a beautiful face.

He felt almost sick to his stomach. Dominique had lost her father and mother in less than a year and could trace both deaths back to his father. No wonder she'd looked at him as if she wanted to claw his eyes out.

He pressed the intercom on his phone. "Lucy, can I see you for a sec?"

Moments later his new assistant strode in, not a strand of her short, dark hair out of place. As always her gaze strayed to Abram for a fraction longer than necessary, but his brother had his back to her and didn't turn at her entrance.

"There's a property that's part of our rental program," he said, scribbling down the address. "I want it taken off immediately and all current reservations cancelled. We'll refund everyone and have Rita try to relocate them to another rental property of ours. If she can't, still comp them wherever they end up staying and include something extra for the inconvenience. A bottle of champagne, whatever. I want this done by the end of the day. No excuses from Rita."

Normally Lucy did whatever he said without question. Now her eyes widened a fraction. "Rita's going to lose it," Lucy said, a small grin tugging at her lips.

"She can deal with it." Rita was the real estate agent for Abram and him, and in charge of almost all of their company's properties. "But because you'll have to deal with her bitching, take her out to dinner one night this month. Anywhere she wants. No limits."

Lucy's grin widened. "I have a feeling you might regret that when she orders a two-thousand-dollar bottle of champagne."

He just snorted because Lucy wasn't kidding. "Probably so. Just make it happen." He didn't care how much it cost him to fix this.

"I will." Still grinning, she left, pulling the door shut behind her.

Abram turned around then, his expression unreadable. "Are you doing what I think you're doing?"

"We owe her."

His lips flattened, but to Viktor's surprise, Abram didn't argue. "What you're doing is insane."

He lifted a shoulder. He'd done a lot of shitty things in his life, but seeing the face of one of his father's victims—maybe she hadn't been victimized directly, but Dominique's life had been impacted greatly because of Ilya—made him need to act. To pay her back somehow. Nothing could bring back her family but he was still going to try to make things right. "You think I'm wrong?"

"No. I just don't think she's going to take what you're offering."

Maybe not, but he would still try.

CHAPTER FOUR

"What's going on with you?" Porter's voice made Dominique jump in her chair and nearly knock her bottle of water off her desk.

She steadied it with one hand, her heart beating faster than normal. "Nothing. Why?"

He eyed her curiously. "You've been acting off since that file was delivered. What's in it?"

Damn it. Of course he'd get straight to the point. After seeing Viktor Ivanov yesterday she'd been feeling out of sorts and then the file she'd received this morning had completely knocked her world off its axis. She didn't know what to think of it—didn't know why Ivanov had sent it to her. "It's personal."

Porter gave her a pointed look. "I know that. What's in it?"

"I'm…not telling you." She felt bad, but she just couldn't.

He frowned and sat on the edge of her desk. "If you need help with anything, you just have to ask." The true concern in his voice nearly undid her.

But she couldn't tell him what was in the file without telling him more about her past. Okay, considering how hard she'd been vetted, she figured Porter already knew about her past, but still, that didn't mean she wanted to talk about it. Even if she did open up to him, she couldn't do that without crying. No way in hell was she going to break down here and in front of her boss. Talk about mortifying and unprofessional. Red Stone Security was a male-dominated workplace, and while she loved her job she didn't want to be seen as anything other than professional. And crying at work? Not happening.

"I'm good, promise... Has my work been suffering today?" She'd been on autopilot all morning and now felt really guilty. If she'd been slacking she'd make up for it tomorrow.

He blinked. "What...no. Jeez, Dominique. I'm talking to you as a friend, not your boss. You're on top of everything as usual. I just want to make sure you're okay. With what happened to Raegan I think we're all a little on edge. I just wanted to make sure things are good."

"I swear I'm fine. I...would you mind if I left work an hour early today? I skipped lunch, so—"

"Just go now. I'm about to clear out anyway. We can afford to sneak out early one day."

The truth was, this week was one of their slower ones. All his guys were on long-term security jobs for the next month so her duties were standard and she could do them in her sleep. That would change in a few weeks when the guys started moving to new contracts. Still, it felt weird to leave early, but she was going to do it. For her sanity, she needed to. "I really appreciate it."

Once he'd returned to his office she shut down her computer and headed out. Instead of leaving, she rode the elevator up a few floors to Lizzy's floor. To her surprise, Lizzy's assistant got her in to see Lizzy almost immediately.

"Hey, chica. What are you doing up here?" Lizzy was stretched out on a chaise lounge with her laptop next to a window instead of sitting at her desk. And she was wearing yoga pants and a T-shirt.

"Is there a new dress code I don't know about?" Dominique laughed as she headed over to the chaise and perched on the end of it.

"Ha ha." Lizzy was sitting cross-legged and slid her laptop to the side. "I can't go to the gym after work so I ran up and down the stairs during my lunch break. Just haven't had time to change and since I don't have meetings today I'm staying comfy."

Dominique figured that Lizzy could pretty much do whatever she wanted, and not just because she was married to Porter. The woman was one of their online security experts and a more than decent hacker. In fact, Dominique had heard some of the guys call her scary good. Something she was really hoping for right now. "That's a little insane."

Lizzy shrugged. "If I don't let the energy out, *I* go insane."

"Fair enough... Can I ask you a favor that you can't tell your husband about?"

Lizzy's expression turned serious. "Depends on the favor."

"It's not work related. I just...need to know where someone is right now. I need to talk to him and it has to be in person."

Lizzy frowned, absently pushing back a loose strand of her long, dark hair. "Why not call this person?"

She could. Heck, she probably should. But no, this needed to be an in-person conversation. Dominique needed to see Ivanov's face, gauge his reaction. "It's...personal." Dominique was friends with Lizzy but she never forgot that Lizzy was also her boss's wife. Shaking her head, she stood. "I know I'm putting you in a weird position and that I'm asking you to invade someone's privacy. Can we just forget I asked—"

"Who do you want to track down?"

She shifted from foot to foot, debating if she should just leave, but she really wanted to know where he was. And to talk to him right freaking now. "Viktor Ivanov."

Lizzy blinked in surprise. "Is this about Raegan?"

"Not remotely. Nothing to do with her, the club, or work. It's very personal. This is his number." She held out a sticky note she'd scribbled the number on earlier.

Lizzy gave her a mischievous grin. "Personal, huh?" She pulled her computer back into her lap and her fingers started flying over the keyboard at an alarming pace.

Dominique wanted to correct her, to tell her not personal in the way she implied, but held her tongue as Lizzy worked. When she started to move around to see what her friend was doing, Lizzy shook her head.

"Uh-uh. Just sit down while I work. Plausible deniability, my friend. If you don't see what I'm doing, you can't admit to any wrongdoing." She didn't glance up once as she said it, her expression almost gleeful.

"Are you breaking the law?" It was a dumb question. Of course Lizzy was. Dominique had heard the rumors, knew that Lizzy could pretty much hack anything. It was the whole reason she'd come to see her.

Lizzy just snorted then grinned. "He's at one of his hotels." She rattled off the name and address, but Dominique already knew where it was.

She'd lived in Miami her whole life and knew the city well. "Thank you."

Lizzy didn't look up, just typed in a few more commands. "Looks as if he's currently in the ground-floor restaurant. East side. Well, his personal cell phone is. I'm assuming it's with him."

Dominique blinked. "You're terrifying."

"Thanks," Lizzy said, looking up. "Are you in trouble?"

"No." She felt like a mess though. "It's just personal. I promise."

Lizzy slid her computer to the side and stood. "What I know about Ivanov isn't much, but I've heard enough that he's a dangerous man."

She nodded. "I know."

"Be careful."

"Thanks. I will. If, uh, he leaves, will you call me? I'm headed over there right now."

"I'll keep an eye on his phone and let you know. Do you need an escort or anything?"

She shook her head. She didn't need an audience for this, didn't want anyone to know her personal business. None of her friends from work knew what had happened to her parents—or if they did they'd never brought it up—and she planned to keep it that way. She didn't want pitying looks. "If you need to tell Porter about this, it's okay."

Lizzy just nodded, which wasn't really an answer whether she was going to tell her husband or not. Dominique didn't really care though. She needed to talk to Viktor Ivanov right now and ask him why the hell he'd sent her a contract signing over the rights to her childhood home. He supposedly just wanted to give it to her.

For free.

There had to be a catch. Even if there wasn't, she sure as hell wasn't taking it. She was going to get to the bottom of this and find out what the heck he was up to. Because a man like Ivanov wouldn't give away such a valuable piece of property for nothing.

Dominique was a mix of nerves and anger by the time she made it to Viktor's hotel. Or one of them, apparently. She'd known he was successful, but when Lizzy had said 'one of his hotels' she'd realized that he must be wealthier than she'd thought.

She had her car valeted because she couldn't even think about dealing with parking. After a confirming text from Lizzy that Ivanov was still in his restaurant, she headed into the lobby. The decorating was minimalist but everything was high-end. A huge chandelier hung right in the middle of the foyer of the five-star boutique hotel, glittering prettily above everything. She was almost certain the place didn't have more than a hundred rooms. The interior had an Old World feel to it and was truly beautiful. She'd read about it in one of the luxury publications she kept up to date on for Porter. She just hadn't realized Ivanov was the owner.

Before she'd taken two steps, a man wearing black pants, a white button-down shirt and a simple black jacket with the hotel's logo on it approached her, a warm smile on his face. "Welcome. How may I help you?"

She gave him one of her most winning smiles. She hadn't really thought this through before coming down here. She'd just been so impatient to see him and hadn't wanted to wait—or call. For some reason that had seemed intimidating. Now, she realized, seeing him in person after she'd told him that his family disgusted her was nerve-racking. Gah, what had she been thinking? "I'm here to see Mr. Ivanov."

Before the man could respond another man appeared as if out of nowhere, moving silently across the marble tile as he approached. She'd seen him at the Celebration of Chefs on Saturday with Ivanov and thought they might be business partners. He was just as big and definitely as intimidating as Ivanov. The man smiled at her, sort of, and dismissed the hotel employee with a few short words.

"I take it you're here to see my brother, Miss Castle."

She blinked at his words, surprised he even knew who she was. "You're Viktor's brother?" She hadn't realized that he had any siblings. Once upon a time she'd done her research on him too. But that had been years ago, when she'd been obsessed with finding out everything about the man who'd destroyed her family. She'd moved on since then, had avoided reading anything about Ivanov once his father died.

"Half-brother. He's working but he'll make time for you." Without waiting for her to respond he turned on his heel and headed toward the open entrance to a restaurant. There was a sign outside that said it was closed until four o'clock.

"I can come back later," she said as she hurried to catch up with him. Looking at the man now it seemed obvious he and Viktor were related. He was just as big, with similar blue eyes. He even had a similar haircut, buzzed close to his head. "I should have called."

He stopped as they reached the entrance. "How did you know he was here?"

Feeling her cheeks flush, she just shrugged. "Lucky guess."

He gave her an assessing look before turning away again and motioning for her to follow him.

She gritted her teeth at his rudeness, but whatever. She'd just shown up here without calling—after illegally tracking Ivanov down. Dominique wasn't going to throw stones about manners.

He led her across a mostly empty restaurant with white tablecloths on all the tables except a circular booth Viktor was sitting at. There were two men about ten feet away from him, standing quietly by the bar. His bodyguards, she guessed, if the way they sized her up was any indication.

His half-brother held up a hand to them, said something in Russian she didn't understand. Unlike Viktor, he didn't have an accent when he spoke English.

Viktor stood, his eyebrows raised as he looked at her, his gaze sweeping her from head to toe. There was a mix of lust thrown in too, which completely screwed with her head.

He started to say something, then one of the men said something under his breath to the other one in Russian, the look the guard gave her easy to define. She might not understand the language but the way he leered at her made her skin crawl.

On instinct she took a step back but to her surprise Viktor moved into the guy's personal space, getting right up in his face. It was amazing—he didn't even touch the guy but it was clear he didn't have to. The guard's body language showed fear, if the way he tried to shrink back in an attempt to be invisible was any indication. Viktor murmured something too low for her to hear, but whatever it was, the man paled a deathly white and nodded once before practically running from the restaurant. He gave her a wide berth and avoided eye contact as he left.

The remaining man looked just as uneasy.

"Leave us," Viktor said to his brother—whose name she still didn't know—and the remaining man.

Once they were gone, he motioned that she could sit across the booth from where he'd been sitting.

She swallowed hard, wondering why she'd thought it was a good idea to just show up here. Viktor was huge and had a ruthless reputation. Clearly she needed to get her head on straight. She paused, unsure if she should sit or not.

"You don't have to be afraid of me," he snapped.

She jumped at the harsh tone.

He scrubbed a hand over his face. "I'm sorry. It's been a long day. Please sit."

Pushing out a breath, she did—because she wanted answers.

"Why the heck did you send over that contract to me this morning?" The question came out as a half shout, making her cringe at herself. "Sorry, I'm just... Well, why did you?"

He was sitting ramrod straight, looking uncomfortable as he watched her. As if he didn't want her here any more than she wanted to be here. "It has come to my attention that my family owes you a debt."

She clenched her jaw tightly. A *debt*? A house wouldn't come close to making up for what she'd lost. "So you're just offering to give me my childhood home?" A place that held a lot of good memories. It was like he was dangling the best carrot ever in front of her but there was no way she could take it.

He nodded once.

"In exchange for what?"

He blinked. "Nothing. It's a gift."

"You can't offer a gift like that and think I'm going to believe you want nothing in return!"

He shifted against his seat, looking uncomfortable. Something told her he wasn't often uncomfortable. "I don't want anything. It's yours. I didn't get much from my father when he died, but your parents' house was part of my trust. I didn't...know what he'd done until yesterday."

Even if he sounded sincere she still didn't know if she believed him. And she regretted coming here. She should have just ignored the contract, ignored everything. Especially since it seemed clear that he must know about her parents, about her mother. It made her feel vulnerable in a way she hadn't in a long time. "I don't want it."

"It's yours. My father hurt a lot of people." There was a strained note in his voice, but she didn't know him well enough to be sure. "I know the house doesn't make up for *anything*, but I can't keep it. Not now. It's been on a rental program for years since it's on the beach. It has high ratings and does well in the summers so if you do the same thing with it you'll make a nice yearly income from it. I can recommend a property management company to run it if you'd like."

No. This was not happening. The world didn't work this way.

Unable to find her voice she abruptly stood. She didn't want the house, didn't want anything from him and it pissed her off that he thought giving her the property would somehow make up for what his father had done.

And yet, part of her felt conflicted. He was supposed to be a monster just like his father, and now she didn't know what to think. She turned, ready to run out of there, when his hand lightly clasped her wrist.

She turned back to him but wouldn't meet his gaze. Instead she stared at his broad, muscled chest. Now she was glad he was taller than her so she didn't have to look into his eyes. And she hated that she noticed how attractive he was.

"Please take it," he murmured. "Sell it, do whatever you want. But take it." There was a sort of desperation in his voice, as if he meant every word.

He just wanted her to take it so his conscience could be eased. And that wasn't going to happen. "That house…is the last place I remember being happy with my parents." Her voice broke on the last word and to her horror she started crying.

No! This was even worse than crying at work. Breaking down in front of the man she'd thought was a monster for so long, a man who was supposedly giving her such a huge gift with no expectations—she tried to rein in her tears, but when he made a distressed sound and awkwardly patted her on the back in a half-hug she couldn't stop herself no matter how hard she tried.

Almost against her will she found herself leaning into the very man she'd always thought of as her enemy.

CHAPTER FIVE

Viktor had never felt more at a loss in his life. He had no experience with crying women. He didn't know if she wanted any comfort and he didn't want to risk her shoving him away if he pulled her into his arms. Even if the thought of holding her close was something he'd been fantasizing about. No matter how stupid. So he awkwardly patted her back. If she was his he'd do more than this—he'd pull her into his arms, wipe away her tears and bring her pleasure, make her forget why she was in pain.

"Do you want to sit?" he murmured. Maybe he never should have sent that contract over. Maybe he should have contacted her first. But he hadn't thought she would want to see him or talk to him. Not after their last meeting. He'd just wanted to make things as right as he could. Upsetting her was the last thing he wanted to do, but clearly he'd made a mistake.

She nodded and swiped away her tears before collapsing on the edge of the booth seat.

Instead of sitting across from her he grabbed a chair from a nearby table and sat in front of her.

Her pretty brown eyes widened slightly but at least she wasn't crying anymore. There was still some dampness on her cheeks and he wanted to wipe it away, to touch her soft skin, take her pain away. But he didn't.

In his periphery he saw his brother reenter the restaurant. When he met Abram's gaze his brother tapped his watch. Viktor shook his head. He didn't care about his upcoming meeting. This was more important.

His brother's expression darkened but Viktor turned away from him and focused on Dominique. "The last thing I wanted to do was upset you," he said quietly.

"I think I believe you." She gave him a half-smile he felt all the way to his core. "I'm sorry I thought you were just like your father."

"It's a fair assumption." One most people made. For the most part people weren't wrong, at least not when it came to business. He *was* ruthless. He just wasn't a gangster and he didn't get off on hurting women. Unlike his father. "I'm sorry about your parents."

At his words her expression shuttered but he could see pain in her eyes. She couldn't hide that. And he wished his father was still alive so he could kill him all over again for what he'd done. "You know what he did to my mother?"

"I can guess." Because his father had been a monster. It was the reason he'd killed Ilya. Something no one knew. Not even his brother. He'd do it again too.

"I only found out after she killed herself." She swallowed hard and paused. He wanted to comfort her but didn't think she would want his touch. "She wrote me a letter. He…he said he made videos of them. So even after she'd paid off his bullshit debt he said she had to keep 'servicing' him or he'd put those videos on the internet for everyone to see." Tears tracked down her cheeks again and the sight was too much.

Fuck it. He couldn't sit here and do nothing. He pulled her into his arms and to his surprise she leaned into his hold, burying her face against his shoulder as she laid her hands gently on his chest.

He closed his eyes for a moment, savored the feel of her leaning against him, almost as if she trusted him. "I'm so sorry."

She sniffled and pulled back, wiped at her face. "It's not your fault. Even if I wanted to make you out to be a monster too." Guilt flickered across her features.

"I'm still sorry. If he was alive, I'd kill him." The words came out savage. Instantly he wished he could take them back when her eyes widened in shock. But screw it, he was who he was. There was no need to hide it, especially since he'd never have a chance with her. Not now. Not with the history between their families.

"I can't tell if you're joking," she said, giving him a watery half-laugh.

He wasn't, but wasn't going to tell her that. The only times he'd killed had been in self-defense, but not many people knew about that. They suspected, sure. Which was another reason for his reputation. "Please take the house."

She was already shaking her head before he'd finished. "I can't, but thank you anyway."

Viktor reined in his frustration. He couldn't very well order her to take it even if that was exactly what he wanted to do. He was going to make sure it ended up in her hands. After reading the file Abram had given him he'd learned that she lost her college savings fund because of her father's gambling, as well as her trust. She'd paid her way through college working two jobs and had only acquired minimal debt—which she'd just recently paid off. She had a strong work ethic, something he admired. Before he could respond he saw Lucy headed his way.

Viktor knew his brother had likely sent her in here because of the stupid meeting he needed to get to. He wanted to wave her away, but simply couldn't do that to Lucy—something Abram knew. She smiled politely at Dominique before focusing on him. "Abram wanted me to remind you that you've got that meeting to get to."

"Reschedule it. Reschedule everything this afternoon."

Lucy simply nodded and left.

Dominique's tears were completely dried as she looked at him. "I should go. I've taken up too much of your time. I really am sorry I judged you so harshly. It was incredibly unfair of me to lump you in with your father."

"It's fine." It wasn't like he was a good man.

"No. It's not." She took one of his hands, squeezed it once before standing.

Everything inside him stilled at the feel of her touching him. He wanted more and hated that he didn't have a chance with her. He stood with her, not wanting to let her go. "If you ever want to see the house, I'm not going to be doing anything with it. It'll be waiting for you whenever you're ready."

Her full lips pulled into a thin line as she sighed. "I'm not going to change my mind, but thank you. I'll show myself out."

Viktor just nodded and watched her leave, even if he wanted to escort her out simply to spend a few more minutes in her presence. But that was stupid. She might not think he was a monster anymore, but she would never look twice at him as a potential...*boyfriend* seemed like such a juvenile word. Regardless, she wouldn't look at him as a love interest.

He closed his laptop and headed out. His brother could deal with the rest of the day's meetings. Viktor was too edgy.

A run and a swim and maybe some time on the punching bag might expel some of this energy. But he doubted it.

He needed to get Dominique out of his system but he wasn't sure how. He hadn't even had a taste of her, yet thoughts of her consumed him. She hadn't seemed to think he was a monster after today so maybe...he did have a chance with her. Maybe they could be friends. He nearly snorted at the thought.

Even if he didn't have a shot with Dominique, he'd call later to check on her, to try to convince her to take the house again. Why didn't he believe his own lie? He wanted to see if she'd let him take her to dinner, to get to know her more. He'd give her a day then test the waters.

Walking away from her was something he just couldn't do.

"Here's the paperwork to fire Peter." Lucy set the stack of papers on Abram's desk, a half-smile tugging at her very kissable lips.

As if she was trying not to smile.

"What's that look?" Abram frowned as Lucy stepped back.

She blinked. "What do you mean?"

"You look...happy. Are you glad we're firing him?" Abram had been planning to anyway, but today's behavior had been the final straw.

Peter had been hired as professional security and had thought it okay to make a rude, sexual comment about a woman he didn't know, right in front of her. It didn't matter that Dominique couldn't speak Russian—Peter didn't know that. For all he knew she could have been a client. That kind of behavior wouldn't be tolerated.

"Why? Are you going to judge me if I say yes?" Now she was full-on grinning. "I don't even care," she said before he could answer. "I hated that guy. I'm so glad Viktor is firing him."

Abram frowned at her words, an alarm bell going off in his head. Lucy seemed to like everyone, even the most obnoxious of their clients. She was sweetness and fucking sunshine almost all the time, usually to people who didn't deserve her warmth. "You never said anything."

She shrugged, taking another step back toward the door. They'd been all over Miami today at various properties they owned, including a hotel he and Viktor favored. He figured Lucy would be leaving soon. Or he'd tell her to. It was well past time she called it a day.

"If I complained about every jerk who made me feel uncomfortable when he looked at me, I wouldn't be able to work anywhere. He was just one of those guys you know is a pig, so I'm glad he'll be gone." She lifted her phone at an incoming text, frowned at it as she typed in a response.

Feeling irrationally territorial, Abram stood from his desk. "He made you feel uncomfortable?"

"What...yes. And now he's gone. Or he will be." She gave him one of those megawatt smiles that were rarely reserved for him. "Hey, I'm gonna grab dinner at the diner down the street before heading back. Want to come with me?"

It was the first time she'd ever asked him and he'd be a fool to say no. Nodding, he grabbed his cell phone from his desk. "Sure. What do you mean, heading back?"

"I've got some stuff I want to get ahead of before tomorrow.

You've got three meetings, and after today Viktor has way more on his plate because he cancelled his afternoon meetings." He could hear the slight question in Lucy's voice but would never talk about his brother's personal life to anyone.

"Are we working you too hard?" he asked as they headed for the elevators. This late in the evening the place was almost empty.

She frowned, smoothing a hand down her black pencil skirt. One that showcased her perfect, pert ass. Today she had on five-inch red heels that defined her calves. Calves he'd love to have resting on his shoulders while…

"No, why?"

"If we're not here, you shouldn't be here."

She snorted. "Abram, I love my job so stop worrying. You guys pay me great, and yeah I work crazy hours but it's worth it. Eventually we'll need to hire someone else but for now I'm good."

The sound of his name on her lips for the second time ever—the first she'd said it all on her own—made everything inside him go still as they stepped into the elevator. He finally found his voice as they reached the bottom floor. "If someone ever makes you feel uncomfortable at work again, let me know." There was no room for argument in his voice and he knew it sounded more like an order than a request but he didn't care. He'd wanted to say something back in his office about it, but then she'd asked him to join her for dinner and he'd pretty much lost the ability to talk. He knew she was just asking because he was the only one here, but still, a guy could dream this was more for her.

For a moment, his adorable pixie gave him a confused look. "Oh…ah, okay. I will, promise."

He nodded, taking her answer at face value, but he still planned to do another look at their newer hires. They'd made a mistake hiring Peter. On paper he'd been perfect, but at work he'd been subtly rude and not exactly lazy, but also not an outstanding employee. Abram and his brother owned a variety of companies and had enough different investment properties that they couldn't vet everyone. But the people who worked directly for them better be exemplary.

They'd earned their reputation for a reason and they couldn't afford to look weak now. Not ever.

And if anyone ever made Lucy feel uncomfortable or even looked at her wrong? They were gone.

"Viktor appears to have a new weakness," his contact said quietly into the phone.

There was some sort of thumping in the background, a vibration. "Where are you?" he demanded.

"I'm in a bathroom at a strip club," he said after a moment. "The door's locked. No one is in here with me. You want what I got or not?"

"What's his new weakness?" He didn't want to get his hopes up, but a rush of adrenaline surged through him.

"Not a what, a who. A blonde woman. I'm not sure who she is yet. She met with him today at one of his hotels. Abram seemed to know her too. Viktor fired one of his security for saying something to her. I don't know the whole story, but Viktor also threatened him with dismemberment if he even looked at her again. That's what I heard anyway. After she left, he cancelled all his meetings and worked out for three fucking hours. It was like he was in a rage." There was a touch of fear in his voice.

This could be what he'd been waiting for. "You don't know her name?"

"No, but I snapped a picture of her when she left. She's fucking hot. Tall, blonde, killer body and full lips I could imagine sucking my dick."

He rolled his eyes. He didn't give a shit what the woman looked like, just how he could use her against Viktor. "Send the picture to me."

"I'll text it as soon as we hang up."

"This is good. Keep me updated if you see her around more. I'll wire you our normal fee." This information was definitely worth what he paid the man.

"Thanks." He could hear the glee in his contact's voice.

The man only cared that he got paid, which was good for him. As long as that loser kept feeding his stripper and God knew what else habit, he'd keep feeding him information.

He just hoped this woman truly was a weakness to Viktor—that he'd finally found something to use against the untouchable Ivanov.

CHAPTER SIX

Dominique picked up her cell phone, then set it down. Again. Next she picked up her glass of white wine and took a sip as she stared out over the balcony of her condo. The complex's pool was surprisingly quiet this evening.

She'd been on autopilot again today at work and for the first time ever had actually been counting down the clock until she could go home.

Her friends had their own stuff going on right now and even though she knew she could talk to them about anything, she didn't want to. She'd always kept her past private and while she figured her boss knew about her family, considering Red Stone's vetting process, she didn't like to broadcast that painful part of her life.

Now…she had a chance to own her childhood home, a place that held so many wonderful memories. It felt wrong to take Ivanov up on his offer because it was such a huge gift.

And after doing some research—some of which Lizzy had helped with—she'd found that yes, he was pretty ruthless when it came to business, but he didn't appear to have his hand in any illegal things. Lizzy said at least not anymore, but that he may have at one time. He also gave a lot to charity, specifically ones that supported education and literacy. Which shouldn't matter. But it did.

Even after meeting with him yesterday she'd wondered if her judgment was off, if he really was just like his father. But from everything Lizzy had found it seemed as if he'd hated the man. And he'd seemed so sincere when he'd been talking to her yesterday. She couldn't help but wonder if her judgment was off because of her growing attraction to Viktor.

She picked up her phone again and dialed his number. It rang once and she almost hung up but he answered immediately.

"Hello?"

"Mr., uh, Viktor. It's Dominique Castle."

"I know."

"Oh, right. I…just wondered if the offer to see the house was still open?" Because even if she didn't take it, she still wanted to see it. Maybe it would give her a sense of closure on that part of her life.

"Of course. Did you want to see it tonight? I can meet you there or pick you up."

His question and offer made her pause. She desperately wanted to see it, but… "I can drive there myself and I'll be telling a friend where I'm going and who I'm meeting with." After yesterday, some intrinsic part of her trusted him, but meeting with a man she didn't really know somewhere alone in the evening? Yeah, she was going to be smart about it.

Thankfully he didn't seem insulted at all as he let out a short, amused laugh. "Good. I'll be bringing my assistant as well. I'll be there in half an hour."

She couldn't believe how easy this was, how accommodating he was being. She'd expected to have to wait—and she hadn't expected the small thrill at the idea of seeing him again. Which felt insane. "Thank you."

Once they disconnected she stared at her phone, wondering what the heck she was doing. Viktor Ivanov wasn't a man she should be attracted to, but she couldn't wait to see him face to face. And it had nothing to do with the house.

Viktor stepped out of his office, not surprised to see Lucy still at her desk. He knew she had plans to leave soon since it was well after seven, and he hated to ask her to work even later but he wanted her with him for this meeting.

"Lucy, would you mind coming with me to visit one of our properties? I'm meeting a woman there and think she'd feel more comfortable if you were with me."

"Is this the same blonde from yesterday?" Lucy asked, her smile just a little mischievous as she stood.

Over the last couple months Lucy's relationship with him had become a little more relaxed. He'd never had employees comfortable enough to treat him like anything other than a boss and he'd never had female friends. But he liked the dynamic of their relationship. "Maybe."

"I knew you liked her," she said, her smile growing wider as she pulled her purse out of one of her desk drawers. "I saw you checking her out at the Chef event. I'm never wrong about these things."

Lucy was far too observant—which was one of the reasons he'd never regretted hiring her. "It's not like that." Even if he wanted it to be. "We are…acquaintances."

She snorted as Abram stepped out of his office, a frown on his face. "Where are you two going?"

"To show Dominique the house."

Lucy's eyes widened slightly. "The one right on the beach you had Rita cancel all those rental reservations for? That place is gorgeous. Are you selling it to her?"

His brother was the only one who knew why he wanted to give it to Dominique, not sell. That wasn't something he'd share with Lucy or anyone else. "Something like that."

"I'll come with you," Abram said, stepping back into his office.

"No." Viktor didn't want his brother there. That would only make Dominique uncomfortable.

His brother stared hard at him, the tension between them clear.

Lucy cleared her throat. "I'll meet you downstairs," she murmured, her heels clicking as she hurried out into the hallway. Abram's gaze strayed after her for just a moment, the longing in his eyes clear. Viktor didn't think his brother would ever make a move on her, and not just because he was her boss. He seemed to view Lucy as unattainable. Viktor could relate to that sentiment.

"You don't want me with you?" Abram asked once they were alone.

"Not tonight."

"What if this woman wants to hurt you? You don't know that she doesn't blame you for our father's sins. Maybe this is a plot to lure you there alone."

Viktor sighed, scrubbing a hand over his face. He was glad his brother cared enough to be concerned, but he wasn't worried about Dominique trying to attack him. "You think I can't handle myself against a woman?"

"I think your judgment is clouded. This house is worth so much…" He trailed off, shaking his head. "I understand why you're doing it, but what if the offer insulted her and now she wants to hurt you?"

"Is this about me bringing Lucy?" Because his brother couldn't seriously think he'd be ambushed by an untrained woman.

Abram just clenched his jaw.

"Well?" Viktor demanded.

"I think we're pushing her too hard. She's putting in seventy-hour workweeks with us. And now you're bringing her with you when she should have left an hour ago? I want to hire another assistant so she doesn't burn out."

Ah, so it was about Lucy. "I agree. You want to tell her or should I?"

Abram lifted a shoulder. "Maybe you should. And she should be the one to approve the final hiring—after we've vetted them."

"Agreed." Lucy would be working closely with whoever they hired so they would need to get along. His brother was right too. They had been pushing her too hard. Some days he felt as if all he did was work. But he'd rather be at the office than go home to an empty house or out to some bullshit event where he didn't like most of the people there to begin with.

As expected he found Lucy waiting downstairs in the lobby, talking with one of the security guards. And as usual she was a chatterbox on the way to the beach house, talking about what they had on the books for the rest of the week and the next, some figurative fires he and his brother specifically needed to put out and other stuff he half listened to.

He was glad she was talking, filling the space with noise so he could try to ignore the anticipation humming through him at the thought of meeting with Dominique.

It was completely stupid to be excited to see her, but after she'd been so visibly vulnerable yesterday she'd gotten even further under his skin.

When he steered into the driveway he saw she was already there, leaning against her car. She had on sandals, white shorts that showed off miles of her tanned legs, and a flowy summer top. It was clear she'd come straight from home or somewhere not work. The last two times he'd seen her she'd been wearing professional dresses that came to just below her knees. Though nothing could hide her incredible body.

He nearly groaned at the sight of her, but kept himself in check. "Once we're inside, can you give us some privacy?" he asked Lucy quietly even though Dominique couldn't hear him. Yes, he'd brought Lucy to put Dominique more at ease but he could admit that he wanted time alone with her. Didn't matter if he didn't have a shot with her. A deeply buried part of him wanted her to see him as a man and not a threat.

"Of course."

Dominique had pushed away from her car and was standing at the front of his SUV, her body language nervous. When he got out, she forced a smile, clearly uncomfortable.

"Thank you for doing this." He hated that uncertain note in her voice.

And he wanted her to just take the damn house. He didn't understand why she was being stubborn about it. She'd only said she wanted to see it tonight. She hadn't mentioned anything about taking ownership.

"It's no problem," he murmured, trying not to stare at her. "Dominique, this is Lucy, my assistant."

After they made polite introductions, he asked Lucy to open the front door and told her they'd be inside in a minute.

"She just thinks you're a potential buyer," Viktor said. "I didn't tell her anything about who you are or why you're here." Though he knew Lucy was curious because there was no sane reason to sell this place. Not when it was making the company a lot of money.

Dominique let out a short sigh and gave him a small, appreciative smile. "Thank you." She turned to look at the huge, two-story house and he allowed himself to drink in her profile.

She'd pulled her long hair up into a tail and she wasn't wearing much makeup. She looked different than she had Saturday night and in her work clothes. A little younger than he'd originally thought—though he knew she was twenty-five now from his files. And a lot more vulnerable. When she wrapped her arms around herself and shivered he knew it wasn't from the July weather. He wondered if being here hurt her and he hated that it was a possibility. He didn't know how to comfort her though. Or even if he should try.

"If it's too hard to go inside we can come back later. Or I can just give you a key and you can come by whenever you want." It would probably be easier on her that way, going inside alone.

Her head snapped around to look at him. For a long moment she watched him with a wealth of emotions bleeding into her dark gaze, one of which was anger.

Which surprised him. His brother's words came back to haunt him and for the briefest moment he wondered if she did want to hurt him in some way. Not that he was worried about her physically taking him on.

"Part of me hates how nice you're being," she finally whispered. "I hated you for a long time. I thought...you were just like him." She turned away before he could respond and headed up the walkway to the front door.

Scrubbing the back of his neck he followed after her and tried not to watch the sway of her perfect ass. Tried and failed.

What the hell had he been thinking, coming here? He should have just let Rita or Lucy handle it. Or just sent the fucking key straight to Dominique.

Being around her and knowing she likely only tolerated him was torture. Especially when all he wanted to do was kiss her.

Dominique sat on the edge of the queen-sized bed in her old room that looked nothing like it used to. A leopard print comforter with giant throw pillows covered the bed. An oversized canvas print of palm trees and the ocean hung on the wall above the dresser and small television. As far as beach rentals went, it was nice. The decorator certainly liked loud prints and colors, if the other rooms were anything to go by, but she could see the appeal for renters. For them it was a fun place to stay in for a week or two.

It had been a wonderful place to grow up in. Closing her eyes, she had a flash of her mom standing in the doorway, telling her that she'd made double chocolate chip cookies and that Dominique better grab some before her father ate them all. Her mom had loved baking. She'd tried new recipes practically every week. Their house had always smelled like cookies.

That was before everything had gone wrong.

As stupid tears pricked her eyes, she angrily swiped them away. She'd been here too long tonight. She knew she should just leave but hours later, she couldn't seem to force herself out of this room.

Part of her was irrationally angry at Viktor for offering her this, for dredging up a bunch of old memories she'd done well to keep locked down. But she knew that was stupid. He didn't seem to have any hidden agenda, just a need to make things right. If anything, he seemed almost desperate for her to take the house, something she still wasn't sure about.

At a slight noise in the doorway she nearly jumped when she saw Viktor standing there, looking almost hesitant. Now that she didn't hate the man she could truly appreciate how attractive he was. She might have compared him to a thug before, but the truth was she *liked* that look.

He had a darker edge to him that she found insanely sexy. His dark hair was cropped close to his head and those eyes—she could definitely get lost in that pale blue gaze. His height and build were enough to make her weak in the knees. Not many men towered over her and she liked that he did. Her experience with sex might be lacking but she had a feeling he'd know what he was doing in the bedroom. How could he not? The man was always in total control and built like a—

He cleared his throat and she realized she was staring at his mouth. Great—she was totally perving on him at the most inopportune time.

"I had one of my drivers pick Lucy up. It's getting late and she's got early morning meetings."

Which meant he probably did too. Of course. Cringing, she stood. "I'm sorry. I didn't mean to take up—"

He shook his head sharply. "Don't be sorry. I just didn't want you to be surprised when you realized she was gone. I can wait outside for you. Take as much time as you need."

"You're very thoughtful." She hated that the words came out as an accusation. But around him she felt like a mess. It was hard to reconcile him with the man she'd always thought he was.

To her surprise his lips quirked up, softening his expression just a bit. "You're the first person to ever say that to me."

She couldn't feign surprise at that. He seemed like a hard man, and in business she knew his reputation was brutal. "This used to be my room," she said, changing the subject. "Though I had posters of surfers on my walls." She half-smiled, looking around the transformed space. "And my walls were purple."

"You surf?" He took a few steps into the room.

"Not really. I mean, I did in high school a little. Longboard, mostly. The posters were of surfer guys. *That* was where my interest was back then."

He snorted, the sound taking her off guard. "That wasn't so long ago."

She lifted a shoulder. "Eight or nine years. God, it feels like a lifetime ago… I hated both of them for a long time," she blurted.

He stepped farther into the room and, to her surprise, sat on the bed next to her. "Your parents?"

"Yeah. My dad for getting killed in a stupid bar fight and leaving us. Then my mom for… I was such a spoiled teenager. Well, not too terrible, I guess, but I was pretty self-involved. I loved my mom but I only cared about getting out of that place we were living in, about spending time with my friends. I hated what happened to us, hated that I got stuck in a new school for my last year of high school because we couldn't afford my private school anymore. I never really thought about how much it affected her. I used to think if I'd paid more attention I'd have known that something was really wrong, that she…" Dominique swallowed hard, lifting a shoulder. She couldn't finish the sentence. It was hard enough thinking it, let alone saying it out loud.

"She was your mother. She was protecting you. It's what mothers do." He reached out and swiped his thumb across her cheek.

Dominique hadn't even realized more tears had slipped past her defenses. The feel of him gently touching her almost undid her completely, but he quickly dropped his hand.

"You sound like you know that from experience."

He looked straight ahead instead of at her. "My mother died when I was seven. My memories of her are…good ones. She was a sweet woman who got involved with a very bad man."

The pain in his voice was so raw she squeezed his forearm on instinct, wanting to comfort him somehow. When he stiffened under her touch she pulled back, not wanting to make him uncomfortable. And she felt a little bad at noticing how incredibly muscular he was and wondering if the rest of his body was just as toned and ripped. She was pretty sure he was, because it wasn't like his suit hid how strong he was.

Looking away from him, she said, "When I was five I wanted a princess party, complete with a prince and princess." She wasn't sure exactly why she was telling him other than she wanted him to know what this house meant to her, what his offer essentially meant. "The 'prince' got food poisoning or something at the last minute so my dad stepped in and wore the costume and stayed in character the whole time. The party was by the pool here, including a pink princess house, and all my friends got princess costumes and tiaras to wear and take home. It was so ridiculously over-the-top for a five-year-old." She shook her head, laughing slightly. "My dad was always like that with everything. He grew up poor so I guess he just…I don't know." She sighed, swiping at more tears. "I swear I'm not normally a crier."

Viktor wrapped an arm around her shoulders, his hold almost awkward, but she appreciated it. Hell, she needed the comfort right now. She leaned into him, trying to ignore that spicy masculine scent that went straight to her head. He was just becoming more and more attractive to her every moment.

"You can cry all you need." His accent was slightly thicker now.

She laid her head on his hard shoulder, soaking up some of his strength. "You really are nothing like I expected," she murmured.

"I don't hear that a lot." His voice was dry. "Usually people say I'm worse than they expected."

Laughing again she lifted her head to look at him. Their faces were only inches apart, making her suck in a breath at the close proximity of his mouth.

His very kissable mouth.

She swallowed hard, stared into those intense blue eyes. For a long moment she wondered what it would be like to kiss him, to feel his lips on hers. That thought would have seemed insane a day ago. Now…

He cleared his throat and whatever weirdness was going on between them was instantly broken.

"My father was nothing like yours," he said quietly, looking straight ahead again, his posture stiff.

Something about the way he was almost awkward was…sexy.

Something she shouldn't be thinking about. "Even with…you? Was he not a good father?"

He let out a harsh laugh, the sound full of bitterness. "When I was fifteen he threw me into a ring with one of his fighters to 'toughen me up,' as he put it—he ran an illegal fighting ring for about a decade. The guy went as easy as he could on me without making it too obvious. He didn't want to kill me, but I ended up with a broken nose, three broken ribs and…" He trailed off, shaking his head. "At least you have good memories with your family."

She was too shocked to respond. How awful to have such a brutal man for a father.

"Take the house, Dominique. It's the best 'fuck you' to my father you can make. Take it and do what you want with it."

Forget the house. She wanted to reach out and comfort him somehow.

As if he sensed her thoughts he abruptly stood and headed for the door.

"Have dinner with me tomorrow night?" she blurted. When he turned to look at her with raised eyebrows she continued. "To talk about the contract." Which, okay, was a complete lie. She wanted to spend more time with him. That knowledge disturbed her but she couldn't fight the pull toward him. The house was something she didn't even want to think about right now.

He nodded, his eyes flaring with heat, and she wondered if he felt that same pull. She knew he wanted her, had seen moments of awareness from him, but it could be nothing more than just lust. "I can meet you somewhere."

"Or you can just pick me up. I'm guessing you know where I live by now?" It should annoy her, but he was trying to fix what his father had done. Considering that he'd sent her that contract, it wasn't hard to figure out that when he'd done research on her, he would have found out more about her. Her address and phone number were probably at the top of the list.

His face flushed, the action…almost adorable. The man really was ridiculously sexy. "I'd have to look it up, but it's in the file I had put together on you."

"I feel like I should be mad about that."

His mouth curved up ever so slightly. "You should be. Though…you found me at my hotel so you've done some research too." There was a hint of a question at the end. As if he'd been wondering how she'd done that.

Her face heated at his words. She wasn't going to admit that she'd asked a friend to locate him.

"Is seven o'clock good?" he continued when she didn't respond.

"It is." The tingle of excitement in her belly was ridiculous, she told herself. But that didn't matter. She was already thinking about what she'd wear tomorrow night.

Because she wanted to get to know sexy and dangerous Viktor way more than she should.

CHAPTER SEVEN

Abram wasn't sure what he'd done to piss Lucy off, but in the last hour she'd been giving him the cold shoulder—and he had no idea why. Last night he'd been annoyed with his brother for taking Lucy with him and she'd no doubt sensed the tension between him and Viktor. But things had been normal between Lucy and him today. They'd even had lunch together. Sure, Viktor had been with them, but things had seemed like they always did.

And now he felt like a fucking fifteen-year-old girl, obsessing over her. He scrubbed a hand over his face as she stepped into his office, her expression perfectly neutral. It annoyed the hell out of him.

"I'm about to head out. Do you need anything else, Mr. Ivanov?"

He gritted his teeth at the formal title. There was no doubt she was pissed at him now. "What did I say about using my first name?'

She rolled her eyes. "I'll take that as a no. Have a good night."

He was out of his chair and around his desk before she'd taken one step back to the doorway. "What's going on with you? What did I do to piss you off?" Because he was racking his brain and he couldn't think of anything that made any kind of sense.

"Nothing, sir. I'm just—"

"Cut the shit, Lucy."

Anger flared in her dark eyes but she seemed to rein it in. "I'm sorry if I have an inappropriate attitude. I'll make sure to—"

"No, you're not sorry. What the fuck is going on?" he demanded, practically shouting. He was close to kissing her senseless. Anything to get a reaction out of her.

She didn't flinch at his show of temper, something he adored about her. Just put her hands on her hips and glared up at him. "Am I going to get fired for being honest with you?"

"No. And when are you *not* honest?" One of the reasons why she was such a good fit for Viktor and him was that while she was almost always in a good mood, she also didn't put up with their shit. And she wasn't afraid of them. They'd had assistants in the past who jumped anytime they gave an order. It was ridiculous.

"You are such a dick sometimes! I get why you act that way in business, because you and Viktor have built something amazing. But I overheard your conversation with Viktor an hour ago." She was fuming and he didn't understand why.

"So?" He hadn't shut the door to Viktor's office when he'd gone in there. The conversation hadn't been confidential. Viktor was going out with Dominique tonight and Abram was worried about him getting hurt. That woman might have an ulterior motive, for all he knew. It didn't matter that Viktor was his older brother—Abram wouldn't let anyone hurt him. Viktor had gone through enough over the years.

"Oh my God, I want to smack you. 'Do not go out with her, Viktor,' 'She is not the type of woman for you,' 'She just wants to hurt you.'" She repeated some of the things he'd said to his brother, her impression of him mocking.

He blinked. "Is that supposed to be me?"

"It's what you sound like. Why don't you want your brother to be happy? I've heard you say the same kinds of things to him before!" She stomped a heel, as if she was going to advance on him. Which he found insanely hot. "What kind of woman do you think is right for him? Because I did a little research and before you get on your high horse, just *don't*. I know you have files on tons of people," she continued before he could respond, and there was nothing to say anyway because it was true. "I *knew* she looked familiar so I made a call to a friend at Red Stone."

He blinked again. "You did?"

"Of course I did. You're my guys. I look out for both of you."

Before he could fully digest what she'd said, she continued, her rage against him clearly building. "She's a freaking exemplary employee over there and a model citizen. They wouldn't have hired her if she wasn't. So what's wrong with her? And why do you always tell your brother that a certain type of woman isn't right for him? Do you mean women who *aren't* escorts? Because that's pretty shitty, Abram! He deserves more than an escort."

His gaze narrowed. "You know about that?"

She rolled her eyes again, throwing her hands up in exasperation. "Of course I know. I did my own research on both of you before I even applied here for a job. I'm not an idiot." She poked him in the chest with a fingertip. "And I like him. He's such a sweet man. Do you just not want your brother to be happy? Because I simply can't believe you'd be that mean."

He wrapped his hand around the finger she'd shoved in his chest and invaded her personal space. The urge to kiss her, to touch her, was overwhelming. The woman was an addiction and he'd never even tasted her. He backed her up until she was against the door. All he wanted to do was take her right up against it, to shove her skirt up and sink deep inside her. "Of course I want him to be happy. I just worry he'll get his heart broken. He's... It doesn't fucking matter. He's my brother. I get to worry about him! And it's none of your business." And he could *not* make himself let go of her hand.

"Fine. If it's not my business, then this conversation is over!"

"It's not over!" It could never be over with her. He was pretty sure she literally just meant the conversation, but something about her tone made him panic, as if she meant they were over. Even if there was no 'they.'

She gave a half push against his chest. "It is over. And I'm not coming into work tomorrow. I'm taking a day off because if I have—"

Hell no. He wasn't letting her leave, wasn't letting her *not* come in tomorrow. Seeing her was the best part of his day. Even arguing with her was better than anything else. Feeling absolutely possessed, he crushed his mouth over hers. To his utter fucking surprise she leaned into him immediately, moaning into his mouth as her fingers dug into his shoulders. He plunged a hand into her short hair, cupping the back of her head in a tight grip. He'd wanted to taste her for so long and now he didn't want to let Lucy go.

Ever.

This woman owned him, had from practically the moment they'd hired her. It didn't matter that this was wrong on multiple levels. He couldn't get enough of her and now that he knew she wanted him back…

No, no, no. She should be shoving him back, telling him that he was an asshole and that she was going to file a sexual harassment charge against him. That was what she *should* do, he told himself. She was too good for him, far too sweet.

And his *assistant*. They shouldn't be doing this.

But when she moaned again and kissed him harder, completely melting against him, he lost his mind. How many times had he fantasized about doing this, about doing so much *more* than this?

Blindly reaching out, he locked his office door with his free hand and pulled back to look down at her, still cupping the back of her head.

Her dark hair was tousled and her lips slightly swollen, her dark eyes dilated with desire. When she touched her tongue to her bottom lip, tasting him on her own mouth, he didn't fight the groan that escaped. He could imagine her tongue stroking him everywhere, wished she had her mouth wrapped around his cock right now.

They both stared at each other, breathing hard, and even though he knew this was a mistake, he couldn't seem to make himself stop.

And not touching her wasn't an option. This woman pushed him to the very edge of his control. He wanted to protect her in a way he'd never imagined. He wanted to give her anything she wanted, to give her so much pleasure she never walked away from him.

Slowly, he went down onto his knees in front of her. He was going to taste all of her, feel her wetness on his tongue. He'd fantasized too many times what she'd taste like, how she'd sound as he gave her pleasure. She watched him, wide-eyed, her breathing growing more erratic.

"Tell me to stop," he growled, barely hanging onto his control.

Once he put his mouth to her, once he got a taste of her, he wasn't stopping until she came against his tongue.

She shook her head, her expression slightly dazed.

He knew he should demand that she vocalize it, but fuck it. He was a selfish bastard. He wanted to taste her, wanted to show her how good things could be between them. He wasn't above tying her to him with sex, at least at first. He would just get her addicted to him.

Keeping his gaze pinned to hers he shoved her pencil skirt up to her hips to reveal bright red… He slid his hands up the back of her thighs and didn't stop until he cupped her smooth, bare ass. *Yep, thong.*

He groaned. His cock shoved insistently against his zipper but that would just have to wait.

"I've wondered what you wear underneath your clothes," he rasped out.

She still watched him, a mix of nerves and lust clear on her pretty face. "Really?" she whispered.

"All the fucking time," he growled. "I stroke myself off thinking about it, about *you*."

Her shiny lips parted, her chest rising and falling, but she didn't say anything. Just watched him. He wanted to see her completely naked, to have her stretched out underneath him as he worshiped her entire body.

He wanted to see her lose every bit of her control and to stake his claim, to ruin her for any other man. Hell yeah, he wanted her so damn addicted to him that he was all she could think about. Because the truth was, *she* was all he could think about. He'd forced himself to keep his distance whenever he could, but there were times when he hadn't been able to stay away. He'd search her out, ask for stupid menial tasks just so he could talk to her, see her face to face.

Even though he wanted to thrust into her over and over and lose himself inside her, for now he'd settle for making her come against his tongue.

"You wet, baby?" he rasped out, his heart thundering against his ribs. She was so fucking gorgeous, all aroused and waiting to see what he did next.

Her eyes were a little glazed over, as if she couldn't believe they were doing this. Well, he couldn't either.

She nodded, her cheeks flushing pink as she licked her lips.

Still keeping his gaze on hers, he slowly pulled the front of her thong to the side before sliding his finger between her soft folds. Just a tease, a bare touch that made him shudder.

She was soaked.

He swallowed a rough groan. "Does arguing with me get you hot?"

"You get me hot," she breathed out, her words unsteady. Her fingers slid through his hair, her touch tentative.

It was exactly what he'd wanted to hear. Inhaling her sweet scent he leaned forward and swiped his tongue along her folds. Moaning, she jerked against his face and he lost it.

Grasping one of her ankles, he lifted her leg over his shoulder, spreading her open wider for him.

"Abram…" Her voice was nervous, unsteady.

"You want to stop, baby?" He hated to even ask, but he wanted her comfortable, for there to be no room for regret.

"No." But she still seemed nervous.

He sucked with words, had no idea how to reassure her. He just wanted to make her feel good. That, he knew he could do. Leaning forward again, he flicked his tongue over her clit and she let out the sweetest moan of pleasure.

He teased the sensitive nub again, adding more pressure even as he slid a finger inside her. "You're so tight," he moaned against her.

He imagined what she'd feel like wrapped around his cock, milking him until he was completely sated. Though for how he felt he didn't think he'd ever get enough of Lucy. Thoughts of her had been consuming him for months. She was his secret addiction. He hadn't been lying; he jerked off to thoughts of her more than he would admit.

Lucy gasped and rolled her hips again, her inner walls clenching around him as he added another finger into her tight body. She was biting her lower lip now, her cheeks flushed, eyes glowing with need.

Her fingers dug into his scalp as he continued teasing her clit, flicking his tongue against it over and over. The more pressure he added, the more she jerked against him, practically riding his face.

He wanted to lie flat on his back and let her do it from above, to completely bury his face in her sweet pussy.

"*Abram*." Her body jerked and he knew she was going to come, could feel the way her inner walls convulsed faster and faster. "Oh…"

When her fingers dug into his scalp he savored the sweet bite of pain as she fell over the edge, her breathing out of control, her cries of pleasure music to his ears as she reached climax.

He didn't stop licking her until she gasped "Too much," the words coming out breathless.

Feeling almost drunk, he looked up to find her staring at him through heavy-lidded eyes. She looked as if she'd been thoroughly fucked, which she had, by his tongue. Too bad it hadn't been his cock yet. But it would soon. Tonight, if he had any say about it.

But not up against his office door. She deserved better than that. He wanted to take her back to his place, to completely worship her body, bring her orgasm after orgasm. Then he wanted to talk about their future, because he couldn't let her walk away after this.

They both jumped at the sound of a soft knocking coming from the outer office. "Hello? Mr. Ivanov?" a male voice called out.

"Oh God," Lucy rasped out, her expression morphing to one of horror. Her eyes widened as she slid her leg off his shoulder. Her legs wobbled and he set a hand on her hip to steady her, a rush of masculine pride roaring through him. He'd loved making her come against his tongue, loved that he'd made her unravel. Avoiding his gaze, she shoved her skirt down with trembling hands as he pushed to his feet.

He pulled out a handkerchief and wiped his face. His fingers smelled like Lucy and sex so he just shoved his hand in his pocket. He didn't want to lose that scent.

He also didn't want her to regret anything because he certainly didn't. "Lucy—"

She shook her head. "I don't want to talk about this here," she rushed out, her cheeks crimson. She quickly turned away from him, smoothing her hair down before she jerked the door open.

One of his drivers and another employee who worked in HR were standing in the doorway. *Fuck.* He couldn't chase after Lucy now, not when it was clear two employees needed to talk to him. He didn't want to embarrass her and he wasn't sure if they'd heard anything. From their expressions he didn't think so, but who the hell knew.

He nodded once at Kir. "I'll be down in twenty," he said.

The HR employee asked, "Got a few minutes?"

"Yeah." Even if all he wanted to do was chase after his very sexy assistant who was covertly trying to make her escape. She'd gone into Viktor's office but Abram knew that as soon as he stepped back into his own she'd be leaving for the night.

To escape him and what had happened here.

If she thought she could run from him, she was very much mistaken. Now that he'd tasted her come, felt her climax against his face, he didn't think he was ever letting her go.

Viktor wiped his damp palms against his pants as he headed up to Dominique's condo. He hadn't been this nervous in…

He'd never been this nervous. It was ridiculous.

She was on the second floor of a small, Mediterranean-style complex. It was in a good area and had decent security. Not good enough for her though. He'd never been particularly protective of anyone before. Well, other than his mother, but he'd been a child when she'd died. And of course Lucy.

But the protectiveness he felt for Dominique was very different. He wanted to put himself between her and anything that might ever threaten her. He wanted to make sure she never got hurt again.

When he reached her door it swung open before he could knock.

As usual his heart rate kicked up at the sight of her. She had on a green and white summer dress that fell a little lower than mid-thigh. With her legs it was pretty much guaranteed that anything showing off all that skin looked good on her. She'd left her pale blonde hair down so that it fell in soft waves around her shoulders and face.

"I was waiting for you," she said, her light laugh just a little nervous. "Did you want to come in for a drink before we head out?"

He wanted to say yes, but shook his head. Viktor didn't want to know more about her, to see more of her life, because it would just show him what he couldn't have.

He was only here tonight because she wanted to talk about the contract. Okay, that was a lie—he wanted to spend time with her. But he knew that she was only here for one reason. So he wouldn't pretend otherwise. And going into her place and having a drink before they went out sounded like something people on dates did. This wasn't a date. "I wasn't sure where you would want to go so I chose a place on the beach. Cuban food, and mainly locals eat there."

"Sounds good." She grabbed her purse, which was more of a small pocketbook than anything, before shutting the door behind her.

"Don't you need to set your alarm?" he asked as she locked her door.

Her eyes widened slightly as she turned to him. "Ah...I don't have a system. Well, my place is wired for it. I just don't have a paid service right now."

He frowned as she fell in step beside him.

"What?"

He lifted a shoulder. It wasn't as if she was his. He had no say over her life. "Nothing. I brought a couple copies of the contract," he said. "If there's something you don't like we can fix it, but I think you'll be okay with it. You should still have an attorney look at it, regardless."

"I lied," she blurted as they reached the stairs. "I don't want to talk about the contract."

Ah, here it came. Keeping his expression neutral, he braced himself for what she was going to say. His brother had been right. Maybe she'd asked him out tonight to—

"I just wanted to spend time with you. As in…a date." She cringed, guilt flickering in her dark eyes. "I'm sorry. I should have just been honest with you."

He blinked in surprise, wondering when she'd drop the punch line, but he realized she was being serious. "You want to go on a date with me?"

She nodded, looking almost miserable. "I shouldn't have used the contract as an—"

"It's fine." His words came out more harshly than he'd intended. Viktor cleared his throat. All his muscles tightened as her words sank in. She wanted to go out with him. For no other reason than she wanted to spend time with him. "I would like to take you out as well." He inwardly cringed at how formal he sounded. But everything about this woman made him forget how to function.

Her cheeks flushed the sexiest shade of pink. "Okay, then. No contract talk tonight?"

"None."

"Good." She lightly curled her fingers around his upper arm and gave him a soft, almost shy smile that made him half desperate to kiss her. He could easily imagine her hands stroking over his naked body and had to shut that thought down. "I'm hungry. Let's get out of here."

He was hungry too, but not for food. Keeping that thought at bay, he nodded once. The feel of her fingers grazing him ever so lightly was heaven and hell.

This woman made him want too much.

That was a very dangerous thing. The last time he'd fallen for a woman he'd learned too late that everything they'd shared was a lie. That she'd felt nothing for him. The shame of that memory flared inside him now, nearly consuming him. It also reminded him why he only used escorts. There was never any question of where they stood.

But when he looked at the beautiful woman on his arm he knew that he wouldn't be able to simply walk away from Dominique, no matter how great the risk.

Even if she did have ulterior motives, a dark part of him didn't care if she used him. He'd let himself be used by her if it meant he got a taste of her in the bargain.

CHAPTER EIGHT

Dominique couldn't fight the jitters humming through her as Viktor opened the front door of the restaurant leading out into the parking lot. Dinner with him had been fun, even if he had seemed awkward at times. If anything, it endeared him even more to her.

He truly was nothing like she'd expected.

When he placed his big hand at the small of her back she could feel the heat of his touch straight to her skin. And she wondered what it would feel like to have him touching her bare skin. She'd been thinking about it all through dinner and questioning if she'd lost her mind. More than anything, she wondered if he'd be sensual, gentle…maybe a little rough.

"Thank you for dinner," she murmured. Her flat sandals crunched over the gravelly parking lot as they made their way to his SUV. She was glad that he hadn't had a driver tonight, that it was just them. She kept obsessing, wondering if he was going to kiss her—and really hoping he would. Everything about him screamed sex and power, and she really, *really* wanted to see what it would be like to lose herself with a man like Viktor.

He grunted a non-response before clearing his throat. "I'd like to take you out again. Tomorrow."

Yep, those butterflies were out of control in her stomach right about now. "I'd like that too," she said as they reached the passenger-side door.

Instead of opening the door for her, he gripped the handle and looked down at her, his body turned toward hers. She wondered what it would be like if he pressed her up against the vehicle and kissed her senseless, just took complete control. She squeezed her legs together at the thought. Everything about Viktor screamed power and control, and she found that she liked that. A lot. In college she'd dated a little, and when she hung out with her girlfriends they usually brought guys.

Now, the guys she'd dated or gone out with seemed like boys. There was nothing boyish about Viktor. He had a hard, dangerous edge to him that shouldn't fascinate her so much, but...she couldn't help herself.

When he reached out to cup her cheek, she sucked in a slight breath. His palm was callused and she liked the feel of it against her skin. There was nothing soft about this man. Her nipples beaded tightly against her bra at his simple touch.

His gaze fell to her mouth as he stroked a gentle thumb across her cheek. There was something intense about the moment as he looked down at her. When he looked at her like that she felt as if she was the only person who existed for him.

On instinct, she arched her body into his, erasing the space between them. He seemed to be keeping a wall up between them, but if he was going to kiss her, she wanted to feel him pressed up against her, feel that huge body on hers. And she really hoped he would take control. She might not know exactly what she wanted in a relationship or even sex, but deep down she thought that might be something she needed to be satisfied with a partner. For most of her life she'd towered over men, and while she was confident in who she was, she wanted a man who made her feel treasured and who could take complete control.

He murmured something in Russian, the words harsh sounding before he lowered his mouth to hers.

She closed her eyes as his lips barely touched hers—and cried out as a hard hand shoved into the middle of her back, sending her flying into Viktor. Her purse was ripped from her hand as she slammed into him. His back collided with the side mirror as her nose rammed against his chest. Tears stung her eyes from the abrupt impact.

She held onto him, trying to steady herself, but he grasped her upper arms and quickly shoved her behind him just as she heard the squeal of tires and flying gravel. Had someone been waiting in a car for this?

"Stay put," he ordered, pulling out a gun before racing to the back of the SUV.

Shock punched through her at the sight of the gun, but she swiped at the tears on her cheeks and stayed crouched by the front tire.

He let out a string of angry Russian words she was pretty sure were curses, before turning back to her. "He's gone. He had a getaway driver."

On trembling legs she pushed up from her crouch. Her nose felt sensitive but she was just glad she and Viktor were unharmed. "You carry a gun?" she blurted out even though yeah, it was pretty freaking obvious he did.

Ignoring her question, he tucked it under his shirt and out of sight. She probably shouldn't be surprised but it somehow took her off guard. That wasn't the thing she should be worrying about right now though. But she was feeling off balance in a big way. Trembles racked her body as she thought about what could have truly happened, how much worse things could have been. Someone could have stabbed or shot them.

Moving to her, he ran his hands up and down her arms, his gaze sweeping over her from head to foot in a purely clinical way. "Are you okay?"

"Yeah, I…we need to call the police. And I need to cancel my bank card immediately. Are you okay?"

He blinked, frowning at the question, as if she'd asked the most insane thing ever. He pulled out his phone. "Do you know your bank's number?"

"Yes… Crap, I've got to cancel my phone now too. God, that was insane. Did you get a look at who took my purse? Oh, maybe they have security footage here the cops can use."

Viktor simply nodded, scanning the parking lot, and opened the passenger door for her. "Get inside." The words came out like an order. "Ah, please," he added when she raised her eyebrows at his brusque tone. "I want to keep you safe."

The way he said those simple words did something strange to her insides. He said it as if he truly meant it. As if her safety was the most important thing to him.

She slid into the seat, and for some reason wasn't really surprised when he actually buckled her in. The way he just took charge sometimes made her melt. Heart still beating out of control, she started to dial her bank as he rounded the front of the vehicle.

To her surprise he pulled out another phone and made a call, speaking in Russian as she made her own phone calls. First she canceled her bank card and then reported her phone stolen. This was a huge pain in the ass but she was just glad they were okay. Once she was done, he was wrapping up his call as well. She handed him his phone as he started the engine.

"Wait, what about the police?"

He snorted, the sound laced with the slightest bit of derision. "I'm not calling the cops."

"Why not? I was just *mugged*." They needed to make a report.

"I want to get the locks changed on your condo tonight. I've already called someone and I'm having it taken care of immediately."

"My locks… Oh my God. They've got my address and my keys." At least she hadn't had any work keys in her purse. She'd just brought the basics tonight.

"What else did you have in there?" he asked, steering out of the parking lot.

She wanted to argue with him about not calling the police, but answered. "My phone and debit card, both of which are taken care of now. A little cash and some makeup stuff."

"No work stuff?"

"No."

"Okay. Good."

"Now why aren't you calling the police?"

"Because they won't be able to do a damn thing about tonight. Did you see the man who took your purse?" he asked, even though he had to know she hadn't seen a thing.

Biting her lip, she shook her head. "I didn't even get a glimpse of him." One moment she'd been almost kissing Viktor and the next someone had shoved her into him. "Where did he even come from?"

"He must have been waiting for us. There was someone waiting with him which means a team timed this perfectly, waiting until we were distracted." Viktor's voice was tight with barely concealed rage. "I should have kept you safer. I'm sorry."

There was so much self-recrimination in his voice it made her pause. "Viktor, it was just a random mugging. It's not your job to keep me safe. I'm just glad we're okay."

He seemed troubled. "I...don't necessarily know that it was random."

A new thread of fear slid through her veins. "What? Why would you think that?"

He glanced in the rearview mirror before switching lanes. "Mud was rubbed across the license plate, and the way it was almost choreographed..." He shook his head, his expression darkening. "I have a lot of enemies and you were out with me." Again, there was that note in his voice she didn't like.

"Some jerk stole my purse. It's no one's fault but his. And I can't imagine someone mugging me simply because I was out with you. That doesn't even make sense." He had to see that.

But instead of agreeing with her, he just did that grunting thing and took the next turn.

Sighing, she leaned back against the seat, fighting the rush of nerves that had invaded her and didn't seem to be going away. Something so much worse could have happened tonight. What if her mugger had been carrying a weapon? She fought off a shudder, and to her surprise, Viktor reached out and squeezed her thigh, ever so lightly.

"I'm going to find out who did this." There was a blade-sharp edge to his voice that took her off guard, but she just nodded.

The truth was in his voice and part of her felt bad for her mugger.

Because if a man like Viktor *did* find him... She was pretty sure he'd hurt the guy. And she didn't know what to think about that.

Didn't know what to think about anything lately. Viktor had completely knocked her world off its axis and she was only now coming to terms with the fact that she was insanely attracted to him. A man who most definitely had a shady history in business and was the son of a man she'd considered her enemy for a long time.

Even though she was worried about her stolen purse, she still couldn't help but wish that they'd gotten to follow through on that kiss. What would it have felt like to have Viktor's lips teasing hers and his body pressed up tight against hers?

She wasn't even sure what she'd like. Her sexual experiences consisted of kissing and what her mother would have called 'heavy petting.' All over the clothes.

After her mom had killed herself Dominique had retreated into herself, just working through college and barely even going out with friends the first couple years. The only people she'd even let into her life had been her extended family. Looking back, she realized that she'd been depressed. It had taken a long damn time to crawl out of her self-imposed prison. Not only that, she'd been afraid of sex for a long time. Her mom had been used sexually, had felt so ashamed that she'd killed herself. Even after Dominique had managed to start living again, she'd still shied away from sex.

So now she was a twenty-five-year-old virgin and for the first time she wondered if that would be an issue. The men she'd dated in the last few years had all been metrosexual types and more often than not the kind of men who used more beauty products than her. None of them had ever gotten her remotely hot enough to even consider sex. She'd go on a date or two and realize that nope, the guy wasn't for her. It wasn't like she was saving herself for marriage, but she wanted her first time to mean something, to be with someone who got her so turned on that she couldn't think straight—

"I promise I'll find who took your purse." Viktor's hard voice cut through her thoughts, his gaze on her intense as they idled at a stoplight.

"W-what…oh, okay. That's good." She stuttered over her words, embarrassed that she'd been so caught up in her own thoughts she hadn't been paying attention to anything else. It was clear he thought she was worried about her stupid purse when all she wanted to do was tell Viktor about her lack of experience.

But she wanted to wait to see if they even had a second date after this. That wasn't the kind of thing she could just blurt out. If things moved forward she'd definitely tell him. Especially if things got more heated between them.

And she really, really hoped that they did.

"Keep your eyes to yourself," Viktor growled out, careful to speak in Russian to Dimitri, the friend he'd asked to come over and change out Dominique's lock.

Viktor could have done it himself, but this particular friend had been a thief in another life and had the right tools and hardware on hand—because Dimitri now owned a string of hardware stores around Miami and in Homestead. Installing locks wasn't part of his normal job description but he was doing Viktor a favor.

Didn't mean he had to let the guy stare at Dominique. Not that he blamed him, but it still annoyed Viktor.

Dimitri just grinned and went back to installing the lock.

"Thank you again for doing this," Dominique said, standing close to Viktor as she watched Dimitri finish up.

"Thank Viktor, not me." Dimitri didn't look up as he worked.

Viktor's annoyance was somewhat appeased at his friend's words.

Dominique glanced up at Viktor then, her cheeks flushing slightly. Just the sight of her like that made him think of what she'd look like after sex—and during sex. And he'd had way too many fantasies in the past few days about that.

"Thank you," she murmured, sliding her hand around his upper arm the same way she'd done at the beginning of the evening. Her fingers rested gently against his skin, her hold light.

He loved the way she touched him and he knew it was because she wanted to. Not because she was paid to. Or…he assumed she wanted to. That doubt still lingered in the back of his head, wondering if she was somehow using him.

He quickly shelved the thought, not wanting his past bullshit to color the time he spent with her. If she was using him, he'd deal with it later.

Right now he wanted to kick his own ass for not being able to protect Dominique tonight. Someone—more than one person—had worked very carefully to make sure they were able to grab her purse and flee with a backup driver for a supposedly simple mugging. Everything about what happened felt off and he was pissed that he'd let his guard down.

As Dimitri worked, he gently pulled Dominique down the exterior walkway, wanting to give them a little more privacy. Her complex had been very quiet tonight, or at least her building and floor. He'd only seen one neighbor arrive since they'd been back.

"What's wrong?" she asked, still holding onto his arm as she turned her body toward his.

With her so close to him, her breasts brushing against his arm as she shifted, it took serious effort to think. He cleared his throat. "I'm going to give you a phone to keep, just overnight, until you can get a new one tomorrow. I don't like the thought of you not having a way to contact anyone and I'm guessing you don't have a landline." Almost no one did anymore.

Her expression softened and she brushed a hand down his chest, just briefly touching him. "I didn't even think of that. Thank you."

All his muscles pulled taut at her touch. It was as if she was trying to make him crazy with need. "I'm also going to have someone watch your condo. Just tonight."

She blinked in confusion, then shook her head. "That's really sweet, but it's not necessary."

"Look… I don't know if the mugging tonight was random or not. I don't like how it happened." He didn't like telling her this much—didn't want her to know what kind of man he was, how many enemies he had. But he wouldn't risk her safety for anything. "I've made a lot of enemies over the years. People who don't like their businesses getting bought out. I've never had a..." He paused, looking for the right word. He'd never had a woman in his life before, and even if they weren't in a relationship she *meant* something to him. "You and I have been potentially seen together at multiple places. If someone thinks you're important to me it's not out of the realm of possibility that they might target you to get to me."

She blinked at him again. "I...that seems a little crazy."

"Then you can humor me."

Her eyes narrowed slightly. "That sounds a little bit like an order."

He lifted a shoulder. "I'm having someone watch the place whether you like it or not." Yeah, he knew that was high-handed but he didn't care. "I could lie and tell you I wasn't, but I'm not going to lie to you."

"You are...frustrating."

"I've been called worse," he said dryly.

She snorted, the sound adorable. "Fine."

Consumed with the need to touch her, he slid his hands down to her hips, pulling her close to him. There was no way to hide his erection from her and he didn't want to. She should have no doubt how she affected him. "I want to kiss you right now," he murmured.

Her eyes were dilated and her breathing grew erratic at his words. She set her hands on his chest. "Why don't you?" Her voice was a whisper.

"Because when I do, I don't want an audience." His employee was waiting at the end of the hallway, watching Dominique's place. Not to mention Dimitri was a few doors down and there were any number of nosy neighbors potentially watching.

She hitched in a breath at his words, her gaze falling to his mouth.

"Can I take you to lunch tomorrow?" He kept his voice low, somehow resisting the urge to lean down and claim her mouth.

She nodded, that almost dazed look back as she met his gaze. "I'd like that."

Yeah, he would too. Way too much. Pushing against his own self-control, he reached up and cupped her cheek, slowly slid his thumb over her full bottom lip. What he wouldn't give to kiss her right now.

Just the thought was tempting, but he hadn't been lying. He didn't want anyone to see him kissing her. Didn't want anyone to hear her moans of pleasure, no matter how small. She made him feel ridiculously possessive and those sounds were just for him.

He was moving into unknown territory with her but he knew that once they crossed the line into a physical relationship he was going to consider her his.

CHAPTER NINE

"You staying in the building for lunch, or heading out?" At the sound of Lizzy's voice, Dominique looked up from her computer.

"Ah…" She glanced at her cell phone, surprised it was lunch already. She'd been working nonstop all morning. "I've got to grab a new phone at lunch. I'm just going to walk down to the store."

Lizzy frowned as she sat on the edge of Dominique's desk—as per usual for her. Today she had on flip-flops, jeans and a T-shirt that said 'Unicorns love bad girls' with a picture of a unicorn wearing a biker jacket under the text. "What happened to your phone?"

Dominique didn't want to lie to her friend, even if she still felt weird about not calling the police. "It was stolen. I was actually mugged last night. My purse was taken and my phone was in it."

Lizzy's eyes widened. "Are you okay?"

She nodded. "Yeah, annoyed but fine."

"Still, that sucks. Where did it happen?"

"Outside a restaurant. I was with…Viktor when this guy just snatched it."

"I'm surprised he didn't kill the guy. What did the cops say?"

Dominique bit her bottom lip. "He didn't call them. Said they couldn't do anything about it and then he got someone to change my locks since my license and keys were in my purse."

Lizzy's expression morphed to one of something that looked a lot like respect. "Good for Ivanov."

"You don't think it's weird he didn't want to call the cops?"

Her friend lifted a shoulder. "Maybe. I don't know. It depends on a lot of things and I don't know how he feels about cops in general. But I can guess. If you tell me what restaurant it happened at I might be able to find out more information for you. I could hack into some CCTVs if you want." She rubbed her hands together, looking way too excited and a little scary.

"If you start cackling like some sort of evil villain, I'm out of here. And I'm not going to tell you where it was. I'm not supporting your hacking habit."

"I'll find out on my own, you know."

Dominique lifted a shoulder, fighting a smile. "If you have extra time to figure it out, go for it. It was just a stupid mugging and everything is thankfully replaceable." She was really glad Viktor'd had her locks changed though. She'd been able to sleep easier last night.

Lizzy just grinned. "Fine... So, have you talked to Raegan this morning?"

"Yeah, she texted me that she and the sexy cop are a thing again." Dominique wasn't sure what to think about that, considering the guy had ghosted on Raegan for a few days. But if the man made Raegan happy, that was what mattered.

"He's a good guy. Relationship challenged, that's for sure."

Dominique laughed. "What guy isn't?" Not that she really had a leg to stand on—she'd never even been in a serious relationship either. "Listen, I've gotta head out if I want to beat the rush. Your man should just be getting off his conference call." She glanced at the phone, saw Porter's light still on. "Or he will be in a minute or two."

Lizzy's expression went pure wicked as she headed for the adjoining door. "If getting your phone takes your whole lunch break, just extend your lunch so you get to eat. I'll tell Porter you'll be longer than usual." Without waiting for a response she opened the door and ducked inside. The lock snicked into place behind Lizzy.

At that, Dominique grabbed her purse and practically raced out of there. It was pretty rare that Lizzy came down to their floor during work hours and Dominique didn't want to stick around for whatever was about to happen.

The elevator made four stops before finally reaching the lobby. It was weird not having her phone. She felt almost naked without it. Even though she'd had her phone locked she'd still changed all her passwords this morning too. Something she should have thought about last night, but she'd been consumed with thoughts of Viktor.

She blinked when she saw him standing in the lobby near one of the huge pillars, talking to Harrison Caldwell, of all people. He was one of the owners. His father had founded Red Stone, but since semi-retiring recently he'd left his three sons in charge of everything. It didn't matter that Porter was Harrison's brother—Dominique still felt nervous around him. The man had an edge to him. Not that Viktor was any less scary, but…she wasn't afraid of Viktor.

As if he sensed her, Viktor turned and pinned her with those icy blue eyes. Though his look was anything but cold. A blast of heat radiated off him, the hunger in his eyes clear as his gaze swept her over from head to toe.

Her surroundings melted away as she headed toward him. She'd called him early this morning and rescheduled their lunch so maybe he was here to see Harrison. Whatever the reason, she didn't care. She was glad she'd run into him, regardless. Her heart rate was out of control as she drank in the sight of him. He had on dark pants, a button-down shirt, a custom-cut jacket and no tie. She loved the look on him.

"Hey," she murmured as she reached him.

His mouth curved up ever so slightly and she wondered if that was his version of a smile. Whatever it was, she liked it. A lot. Seriously, how had this happened? How had she started to fall for Viktor Ivanov so dang fast?

"You look beautiful," he said quietly.

The simple words took her off guard and pleased her at the same time. She started to respond when Harrison Caldwell—whose presence she'd completely forgotten about—cleared his throat.

"I've gotta go," he said, nodding once at her before focusing on Viktor. "We'll talk later."

Viktor simply nodded before turning back to her. "I thought I'd walk with you to the phone store. Then lunch if you have time."

She was irrationally pleased he'd decided to meet her here. "I think I'll have time. I just saw on Twitter that one of my favorite food trucks is supposed to be a couple blocks from here for the next few hours."

"Food trucks have Twitter accounts?" He sounded dubious.

Laughing, she linked her arm through his. "Everyone does. Even you."

"No, some of my *companies* do… Lucy hired a team of people to head up our social media accounts. I've never looked at them."

"Yeah, I can't see you actually tweeting. Or using Snapchat." She laughed when he just gave her a blank look. "You sure you don't mind coming with me? I might not even be able to sneak in a lunch break if they're too busy."

"You will be able to." He sounded ridiculously confident about that as they reached one of the big glass doors.

A rush of Florida heat rolled over them as they stepped outside. She savored the warmth after being cooped up inside all morning in the air-conditioned space, and slid off her light cardigan sweater. "Why does that sound as if you know that for a fact?"

"I know the owner of this particular store. I made a call."

"Viktor…" She trailed off when he looked down at her, pinning her with such a heated look she felt it all the way to her core. A Florida summer had nothing on him. "What?"

"I like it when you say my name." The words were a sexy growl.

She felt her cheeks flush and couldn't blame it on the weather. Viktor had gotten under her skin, and she had no idea if she was ready for a man like this because she was pretty sure he was way out of her league. Deep down she wondered if he was going to freak out when she told him about her lack of experience. Part of her didn't want to tell him, but she was beginning to really trust Viktor—which scared her too.

"So, it's good information right?" his contact asked.

He tried to keep his tone disinterested, but this was gold and the man had to know it. "Very good." Last night he'd received pictures of the blonde woman and Viktor out at a restaurant and it had looked like a date. "How'd you get the pictures without him seeing you?"

There was a short pause, then, "Because I'm very good at being invisible."

"You're sure?"

"Yes. It was easy to follow him. I placed a tracker on his SUV last night so I didn't need him in my line of sight. I just followed the tracker."

"Have you removed the tracker?" He didn't want Viktor to know anyone was targeting him. Not yet. Not until it was too late for the fucker to do anything about it.

"Of course," the man snapped. "Did you get what you needed from her purse?"

"Yes." After he'd received the location of Viktor and the woman last night he'd sent a well-trained team of two to mug her.

He'd needed it to seem random but also have a team good enough to surprise Viktor. The circumstances had been perfect for the mugging. Viktor hadn't had his driver and he'd been wrapped up in that whore. Unfortunately, now Viktor seemed to have someone watching the woman's place. That seemed a bit paranoid but also confirmed what he'd needed to know—Viktor cared for the woman.

"I overheard Lucy talking to someone on the phone yesterday. I think it was about this Dominique Castle. Lucy was confirming with someone that she works for Red Stone Security," he said.

A thread of alarm worked its way through his system. "Hmm, that could be a problem."

"Why? It's not like you're going to hurt the woman, right?"

The owner of Red Stone Security and his sons weren't the kind of people you messed with. Then again, neither was Viktor. He ignored the question. The woman might get hurt, she might not—but he was pretty certain she would die too. "Maybe it won't be a problem. She is important to Ivanov though, that much I'm sure of. I know for a fact he had someone change her locks last night."

"How do you know that?"

"Because I had someone go to her condo complex last night. She's a beautiful woman," he said, looking at her picture again. "It'll be a shame to waste all that beauty. Keep me updated with anything else. Your payment is on the way." He hung up before the man could respond and traced a finger over Dominique Castle's face.

What kind of woman got involved with a man like Ivanov, he wondered. She'd have to be a whore. No doubt about it. She'd get what she deserved too.

Viktor pulled out his phone as he left one of the hotels he and Abram had recently bought. This was one they wouldn't keep, but would reorganize, get it running right again, then sell for a profit. His driver was waiting outside, the SUV idling as he approached. Viktor waved him off from getting out to open his door and slid into the back seat, calling Abram as Kir pulled away.

"Hey, I'm calling it a day." Normally he'd work another two or three hours but he wanted to see Dominique and she was free tonight. It amazed him that someone like her wanted to go out on a date with him, but he was determined not to fuck things up. He might not know anything about relationships, but he would learn. For her.

"Me too. I'm going to check on Lucy. I'm worried about her." There was an odd note in Abram's voice.

"She's sick. It happens. But…I think it's a good idea." Not that his brother was asking him. Because Abram wouldn't ask for anyone's opinion when it came to Lucy.

"Look, I want to hire a new assistant for me as soon as possible. We can start looking next week."

"Any reason for the rush?" Viktor thought he knew, but didn't want to assume.

His brother cleared his throat. "I don't think Lucy should be working under me anymore, for personal reasons. I want to…be with her. She can't work for me if that's going to happen."

"You finally tell her how you feel?" Viktor had been trying to ignore the chemistry between them but it was so damn obvious.

Abram cleared his throat again. "Sort of."

"We'll talk to HR, make sure—"

"I've already taken care of everything. No matter what happens between us she'll have job security. And we're giving her another fucking raise." He said the last part as if he thought Viktor might argue.

"Agreed. Look…how serious are you about her?" He glanced at his driver, who didn't seem to be paying attention, but he never underestimated anyone. He'd had the same driver for years, until recently when he'd promoted Lyosha to a different position.

"Very."

Good. "I heard her talking to a friend about a Bulgari necklace she said would be her Christmas present to herself one day—"

"I bought it a month ago."

His eyebrows shot up. "Shit, you are serious."

Abram just snorted. "You going out with Dominique tonight?"

Something in his brother's tone annoyed him. He gritted his teeth. "Yes."

"All right. Just…be careful. I called Lyosha, told him to head up an extra security team tonight. They're going to tail you, subtly. She won't know about it, but I want you to have some backup just in case. I don't like that mugging."

Viktor scrubbed a hand over his face. He didn't want to say too much in front of his driver, but he didn't like the way the mugging had gone down either. A two-man team for a simple snatch and grab? What he hadn't told Dominique was that he'd gone to the owner of the restaurant later that night and it turned out all their security cameras had been tampered with right around the time he'd arrived with Dominique.

Which meant someone could have followed him. He'd checked his vehicle for trackers and found nothing, but that didn't mean shit. Someone could have followed him or tracked him another way.

He'd left his life of crime behind but that didn't mean he didn't have enemies. And he didn't think for a second that she'd been the real target. This felt like a message to him. "I don't either," he finally said.

"What if she's involved? Maybe the whole thing was a setup." Abram's voice was tight, agitated.

"To what end?" He didn't believe it, regardless. Dominique had been shaken last night. Unless she was the best actress in the damn world, no, he didn't think she was involved with her own mugging.

"I don't know yet," Abram grumbled.

Viktor hid an exasperated sigh. "Why don't you quit worrying about me and worry about yourself?"

"You're my brother."

"I know." The truth was, he worried about Abram too. All the damn time. He was the only family Viktor had. "Let me know how Lucy is, if she needs anything."

Abram just grunted and hung up.

Shaking his head, Viktor tucked his phone into his pocket. He'd be seeing Dominique in less than an hour and the anticipation humming through him was like a live thing. She'd been on his mind all day, consuming him.

After she'd picked up a new phone today they'd grabbed lunch at a food truck and eaten at a nearby park. While he'd been vigilant about their surroundings, he'd realized that he'd been relaxed with her, unlike how he felt with most people. But it was as if she didn't *want* anything from him other than his company. Hell, she wouldn't even take the house. He'd tried to bring it up once but she'd shut him down fast.

It was clear she still hadn't made a decision about it, and that was fine with him. The longer it took her to figure out what she wanted, the longer he still had a reason to contact her. Not that he seemed to need one other than to simply ask her out.

He wanted more than just dating though. He didn't care if it was too soon—he couldn't just do casual. Not with a woman like her. He'd had casual sex, sex he paid for. He wanted something real. Even if he wasn't sure he deserved it.

The only problem was, he knew shit about relationships and women. He didn't want to come off too strong, but once they crossed a certain line, he knew he wouldn't let her go. He just hoped she was ready for him.

CHAPTER TEN

Feeling a little bit possessed, Abram pounded his fist against Lucy's front door again. He knew she was in there; had seen a light flip on about ten seconds ago. And he knew he was acting like a psycho. He just didn't care.

She lived on a quiet cul-de-sac with beach-cottage-style homes, some two-story but mostly one-story houses. A next-door neighbor stepped out from his front door, eyed Abram with suspicion. The guy was good-looking too, probably in his early thirties.

Shirtless and tanned, he glared at Abram. "You need something?" the man asked, his tone brusque.

"I'm here to see Lucy." He forced himself to remain civil even if it wasn't this guy's business who the hell he was. Still…he was glad Lucy had neighbors who cared enough to look out for her.

The man crossed his arms over his chest and leaned against the railing of the front porch. "Don't think she's home."

Before he could respond, Abram heard the click of the lock opening. Lucy jerked the door open, her expression unreadable as she watched him. She stepped out onto the porch and smiled at her neighbor. Some irrational part of Abram was jealous that the guy got to see her smile. He wanted all of that sweetness reserved for him, not some dick.

"Hey Leo, everything's good over here. This is just a friend. I asked him to stop by to help me with my…computer."

"You sure?" The neighbor's gaze flicked to Abram, clearly not trusting him.

"Yeah, I promise. Tell Maria I'll be bringing over that dish she left a little later this evening."

The man nodded, still not moving from his sentry position.

Lucy grabbed Abram's upper arm and practically dragged him inside, shutting and locking the door behind him. "What are you doing here?" She dropped her arm and placed both hands on her hips as she glared up at him.

"You're not sick." He swept his gaze over her, surprised to see her looking so casual, though he knew he shouldn't be. She was at home, not work or a function. She had on skimpy beach shorts that showed a whole lot of skin, a tank top and the straps of a blue and white bikini tied behind her neck. She'd once told him that she had a small pool in her backyard so he guessed she'd been using it.

She crossed her arms over her chest. "So what? I needed a sick day, so I took it. And you showing up here to check on me is completely inappropriate."

"As inappropriate as me eating your pussy at work?"

Her cheeks went bright pink. She opened her mouth but nothing came out as she stared up at him. Everything about her was adorable, right down to her painted cherry red toenails.

He was glad she wasn't talking because there were some things he needed to say and if he didn't get them out all at once he wasn't sure he ever would. "We're hiring someone new as soon as possible to be my assistant. You'll work directly under Viktor when that happens. I don't want there to be an imbalance of power between us and I can see how it could happen if I'm your boss—though to be fair, you boss me around a lot."

She let out a shaky laugh and he could see some of the tension leaving her shoulders. That had to be a good thing so he barreled on.

"I want to be with you. I want…you to be my girlfriend." Even saying that out loud was too strange. "Which is a dumb, fucking word. But I want to start something real with you and I know that can't happen unless there's a division between us at work." When she watched him with those big dark eyes, not saying anything, he started to panic. "Say something," he demanded—okay, snarled.

Instead of being taken off guard, like any one of his employees would have been, she rolled her eyes. "Jeez, Abram. You've just shown up and dropped a lot on me. Can we sit down and talk?" She motioned to the attached living room.

He didn't want to fucking talk, but he did as she asked. When she sat on the long, white tufted couch he sat next to her, crowding her personal space. He'd been going crazy all day without seeing her, wondering if she was going to quit because of what happened between them.

Thankfully she didn't seem to mind how close he was to her.

"I'm sorry I called in today. I felt really awkward about…what we did." Her cheeks flushed again and he had to restrain himself from reaching out and touching her. "I know it was pretty weak, but I called in sick so I could think."

"What's there to think about?" He'd just laid himself on the line, made himself completely vulnerable. The very idea of doing that for anyone else made his skin crawl. Not that doing it for her was much easier. If she shot him down… He swallowed hard. He hadn't thought that far ahead.

She clasped her hands together in her lap, her back ramrod straight. Even in her beach clothes she looked every inch the princess. "Well…us. I mean, you're my boss and—"

"I won't be your boss soon. And I've had HR and legal draw up papers so that no matter what happens between us, your job will never be affected. You will always have job security, no matter what." He didn't tell her that he wasn't letting her go, that he planned on convincing her to take a chance on forever with him. Even he knew it was too soon to say that out loud.

Her pretty lips parted, her expression softening. "You did all that?"

"Yes. And…" He reached into his jacket pocket and pulled out the long box he'd kept in his office for the last month. He handed it to her, not sure what to say. The thing had been burning a hole in his desk so he'd shoved it in his safe until today.

He'd overheard her conversation with a friend when she'd been on lunch break, talking about how once she'd gotten her retirement accounts maxed out for the next five years in a row, this was going to be her Christmas present to herself. Well fuck that. He was going to give it to her now. He wanted to give her the whole damn world, anything she wanted.

Her eyebrows raised slightly as she started to open the box. She let out a gasp when she saw the gold roped necklace inside. She ran her fingers over the thick chain almost reverently. "Abram, this is beautiful… Oh my God, no." She handed it back to him, her hand trembling even as she looked at the beautiful necklace. "I can't take this. It's over eight thousand dollars." She whispered the last part as if he'd committed a sin.

It was more like twelve grand because he'd had diamonds added to it, but he didn't correct her. "Who cares?"

She blinked. "It's too much. Way too much. And we're not even… What are we?" She linked her fingers together again in her lap.

"I told you what I want. What do you want?"

"You. Since the moment we met."

Relief slammed through him and without thinking he pulled her into his lap. She let out a squeak of surprise and then her cheeks flushed that sexy-as-fuck shade of pink again when she shifted over his erection.

"That's because of you," he murmured. He'd been walking around with a hard on for months because of her.

Sitting sideways in his lap, she turned more to face him, placing her gentle hands on his shoulders. He'd never thought to fall for anyone, but definitely not someone as delicate-looking as Lucy. He'd learned early on that she might look fragile, but she was a force of nature. He adored everything about her.

"So you and I…will be exclusive?" She sounded almost unsure about that.

He snorted. "I've been exclusive to you since we hired you." Because the thought of being with anyone else had been impossible. After he'd met Lucy, gotten to know the sweet woman who'd completely stolen his heart, everyone else paled in comparison.

Her lips parted slightly. "But I saw… I saw a jewelry box in your desk drawer a month ago. Just like that one. I thought maybe you were seeing someone…" She trailed off and for the first time since he'd known her, he could see true vulnerability in her dark eyes.

Without looking at it, he clasped it, slid it into her lap. "This is the *same* one. I bought this for you. I've never bought jewelry for another woman. Ever." He'd never even thought to. He'd had bed partners, that was it. No one he wanted to spend time with outside of the bedroom. Until sweet, sexy Lucy who'd become a bright light in his life.

"Oh." She bit her bottom lip, still looking unsure.

It drove him crazy. "What?"

"Nothing, just trying to wrap my head around all this. I've been into you since we met and I don't know, I tried to convince myself it was a stupid crush. Then when I saw that necklace I was…insanely jealous. Which I feel stupid admitting. It was gone the next day from your drawer so I assumed you'd given it to someone."

He decided not to tell her that he found her jealousy hot, but he liked knowing she gave a shit. "Is that why you've been frustrated with me the last month?"

"No. Maybe…yes."

He opened the box and lifted out the piece of jewelry, clasped it around her neck. "I want to fu—make love to you with just this on." It was totally barbaric but he wanted to claim her while she wore something he'd given her. Like he'd marked her.

She made a soft little moan and shifted in his lap, her eyes going heavy-lidded.

"You like the idea of that?" He knew he should offer to take her out to dinner, to do things a normal couple would do. But the need to be inside her, to claim her, was overwhelming.

Her breathing grew shallower as she lifted a hand to the necklace, gently ran her fingers along it. "This is too much," she whispered, but there was no conviction in her voice.

"That's not an answer, baby. You like the idea of me taking you wearing just this?" He leaned down, nipped her earlobe between his teeth. "Maybe fucking you from behind in front of a mirror so you can see us? See how sexy you look when I make you come?" He wanted to do more than just fuck, but the way Lucy reacted to his words told him she *liked* the way he was talking to her.

She clutched onto his shoulders, her breathing erratic as he scraped his teeth along the column of her neck. "There's a big mirror in my guest bedroom," she whispered again, her voice shaky.

The statement ricocheted through him, making him jerk against her. He pulled back slightly so he could see her face. "You want..." For some reason he couldn't finish the thought. Being here with her now was too surreal. In no reality did he end up with a woman like Lucy but here they were.

Her lips curved up into a mischievous grin as she slid off his lap. He made a move to pull her back but she dodged his hands and stripped off her tank top before turning away from him. Even the sight of her bare back got him insanely hot.

He was on his feet in a millisecond, following after her as she tugged the strings to her bathing suit free, letting her top fall to the ground as she headed down a brightly painted hallway.

All he could focus on was her back and the soft curve of her hips as she pushed open a door into a dimly lit bedroom. Sheer curtains were pulled together over the single window, letting in some of the waning early evening light. He leaned against the doorframe, fascinated with her, as she shimmied out of her shorts and bikini bottom without looking at him.

Her breasts weren't large, enough to fill his hands, and though she was petite her hips were full and perfect. Everything about her was perfect.

"Will this do?" Her sexy voice brought his gaze back up to hers.

He realized he'd been staring at the juncture between her thighs—the little bit of hair covering her mound. He'd been remembering how she tasted, how she'd felt as she'd come against his face and fingers. She'd pointed to the huge wood-framed mirror propped up behind a daybed with all sorts of frilly female stuff on it and around it. The room had a sort of Parisian theme to it. Something he most definitely didn't care about.

Keeping his gaze pinned to hers, he shoved away from the doorframe and slid his jacket off. She watched him carefully, her eyes wide and her body language just a little bit nervous, if the tremble that shuddered through her was any indication.

Moving slowly, he let her watch his every move, his hands going to his belt buckle. She sucked in a breath as she tracked his actions. When he was fully naked he grabbed a condom from his pants before stalking toward her. The most primal part of him liked it when she backed up to the daybed, her breathing raspy and unsteady.

There was nowhere for her to go, not that he thought she actually wanted to be anywhere but here. Her pale brown nipples were beaded tightly and he wanted to taste them, to taste all of her again.

Yesterday hadn't taken off any of the edge from the need to have her. It had only stoked the wildfire burning inside him. When he reached her, his cock jutted up between them, pressing against her belly.

She sucked in a breath as she looked down between their bodies, and to his pleasure, she grasped his hard length, a smile on her face. "You really are big all over," she murmured, more to herself than him.

Seeing the anticipation on her expression, the way her dark eyes went heavy-lidded as she stroked him once, made him groan as much as the feel of her fingers wrapped tightly around his cock did.

Even though he could easily come in her hand, he placed his over her smaller one. There was no way that was happening this first time. He would be inside her when he did. And she would most definitely come first.

When she looked up at him, he lowered his mouth to hers. Instead of crushing his lips against hers, which was what his body was demanding, his instinct said to take things slower with her.

At least this first time. He'd already made her come up against his office door; now he wanted to savor her, make sure she remembered their first time together.

The first time of many, if things went the way he hoped.

She slid her hands up his bare chest, her fingers digging into his pecs as he pushed her back onto the daybed. The thing was way too small but it would do for now.

He didn't know where to start now that he had her stretched out before him.

"Fuck, you're gorgeous," he rasped out as he straddled her on the narrow bed. It dipped under his weight, making her giggle.

The light sound eased something in his chest.

"What happened to…taking me from behind?" she whispered, watching him carefully, her eyes slightly dilated.

He noticed she didn't say the word fuck and found that insanely adorable. "We'll get there." He dipped his head to one of her breasts, sucked on her already hard nipple.

Moaning, she arched her back, sliding her fingers through his short hair even as she wrapped her legs around his waist, plastering herself to him. His cock was thick and heavy between them. The way she enveloped herself around him made all those possessive instincts he hadn't known he even *had* flare to life.

"Abram." His name sounded like a prayer on her lips and all he'd done was tease her nipple.

He bit down gently on the hard bud and she squirmed under him, her fingers now digging into his back.

Yeah, he could get used to hearing her say his name; wanted her to say it as he thrust inside her.

He reached between their bodies and cupped her mound even as he moved to her other breast, swiping his tongue around her nipple. He slid a finger between her slick folds, making her moan even louder as she rolled her hips against him.

His cock ached, begging to be inside her, but he needed to work her up a little more. Lifting his head from her breast, he crushed his mouth to hers.

She twined her tongue with his, just as hungry for him as he was for her. He could feel it in her every movement and hear it in every little gasp she made. When she gave his bottom lip a playful nip, lightly scraping her fingernails down his back, his balls pulled up even tighter.

Though he wanted to keep kissing her, teasing her, he wanted her to come even more. This first time would take the edge off.

Pulling back from her, he stared down at her for a long moment. Her breasts rose and fell as she watched him, her dark eyes filled with hunger. When she reached for his cock, he grasped her wrist and pulled her up to a sitting position.

"On your knees. Face the mirror." He barely managed to get the words out, to keep a grasp on his control.

She did as he said, her movements unsteady and a little jerky. He liked that she was as affected as him. When she met his gaze in the mirror, he swore his heart stopped for a moment.

Her short, dark hair wasn't neat like it usually was, but mussed. Her lips were slightly swollen, and the look in her eyes was more than just lust. She looked like she needed him. Maybe as much as he needed her.

Moving in behind her, he took a moment to appreciate the differences in their bodies. She was so petite and slender, but with a steel backbone. He wasn't worried about hurting her, knew he could never do that.

He ran his hands down her sides, hated how callused his hands were, but she didn't seem to mind. She shuddered, holding onto the vintage metal frame of the daybed as she spread her legs just a little wider.

Even her pose, the way she was bent forward, waiting for him, made his breath catch. He was never letting her go.

He'd felt how slick she was but he still reached between her legs from behind, groaned at the feel of her. "You're so wet."

"I'm wet all the time for you." Her words came out low as she watched him in the mirror, her fingers clutching the frame. "You make me crazy at work and I *still* get turned on by it."

"Good." Because he got turned on by her all the damn time. Didn't matter what she seemed to be doing. He quickly rolled on a condom before guiding his cock to her entrance.

Soon, he planned to be inside her bare, with nothing between the two of them as he emptied himself inside her.

He didn't push inside her just yet though. Reaching around, he cupped both her breasts, teasing both her nipples with his thumbs as he watched her expression.

She sucked in a breath, pleasure playing across her expression as her head fell back against his chest. He loved seeing her like this, open to him.

And all his.

He worked her up until she was squirming and pushing her ass back against him, silently demanding he do something.

Without pause he thrust into her in one long push.

"Abram." She froze for a moment, her breathing shallow as she adjusted to his size.

He felt her inner walls tightening around him, already milking him. She was so damn tight and yeah, he was big. Nothing to be done about that. He buried his face against her neck, inhaled her sweet scent as he reached around and found her pulsing clit.

She needed to come, and fast. Because his control was slipping. Lucy'd had him on edge for months. Now that he was inside her, he knew he wasn't going to last long. Not this first time.

When he slid a finger over her clit, she moaned and jerked back against him. At the same time he felt her clench around him even tighter.

Using her body's cues, he stroked her clit, increasing the pressure the louder she moaned until he knew she was close.

"Oh God, oh..." She jerked against him as she rolled into climax.

He began thrusting inside her and she cried out even louder, her inner walls rippling around him as she found her release. He couldn't watch her in the mirror anymore as his own orgasm built and crested as months of need for her slammed through him.

He wasn't sure how long he thrust into her but his orgasm seemed to go on forever as he lost himself inside her.

When he looked at her in the mirror again, the satisfied expression on her face made him do a mental fist pump. It was the most beautiful thing he'd ever seen. And he'd put it there.

"We could have been doing this for months now," she murmured, giving him the most sensual look in the mirror.

He nipped her shoulder gently. "I think we should make up for lost time, then."

CHAPTER ELEVEN

"I can't even pretend I'm not impressed by this." Dominique looked around the empty five-star restaurant before focusing on Viktor again, her expression warm.

He'd never been on the receiving end of such raw openness before. Viktor would be lying if he said he wasn't glad she was impressed. He'd do fucking cartwheels if it made her happy. Anything to see Dominique smile.

He cleared his throat. "With the place under renovation I thought it would be nice for just the two of us to come here." He and Abram had shut down one of the hotels they'd recently purchased to renovate a good chunk of the place. But the restaurant right on the Atlantic was one of the only parts of the hotel that didn't need *any* work. So he'd brought in the chef—one of the few employees he planned to keep on staff while he restructured—to impress Dominique tonight.

He'd never cared about impressing anyone before. Even when he was younger, he'd just cared about people respecting and yes, fearing him. With Dominique... She brought out a completely different side to him. He was still adjusting to that.

"I'm glad you like it," he murmured, reaching across the linen-covered tabletop to slide his hand over hers.

Her cheeks flushed and he found himself getting hard. Again. She had an innocent quality to her that surprised him. Even more, he was surprised he liked it. When he'd had Abram run her information, when he was still wondering who she was and why she hated him, his brother hadn't found a record of any serious boyfriends.

There was no way a woman like Dominique could be a virgin, but he guessed she didn't have much experience. Which, yeah, he liked the thought of that too. But he didn't care how many guys she'd been with. That shit wasn't important. The only thing he cared about was locking her down now. Convincing her that they might have a shot at something real. The only problem was…he wasn't sure he could give her the kind of sexual experience she deserved. His only experience was with women he'd paid. Dominique would know nothing about that. The truth was, he knew it would disgust her. Which was why he had to tell her.

She was an absolute knockout but it was more than that. She was simply…sweet. He didn't know many people who he considered to be sweet. Given their family's history, she should truly hate him, but she'd given him a chance. One he still wasn't sure he'd take.

"Can I ask you a question?" Her voice was tentative, a little nervous.

Instinct made him want to put his guard up, but she'd opened up to him about her mother and he found he wanted to trust her. He withdrew his hand, wrapped it around his glass of vodka. "Of course."

She trailed her finger down the stem of her wine glass. She'd worn a simple black dress tonight with diamond studs in her ears and no other jewelry. Still, she shone as brilliantly as a star everywhere she went. The extra security team tonight had certainly taken notice of her. It was hard not to. But he'd made it clear to Lyosha that she was *his* woman, that everyone should treat her with respect. His longtime friend and head of security had shown a flicker of surprise, but in true Lyosha form had said he'd make sure everyone knew.

"It's none of my business. I'm just curious about you. But if you don't want to answer you don't have to." She rushed out the words, as if she'd been practicing.

"Just ask," he murmured, tension rising inside him. Maybe his brother had been right after all. This would be where she started to ply him for information in an effort to use it against him.

"How is it that you and your brother, ah, half-brother, have the same last name?" She cleared her throat. "I know that your father's last name was..." She trailed off, pain flashing in her expression before she masked it. That was one thing he'd come to learn about her—she didn't hide her emotions as well as she probably thought she did.

Her question wasn't what he'd expected, and easy to answer. He'd been worried she'd want to know more about his past, more about his relationship with his father, or how Viktor had gotten to where he was today. Something she could use against him. But this... She could have found this out from a search.

Even though he knew she could be testing him, that this might be some sort of warm-up question, the tension in his chest eased ever so slightly. "When my father died I took my mother's name. Ivanov is a very common Russian family name—one of the most common, in fact. Abram's mother had the same last name as well. It's a lucky coincidence." One he was happy for. He liked having that link to Abram. He didn't care that they were technically half-brothers. That shit meant nothing to him. They were true brothers in every sense of the word.

Dominique gave him a knowing smile. "You two are close."

He nodded. "He's a good brother." Even if he did worry too much.

"I...don't know if he likes me very much." She stumbled over the words. "At the hotel the other day, he seemed to know who I was and..." She lifted a shoulder but he could see that it mattered to her.

"Abram is very protective. He thinks...you might be out to hurt me."

She blinked, those gorgeous dark eyes genuinely confused. "Me, hurt you?" Then she laughed, the sweet sound rolling over him like a warm wave.

He realized she thought he meant physically, but he didn't correct her. Viktor half-smiled and lifted a shoulder. "He can be paranoid."

"He's your brother. It's good he worries about you. My cousin,

Quinn, is like an older brother to me. Now more than when I was younger."

"Why now?" He'd seen the name Quinn in the file his brother had compiled on her, knew the guy had been a cop and now worked for Red Stone.

"Ah…this might be veering into more heavy stuff than first date conversation."

"This is our second date." There would be a lot more, as far as he was concerned. He reached for her hand again, was glad when she instantly linked her fingers through his. Even her hands were beautiful. She had long, elegant fingers he could easily imagine wrapped around his cock, stroking him until he came.

She laughed lightly and squeezed his hand. "Yeah, you're right. But this is probably oversharing."

"I think we're past that point." His voice was dry.

"True… Okay, fine. After what happened with my mom, Quinn is the first person I called. He, uh, he'd just started working for Red Stone but he'd been a cop before so he swooped in and just took over everything." The adoration on her face was clear. "Even though I was eighteen he refused to let me live on my own. My mom had…cut out that side of the family, her side, because, well, whatever."

"You don't have to tell me any more." The distress that had started to trickle into her expression sliced at him. He didn't want her uncomfortable or in pain. Ever. Which was a stupid thing, considering he couldn't protect her all the time. But he didn't want to be the cause of her distress.

"It's okay, really. I kinda want you to know this about me." She faltered for a moment, but continued. "I moved in with his parents for the first few years I was in college. I, uh, didn't realize it then but I was dealing with depression over everything and they really kept me afloat. They—Quinn and the rest of my family too—were like anchors. I was too caught up in my own bullshit then to be grateful but I know now how lucky I am that they were there for me."

"You are lucky." With the exception of his mother, he'd never had anyone he loved or trusted until Abram. He was glad she'd had family to support her. Her life could have turned out very differently otherwise. He'd seen it happen too.

"This brings me to something I've wanted to tell you." Her cheeks flushed pink, but she trailed off as their server quietly brought their desserts.

Dominique's eyes widened slightly in pure pleasure as the man placed the plate in front of her. Viktor didn't look at his own. He didn't care about the damn food. Hers was a chocolate cup filled with some sort of cream and fresh fruit. There were also fresh strawberries fanned out around it. The entire display was drizzled with chocolate.

"I've always wondered how they make these," she murmured. "The cups are so delicate."

"Balloons," the man said before darting his gaze to Viktor, just a touch of fear in his gaze.

As if Viktor would be angry he'd talked. Jesus, he wasn't that fucking scary. He tried smiling at the man but was pretty sure he failed when the guy flinched. "Balloons?"

The man nodded and looked back at Dominique, his expression quickly morphing to one of appreciation as he talked to her. "The chef dips small balloons into the melted chocolate halfway and they dry in this shape. Once they're done he carefully lets the air out and removes the balloon."

"That's so interesting. I'm going to have to try it," she said.

The man beamed at her before disappearing back to the kitchen.

"You cook?" Viktor asked once they were alone again. He didn't reach for his fork, just watched the expression of pure joy flicker across her features as she took that first bite.

She let out a little moan of appreciation as she nodded. "You want a bite?"

He shook his head, his dick going ridiculously hard. If she took this much pleasure in dessert… He could just imagine what she'd look like when he brought her to orgasm. He'd thought about how he'd do it too, way too many times. He'd never brought a woman to his house but he was obsessed with the idea of her stretched out on his bed, all his for the taking. He wanted to take his time with her, to have her begging for him to fill her.

"You're missing out. And yes, I do like to cook—baking, mostly—though I don't get to as much as I'd like because of work."

His gaze strayed to her mouth as her tongue darted out to swipe cream off her bottom lip. He had to actually bite back a groan at the sight. He'd been with women who knew how to seduce, how to do everything right—because it was all choreographed and fake. With Dominique, he knew there was no artifice.

Even if she was driving him crazy.

He had the irrational urge to shove everything off the table and take her right here. Which was beyond insane. But she made him want to lose control, something he didn't like. He rubbed the back of his neck and glanced around the restaurant.

The extra security was in place and very discreet. After that mugging he didn't care if he was being paranoid. He wanted to make sure Dominique was safe. He just hated that he had no control over what happened to her when she was at home. He couldn't very well insist she keep a security guard with her. Even *he* knew that was insane and would push her away from him.

So he planned to be with her as much as he could. At least then he could protect her. Past that, however, he was in completely new territory. Sex before had always been detached, unemotional. Now…he wanted something different with Dominique. He wanted to make sure she was completely satisfied. Unfortunately he wasn't sure how fast he should move. The more primal part of him said he was moving way too fucking slow. That they should be in bed right now. She should be flat on her back while his face was buried between her legs.

He scrubbed a hand over his face. "You said you wanted to tell me something before?"

She set her fork down even though half of the dessert was still unfinished. "It's not a big deal." But something about her body language said otherwise.

He instantly went on alert, that familiar cynicism building inside him. He hated that he kept expecting something to go wrong, that he was expecting her to stab him in the back.

"It sort of ties in with what I was telling you about my family stuff… I just don't have a lot of experience with dating." Her cheeks flushed that sexy shade again as she watched him.

He felt like she was leaving something out, that he was missing something as she stared at him with those big eyes. "I don't either."

She huffed out a little laugh. "Somehow I think you have more experience than me." This time her cheeks went crimson and he wanted to know exactly what she was thinking.

"I've never had a relationship." The words were out before he could stop himself. If she was running some scam on him and *did* want to hurt him, she'd have already done her homework on him. She'd already know what he was telling her. Still, saying the words out loud made him feel too exposed. He knew he was probably going to regret telling her this, but fuck it. She'd been open with him—even if it was part of some con game she was running. "The first woman I ever thought I loved turned out to be a paid escort. Paid by my father to keep tabs on me."

Dominique let out a horrified gasp, her eyes widening. "What?"

His lips pulled into a thin line as he shoved the anger and shame back down. He'd moved past that part of his life. "He was a bastard through and through. Thought I wanted to take over his organization."

Viktor snorted at the thought. Nothing could have been further from the truth. Back then he'd been working on a way to escape, to get out and start his own legal businesses. He'd wanted nothing to do with his father.

"In my twenties I used to fight in his illegal rings." Partially for the money he'd made betting on himself, and partially so others in his father's organization would never forget that he could easily kill them. He'd always known he'd one day break off on his own and all those men would remember how he'd beaten men bloody. The visceral reminder was better than anything he could ever say. He cleared his throat. "She was at one of them—by chance, I thought."

She'd been so damn sweet—though it had all turned out to be a lie. Everything about her had been a lie.

The humiliation he'd felt when he'd discovered the truth was something he'd never forget. "Since then I've only used escorts. You're the first woman I've ever wanted to take out like this, on a real date." *More than date.* But he left that part out. It didn't matter now anyway. Now that she knew the truth about him she'd get up and walk out of here and never look back. Which was what he knew he deserved. He might be a bastard but he wanted her to know everything about him so she could just leave. He didn't deserve a woman like her. Better to cut this off now before he fell even deeper.

"Oh, Viktor." She reached across the table and slid her fingers through his, holding his hand tight.

Her reaction made him still, even as a tiny spark of…hope flared inside him. She didn't seem disgusted by him and he'd given her an easy out. An easy way to tell him to fuck off and never call her again. "You understand what I'm saying, that I've only ever fucked escorts." His words came out harsh.

She flinched when he said 'fucked' but she nodded. "Yeah, I totally got that. I'm so sorry that your father…that you got hurt like that."

He pulled his hand back. "I wasn't hurt," he snapped. He'd been stupid and naïve, and it had taught him a valuable lesson. But something told him that if Dominique ever hurt him that same way, he might never recover. She fucking terrified him in so many ways.

The look in her eyes was something a lot like sympathy as she picked up her wine glass. "I'm still sorry."

He started to respond just as a burst of staccato gunfire erupted from just outside the restaurant—in the lobby of the hotel.

CHAPTER TWELVE

Dominique jumped as pops sounded nearby. It took a moment for it to register that it was freaking gunfire! Before she could even think about moving, Viktor had a weapon out and grabbed her around the waist, dragging her to the kitchen.

Panic slammed through her as she ran next to him, her heels making it difficult, but Viktor didn't slow. He had a hold on her and wasn't letting go. She was vaguely aware of other men moving out of the woodwork like shadows, guns in their hands as Viktor barked out orders.

It was complete chaos and she wanted to cover her ears, to block out the shooting. This was nothing like the movies. Her ears rang and her heart pounded wildly in her chest as they breached the swinging kitchen door.

The chef she'd met earlier was standing next to an industrial stove, terror on his face as he remained frozen in place.

Viktor shouted at another man who Dominique had met earlier. Lyosha. If she'd thought Viktor looked scary, this guy was even more so. Tattoos crept up under the top of his shirt, covering part of his neck. He might look like a brainless thug but his sharp green eyes seemed to take in everything. And he didn't appear to like what he saw when he looked at her.

Viktor said something to him in Russian and pushed her to him. She wanted to argue but was almost numb. The man's jaw tightened and it was clear he wanted to argue as well, but he nodded once.

"Stay with him no matter what. He'll keep you safe," Viktor snapped at her before disappearing back out the swinging kitchen door.

She took a step after him, not really to go with him, but to keep him with her. Right now it felt as if her insides would break apart from the adrenaline pumping through her. Her fight or flight response was going haywire and she was having a hard time keeping it together.

A strong hand grasped her upper arm. "Come with me." Lyosha pulled her with him.

"Where's Viktor going? What's happening?" She was terrified for him, that he'd run back into where men were shooting.

He didn't respond, just looked over at the chef and shouted for him and the server to follow. The two men hurried after them as Lyosha tugged her through another door, none too gently—but not before checking outside it. She heard the distant pop of another gunshot, then nothing. Fear for Viktor swelled inside her. What if he'd been hurt?

Her heart continued that erratic beat as they stepped out into a small hallway she realized must be used for employees. "Where's Viktor gone?" She wondered if it was a stupid question but she couldn't believe he'd just raced back out toward the gunfire even if he did have a gun. "Has anyone called the police?"

But the man just hurried down the hallway, his gun at the ready as he stopped four doors down. "We'll be safe in here. There's an extra exit if necessary." He stood back and motioned the three of them into what turned out to be a storage room.

Bins marked with different holiday decorations were stacked on tall metal racks that went all the way up to the ceiling. There was another door on the other side of the small space just as Lyosha had said.

"What's going on?" she asked quietly as he shut the door. Her entire body was trembling so she wrapped her arms around herself. "You can talk now that we're safe," she snapped when he still didn't respond.

He pinned her with a hard look. "I don't know what's going on. Someone is stupid enough to attack Viktor and I should be out there with him. Not watching you three," he muttered, his jaw tightening again.

"Then go if he needs your help!" She hated that Viktor had raced right back into whatever dangerous situation without knowing what he was getting into. The thought of him injured or worse sent another jolt of fear through her. Especially after everything he'd just told her. She couldn't believe his own father had done that to him—well she could, knowing who his father had been, but she still hated it. Viktor had looked as if he hated himself as he admitted to her he'd only been with escorts.

Lyosha simply frowned at her but didn't respond, just pulled his phone out of his pants pocket when it buzzed. After a short conversation in Russian he shoved it back into his pocket then opened the door a fraction.

Hope bloomed inside Dominique that Viktor was there, but another man…Kir was there. The blond-haired, blue-eyed man seemed to have an easy smile for everyone. Now his expression was tight but after murmuring quietly to Lyosha, the other man stepped back and let Kir in.

"Protect the woman with your life." *Or else*, seemed to be the unspoken words that followed. Lyosha's words were sharp, deadly, and sent a frisson of fear down her spine.

Yeah, she was glad he wanted Kir to keep her alive, but the way he spoke was scary. Okay, everything about him was terrifying.

Kir turned to look at all of them as Lyosha left, and half-smiled. "Everything's okay. We'll be in here for just a little bit," he said calmly, his words having a soothing effect on all three of them. "The threat has been neutralized so don't worry. And Viktor's fine," he added before she could ask. "He sent me here to keep an eye on you. To keep you safe."

That was all she needed to hear—that Viktor was okay. Yeah, she had a lot more questions but knowing he was unharmed allowed her to take a deep breath and let some of her panic go. She leaned against one of the racks and turned to look at the other two men who were standing in what looked like a state of shock. Especially the chef. His dark eyes were wide and his entire body was trembling as he more or less stared blankly at her.

She pulled one of the bins off a rack. "Why don't you sit?"

He nodded and did as she said as if he was on autopilot.

"You should probably ask for a raise after tonight," Dominique said to the server, hoping to dispel some of the tension in the small room.

Kir was standing guard and clearly not interested in making the two men feel better, and when she was nervous she tended to talk.

The server let out a shaky laugh but she could see some of the tension leave his shoulders. "No kidding. I'm Eric, by the way."

She forced a smile, glad he seemed to be handling things okay. "I'm Dominique."

Viktor eyed the fallen bodies, anger a live wire inside him, pulsing and ready to strike out at whoever had ordered this.

He didn't recognize any of the men, and from experience he knew that these guys would be hired muscle. There were six men in all, each one wearing a bulletproof vest and armed to the teeth. They didn't have on more tactical gear, however. Which made Viktor think they weren't that well trained. Careful not to move the body too much, he pulled down the shirt of one and saw what he knew was a prison tattoo.

When he saw Lyosha striding across the lobby strewn with dead bodies, he frowned. "Why are you here?"

"Kir is with the woman and the others. They're fine." His words were almost dismissive, but Viktor knew better. He could see the worry in Lyosha's gaze, faint that it was. "My priority is you. Are we calling the police or not?"

He looked around again. His men were all law-abiding citizens and worked for the security division of his company directly under

Lyosha. He was their boss and from experience he knew they'd do whatever he said. "Someone could have heard the gunfire and called it in," he finally said. He absolutely hated involving the police but sometimes it was better to show that he had nothing to hide. And getting rid of half a dozen bodies was doable, but not easy. He'd rather let the police take care of them and have all this on the record.

Lyosha nodded, clearly on the same page. "I'll photograph all the dead men, remove any personal items—if there are any—and take their fingerprints before we call."

"Good. I need you to take Dominique out of here. Kir can make sure the other two get home safely. I'm going to tell the police I was going over the layout of our new plans when we were blindsided. It will be like Dominique and the other two were never here."

Lyosha nodded again. "Good. The chef is about to piss his pants, if he hasn't already. I'll make sure they know they'll be compensated for their silence."

Viktor nodded. It would be easier this way, less messy. He didn't want Dominique dragged into anything and she didn't deserve to get hauled to the police station where she'd be questioned for hours. No, she should be at his home, safe and resting. Her condo was easy to breach so that wasn't an option. He needed her where he could control the environment more. "I'll go talk to Dominique but I want you to take her to my home."

Lyosha's eyebrows raised. "I should be with you."

"I need someone I trust with her. I need to know she's safe while I'm dealing with the cops." And Lyosha had been his driver for years, had joined him after he'd split from his father's organization.

"Fine. But are you sure you can trust her?" There was no malice in the question, the only reason Viktor reined in his temper.

"Why?" Viktor wondered if his brother had said something about their history, but he immediately dismissed that. Abram would never betray his confidence.

Lyosha glanced around at his men and barked out an order for them to start taking fingerprints of the dead guys, before he turned back to Viktor. "I know the type of woman you like." He rubbed the back of his neck, clearly uncomfortable. "No disrespect. I just don't know if you should completely trust someone like her, even if she's yours now."

He blinked, realizing Lyosha had misunderstood him before. "She's not an escort—never was. She works for Red Stone. She is my…she's *mine*."

Now Lyosha cursed, as if that was worse than what he'd originally assumed.

Just to get another rise out of him because it was so rare, Viktor added, "She's Porter Caldwell's assistant."

"You're fucking insane," he muttered. "She works for those Boy Scouts?"

He didn't answer, just tilted his head in the direction of one of the employee doors. He needed to see for himself that she was okay and then convince her she should go with Lyosha. From what he knew of her, he figured Dominique would argue and want to stay, but it wasn't happening. He wanted her gone, mainly because he didn't want the police to tie her to him. He'd been legit for a while but he didn't want to give some asshole cop an excuse to harass the woman he'd fallen for.

Hurrying down the hallway, he texted Kir to let him know they were on their way. As they reached the door to the storage room, Kir peered out, his weapon in hand.

The door quickly shot open and Dominique practically shoved Kir out of the way as she hurried to him. Later he'd have to tell her that she couldn't do that—that in a situation like this she needed to remain behind one of his men at all times until they knew for a fact that everything was clear, but…he liked the worry for him he saw on her face.

Not the actual worry, but he liked that she cared for him enough to be concerned.

"Are you okay?" She grabbed his upper arms, looking him up and down, her body slightly trembling.

"I'm fine." He pulled her into his arms, needing to comfort her, to actually hold her. She was heaven in his arms, soft and sweet and his.

It was a foreign sensation to comfort another person, but he smoothed a hand down her spine and murmured to her in Russian. He knew she wouldn't understand and he truly didn't give a shit that Lyosha and Kir could understand him. If she played him for a fool he'd deal with the fallout. Right now, the only thing he knew was that his woman was upset and he needed to reassure her.

"What happened?" Her voice was muffled, her face buried against his chest.

"Not sure yet." He couldn't give her any details, not now. Getting her out of here was the most important thing.

She pulled back to look at him, just a hint of tears glistening in her dark eyes. "I was so worried about you," she whispered.

He cupped her cheek and brushed his lips over hers. He knew they didn't have time for this, but he just wanted a taste, to reassure her the situation was under control. "Everything's okay," he murmured, pulling back. "I need you to go with Lyosha. He's going to take you to my place. I've got to stay and talk to the cops but I'll tell you anything you want to know when I get there."

She took a step back, her eyebrows drawing together. "I should be here to talk to the police too."

"No." She frowned at his abruptness but he needed her gone. *Now.*

"Viktor—"

"Kir's taken the other two. They're fine leaving." Lyosha's voice made them both turn.

Viktor noticed that Dominique stepped closer to him—away from Lyosha. "See, they're gone too. It'll be easier with you gone as well. No questions from the police, no making a report, nothing. You can go and relax and—"

"And leave you to deal with everything by yourself?" she demanded, turning her full attention to him again. "I'm staying." She crossed her arms over her chest.

"No. You're not." Damn it, he needed her safe. He was used to people following his orders. Always. "If you stay you'll have to lie to the police about the other two not being here. Because they're gone now."

She bit her bottom lip and looked over at the doorway of the storage room. The others had left through the other exit, likely already in a vehicle driven by Kir. "Fine. He can just take me home, then."

"You're going to my place where I know you're safe." That wasn't up for debate. None of this was. He also wanted her where they could pick up where they'd left off. He wanted her in his bed and moaning out his name as he brought her to climax.

She poked at his chest. "Unless you're planning on kidnapping me—"

"I'll do what it takes to keep you safe," he ground out. "I have no idea what tonight was about, who those guys were. So you're going with Lyosha to my place."

Her eyes widened. "What if I say no? You'll seriously just kidnap me?"

He bent down, got right in her face even as he hated the anger—and fear—he saw there. Because it was directed at him. "I will do what it takes to keep you safe," he repeated. "If that means tying you up and hauling you to my home, I'll do it. Don't test me."

She watched him for a long moment, then glanced at Lyosha, who was looking anywhere but at them. Finally she turned back to Viktor and shoved him in the chest. "You're a bastard."

"I know. But I'll be damned if you get hurt because of me." He wanted to comfort her, to kiss her, to do something other than basically kidnap her, but he didn't have time right now for reassuring words. "I'll be there as soon as I can."

After a quick nod at Lyosha, he headed back the way he'd come. Dealing with the cops always made him edgy, but it was something that had to be taken care of.

As soon as it was, he'd go home and face Dominique's wrath. He hated that she was angry at him, but he'd rather deal with that than see her dead from a bullet.

He would keep her safe. Even if she hated him for it. Because after tonight he knew she meant way too much to him already. All he wanted to do right now was take her back to his place and make love to her until they both passed out. To claim her so that she knew who she belonged to.

CHAPTER THIRTEEN

"You should get some rest." Lyosha, who'd brought her back to Viktor's palatial place, had taken off his jacket so that his shoulder holster and guns were showing. He was standing at the window in the living room—*one* of the living rooms—that faced the big driveway.

She'd been worried they should stay away from windows after that attack but he'd assured her that no one would get past the front gate and security.

At first Dominique had been terrified of the guy, and while she was super annoyed with him for forcing her to come here, she'd realized he definitely wasn't going to hurt her. He'd been careful to not even touch her on the way here. And he'd actually been pretty decent, trying to get her to relax. As if that was possible.

"I'm not doing anything until I talk to Viktor," she said. *And rip him a new one.* She couldn't believe him; couldn't believe he'd pretty much kidnapped her and had her sent here by one of his men instead of letting her talk to the police. From everything Lizzy had told her, he wasn't doing anything illegal with his businesses so she couldn't understand his reluctance to let her talk to the police. He'd clearly done nothing wrong—he'd been a victim. Some guys had opened up fire at one his hotels. The whole thing was crazy.

The man made *her* crazy.

"You should listen better," he muttered. A flash of light illuminated him by the window, as if from headlights. The long driveway ended in a huge half-circle in front of the house but there was a four-car garage as well.

Hope bloomed inside her that it was Viktor. It was well after midnight so he should be back anytime. Or she assumed he would be. She snorted at Lyosha's words. "You think I should be a better kidnapping victim?"

He made an annoyed sound in his throat. "You should listen better to Viktor. He's just looking out for you. He needs his woman not to question him."

A burst of surprised laughter escaped. "Oh my God, you did not just say that. Like what, I should be one of his employees and just jump when he says something? Relationships don't work like that. Not since the nineteen fifties." Not that she knew from experience, not really. But she'd at least had a good example from her parents—until everything went pear-shaped. And it wasn't like she and Viktor were even in a relationship. She'd thought they might be heading that way—until tonight. Now she just wanted to smack him.

"No, you're a woman. You need to let him take care of you." Frowning, he pulled out his cell phone. Whatever he read on the screen had the tension in his shoulders completely easing up.

"Oh sweet Lord, so you're a sexist," she muttered. "Just great." She stood, determined to find Viktor. Because she was pretty sure he was back, if Lyosha's body language and the flash of headlights were any indication.

He pinned her with a penetrating stare. "I'm not sexist. I just think—"

"I really, *really* don't care what you think. Where's Viktor?"

He lifted a big shoulder.

"Fine. I'll find him myself." She swiveled and headed out of the room. She'd taken her heels off hours ago but was still in her dress. The hardwood floor of the foyer was cool against her feet. She hadn't gotten a tour of the place but she could pretty much guarantee Viktor wasn't up the stairs to her right.

There was a huge formal dining room across from the living room she'd just been in, and another door on the other side of it. It had to extend to the rest of the house, and since the garage was on the other side—

"Come on." Lyosha fell in step with her. "I'll take you to him."

She hurried after him as he continued to the dining room at a fast clip. "I'm surprised you're taking me."

"It's better than you running all over this place, getting into things that don't concern you." He shot her a dark look as he opened the swinging door connected to the dining room.

She just rolled her eyes and strode past him into what turned out to be a huge, gorgeous kitchen. Everything in it appeared new.

She didn't get a chance to appreciate any of it before Lyosha ushered her through it to a hallway. Then another one, until he knocked on a heavy-looking wood door with intricate carvings on the outside. It was custom and beautiful.

Viktor opened the door a moment later and much to her annoyance her heart skipped a beat at the sight of him. She could see Abram behind him, leaning against a big desk. Viktor's eyes widened at the sight of her, then he glared at Lyosha. He growled something in Russian but thankfully Lyosha answered in English.

"I told her to take one of the guest bedrooms and offered her new clothes. She said no." He looked at her, seemingly for confirmation.

She nodded, even though a small part of her wanted to throw him under the bus. He was just doing his job and she wasn't going to hold it against him. Even if he annoyed her with his sexist bullshit. "We need to talk," she said to Viktor as the door opened even wider.

His brother stepped past her, giving her an unreadable look as he motioned that Lyosha should come with him.

Viktor moved back so she could enter. "I'm sorry you got dragged into this." For a moment he looked as if he would reach for her, but he let his arms drop. His voice was as exhausted as his expression.

Which made her feel bad. She wanted to comfort him, to wrap her arms around him. But not until they hashed some things out. "I'm really not happy with you, but first…were any of your men hurt? Are you okay with the police?"

"None of my guys were injured and yes, I'm fine. They just had a lot of questions and had to deal with the bodies. It was very time-consuming."

"I'm glad you're okay." She smacked his upper arm once. "But I'm not okay with you kidnapping me."

His jaw tightened as he looked down at her. Without her heels on he actually towered over her. Instead of using his height difference against her, he sighed and went to sit on the edge of the desk. "I'm sorry, Dominique."

The way he said her name sent a shiver of awareness through her. She fought against her reaction. She came to stand in front of him, hating how tired he looked. "Why didn't you let me stay?"

"I just… I didn't want you there, not with the cops and the whole parade of people I knew would be there."

"Why not? You're not into anything illegal, right?"

"Not anymore."

She nodded once. "I know that."

His lips curved up, his smile wry. "Your guys down at Red Stone tell you that?"

She lifted a shoulder. "More or less. So what's the deal, for real? You think I can't handle a few questions from the police?"

"I didn't want you to *have* to. I didn't want you on their radar at all." His words were as harsh as his expression. There was no give there. Now he didn't look tired, just angry and frustrated. "I didn't want you linked to all that death, to me."

"That's stupid. I'm a big girl, I've dealt with a lot in my life and—"

"I know!" He shoved up from the desk but she didn't back down. "I just didn't want you to have to deal with anything else. There was nothing you could tell them, no need for you to be there. I just…wanted you safe." He practically growled the last couple words, his big, sexy body vibrating with tension.

"That's not fair."

He blinked. "What isn't?"

She leaned into him, wrapping her arms around him, taking him off guard if the way he jolted at her touch was any indication. "I've worked up a lot of anger at you the last few hours. I'm still not happy and I seriously hope there's not a next time for this kind of thing, but if there is, just include me in whatever happens. You don't need to protect me."

He smoothed a hand down her spine. "I want to."

She liked the way he held her, how secure he made her feel. "Will you tell me what happened tonight? Or who attacked your hotel?"

Sighing, he pulled back and motioned to one of the chairs. She didn't want to move away from him so she tugged him until he sat, then she sat on his lap. He seemed surprised by it but she didn't care. She might be annoyed with him, but she still couldn't seem to get enough of him.

He wrapped his arms around her, holding her tight. She wasn't sure what cologne he used but the subtle, masculine scent wrapped around her as he sighed. Looking into his face now, it was hard to remember that she'd once been afraid of this man, that she'd hated him.

"Men with guns attacked my hotel. There were half a dozen of them and I don't know who they are or who they worked for. But we're looking into it. We…took their fingerprints. I know the police will do their job, but my people are better equipped. And I need to know who did this." His jaw tightened, his rage clear.

Dominique placed a gentle hand on his chest and shifted slightly against him. His grip around her tightened, his eyes darkening a fraction. His erection was evident but she couldn't focus on that now. "Do you have any ideas?"

He paused and she could see the indecision on his face. "Ideas, yes. The attack was bold, which does narrow it down."

"That's good, right?"

He nodded, his expression wary as he watched her. "I'm not letting you leave my place."

She blinked. "What?"

"Until I figure out who was behind the attack, you're staying with me." His grip on her tightened as if he thought she might bolt.

"Will someone at least go to my place to get my clothes?"

He blinked, his grip loosening a fraction. "You're not arguing?"

"Well, I don't like your tendency to tell me what to do."

"I think you like it a little," he murmured, his voice dropping an octave. His gaze dipped to her mouth, his expression going heated.

She felt that look all the way to her core. Heat flooded her as she shifted against him again. "Maybe I like it in the bedroom." She was pretty sure she would anyway. "But not outside it."

"Hmm."

"Look, I don't want to die, and if someone's targeting you—and they obviously didn't care that I'm with you—then I'll stay here for now. But I'm going to work Monday." She needed to make sure he knew that before they started kissing and she completely lost any sensible thoughts.

His lips pulled into a thin line but he nodded, one hand sliding up her leg, dipping under the hem of her dress as he moved over her upper thigh.

She sucked in a little breath, enjoying the feel of his callused fingers stroking her skin. She wondered how high he would move.

"I called Porter, told him a little of what's going on and that we'll see how Monday goes. But Red Stone is one of the safest places in the city. You should be fine to go to work."

Annoyance surged through her at his 'do what I say' attitude but it was hard to care as his hand crept higher. His touch was so gentle, his fingers just barely skimming her skin, but he still scorched her, sending tingles of awareness straight to all her nerve endings.

He knew he was making her crazy. His blue eyes looked somehow darker in the dim light of his office, the hunger rolling off him palpable as he watched her carefully.

She sucked in a breath when he reached the silky edge of her panties. She was already wet for him, her nipples hard against her bra cups. Anticipation hummed through her as she waited for him to move just a bit, to touch her exactly where she wanted, where she ached for him.

"Stay in my bed tonight?" he asked, his voice hoarse, his gaze focused on her mouth as he teased a finger under the edge of her panties. He was basically touching her hip, nowhere near where she wanted him to be, and yet she had goose bumps all over.

Swallowing hard, she nodded. She definitely wanted that. And she knew what he was asking. Which meant... "I need to tell you something. It's not a big deal, really." Oh God, this was harder than she thought. A small part of her didn't want to say it at all but he needed to know. "I'm...a virgin."

He blinked once, as if he hadn't heard her right. Lightning fast he slid his hand out from under her dress and smoothed it into place. Then he patted her leg as if he didn't know what to do with his hand. He looked a little like a deer caught in headlights as he cleared his throat.

"I still need to do a little work," he said, moving to stand, sliding her off his lap as he did. "But I'll make sure Lyosha gets you settled in a guest room."

His words were like a slap of ice water against her face as what he said registered. He was sending her away to a guest room; basically rescinding the offer of taking her to his bed. Because what, he couldn't handle her being a virgin? Embarrassment flooded her as he strode from the room, practically running away from her. She hadn't thought he'd care. Not so much that he'd flee from her as if she had some disease.

Stupid tears pricked her eyes as she sat on one of the chairs. Part of her wanted to go after him, but she didn't know what to say. It was clear he had no interest in her now. That hurt worse than she could have imagined.

CHAPTER FOURTEEN

Viktor scanned another file of potential suspects, still trying to narrow down who the hell hated him enough to come after him so boldly. This had personal written all over it. Personal and...a little amateurish. The attack hadn't been as well thought out as it could have been and the point of entry was stupid, considering all the other entrances for the hotel.

He clicked to another file but wasn't truly seeing anything, not enough to digest any real information. All he could think about was Dominique and her words to him. It seemed impossible that she was a virgin. He hadn't known what to say, how to respond. She might as well have sucker punched him.

"She's settled in." Lyosha's voice made him look up from his computer. The other man leaned against the doorframe of Viktor's office, his expression annoyed.

Viktor frowned. "What?"

"Why are you still here and not upstairs? Or why isn't she in your fucking bed?"

He gritted his teeth, ignoring the questions. Leaning back in his chair, exhaustion crept in on him. "I need to read over these files."

"You already know what's in them."

It was true. "Why do you care what I'm doing?"

Lyosha lifted a shoulder. "Just wondering what you did to make your woman cry."

Viktor was standing before he realized he'd moved. Guilt punched through him. "She was crying?"

"No. But it's good to know you care if she does. And for the record, she looked like she wanted to. What the fuck are you doing down here?"

There weren't many people who talked to him so freely but Lyosha had been his friend for many years. Didn't mean Viktor wanted to have this conversation. Not with him, not anyone. "You didn't even trust her a few hours ago," he muttered, sitting back down. He should just go to bed, but he didn't want to go alone—because he knew he wouldn't sleep. He'd be too busy fantasizing about Dominique. And as soon as he had a thought, just as quickly he'd feel like a fucking perv. She didn't deserve someone like him for her first time, someone whose hands were stained with blood. Still…the thought of being her first, introducing her to sex… *Damn it.* He scrubbed a hand over his face. He was too damn conflicted.

"Don't tell her, but I like her. It's clear she cares about you." Lyosha's mouth curved up in his version of a smile. "I had fun messing with her earlier about her role as 'your woman.' For a moment I thought she might hit me."

Viktor could imagine what his friend had said. "You're an asshole."

"I know. Now what's the problem?"

Yeah, not having that conversation. "Shut the door."

Lyosha immediately went into work mode, stepping inside and shutting it quickly behind him. "What's up?"

"I looked over your report and agree with the top three suspects, but…I think they might be getting information from someone who works for me and Abram." He couldn't be sure, but he didn't like how Dominique had been mugged while out with him. Then that bold attack with her there at the hotel. Not many people had known about his plans last night—and even fewer the night of the mugging. The three people he suspected he'd done business with before and things had gone south when Viktor had bought them out—legally. He hadn't actually screwed any of them. They'd been paid fairly, but some people couldn't take what they perceived as losing.

The other man nodded. "I've already started running security checks on anyone who has direct access to you or Abram. Digging into financials and phone records to start. If I learn nothing from either of those, I'll move on to another step but I think I'll have something by tomorrow morning." He glanced at his watch. "Later this morning."

"What about the fingerprints or facial IDs?" One way or another they were going to figure out who'd come after him. Getting that information from the dead, would-be hit men was a good place to start. If the dead men had been paid already he'd just follow the money trail back to the payer.

"Still working on it. Those programs take time to run all possible matches. I've got an alert set up on my phone and yours. You'll get a notice when something pops up."

"Good. Go get some sleep." Normally he didn't have so much security at his house, just a basic two-man team. But for now he was keeping everything locked down tight. Even Abram was here and had brought Lucy just in case she was targeted.

Lyosha snorted as he pulled open the door. "You too."

Once Viktor was alone he shut his computer down and tried to convince himself to go to his own bedroom. Alone.

His room was attached to his office so he *should* just step right next door. Instead he found himself heading for the guest room Dominique was in.

He'd been an asshole before but he hadn't been able to handle what she'd told him, hadn't even known what to say. Hell, he still wasn't sure he could deal with it.

What did he know about virgins?

His hands were dirty in more ways than one. He broke out into a sweat just thinking about touching her now. Even though he desperately wanted to, Dominique deserved better than him.

Even when he'd told her about his sexual past she hadn't judged him, she'd just looked as if she wanted to give him a fucking hug. Which was almost worse. He'd told her to give her a way to walk out on him. But she hadn't taken it.

Then he'd walked out on her like an asshole when she'd been honest with him. Made herself vulnerable with him.

She didn't deserve that.

When he reached the door of the bedroom he knew she was in he had to wipe a damp palm on his pants. He immediately cursed himself for the weakness. The woman had turned him into someone he didn't recognize but it was hard to give a shit when she opened the door wearing a T-shirt that was most definitely his. Lyosha must have given it to her. It barely came to mid-thigh. He wanted to drop to his knees, shove that shirt up and press his face to her belly, beg her forgiveness, then make her melt and settle his mouth over her pussy. He wouldn't stop until she'd gone over the edge and was crying out his name.

Her mouth tight, she crossed her arms over her chest—and given the outline of her full breasts, it was clear she wasn't wearing a bra. "Is everything okay?"

He shook his head and pushed into the room past her. The bed was slightly rumpled and only a single lamp was on, casting the room into shadows. "No."

She gasped, dropping her arms. "What are you doing?"

He shut the door behind him and forced his gaze to her face—even though the sight of her long, bare legs called to his most primal side. He wanted them draped over his back, her feet digging into him as he made her come against his mouth. Even though the sane part of him told him to walk away, to just apologize and leave, he didn't think he could. Not when he was standing here, looking into her beautiful face and knowing he'd never meet another woman like her.

"I came to apologize. I acted like an asshole."

She nodded. "Yeah, you did."

"I'm sorry. I...it wasn't about you. When you said you were a virgin I worried about hurting you." More like tainting her with who he was.

To his surprise, she rolled her eyes and went to sit on the edge of the bed. "People have sex every day. I'm not some petite doll you have to worry about hurting. Something you already know. So I accept your apology but I don't buy that crap about not wanting to hurt me. You made me feel really bad about myself." She wrapped her arms around her middle again, the simple action putting a wall up between them.

He'd done that and he hated it. He didn't want there to be anything between them.

He scrubbed a hand over his face. "I know," he rasped out. "I'm truly sorry. I'm in new territory here and you scare the shit out of me." The admission cost him but she was worth it.

Her eyebrows drew together. "*I* scare you?" Her voice was incredulous.

Nodding, he went to sit on the edge of the bed. Her sweet scent was subtle, but the exotic, floral notes teased him. "I've never been with a woman like you. I've never known a woman as sweet as you. I keep giving you reasons to walk away and you keep surprising me. I've…fallen for you pretty hard." Laying himself completely bare was almost too much.

Her dark eyes softened just a fraction. Taking it as a good sign, he scooted a few inches closer. The need to touch her was overwhelming, but he resisted.

"You deserve someone better than me for your first time." Though if they *had* a first time, he was going to try damn hard to make sure it was the best she ever had. No. He wanted to make sure he was her *only* lover from this point forward. Strangely, the thought of being in a committed relationship didn't scare him as much as he expected. What did scare him was if she didn't want the same thing.

"Why would you say that? Yeah, you're a little rough around the edges sometimes—and annoyingly bossy—but you're a good man." She closed the distance between them until their knees were touching. "You hurt me earlier but I still haven't changed my mind about us, about…" She trailed off, gesturing between them, but she didn't need to finish.

His gaze strayed to her mouth. Just the thought of brushing his lips over hers, of pinning her beneath him as he brought her to orgasm, was making it hard to think. To breathe.

He wasn't a good man. The words stuck in his throat. He wanted to tell her the things he'd done, that he'd killed his own father. Killed others. Always to protect himself, but he still had blood on his hands. He couldn't force the words out though. Not when she was looking at him with those big, dark eyes and all he wanted to do was kiss her, to make her his.

He cleared his throat. "I haven't been with anyone in over a year." He'd gotten tired of paying for sex, of feeling no connection. "And I've been tested. I'm clean—and I have all the paperwork. You can see it whenever you want." He mentally crossed his fingers that she still wanted him at all. It had sounded like she did, but he didn't want to make an assumption.

When she pushed up from the bed, his hopes withered into nothing. She was going to tell him to leave. He prepared for the blow, for her to tell him that it wasn't happening.

Until she stripped the T-shirt over her head, revealing the body he'd been fantasizing about since the first night he'd seen her.

His cock shoved at his pants as she dropped the shirt to the ground. He devoured her with his eyes, afraid to touch her.

Her breathing was erratic and the pulse point in her neck was going crazy. Long, blonde hair cascaded around full breasts he wanted to cup, kiss, stroke. They rose and fell, her pink nipples already hard. Her slender waist flared into full hips and her pussy was covered by a thin scrap of black, lacy material she would soon be losing.

He swallowed hard, met her gaze as he stood. A good man would probably tell her they didn't need to do anything tonight. She'd been through a hell of a lot in the past few hours and despite what she'd said, he knew he didn't deserve her.

But it was already too late for that. There was no way he was walking away from her.

He cupped her cheek and realized his hand was trembling. If anyone could fuck him up, it was her. He'd looked down the barrel of a gun before with a certainty he was going to die and hadn't felt a sliver of the fear he did now.

Well, more than the fear that he'd screw things up—or that she'd eventually walk out on him when she realized she could do better.

Even with all that jumbled in his head, he'd never been so turned on in his life.

He'd never had slow or sweet sex, wasn't even sure he could. Even with his ex, the one person he'd thought had loved him, it had been rough and hard. He didn't want that with Dominique.

"Tell me if you don't like something and we'll stop. Promise me." He growled the words, needing to hear her say yes before he completely lost himself in her.

She just gave him a sensual smile and pressed her body to his, standing up on tiptoe to kiss him.

He let go of everything in that moment. He trusted that she'd tell him if they went too far. He covered her mouth with his, cupping her cheek with one hand and gripping her hip in the other. The thin strap of her panties was the only thing between his hand and completely bare skin.

That was going to change now.

Moving quickly, he grasped her ass and lifted her onto the bed. She stretched out on her back, her stomach muscles pulled tight as he crawled over her, caging her in. He was ready to devour every inch of her.

He might not know anything about being with a virgin, but he knew she'd need to be ready for him. Which meant his clothes were staying on until she'd come. He wanted to pleasure her first, to bring her to climax with his mouth before he even got undressed. He'd prove to her that this was about more than just fucking.

"I don't know where to start," he murmured, meeting her gaze. "I want to kiss all of you at the same time."

It must have been the right thing to say because she half-smiled and pushed out a breath as she stroked her hands over his chest. Which was unfortunately still covered.

He wanted to feel her skin to skin but that would happen soon enough. Reaching between their bodies, he barely cupped her covered mound. "Would you like it if I kissed you here?"

Her dark eyes dilated and her cheeks flushed as she made a moaning sound that could have been a yes. That was good enough for him.

Though he wanted to simply bury himself inside her, he forced himself to go slow, to savor this—for both of them. He wanted to work her up to sex, to make sure tonight was all about her.

He was so used to taking charge in the bedroom, to getting exactly what he wanted, that this was virgin territory for him too. With Dominique, she was in control of him even if she didn't know it.

He covered her mouth again, kissed her until she was arching underneath him, her body plastered to his. He'd never had this before, this slow sweetness of just kissing. He loved the almost shy way her tongue flicked against his even as her fingers dug into his back with force, telling him she wanted him exactly where he was. On top of her.

She was soft and slender beneath him, the complete opposite of him and he loved it.

Driven with the need to stroke his tongue against her pussy, he somehow tore his mouth from hers, feathering kisses along her jaw and down the long, elegant column of her neck. Everything about her was elegant, right down to her slender fingers.

She slid them against his scalp, through his closely cropped hair as he moved lower, lower, lower... She moaned as he sucked on a taut nipple.

He lifted his head, watching her reaction. Everything about her was real, right down to her sensual moans. He loved that none of this was scripted, that she was truly enjoying herself. He sucked just a little harder, wanting to see what her reaction would be. He wasn't sure how much experience she had at all so he needed this to be memorable for her.

"Viktor..." Her fingers tightened as she arched her back, trying to shove herself deeper in his mouth.

He groaned against her soft skin, gently palmed her other full breast. She was like the sweetest offering, a dessert he wanted to savor all night. His first time had been with an escort even if he hadn't known it. This was nothing like that. This was…heaven.

His cock was heavy between his legs, aching to fill her body.

But he couldn't screw this up. He needed her wet and begging for him, so turned on that the bite of pain when he entered her wouldn't matter. He had no clue how much it would hurt—he just had to make this good for her and hope it minimized her discomfort later.

Taking him by surprise, she shoved at his head. "You're killing me," she rasped out. Her body writhed under his in the most sensual way, her legs clenching around his waist, her grip tight.

She was basically rubbing herself against him, looking for a release—one he was going to give her with his mouth, fingers, cock.

He moved down to her belly, layered more kisses along the flat plane of her stomach as she lifted her hips, silently begging him for more.

She might be a virgin but she seemed to know exactly what she wanted. He wondered if she'd ever had someone go down on her, but didn't want to ask for a multitude of reasons. This time was just about them.

Crouched between her legs, he kept his gaze pinned to hers as he hooked his finger in her panties and began dragging them down her smooth, tanned legs. She had fine, pale blonde hair on her mound. "Tell me what you want," he demanded. "Say the words." Because he needed to hear them. Some primal part of him wanted her to spell it out.

Her cheeks were flushed, her eyes heavy-lidded. "Kiss me."

"Where?" He wasn't sure why he was pushing, but he wanted to hear the word on her lips. He'd push her more, later, once she was ready. For now, he just wanted to hear—

"My pussy." She whispered the words, as if someone might overhear.

He jerked at hearing the words roll off her tongue, wanted to capture her mouth again and plunge right into her, but first…

He inhaled her sweet scent as he ran a finger down her slick folds. She was soaked, and the knowledge did something primal to him. She made him feel like a fucking caveman with the need to claim her, to make sure everyone knew that this sensual woman was his.

Leaning down, he flicked his tongue over the tiny bud already swollen and peeking out from her folds.

She jerked against him, a shudder racking her.

"So sensitive," he murmured before teasing her with his tongue again, this time with more pressure.

Her hips rolled against his face as he continued kissing and licking her clit. The moaning sounds she made were the most erotic thing he'd ever heard. She wasn't acting. This wasn't a show for him. This was her completely enjoying herself. Her fingers dug into his head and he savored the nip of pain.

When he finally slid a finger inside her, he shuddered at her slickness. She was so damn reactive and this was all for him. He knew he shouldn't care that she'd never been with anyone, and if she had, he wouldn't have given a shit. But to know he was going to be her first made him crazy.

Made him feel honored in a way he was certain he didn't deserve.

But he could be the right man for her. That he knew with a bone-deep certainty. He could give her everything she wanted, take care of her, keep her safe. He knew that no one was entirely safe but he'd make damn sure she had the best of everything.

As he slid another finger into her, she groaned. "Viktor, more. Please." The sweet way she begged made him crazy.

He decided to stop teasing. She was so wet she'd be able to take him fully. But he needed her to come first. She had to have pleasure before that pain. He wouldn't allow anything else.

Increasing the pressure of his tongue, he circled her pulsing clit, relished the way she writhed against his face, her cries growing louder as he teased her. He moved his fingers in and out of her, her tight sheath clenching around his fingers quicker and quicker.

She was close.

He needed her to come. Needed it so bad he was practically shaking.

"Oh… Oh, Viktor…" Her back arched and she dropped her hands from his head, clenching those fingers—the ones he'd imagined wrapped around his cock too many times—into the covers.

He tweaked her clit with just a little more pressure. She was so close. Her inner walls tightened around him faster and faster and he knew the exact moment before she was about to fall over the edge.

Her entire body tightened right before she cried out and let go. His fingers grew even slicker as she found her release. He savored the little ripples of her tight pussy as she reached orgasm.

Lifting his head, he watched her ride through it. Her eyes were closed, her cheeks and chest flushed pink as she continued coming. Eventually she stilled against the covers, her breathing erratic as she opened her eyes to look at him.

Her lips curved up in a sensual smile of pure bliss, looking thoroughly satisfied. "That was amazing," she murmured, instantly reaching for him.

The way she moved for him, her arms outstretched, made his heart swell until he felt it would explode.

He stripped off his shirt and pants, getting undressed in record time. He grabbed a condom from his pocket but she frowned at it and sat up as he crawled back into the bed.

He was rock hard, his cock jutting out so thick and heavy that for the first time in his life he wished he was a little smaller.

She took the condom from him and tossed it away as she grasped his hard length. "I'm on the pill and I don't want a barrier between us the first time."

He couldn't believe she was putting that much faith in him. The fact that she was made him realize that this was a woman he could trust, a woman he was never letting go.

He looked down between their bodies. Watched, mesmerized, as she stroked him oh-so-slowly. Way too gentle for what he normally preferred, but just having her hand on him, he was pretty sure he could come right there if she continued.

He didn't respond about the condom. If she didn't want one, he trusted her to be on the pill. The truth was, he wanted to be inside her bare too. Even the thought was almost too much for the last shred of his control.

Crushing his mouth to hers, he covered her body with his. He grasped her wrist, pulled her hand away from his cock because no way was he coming in her hand. Not this first time.

He'd never wanted a woman like this. Ever. He felt fucking possessed as he positioned himself at her entrance and slowly slid inside her inch by inch. He pulled back just a little so he could see her face, could make sure he wasn't hurting her. Her dark eyes were dilated as he moved into her, her breathing erratic and the pleasure in her gaze crystal clear. She was slick and so tight it took all his control to do this right.

Which was hard when his balls were pulled up tight and all he wanted to do was empty himself inside her. Especially after she'd said she wanted him inside her with no barrier.

Yeah, this woman was his. In a way he hadn't fully comprehended until now. He knew that having her in his life would give him a weakness he'd never had before.

But letting her go wasn't an option. He couldn't live in a world with her and not have her in his life. *Nope. Not happening.*

"You're mine," he growled against her swollen lips. The words came out guttural as he held back the urge to slam into her.

She sucked in a breath, her eyes glazed over with passion as he gave the final push inside her. There was a slight resistance that gave way before he was buried fully inside her.

Her inner walls tightened around him but he didn't move, just watched her carefully, heart pounding. "Is this okay?"

Her lips curved up ever so slightly, her breathing uneven as she nodded. "It's different. I feel very full but…no pain. Promise," she whispered.

The truth in her eyes was clear so he pulled back slowly, gritting his teeth at how good she felt, how tight.

Everything about this moment was so intimate. He wanted to look away, felt too vulnerable as she stared up at him, but he couldn't. This was more than sex to him. More than he could put into words.

He wasn't sure he wanted to. Being with her like this had ripped him in two so that he felt like a different person. A better person with her.

She stroked her fingers down his back as he thrust in and out of her. The sensation of being inside her was too much and not enough. He didn't think he'd ever get enough of her.

She was an addiction he was more than glad to succumb to.

He wasn't sure if she'd be able to have a second orgasm, but he was damn sure going to try. Slowing down his thrusts, he reached between their bodies and tweaked her clit, rubbing with enough pressure he knew she'd like it.

She jerked against him, sucking in a sharp breath as her inner walls started rippling around him. He felt her climax start to build almost immediately, could hear it in the way her breathing grew erratic and out of control.

When she reached down and grabbed his ass, digging her fingers into him in a purely possessive way as she cried out his name, he let go. There was nothing else to do.

Her name was on his lips as they both came. He thrust into her long and hard as he found his release. It felt as if he climaxed forever. He buried his face against her neck, breathing her in as his orgasm finally subsided.

She wrapped her arms around him tight, holding him so close he never wanted to let her go. Her embrace made him feel honored and possessive at the same time. "That was wonderful," she murmured, her voice just a little sleepy.

He couldn't find his voice so he just held her, trying to come to terms with how his life had just shifted.

And he was done worrying that she was going to stab him in the back, that she was working some angle against him. This, what she'd given him… He simply knew now that she wasn't waiting to hurt him.

The only way she could hurt him was by walking away.

CHAPTER FIFTEEN

"I could lie here all day," Dominique murmured against Viktor's solid chest. She wasn't sure what time it was but it was early. At least it was Saturday so she didn't have to worry about work.

His hand stroked up and down her back in a lazy rhythm. Though he was hard, he hadn't made a move to touch her since their last bout of lovemaking. Which was good because she was too sore. She traced her finger over the curves of one of his many tattoos. When he'd completely bared himself to her she'd been surprised by how many he truly had. Not to mention the multitude of long faded scars that covered his body—mainly his torso and arms. One day she would ask him what the tattoos meant and how he'd gotten the scars.

After their first time he'd been so sweet, surprising her by getting a warm cloth and cleaning between her legs. It had been so intimate, so…unexpected. She'd quickly learned that he did a lot of unexpected things. He'd made her so angry last night, just taking over and ordering her back to his house, but she could see that it was from a place of protectiveness. And it certainly didn't make her like him any less. If anything, his bossiness turned her on. Not that she was going to tell him that. Not yet anyway. He'd probably turn into a super caveman if she did.

"I would like that very much. How are you feeling?" He reached between her legs, cupping her sex in a purely possessive move. His big hand was gentle though.

Feeling her cheeks heat up, she shifted her head so she could look at him. "A little sore, but good."

His blue eyes heated with hunger but he withdrew his hand and wrapped his arm around her, just holding her close. "I thought you would be."

They'd had sex again a couple hours after that first time. He'd slowly taken her from behind as she gripped the headboard, teasing her clit as he moved inside her. Even thinking about it made a shudder rack through her entire body.

She set her head back on his chest, feeling more content than she had in a long time. "Why do you hire so many Russians? I mean, I know you are Russian. I just wondered if there was a reason," she said after a few minutes. There was so much about him she wanted to know.

"That's a long answer." The rumble of his chest under her head vibrated through her.

She smiled against his hard body, wishing she wasn't so sore right now. "I don't have anywhere to be."

He didn't respond for so long, she thought he wouldn't at all. "I had already started to break away from my father before he…died. He was a violent, vindictive asshole so I had to move slowly, setting up various accounts and a lot of stuff I won't bore you with. For lack of a better term, he was a gangster. He'd created his own little empire right here in Miami but not all the men who worked for him did so willingly. From the time I was a kid I watched him carefully—watched his people carefully. I knew who would break away from him when I made my move."

"He died before that though, didn't he?" Viktor had told her that his father had left him her family's house as part of his trust and she couldn't believe that he would have done that if Viktor had cut ties.

She felt Viktor move slightly, as if he was nodding. "Yeah. There was another man who'd always been in competition with me." He paused again, and she guessed he was choosing his words carefully. "He wanted my father's empire, wanted me out of the way. I wanted the same thing essentially so I made a deal with him. I took the men I knew who were loyal to me and we severed ties from that life in a clean break. I'd already started working legitimate side businesses, so the transition wasn't difficult. As long as I didn't try to take any of his criminal enterprises we had no problem."

She looked up at him. The room was dim except for a few streams of light coming in through one of the curtain-covered windows. "He just let you go?" She didn't know much about the criminal lifestyle but that sounded too easy.

Viktor gave her a dark smile. "He had no choice. Not unless he wanted a war."

She bit her bottom lip. "Is there a possibility he's the one who attacked you last night?"

He snorted, his expression easing. "No. He's actually at the bottom of my list. We haven't had contact in years. I stay out of his way and he stays out of mine. The people who attacked last night weren't pros."

"You still keep pretty intense security at your house." She knew that even the Caldwell brothers didn't have the kind of security he did. Not actual armed guards anyway.

"I never let myself get complacent. I can't afford to." He cupped her cheek, his touch gentle. "I'll never risk your safety either. Don't doubt that."

"I don't." She might not have known him that long, but she didn't doubt him. He made her feel…happy in a way she hadn't been in a long time. Which was hard to swallow. She turned her face away from his hold and lay back on his chest.

He stiffened slightly. "What?"

"Nothing… Okay, I feel a little guilty being so happy with you. It makes me think of my mother and then I get so angry at *her*." Shame swelled inside her for feeling angry at all. "She left me. I feel like…she didn't love me enough. Like I wasn't worth sticking around for. Which is stupid, I know." Her throat grew tight as the mix of long-buried emotions shattered inside her. She hated feeling like that.

His hold tightened ever so slightly. "My father was an evil man who ground people into the dirt. The fact that she endured being with him... She loved you very much, Dominique. That's something you should never doubt."

His words soothed all the jagged edges. She didn't respond, just let him hold her. She wasn't sure how long they stayed there but when her stomach rumbled loudly she buried her face against his chest.

He laughed, the sound so sweet to her ears because he rarely seemed to do it. "I think it's time I got you fed." He reached a hand down, palmed her ass before squeezing possessively. "Then I plan to eat you. Slowly."

His words set her on fire, but if she was going to have enough energy to keep up with him, she knew she should eat something. Then...she hoped they headed right back to the bedroom.

Last night had been amazing. She hadn't expected her first time to be so good. Now she was so glad she'd waited. Being with a man like Viktor who'd been so giving, clearly putting her pleasure before his own, had been incredible. She was pretty sure she'd fallen for him. It didn't seem to matter that her head said this was way too fast. Her heart wasn't listening.

He couldn't concentrate on anything today. Not after last night's failure. He'd hired those men specifically because of their shock tactics and penchant for violence. They were supposed to have killed Viktor's men and taken the woman.

Time was running out and he still needed her as a bargaining chip. He'd eventually kill her, but not until he got what he wanted. Then he'd kill her and Viktor. His brother too, because there was no way Abram would let his brother's death go unpunished.

It was Ivanov's own fault, for coming after him first. The stupid Russian liked to hide behind a mask of civility, claiming that the things he did weren't personal, just business. Well it was fucking personal to him.

With a trembling hand he dialed his contact.

The man answered on the fourth ring, his voice tight. "What?"

"What's the security situation like?"

"Tight. Everyone is locked down and..." A door shut, then, "Both women are locked down as well. Both here."

Here meant Viktor's house. "I want the woman." He didn't need to specify which one. The assistant would have been a decent choice, but knowing that Viktor truly cared for Dominique Castle, that she wasn't some whore he was paying, made her the *only* choice.

"Too bad for you."

He gritted his teeth, forced his voice to remain even. "Two hundred fifty grand in your account if you get her to me by this afternoon."

The man sucked in a breath. "That's still not enough for my life. Because he will hunt me to the end of the earth if I take her."

"He won't be around that long. Once I get her I'll be able to bargain with him for what I want. Then I'll pay you five hundred grand, with the promise that I'll kill him *and* his brother. Once that's done you'll be able to start over somewhere with a nice chunk of money."

Seconds ticked by. One, two, three... "I'll do it. I want that boat of yours too. The one in the marina."

Greedy bastard. Maybe he'd kill him too. He would tidy up all loose ends. "Agreed. Bring her to my office. Call me on your way. I'll meet you in the loading area."

"As soon as I get my money, consider it done."

Pleased with himself, he ended the call. He'd pay him the first deposit, but he'd never pay the five hundred grand. No, he'd kill his contact first.

Soon he'd have that bitch and Viktor would be at his mercy. Opening his desk drawer he pulled out a little packet of cocaine, dipped his finger into it and spread it across his gums. Then he took one hit.

Just one to keep him focused. He wasn't an addict. He just liked the way it made him feel, that rush of adrenaline that helped him to keep working longer hours.

Nothing was going to go wrong. Not like last night. With the exception of that snafu, everything else was falling into place.

Once he got Viktor where he wanted him, he was going to kill the bastard himself. He'd make sure Viktor begged him for death by the time he was through with him.

CHAPTER SIXTEEN

Dominique opened the refrigerator in Viktor's kitchen and stared at the neatly stacked containers of food, and bright fruit and vegetables stocked in the crispers. He hadn't been kidding when he said anything she wanted would be in here. He'd apparently prepared for the zombie apocalypse. Which was fine with her.

She might hate that there was a threat hanging over their heads, but she wasn't going to complain about getting to spend time at Viktor's place. The man had completely stolen her heart and she simply liked being with him. Right now he was in his office with his brother and Lyosha, going over…something. She wished they were back in bed together. Sex was definitely as good as her friends had made it out to be and she was having fun exploring it with him.

"I was hoping I'd find you." A female voice made her turn away from the fridge. Which was just as well—she wasn't sure what she wanted anyway.

She turned to find the petite assistant she'd sort of met the other day. "Hi…Lucy, right?" Viktor had mentioned something about her being here too.

The woman smiled as she leaned against the center island. A book, towel and bottle of sunscreen were in her hand and she was wearing a sheer cover-up that didn't do much to hide her bikini. "Yeah. I'm stuck here too until further notice. You okay after last night? I know that you were at the hotel."

Dominique nodded, glad she didn't have to lie. It was clear both brothers must trust Lucy if she knew Dominique had been at the hotel when even the police didn't. "Yeah, I'm good. A little freaked out but Viktor's place is great if we have to stay on lockdown." Only because the man himself was under the same roof.

"Right? Listen, while they're doing whatever they're doing, I'm taking a break for once and soaking up some sun by that monstrosity of a pool. Want to join me?"

Since Viktor had a fortified wall surrounding his property and extra security, Dominique guessed that was the only reason it would be okay for them to be by the pool right now. Otherwise he'd probably go into super caveman mode and not let them outside. "Yeah, I'd love to. I need to find out if Viktor has anything I can wear." Or if the guys he'd sent over to her place were back yet with her clothes. Right now she was wearing gym pants Lyosha had found that were about four inches too long and an oversized T-shirt. She felt a little ridiculous even if she was comfortable. "I'll meet you out there?"

Lucy nodded, her smile genuine. "Great. I'll see you in a little bit."

Dominique didn't want to bother Viktor but she didn't think he'd mind. And she really wanted to get to know Lucy since she'd be staying here too. Not to mention Lucy obviously knew the brothers well and Dominique wasn't above asking questions about Viktor. She wanted to know everything about him.

When she reached the hallway that led to Viktor's office she smiled when she saw his driver, Kir, headed her way. He'd been one of the only security people who was actually friendly to her. Mostly Viktor's guys seemed to walk around with perma-frowns.

"Hey, is Viktor—" Her words died when she saw the gun in his hand. It had a silencer on it and was pointed directly at her.

Everything around her funneled out as she stared down the barrel of the weapon. Before she could think about moving, he was next to her, grabbing her elbow in an unforgiving grip.

"You're coming with me," he said quietly, almost a whisper, his voice hard. "You scream and I'll shoot you in the stomach. It's a bad way to die." He said it as if it was something he knew to be certain.

On instinct she yanked against his hold but he shoved her up against the wall, one hand wrapped around her throat as he pressed the muzzle of the gun to her temple.

"I'll smoke you right here. Nod if you believe me." His eyes were cold, nothing like the friendly man from the last couple days.

She nodded, her throat tight with fear. What if Lucy came back inside and this maniac decided to shoot her?

"You're going to come with me on a short drive. If you're a good girl, you won't get hurt. But if you fight me, I'll just kill you and cut my losses. You gonna fight me?" He leaned closer, his breath hot against her face.

Ice slithered through her veins, making her feel numb and sluggish. Her heart was a drumbeat in her ears as she shook her head. She wouldn't fight him. At least not this very instant. It would be suicide to go up against a man like this. She might not know much about him but he had a gun he wasn't afraid to use and he was most definitely a lot stronger than her.

"Good. Keep your mouth shut and do what I say." He yanked her away from the wall and dragged her down the rest of the hallway.

Her bare feet were silent against the wooden floor, as were his shoes. All she wanted to do was scream for help, to scream the entire house down. But she'd seen the truth in his eyes—Kir would have no problem ending her life. He wouldn't lose a second of sleep over her death. And what if he shot at Viktor...or Lucy? What if an unarmed person came running to her aid and got caught in the crossfire? She couldn't have that on her conscience.

Looking over his shoulder only once, he paused at the door at the end of the hallway. His grip still tight on her arm he opened the door into a large garage. A car, an SUV, a motorcycle and a vintage truck were parked side by side.

Fear hollowed out her chest, making it hard to breathe as he dragged her inside the garage, shutting the door behind them with a resounding click.

"You are going to be the perfect bargaining chip," he muttered more to himself than her.

Instinct told her to fight him, to try to run. She'd always been taught never to get into a vehicle with someone who meant to do her harm. But if she didn't go, she'd be dead for certain. There was nowhere she could run now, no way to overpower him. She'd just have to go along with him and pray there was an opening for escape.

He palmed a set of keys and pressed the key fob. The SUV lights flashed once, a quiet beep indicating it had unlocked.

"You're driving," he ordered, training his gun on her as he hurried her to the driver's seat. "You try anything stupid, I'll shoot your knee first. Now get in." He yanked the door open for her, his weapon trained on her the entire time.

She practically collapsed on the front seat, her legs weak as he slid into the passenger side. He opened the garage with the little remote hooked to the visor.

"Start the vehicle and slowly steer out," he ordered. She risked a glance at him as the door opened. His gun was still in his hand and pointed at her.

Just freaking great.

She swallowed hard and did as he said. The sun was blinding when she first pulled out of the garage

"Fuck," he growled.

She hit the brakes and froze, unsure what she'd done. Then she saw a man wearing dark pants, a casual polo shirt and a shoulder holster with two guns walking toward them.

"No one was supposed to be here during the shift change," Kir muttered. "Don't say a fucking word." Her window started to roll down, Kir controlling it from the middle console as the man approached the driver's side. She realized Kir meant to talk to him.

He couldn't actually think this guy would believe she was leaving dressed like this. Or that Viktor would let her go? No, Kir meant to shoot him. He raised his weapon and on instinct she floored it, the tires squealing as they shot down the driveway.

"Bitch!" He slammed his fist against the dash but surprisingly didn't strike or shoot her. She'd been waiting for the blow. "Don't slow down," he ordered as they zoomed toward the gate. A man stepped out, weapon drawn, but he aimed at the tires.

Pop. Pop. Pop.

The vehicle swerved as the tire blew but she kept her grip on the wheel. The SUV jerked again wildly as she floored it. God, she hadn't even strapped in.

She wanted to scream at the man to move but he kept shooting at the tires.

Kir cursed and jumped into the backseat. She heard the back window rolling down then the muted sounds of gunfire. The man in front of her dove out of the way, behind the huge brick wall that ran the length of Viktor's property.

He wouldn't shoot at Kir because he wouldn't want to hurt her, she realized. It was why he'd aimed for the tires. For a moment she contemplated jumping from the vehicle but at this speed she didn't know if she'd survive.

"When we exit, take a right," Kir ordered, sliding back into the front seat.

She started to put her seatbelt on but he knocked it out of her hand, his expression dark as he sat back and strapped himself in. "Yours stays off. If you try to crash, you're killing yourself."

She gritted her teeth, her adrenaline pumping as she did what he said and took a sharp right. The shot tire was deflating fast, the vehicle getting hard to control as they careened down the street. She didn't have a death wish and right now it was either death from car crash or a bullet to the stomach. She didn't like either of those options.

Kir looked over his shoulder and pushed out a breath. "I think we'll be able to make it." Again, he was more talking to himself than her.

She almost asked where he was taking her and who he was bringing her to, but she didn't think he'd answer. She was nothing to him. If Viktor or one his guys didn't figure out where she was being forced to drive, she was going to have to get out of this on her own.

Ten minutes earlier

"Explain this as simply as possible," Viktor said to Lyosha, who'd just rushed them into his office because he said he had news. Both Lyosha and his brother could take forever to get to the point, especially when it had to do with Lyosha showing off his computer skills.

"All of the dead men were paid from a business account owned by a shell company." Lyosha set his laptop on Viktor's desk so he could see the spread of financial records.

Viktor only glanced at it. "You narrow down the owner yet?" Because that was all that mattered. Once Viktor had a name, the person who'd put Dominique in danger would pay.

"No, but I'm running a program that should help with that."

Viktor scrubbed a hand over his face. He'd been making calls the past hour, reaching out to contacts and calling in favors as he tried to narrow down who'd been stupid enough to attack him in his own hotel. So far his three top suspects weren't panning out. Two weren't even in the country and he knew without a doubt that if either had decided to make a move, they'd be here in person.

The third was dealing with the FBI on suspicion of fraud and illegal smuggling. According to the digging Viktor had done, the man was under almost twenty-four-hour surveillance so it seemed unlikely he was the one behind it either.

"Tell me you have something, then." Lyosha had called him in here—away from Dominique. He knew he needed to be focusing on finding who'd targeted him, but he didn't like being away from her even for a moment. Not after last night. Now that he'd gotten a taste of her he wasn't letting her go and he wasn't above binding her to him with sex.

"Maybe. I got some interesting hits on the financials I ran. Nothing on the phone records but I really didn't expect any. Even these financial records can be explained away, but you still need to see what I've found."

Viktor just grunted. If someone was going to betray him, they wouldn't be stupid enough to use their own phone.

Lyosha started to pull up another screen when his computer dinged. "Hold on," he murmured, his fingers moving quickly across the keyboard. His expression grew tighter, putting Viktor on alert.

They'd worked together a long, damn time. Something was wrong. He knew better than to ask though, until Lyosha was done working.

"Fuck," the other man growled. "Kir's the owner of one of the accounts from the unknown shell corporations."

Viktor froze. "Kir?" Their regular driver? A man he trusted.

Lyosha's expression was grim. "It's not on any of my current financials for him. He was careful to hide it but he's definitely receiving deposits from the same account the dead hit men did."

"Who's the owner?" he demanded, pulling out his cell phone to alert the rest of his security team. Kir was on the premises and he was going to be dealt with now.

"Still don't know—"

His phone buzzed in his hand. It was Dima, in charge of the perimeter security. He answered immediately. "What?"

"She's gone! I don't know if she was willing or not but I don't think she was. Kir and the woman came barreling out of the garage."

The bottom of his stomach fell out.

Viktor grabbed Lyosha's arm and motioned that he should follow. Lyosha was already on the phone, likely with another one of his guys. He grabbed his laptop and fell in behind Viktor.

Dima continued as Viktor raced through his house, his heart pounding out of control. Dominique was gone; she'd been taken. Because no way had she left willingly. He needed to know where that bastard Kir had taken her—and why.

"Brady went to stop the SUV and she gunned it, tearing out of here. Brady thinks Kir meant to shoot him but can't be sure. He said she looked terrified. I managed to shoot out one of the tires."

"Where are you now?" he demanded as he burst through the door to the garage. Two of his security guys were standing in the driveway on their phones. He ignored them and got into the car. Lyosha slid into the passenger seat.

He was vaguely aware of Lyosha barking out orders to someone but he ignored him and focused on Dima as he tore out of the garage in his Tesla.

"I took off after them in one of the SUVs. I've got two guys with me. There's only one way he could have gone to escape... Shit."

Bolts of adrenaline pumped through his system. He clenched his fingers around the wheel, surprised he hadn't ripped the thing off the dash. "What?"

"Just found the SUV. It's abandoned."

"Where are you?"

"Gas station right before the highway." Dima's voice was tight.

Fuck, fuck, fuck. He lived in a private, cut off neighborhood but once you crossed the bridge to the mainland, there were too many damn directions Kir could have taken Dominique. And if he got on the highway... That fear compounded, making him imagine every horrific scenario possible for why Dominique had been taken, what could happen to her.

"We're going to find her." Lyosha's voice made his head jerk around and Viktor realized he was blindly driving in the direction of the gas station but not really seeing anything.

He'd never known what true fear could be until now. Even the times he'd been facing certain death he'd never been afraid like this. Because this was different. This was fear for the woman he loved. He wasn't afraid of his own death but the thought of her dying—no. It wasn't happening.

He'd get her back no matter what it took.

CHAPTER SEVENTEEN

Dominique opened her eyes, blinking against the brightness of the sun… No, not the sun. A spotlight. What the hell?

As the memory of everything came back, her stomach revolted. She'd been kidnapped and forced at gunpoint to drive to some building downtown. That was all she remembered before Kir clocked her in the side of the head. Then…blackness.

She tried to twist around but the movement sent pain splintering through her head. She bit back a groan, unsure if she was alone or not. If she wasn't she didn't want to draw attention to herself.

A new fear blasted through her as she looked down at herself. She was in a chair, her hands cuffed to the armrests and… She tried to lift her legs but her ankles were secured too. At least her clothes were still on.

Kir hadn't said much about why he was bringing her to someone but it was obviously not for a good reason.

Think, she ordered herself. The spotlight in her face was so damn bright that beads of sweat were trickling down her forehead. Blinking, she tried to see past the spotlight and could just make out some random shapes. No, not random… A couple chairs and…huge open windows. Just like in her office. It was hard to tell but she thought she could see a high-rise through the window. She couldn't be sure though.

She yanked against the cuffs and her chair scooted across the floor a couple inches. The scraping sound echoed slightly.

"Well, well, you're finally awake." Snapping footsteps across the concrete floor made her go still. "Smile for the camera, sweetheart."

Viktor slammed his fist against Kir's face again, the darkest part of him savoring the man's cry of agony as his nose broke—again. He reared back to hit him but Abram wrapped his arm around Viktor's neck and yanked him back, tackling him to the ground.

His brother had his arms and legs wrapped around him tight. "You kill him, you kill your chance to find her," Abram growled, struggling to hold Viktor in place. "Don't be stupid. Don't fail her."

The words rolled through him, bringing him back through the haze of his rage. Though it took effort, he stopped fighting his brother, expelling a ragged breath as he looked at Kir's prone body. He wasn't restrained, but he didn't attempt to get up. Not with Lyosha ten feet away on his laptop working furiously and two of Viktor's guys standing guard—men who'd been friends with Kir.

The fucking traitor. He'd betrayed them all.

"You really thought you could betray us and get away with it?" His voice was steady.

Abram loosened his grip and they both shoved to their feet.

"It wasn't supposed to be like this," Kir rasped out, his voice uneven. He'd ditched his cell phone but he hadn't ditched his laptop. Which was how they'd been able to track him.

One of his eyes was swollen shut, his nose broken in multiple places, and blood covered the front of his shirt as he stared up from the floor of the kitchen—in a condo that Lyosha had easily tracked him to. One of Kir's ankles was broken too, his foot twisted at an odd angle.

It wasn't enough. Viktor wanted to break every bone in his body with his bare hands when he thought of Dominique somewhere terrified for her life, being hurt… He locked the thought down before he broke Kir's neck. His brother was right. He needed to stay calm and find out where Dominique was.

He crouched down next to Kir's head. The man stared at him

through his one good eye. "What was it supposed to be like?"

"I was just...giving him info about you. That's...it." He wheezed out the last couple words, his face scrunching in pain.

"Who?" Viktor just needed a name. The name of the man who'd orchestrated the kidnapping of the woman he loved. The man who'd turned one of his employees against him.

"You'll kill...me if...I tell you."

"I'm going to kill you anyway." He leaned closer to Kir, rage infusing him as he looked at the man who'd held Dominique at gunpoint, dragged her away from where she'd felt safe. Where she should have *been* safe. Viktor had no idea what Kir had done to her either. That not knowing was making him insane. "If you tell me I'll make your death quick. If you don't...you know what I used to do to people who crossed me."

The truth was, he'd never been into torture. Unlike his father. But he'd stoked the rumors of his nature years ago so people would be afraid to cross him. Clearly his reputation hadn't been enough to keep Kir from turning on him. Viktor would have to remedy that soon.

When Kir didn't respond, he continued. "See my man Lyosha over there? You know how good he is at finding people. He found you in less than an hour. He's already drained all your bank accounts—even the one you thought you'd hidden from us. Now all his focus is on finding who hired you. He *will* find who it is, that I have no doubt. The only question is, will he find him first or will you tell me? Because once he finds what I need, my offer of mercy is gone. I'll keep you alive for weeks. At least." He leaned even closer so that his mouth almost brushed Kir's ear. "I will cut you apart piece by piece. And then I will make you eat your own dick."

"Found something," Lyosha said

Eyes widening, Kir blurted, "Shane Hollis! He's the one who's been paying me! I took her...to one of his buildings downtown. The top four...floors are..." His breathing was labored and his words starting to slur. "Abandoned. He's keeping her there...for now." He rattled off an address before breaking into a fit of coughing.

Viktor shoved to his feet, looking to Lyosha for confirmation. His head of security shrugged and Viktor realized Lyosha hadn't found anything. He'd just been trying to goad Kir into talking.

It was hard to believe Hollis was behind this. The trust-fund jackass was so weak, ineffective at business—and had a drug problem.

"Keep him alive for now," Viktor said to Dima. He wasn't sure what he was going to do with Kir yet.

Dima nodded, giving Kir a look of pure disgust.

Viktor turned away, all thoughts of Kir's betrayal taking a backseat to finding Dominique. Saving her was all that mattered.

His phone buzzed in his pocket. He yanked it out, answered even though he didn't recognize the number. This could be about Dominique. "Hello?"

"Click on video capability," a distorted male voice said.

The fear inside him raked against his insides like savage, unforgiving talons. He motioned to his brother to keep Kir quiet as he quickly moved out of the kitchen. He stopped in the bare living room and swiped his thumb across the screen.

Dominique appeared, her face scrunched up. She was squinting. Her face was illuminated by a bright light. His throat seized in terror when he saw that she was cuffed to a chair, her arms and legs restrained.

Suddenly the light dimmed and a man wearing a hockey mask crouched next to her, his face right by hers as he fisted the long length of her hair and yanked her head back. The blade of a knife gleamed as he held it up in full view of the camera.

Crying out, she blinked, her eyes filling up with tears as she stared into the camera. He wanted to tell her everything would be okay, but he knew he'd break if he started down that road.

He had to keep his shit together for her, to get her out of this whole. "What do you want?" His voice was somehow calm.

"You took something that belonged to me. Now I have something that belongs to you." The voice was muffled but not mechanical. It was difficult to tell if it was Hollis or not. Leaning closer to the camera, the man loosened his grip on her hair but didn't let go completely as he moved forward.

"Tell me what you want and it's yours." He couldn't even negotiate. Not with Dominique's life in the balance. He'd give this monster whatever he wanted.

"You're going to meet with me at a place of my choosing and sign over property to me. If you involve the cops she's dead."

He snorted in derision. "There will be no police."

The masked man nodded once, setting the knife down. "You will also bring your brother. If you have any backup, however, she's dead. If I even *think* you have backup, she's fucking dead. And I'll amuse myself with her before I kill her." The man reached out and stroked Dominique's cheek. "She's got such a pretty mouth."

A red haze blurred Viktor's vision at the sight of this bastard touching her. "Where do you want me to go?" he bit out.

The man rattled off an address but didn't drop his hand as he continued stroking her cheek. "Don't you agree she's got a pretty mouth? I can think of—"

He screamed as Dominique bit his hand, her teeth sinking into his flesh and holding tight. He backhanded her with his free hand. Her head snapped back and the man hit her again. Her head lolled forward and her body stilled.

Raw terror jumped inside Viktor. Cursing, the man shoved his face in front of the screen so that Viktor couldn't see her anymore.

Viktor growled low in his throat, his hand clenching around his phone. He was going to kill the man. *Slowly.*

"You have twenty minutes to be at that address. Go in through the parking garage. Bring your brother. Or the bitch dies."

The screen went black before he could respond.

"It's a trap," Abram said, moving into the living room with Lyosha.

Viktor nodded once, agreeing. It had to be a trap. Abram and Lyosha had clearly heard everything and Lyosha was still working away on a tablet.

"I got a location on where he called you from," he said. "The phone is a burner but it pinged from a property Shane Hollis owns—for now. It's being foreclosed on. It's different than the address he gave you. On the other side of downtown. It'd take him more than twenty minutes to get there."

He had no time to make a decision. "Can you find out what kind of security the place has? The one he called from?" He was already moving toward the front door. They needed to have left ten minutes ago.

"I can try, but it'll take more than twenty minutes to disable it, if that's what you're thinking."

That was exactly what he was thinking. Hollis, or whoever was under that mask, wanted him to go to a specific address when he wasn't even there. It had to be a trap. "What about the place he wants us to go to?"

He, Abram and Lyosha spilled out into the hallway, talking as they ran to the elevators. His body was moving on autopilot, his only goal to get to his car and find Dominique.

"It's…also being foreclosed on. Owned by Hollis too. This fucker is losing everything his family built," Lyosha muttered.

Viktor's gut told him to go to the place the phone pinged from. As the elevator dinged at the bottom floor, the doors whooshing open, he looked at his brother, who'd been quiet. "If it was Lucy, what would you do?"

"Go with my instinct—which says the place he wants us to meet him is a fucking trap. Probably rigged with explosives or someone waiting to take us out. I think your girl is at the place his phone pinged from."

"Me too." He pulled out his phone again as they hurried into the parking garage of the condo complex Kir had thought was his hideout. He needed to get into that building undetected in twenty minutes and there was only one man he could think of who could make it happen.

It was time to collect his favor from Harrison Caldwell.

CHAPTER EIGHTEEN

Weapon in hand, Viktor stood outside the stairwell door to one of the top floors of the Hollis-owned building. Lyosha and Abram were silently waiting on the stairs as he confirmed one last time with Harrison that they were good to go.

"We've completely taken over the security feeds. The top eight floors aren't being monitored but there's no way to know if he saw you infiltrating from the parking garage. From this point forward if he does have security capability, he'll only see what we show him." Harrison's voice was clipped over the phone line.

Viktor nodded at Abram and Lyosha and they moved silently up the stairs. Instead of using the elevators they'd chosen the stairs so they wouldn't be seen. The building hadn't been finished—Hollis had run out of money—so there was no security in the stairwells either. Not that it would have stopped Viktor from coming here.

Nothing could do that. "Thank you."

"I've called in a favor to the PD. They're going to move on the other building as if there's a bomb threat."

Which there very well could be. Viktor had no idea what Hollis had in store for him and Abram at the meeting place he'd insisted on. "Wait until I've got Dominique safe." Because if the cops moved in and Dominique was in there instead, or if Hollis got wind of the police involvement, he could kill her.

Harrison snorted. "Contact me in fifteen minutes or I'm sending the cops in."

Viktor didn't bother responding, just ended the call and checked to make sure his phone was on silent. This was it. He, Lyosha and Abram were sweeping every floor, starting with the empty four on top.

Heart pounding, he eased open the door and peered into a hallway. Sunlight streamed in through the open doorways. A couple soda cans sat in a cluster near the closest entry—with no door. The floors weren't done; the steel and concrete frame was visible down the majority of the hallway. Insulation was also visible through the nearest open doorway, as if the construction crew had started installing it, then stopped mid-job.

He took a step into the hallway but froze at the slight echo of his footstep. Inwardly wincing, he slipped his shoes off and tucked them out of sight in the nearest room. Weapon up, he moved silently room to room, sweeping each one with a glance. There was no furniture, nothing to hide anyone.

When he heard a muffled sound three doors down from the opposite stairwell, he froze, listening. He heard it again.

It was too much to expect that it was Dominique, but the hope burst inside him, a burning wish to find her alive, unharmed.

He glanced once over his shoulder before continuing his path. His heart was an erratic tattoo against his chest as he moved like a predator hunting prey. If Hollis was in there, the man was dead. Viktor wouldn't allow him to surrender.

At the next doorway he heard the scraping, shuffling again. Moving in low, he swept the room with his weapon, immediately dropping it when he saw Dominique restrained to a chair, a gag in her mouth. Alone.

The spotlight was off her, at least.

Her eyes widened when she saw him. A bruise was forming on her cheek and a tiny trail of dried blood streaked down her chin, but she was alive. For the first time in the last hour he felt as if he could breathe again. Pistol still in his hand he hurried across the open room.

Crouching next to her, he turned so that he had the doorway in his periphery. He wanted to comfort her, but if Hollis was nearby Viktor didn't want the man to hear him. Holding a finger to his mouth, he then tugged her gag free. He didn't have a way to get the cuffs off, not without a key or a way to cut them free.

"He's crazy," she whispered. "He's got guys waiting at that other building. If Abram's gone there—"

"He hasn't. I'm going to get you out of here. I can't get these off yet. Do you know where he is?" He kept his voice pitched low.

She shook her head as tears spilled over her cheeks.

He cupped her cheek with his free hand and swiped them away. He wanted to pull her to him but couldn't risk the distraction, couldn't risk losing focus on their surroundings for a moment. "You're okay now," he said quietly before pulling his phone out. He needed to call Harrison and get his brother and Lyosha up here. They needed to get Dominique free then hunt down Hollis.

Even killing that fucker took a backseat to getting her to safety. As the phone started to ring Shane Hollis stepped into the room, hockey mask shoved up on top of his head—and a pistol in his hand.

Viktor whipped his weapon up lightning fast, moving to stand directly in front of Dominique so that his body blocked hers entirely. "Drop your gun," Viktor ordered.

Hollis's eyes were wild, a little too big and red-rimmed. "You stupid fucker!"

"Drop your weapon. The police are on their way up. There's nowhere to go. Just put your gun down and you'll get out of this alive." The guy had hired men to come after Viktor and kidnapped Dominique so he was dead, regardless, but Viktor couldn't risk Dominique getting hurt or worse if the guy started firing.

"There are no cops!" His gun hand wavered slightly.

"Why did you do this? Why target me?" Viktor wanted to keep the guy talking. If the call to Harrison had connected, the other man should be hearing all this.

"You took everything from me!"

"I bought the businesses you put up for sale." *At a fair price,* he thought. Too fair, because he'd wanted to let the guy save some pride.

"Then you wouldn't work with me." His voice was whiny,

matching the trust-fund jackass Viktor had pegged him for at their first meeting. "The fucking criminal wouldn't work with *me*. Me! I'm a fucking Hollis." His gun hand wavered. "My family built—"

Viktor pulled the trigger, hitting Hollis square in the chest. Hollis's eyes were wide as his body jerked back.

Boom. Boom.

Viktor fired again and again until Hollis tumbled backward, his weapon clattering to the concrete floor. He moved to it, kicked it away. Not bothering to check for a pulse, he patted the guy down until he found what he was looking for.

As he pulled the handcuff key out, he whipped his weapon up at a slight sound—then dropped it when he saw Abram and Lyosha rushing toward him.

Palming the key he hurried to Dominique, who was silently crying. After he'd freed her, she lunged at him before he could pull her into his arms.

"I thought he was going to kill you," she sobbed, her voice cracking. "He was so smug, so sure you'd walk right into his trap. He said…he said he was going to bring you here and make you watch as he—" Her voice broke then, her body racking with silent sobs as he lifted her into his arms. She wrapped her arms around his shoulders and buried her face against his neck as he carried her fireman-style out of the room. He couldn't move fast enough. He wanted her away from this death and pain.

"There's no one else here. Cops are on the way. So is Harrison," Abram said as Viktor stepped over Hollis's dead body.

"I'm taking her downstairs." Away from all this.

He didn't pause to talk to either Lyosha or his brother. The only thing that mattered was getting her to safety, getting her home—his home. Where no one would ever hurt her again.

He paused halfway down the hallway and turned to his brother. "Call Dima. Tell him to take care of it." Meaning Kir. No way was that fucker walking away after this. He wouldn't do jail time. He'd just disappear forever. But Viktor would make sure that word spread in the right circles that he'd died because of his betrayal. A gruesome, horrific death. He had no problem spreading false rumors about himself, not when those rumors would keep Dominique safe. So anyone who thought they might target him or his loved ones in the future would think twice.

"Already done. We'll make it look like—"

Viktor shook his head sharply to cut Abram off. He didn't want Dominique to hear any of this. She needed to be completely truthful in everything she said to the police. She was a victim and an employee of Red Stone Security so he had no doubt the police would treat her right. But he didn't want there to be any doubt about what had happened today.

She'd been kidnapped by Kir, then brought to Shane Hollis. For all the cops would think, Kir had disappeared, going on the run for his life. Viktor didn't want her to know what would happen to Kir—at least not until after she'd talked to the police.

CHAPTER NINETEEN

Abram shifted slightly against the bed, watching Lucy as she slept. Today had been a new level of insanity for him and his brother. And that was saying a lot.

After dealing with the cops and hours of endless questions and paperwork, Viktor and Dominique were holed up at Viktor's place and Abram had brought Lucy to his. He needed to know she was safe, protected.

And he wasn't going to let her go anytime soon—or ever. She might not realize it yet, but that necklace was only the first piece of jewelry he'd be buying her. Soon he planned to have a ring on her finger. All the muscles in his body were pulled taut, his cock rock hard, as he watched her. He should just get up, let her sleep, but he liked being near her.

He hadn't told his brother yet, but he was going to insist that they all take Monday off. Everyone could use a break, as far as he was concerned, and he planned on keeping Lucy on lockdown, naked and happy the entire day

"I can hear you thinking," Lucy murmured, not opening her eyes even as a seductive smile curved her lips. "Everything okay?"

"Yeah," he rasped out. He slid his palm under the sheet and over her bare stomach. He hadn't wanted to wake her before but touching her grounded him, reminded him that she was real and all his.

Cracking open her eyes, she turned, sliding her arm around his waist and pressing her bare chest to his. "You sure about that?"

He loved being skin to skin with her. Before Lucy he'd never had a woman at his place. Now…he wanted to wake up to her face every morning. It was a strange thing, this need to have her in his life, to see her every day. He'd felt this way since he'd met her but he still wasn't used to it. "Just thinking that it could have been you kidnapped this morning. Viktor kept his shit together better than I would have." It was a testament to his brother's control. Abram couldn't even imagine Lucy being stolen from him. It made his entire body break out in a sweat.

"Nah, you'd have taken care of business like you always do," Lucy murmured into his chest, her voice thick with sleep. "I'm just glad Dominique is okay. She's a good fit for your brother."

"Yeah, she is." And he felt like a bit of a dick for the way he'd talked about her to Viktor when it was clear the woman deeply cared for him. Not that he'd change his reaction. He'd just been looking out for his brother—and he'd do it again.

"So what's going to happen with Kir? You think the police will ever find him?" She leaned back a fraction, her hair rustling against the pillow as she met his gaze. She was slightly more awake now and he was glad—because he wasn't letting her go back to sleep until he'd gotten a taste of her.

"I think…" He paused, choosing his words carefully. "You don't need to worry about him ever again. He won't be a problem for us. I swear it. And…it's highly unlikely the police will find him." Abram felt no guilt that Kir was dead either. The man had betrayed him and his brother in the worst way possible.

Her eyes widened slightly then she shook her head, her expression wry. "I should probably be horrified by that, but I'm so freaking glad we don't have to worry about him." She yawned, stretching so that her back arched and her breasts rubbed against his chest again.

He'd been trying to show some restraint. He hadn't woken her up or pounced the moment he knew she was awake—but his self-control was pretty thin where she was concerned. He wanted to test her slickness then slide right into her. Fuck foreplay right now. He craved being inside Lucy.

Moving his hand lower, he cupped her pussy.

She sucked in a breath, her eyes going heavy-lidded with hunger. "You're a machine."

"I can stop if you want."

"Okay, stop," she whispered, watching him carefully, a grin pulling at her mouth.

He inwardly smiled. She wanted to play. He slid a finger inside her to find her slick. "You sure about that?" Breathing erratically, she shook her head so he added another finger. "I love you." The words were out before he could analyze them or try to talk himself out of saying them. He wasn't used to being vulnerable in front of anyone.

Her dark eyes widened and for a brief moment he worried he'd fucked up by moving too fast, but the smile she gave him was blinding. "I love you too, you sexy, frustrating Russian."

Relief like he'd never known surged through him, hearing the admission from her. Yeah, she was definitely his.

He nipped her bottom lip between his teeth, keeping his fingers buried inside her but not moving. For now, he just wanted to take his time with the woman he'd fallen in love with. Today had only cemented his feelings for Lucy. When he imagined what it would have been like to be in his brother's shoes, it clawed him up inside. He would never let anything happen to Lucy, never let anyone take her from him. She was his, and he was hers.

"You're taking Monday off. We're going to spend it in bed."

"Hmm, bossy, bossy," she murmured. "I'll take Monday off only if you promise to make it worth my time." The seductive grin she gave him made his cock jerk.

"I promise you'll want to call in sick Tuesday too," he murmured before capturing her mouth fully with his.

Dominique opened her eyes and groaned as she rolled over in Viktor's huge bed. After the insanity of today even her brain felt tired. The endless questions from the police, going through everything a dozen times, and then the worry that Viktor would somehow be in trouble for killing Shane Hollis was beyond overwhelming.

She'd thought she'd sleep until morning but it was only ten p.m. She'd only gotten about two hours of sleep. Frowning, she sat up in bed, the sharpest sense of disappointment hitting her that she was alone.

Sliding out of bed, she winced at the ache in her face. At least she didn't have any broken bones, just some bruising from the cuffs and on her cheek. And she and Viktor were alive, the only thing that mattered.

At first she was terrified when she'd learned that Kir, the man who'd kidnapped her, hadn't been located by the police, but Viktor had stressed that he wouldn't be a problem to her ever again. It hadn't been hard to read between the lines and the truth was, she didn't want to know what Viktor had done to him. She was just glad the guy was out of their lives.

She peeked into his office and found it empty so decided to go exploring. He wouldn't have left the house. Or she really hoped he hadn't.

A chill snaked through her as she stepped into the hallway, the wood floor cold against her feet. She knew the chill had nothing to do with the house though—she just couldn't seem to get warm. Viktor had already had her clothes brought to his place so at least she was in her own pajamas.

The only thing she really cared about was finding Viktor. He'd saved her and she was completely and utterly in love with him. She needed to tell him. It didn't matter if it was too soon or if he didn't return her feelings.

After a few minutes she found him in the kitchen, slightly bent over as he pulled something from one of the shelves in the refrigerator.

"That's a sight for sore eyes," she murmured, taking in the tight lines of his back and all those beautiful tattoos. The man should never, ever wear a shirt.

He jerked at her voice, a plastic container in his hands as he turned. "You're awake." He set it down on the island, hurrying to her side and practically carrying her to the nearest seat at the island.

"I'm okay," she murmured.

"I thought you'd be out for a while." Guilt flickered in his gaze. "I didn't want you to wake up alone."

"It's okay, seriously. I'm…actually kinda hungry."

"I was about to heat up chicken parm. You want some?"

"That sounds amazing." She'd only been able to stomach a little soup when they'd finally gotten back to Viktor's place. As if on cue, her stomach growled.

He half-smiled and brushed his mouth over hers. She felt it all the way to her toes, but he moved back too quickly for her to fully enjoy it.

"How does a glass of red wine sound? It might help you sleep since you won't take your medicine." His voice was slightly annoyed as he started scooping the food onto two plates.

The doctor who'd looked her over at the hospital had given her a prescription for pain meds, but she hadn't taken anything except ibuprofen. "That sounds good." It was weird seeing him acting so domestically, moving around the kitchen with such ease. "Did you cook this?"

He snorted and shot her an amused glance over his shoulder. "No. I have someone who comes in once or twice a week with casseroles and pre-makes things for me for the week."

She laughed lightly. "Can I help with anything?"

He simply frowned and turned to the microwave as it dinged. "You are not to do anything for at least a week."

"Pretty sure that's not what the doctor said."

"It's what I say." He pulled out the plate and tested it before bringing it over to her. "And you will follow orders." There was no command in his voice, more concern than anything else.

"If you hadn't just saved my life I might take issue with your bossiness," she murmured, taking the glass of wine he offered her.

"And you'll be staying here." There was no room for argument in his tone. He leaned against the island next to her seat, determination in his blue eyes as he looked down at her.

"For the next week?"

"Yes." There was something in his tone she couldn't quite read.

"I'd like that...if you're sure." Things between them had happened so quickly, and while she knew her feelings for him were true, she also didn't want him to get sick of her. He was such a hard man to read. Even though he'd made himself vulnerable with her a couple times, she still wasn't sure if his feelings for her were as strong.

His eyebrows pulled together. Instead of responding he turned and put his own plate in the microwave. "I've got security stationed around the house but no one inside. And Abram and Lucy have gone back to his place."

"I thought those two were together," she murmured, blowing on her food. "Any new developments I should know about?"

He shook his head and leaned against the counter, watching her with that brooding stare she found she liked way too much. "Nothing new."

"What's wrong, then?" Because she was coming to learn his moods, and right now something was bothering him. A lot. "We're not in danger, we're alone, and we've got awesome food."

He rounded the island and pushed right up into her personal space. She dropped her fork as he cupped her face in his hands, his hold so incredibly gentle it made her want to cry. "I keep seeing you tied up, him hitting you and..." He swallowed hard, the raw vulnerability on his face clawing at her.

Through everything that had happened, he'd been a rock. She'd been a complete sobbing mess once he'd gotten her out of that building. It was like the floodgates had opened and she just couldn't stop crying. She'd been so damn grateful to lean on him. He'd been next to her through all the police questions, stoic and unshakeable.

She moved off the chair, pulling him into a tight embrace, resting her head against his chest. "I'm not going anywhere. I'm here, safe, and nothing is going to happen to us again. I know I said it already but thank you for coming for me. Thank you for saving me. Thank you for being you. I…love you." She pulled back as she said the words, so she could see his face as she admitted the truth. "I'm not saying it because of what happened. I'm saying it because it's the truth. I love you, Viktor."

He stared down at her, as if he couldn't believe what she'd said. "I…" He cleared his throat. "You're moving in with me."

She blinked at his brusque tone as well as his words. "What?"

"I don't want you here for just the week. I want you here always." His big body was trembling under her hold and she realized this was how he was telling her that he loved her.

Or she really hoped that's what he meant. Because what she felt for him was consuming. She would need to hear the words eventually but for now, happiness bloomed in her chest. "We'll talk about it at the end of the week."

He just gave her a sensual look before brushing his mouth over hers in a teasing, stroking kiss that once again was over way too quickly. "Eat your food."

She did as he said, and once they were done he carried her to his bed where he tucked both of them in and wrapped his arm snug around her middle. She could feel the hard length of him pressed against her back but he made no move to do anything about it.

She was too exhausted anyway and she was grateful that he was simply holding her. She needed his strength.

"I love you too," he whispered against her hair a few moments later, his big body going rigid as he spoke. "And I'm not letting you go."

Hearing the words soothed all the ragged edges inside her. She linked her fingers through his, squeezed tight. "I'm not letting you go either," she murmured as she felt herself start to drift, knowing that she was safe in Viktor's arms.

EPILOGUE

Four months later

Dominique sat on the edge of her and Viktor's bed, watching him standing like a statue in their walk-in closet, staring at his clothes. He was only wearing pants, and she didn't mind the view. Still, the man normally just picked something in minutes. His clothes were obsessively organized anyway, unlike her side of the closet.

"I've never seen you like this," she murmured more to herself than him.

He'd pretty much steamrolled her into moving in with him four months ago—and the truth was she hadn't wanted to spend any nights away from him so it hadn't exactly been a hardship. Incredible sex every night and some mornings with the sweetest, sexiest man she was crazy in love with? *Yes, please.*

He turned to her and blinked, as if coming back to himself. "This is a big deal."

"You've met Quinn and Athena before." Her cousin Quinn had been unsure about Viktor at first, but considering he'd literally saved her life, Quinn had been mostly welcoming.

"Thanksgiving is different. And it's at Athena's family's house."

"Yeah, they're kind of insane, by the way." Athena came from a huge Greek family. One of Athena's cousins, Belle, Grant Caldwell's wife, was super pregnant and about to pop. "According to Athena everyone has a bet on when Belle will give birth. They seriously have a pool going."

Viktor scrubbed a hand over his face before he pulled a cashmere sweater from the closet. "I've never done a family holiday before. Even with Abram, we never do anything big." His brother was spending Thanksgiving with Lucy's family and she knew he was worried too.

Dominique slid off the bed at the surprising note of worry in Viktor's voice. Pretty much nothing rattled the man, but she shouldn't be surprised about this. He'd never even had a big birthday party, something she'd found out when she threw him a surprise party a month ago. He'd been stunned, and though he'd kept his serious, typically hard Russian expression in place most of the party, she'd known how pleased he'd been. Even Abram had been impressed with the party—and had finally warmed up to her. He'd even asked Dominique to help him pick out an engagement ring for Lucy, which pretty much told her that he completely trusted her now.

She pulled Viktor into a tight hug, burying her face against his chest before he tugged the sweater on. She could never seem to get enough of him. "Holiday stuff like this is usually fun. There's lots of food, maybe a little drinking and usually watching some stupid sports game on TV afterward."

He rested his chin on top of her head, sighed. "I'm not really worried about Thanksgiving."

Frowning, she pulled back. "What is it, then?" Fear slid through her veins when he didn't answer, just watched her with way too many emotions for her to decipher. He looked almost afraid. Oh God, was there another threat against them—

Abruptly he dropped to one knee and a jewelry box appeared in his hand as if out of thin air.

Her heart skipped a beat as she stared at him—and the box. She'd thought they were probably heading in this direction, but she hadn't expected this so soon. Though she had been hoping for it.

"I can't wait any longer," he rasped out. "I love you, Dominique. I never even thought I was capable of loving someone so much, but…you make me a better person, as stupid as it sounds."

"It doesn't sound stupid," she whispered, staring at his handsome face as he knelt there, the fear and hope on his face making her heart squeeze. She couldn't believe he was afraid though. He should know what her answer would be.

His eyes held hers. "Marry me?"

"Yes." She held out her left hand, only trembling a little as he slid a beautiful solitaire diamond on her finger. Then she fell to her knees, wrapping her arms around his neck as she slanted her mouth over his.

In pure Viktor style, he took over immediately, pinning her to the floor of their closet with a fierceness she craved from him.

When he slid his hands up her thighs, shoving her pretty red dress up to her waist, she knew that they were definitely going to be late. And she was more than okay with that.

Dear Readers, thank you for purchasing the Red Stone Security Series Box Set: Volume 5! If you'd like to stay in touch with me and be the first to learn about new releases feel free to sign up for my monthly newsletter at: www.katiereus.com

DANGEROUS PROTECTOR

CHAPTER ONE

Tegan didn't turn around at the sound of the little bell jingling over the front door. She knew exactly who was coming into Kimmy's Cakes and Coffee at seven thirty in the morning. Callan Fitzpatrick. Recent military vet, quiet and sweet, he'd been coming in here every morning for the past month to flirt with Tegan's boss, Kimmy.

Well, sort of flirt. The two of them were hopeless—and adorable—as they danced around each other. She hoped Callan worked up the courage to ask her friend out.

"I'll have your order in just a sec. Kimmy's coming in later—Brendan's got a fever. So you're stuck looking at me this morning."

"That's not exactly a hardship." A deep, familiar, and oh-so-sexy male voice made everything inside her go still. *Not* Callan, but his older brother, Aaron. The man affected her in ways she didn't even want to think about.

Especially since most of the time he didn't seem to even like her.

Pasting on her most pleasant expression, she turned from the espresso coffee grinder. Like always, she felt a jolt of awareness when she saw him. Something—everything—about him called to her on a level she didn't quite understand. Tall, dark, and perpetually surly. Except when he had his five-year-old son with him. *Then* he was actually human. Unfortunately for her, Aaron was alone today so that meant she got the surly version. Though, so far he actually seemed to be in a decent mood.

"That almost sounded like a compliment." Smiling, the action more nervous than anything, she reached for the stack of to-go cups.

He lifted one of those big shoulders. "Just the truth."

She so did *not* know what to make of that. "Same order as always?"

"Yep." He shoved his hands in his jacket pockets and looked around the shop curiously, as if he cared about the feminine French-style decorations.

Kimmy was obsessed with fleurs-de-lis and they were everywhere. Even the miniature chandelier, which was more for decoration than actual use, had little dangling fleurs-de-lis that glittered when the sun hit the shop just right. Since it was almost Christmas, there were a few extra decorations, including a small tree in one corner with red and white little fleurs-de-lis ornaments Kimmy had made herself with a lot of glitter, paint, and ribbon. Tegan tried to ignore the fact that she'd be alone again this Christmas, but seeing it splashed everywhere, even at work, made it difficult.

Aaron didn't come in here very often, but Tegan still figured his intent observation of the place was to avoid looking at or talking to her. Which made something perverse in her flare to life. She wasn't sure what it was, but his refusal to look at her made her want to *make* him talk to her.

"Coming right up," she said as she moved to the economy-sized coffeemaker. She'd already ground the beans this morning. And unlike the majority of customers who wanted a specialty drink, both Fitzpatrick brothers drank their coffees black with sugar. This would be her easiest order of the day. "Feel like mixing it up this morning?" With her back to him, she glanced up in the mirror over the prep station.

He was looking at her back with a mix of emotions. Annoyance and…hunger? She blinked. That couldn't be right. Well, the annoyance was probably spot on, even if she didn't know what she'd done to bother him. Maybe he just didn't like redheads. Which was ridiculous, since gingers were awesome.

"How so?" he rumbled in that deep voice that flowed right

through her like hot chocolate on a winter day, warming her from the inside out.

She ignored what the sound of it did to her insides. "Go wild, get some cannolis for the guys at work. They would be eternally grateful, trust me." She knew he worked for the same security company her friend Julieta's husband did, though she wasn't precisely sure what he did. Just something to do with personal security.

He made a grunting sound of derision. "No, thanks."

"Fine, but you're taking a few chocolate macarons to give to Dillon. They're on me." Because she adored Aaron's son. The kid was always so serious when he came into the shop and she enjoyed making him smile. Usually Tegan's dog, Kali, did that job with no problem when she was here. It was hard for anyone not to smile when a sweet Siberian husky was giving you kisses and wagging her tail like you were the most important person in the world to her.

His entire body—muscular, trim, and fit—went still. "How do you know he likes those?"

She lifted an eyebrow. "Uh, because I work here and he comes in two days a week with your mom."

He blinked, as if this news surprised him. Uh-oh, maybe it was a grandma-grandson secret since Bree Fitzpatrick *did* let Dillon get whatever he wanted. Like, always. She literally never said no to the kid when he asked for something. Tegan was about to backtrack when he nodded. "Yeah, bag some up."

"Want to get some lemon ones for Bree? She loves them." She held back a grin, wondering if she was pushing him too much.

Those brown eyes that weren't just a plain, boring brown but had amber flecks in them watched her with curiosity. "I can see why Kimmy hired you. You're very good at upselling." Again, she wasn't sure if that was a compliment or not. His tone and facial expressions were impossible to read. Frustrating man.

"Well, yeah, I'm awesome." Now she smiled at him, unable not to.

His lips twitched a fraction, and she couldn't help but wonder what he would look like if he actually gave her a full-on smile. He'd no doubt be knee-weakening gorgeous so it was probably a good thing he was allergic to smiling. "Yeah, throw some of those in, too."

She bagged the sweet macarons into the small pink and white bags. They carried simple brown bags that Kimmy usually gave to male customers, but Aaron was getting the pink. The thought of such a huge, sexy guy carrying these around made her smile. "Sure you don't want some extras to surprise your coworkers?"

He just snorted, which was apparently his version of no.

God, what was wrong with her? She needed to just shut up but she couldn't turn off her mouth or her brain around him. "The lemon ones are melt-in-your-mouth zesty and delicious."

At that, his gaze dipped to *her* mouth, paused, and for just a fraction of a second lust flared in his gaze so bright and hot she felt the burn straight to her toes. Oh, sweet Lord. Then he did that typical Aaron thing and just grunted a nonresponse, slid cash on the counter, and left with his coffee.

She watched his very tight backside as he stalked from the shop. And stalked was the only word for the way he was moving. His back was rigid, his shoulders tight.

She seriously wished she could figure him out. At twenty-seven, Tegan had been on the receiving end of more than her share of appreciative male looks and Aaron had definitely given off that vibe—for less than a second.

Or maybe she was just projecting because something about Aaron Fitzpatrick got to her. Got under her skin in the worst way possible. Before she'd settled down in Miami eight months ago she'd been on the run for two solid years. Sex hadn't been on her agenda. The opposite sex in general had barely registered to her because all she'd cared about was staying one step ahead of the man hunting her. Now that her threat was dead, she had time to actually live again.

So why did her libido have to wake up and take notice of the grumpiest man she'd ever met? When she saw he'd left one of the macaron bags behind, she snapped it up.

After locking the cash register, she stepped out from behind the counter. Normally she wouldn't leave the shop unattended, but they wouldn't get busy for another twenty minutes. While crime wasn't completely nonexistent, it was on the low side on this particular street and in this part of town. It was one of the reasons she'd decided to work here. She wanted way less stress in her life after the last couple of years.

Aaron was across the street, arms folded over his chest as he leaned against his parked truck while he talked to Addie, the owner of a painting shop. She ran Addie's Bring Your Own Brush and had 'paint parties' five or six days a week.

He must have set the coffee inside his vehicle. Neither of them had seen her so it gave her a chance to watch him when he was unguarded. His expression was relaxed, his body language loose and casual. Tegan moved between two vehicles parked by the curb and waited for a car to drive past before she stepped into the road.

It shouldn't bother her so much, or at all really, but he was so relaxed talking to Addie. It was as if he just saved his grumpiness for Tegan. She bit back the sigh that wanted to escape. It didn't matter. As she crossed the road, both Aaron and Addie looked up. Since she was friendly with Addie, Tegan smiled. "Hey, I like what you've done with your hair."

"Thanks." She fingered the newly chopped off locks. Addie had worn her thick brown hair past her shoulders for as long as Tegan had known her, which admittedly wasn't that long. Now it shaped around her face in a sleek bob that showed off her elegant features. "I needed a change."

Addie and her long-time boyfriend had recently broken up, and good riddance to the guy as far as Tegan was concerned. She'd only met him twice and the guy had that skeezy vibe all over him. All fake charm that Tegan knew was just a veneer. After being on the run she'd learned to read people fast. "Well, you look great. Blake can eat his heart out when he sees you."

Addie laughed, shaking her head. "I hope so."

"You forgot these." Tegan handed the bag to Aaron, avoiding his gaze and ignoring the little spark that flared when their fingers brushed.

"How's your painting coming along?" Addie asked when Tegan would have made her quick getaway.

She glanced over her shoulder. There were two joggers heading down the opposite sidewalk. Unlikely they'd head into Kimmy's shop, but she needed to be there in case they did. "Ah…" She turned back to Addie and winced. "Awful, to be honest. Spectacularly awful. I don't think I have that creative gene."

"I don't believe that. I've gotten so many compliments on that website redesign you did. But come to the next class this Thursday afternoon if you're free. I'll figure out where you're struggling. We'll fix it, I promise."

The truth was Tegan would rather just *buy* a cute painting, but it would be pretty cool to actually finish one herself. *Once.* Because after she finished this thing, she was done with painting. And it was unlikely she'd be hanging it where anyone could see it either. Maybe in her closet. "I'll be there. I'll bring some treats, too."

Addie's blue eyes lit up. "Bring those chocolate chip cannolis."

"I will, but I've gotta get back to the shop." She glanced over her shoulder again just in time to see Mrs. Bailey strolling down the sidewalk, bundled up in a scarf, hat, thick jacket, and walking her little shih tzu—who had on a tiny pink hat and matching doggy coat. She opened the door to Kimmy's shop and stepped inside. Duty called.

As she started to jog back across the street, a chilly breeze whipped over her. She hadn't bothered to grab her jacket, but now she wished she had. Wearing jeans, a long-sleeved black T-shirt, and a black-and-white checkered apron wasn't helping much with the chill.

When she reached the sidewalk she stuck her hand in the pocket of her apron. She'd get too warm wearing her jacket inside, but she could use an extra sweater today. She'd just grab the one she'd left in her car. It was a surprisingly cold winter in Florida. She was counting down the days until spring.

Her car was a few shops down as she pressed the key fob to unlock the doors. The moment she did, an explosion of noise and heat ripped through the air. Glass seemed to rain down from everywhere, pinging against cars, the sidewalk, and scraping her neck.

Screaming, Tegan threw herself to the sidewalk, covering her head as she dove. Another scream built in her throat, but it was too tight to escape as another shockwave of energy seemed to roll over her, pulsing through her entire body.

As she rolled for the curb, her stomach slammed into a light pole. Grunting in pain, she tried to push away from it, but couldn't make herself move. Her head throbbed and all the muscles in her body were pulled tight.

Full-blown terror rocked through her as it belatedly registered that had been *her* car that had just exploded.

If she'd been closer to it or *inside* it…

Oh God, she'd parked right outside the children's clothing boutique. If that thing had gone off a couple of hours later…

Tremors overtook her body, making her shake so badly she couldn't move, could barely think. The man who'd wanted something from her that she simply didn't have, had been killed. He *couldn't* be after her.

But someone obviously wanted her dead. You didn't accidentally rig a bomb in someone's car.

When a strong hand took her by the shoulder, she moved on pure instinct and struck out, letting years' worth of raw survival instinct explode as her fist connected with hard flesh.

CHAPTER TWO

Aaron caught her fist in his open palm. "Tegan! It's me!"

All the energy left Tegan's body in a whoosh. It was Aaron, not someone who had come back from the grave to finish her off. Her heart still beat an erratic tattoo against her chest, but her fight instinct was quickly fading.

Aaron bent over her, his far too handsome face a mask of concern. "Tegan, can you hear me?"

Nausea swept through her as she stared up into the most beautiful dark, amber-flecked eyes she'd ever seen. In the distance she was vaguely aware of multiple car alarms going off and the sounds of worried shouts. Probably from shop owners or early morning joggers. At least most of the shops weren't open this early.

"Damn it, Tegan, answer me." He looked away from her then and she heard him shout out orders to someone to call 911. It sounded as if he was in a tunnel as he spoke.

He held up three fingers in front of her. "How many fingers am I holding up? What day is it?"

The ringing in her ears suddenly stopped, as if a switch had been flipped. Groaning, she swatted at his hand. "Three, and Tuesday, I think."

The relief that crossed his face was so stark she felt it like a physical caress. "There was an explosion and you were close. You need to stay still. The shockwaves from an explosion can travel through the body at a rapid speed—including through the brain. It can actually move the brain in the skull. You need to stay where you are." He spoke so clinically, but the note of worry in his voice was impossible to ignore.

"Jeez, Aaron. That's so gross. Are you trying to freak me out more?" Why on earth would he tell her all this? She shoved his hands away and sat up. Pricks of pain stabbed her palms as she pushed against the sidewalk. Wincing, she saw the blanket of glass shards littering the sidewalk around them.

Cursing under his breath, he gently took one of her palms and started pulling the fragments from her skin. "Your car just exploded in a fiery ball. I think that should freak you out more than anything. You could have a concussion, and we need to keep you still until help gets here." Sharp fear punctuated each word. "Not that I like just being a sitting duck," he muttered, looking around and waving off anyone who tried to get too close to her.

"Your bedside manner sucks." She tried not to flinch as he pulled out the glass pieces.

Maybe it was the mention of the word *bed* but his dark gaze flicked to hers and momentarily did that heated thing again before he returned to his task. Or more likely it was just her imagination.

"How do you know that stuff about concussions and explosions anyway?"

He paused and glanced up at the sound of an approaching ambulance. Oh, thank God, help was on the way. "I was in the Corps."

Oh right, she knew that. "I thought the Marines had corpsmen from the Navy as their medical people." She knew she was rambling but didn't care. She was feeling shaky and needed to talk.

"How do you know that?" Job complete, he let go of her hand. Was it just her imagination or did he linger a moment before letting go?

"My dad was in the Navy." Grimacing, she twisted back and forth to see if she had full range of movement. Nothing seemed to be broken. Of course, now she was freaked out about what he'd said. She kept envisioning her brain moving around in her skull like Jell-O, which didn't help her nausea.

"Tell me about your dad." His voice was utterly calm as he held up a hand to a concerned-looking jogger about twenty feet away, ordering the guy to move back in a ridiculously authoritative voice.

She was grateful he was keeping people at bay. He seemed almost vigilant about it, not letting anyone near—probably because he was worried that whoever had set that bomb might be around. Oh God. She didn't even want to think about that right now. She cleared her throat. "Why?"

"Just talk to me. I don't know anything about your past and I'm curious."

"You've never been curious before."

"I need to keep you talking in case you *do* have a concussion."

The sirens were growing louder now. "I should have tried getting blown up months ago if that's what it takes to get you to be nice to me."

"I'm nice." He actually sounded offended.

She snorted then winced at the rush of pain that shuddered through the base of her skull. "Holy balls, my head hurts."

"God, your mouth." The way he said it almost sounded like a groan.

"I think you like my mouth." The instant the words were out she wished she could reel them back in. Oh yeah, *clearly* she had a concussion. Or freaking brain damage.

To her surprise, his lips pulled up in the first honest to God smile she'd ever seen from him. It completely transformed his constantly gruff expression into something that should be considered illegal. "You wouldn't be wrong about that," he murmured.

Wait...what? She swore her heart actually stuttered in her chest. Before she could even think of a half-decent response, he stood from his crouching position and started shouting at someone. Tegan wanted to cover her ears.

Seconds later two uniformed paramedics hustled Aaron out of the way. She wanted to ask him to stay, but knew that was stupid. They weren't friends and even though he made her feel safe, she wasn't going to put herself out there like that. Crouching in front of her, a female paramedic introduced herself and started taking Tegan's vitals, all while asking her rapid-fire questions. While Tegan answered, the two paramedics helped her onto a stretcher.

She was finally able to take in the complete, horrific landscape. On her side of the street, the windows of Addie's shop, a hardware store, and the children's boutique clothing store had all been blown out. Tegan's car was a smoldering mass of metal, shattered glass, and twisted plastic. The vehicles in front and behind it had also been affected by the blast, all the glass blown out and now littering the sidewalk and street. It looked like a war zone.

One of her side-view mirrors lay on the sidewalk, flames flickering along the rounded top of it. Bystanders had been partitioned off across the street as the police worked to create a barricade around the blast site.

Panic punched out to all her nerve endings. "Oh God, is anyone else hurt?"

"Just you that we know about." The blond woman with tattoos peeking out at her wrist moved efficiently as she got Tegan settled into place.

Beyond exhausted, she closed her eyes and lay back against the stretcher. She didn't want to see anyone right now, not even her friends.

"Don't go to sleep on me," Blondie snapped as they started moving her.

"I'm not. I just don't want to see anyone."

"Fair enough until we get you in the ambulance."

Tegan just wanted to curl into a ball and hide. Had she somehow brought her past troubles to Miami? The man who'd been after her was dead. She should have been safe.

As they lifted her onto the back of the ambulance, her eyes popped open at the sound of Aaron's deep, annoyed voice.

"Damn it, be careful with her." He was glowering at the paramedics as he climbed in after them.

A ridiculous surge of elation slid through her to see him.

"Don't tell me how to do my job, Aaron." The woman's mouth

pulled into a thin line and Tegan realized how much they looked alike.

She knew the Fitzpatrick brothers didn't have any other siblings so maybe the woman was a cousin. "Are you coming with me?" she asked him.

Aaron seemed truly surprised by her question. "You thought I was just going to let you go to the hospital alone?"

Well, yeah, she had. "Oh God! The shop—"

"Don't worry about it. I already called Kimmy, and Addie is locking up until she can get down here. She's got an extra key."

Another thought slammed into her and the panic she'd been keeping at bay started to bloom out of control. "My dog—"

"Took care of that, too. Addie said you'd be worried. She's calling your neighbor to let her know what's going on."

"Thank you. I..." Tegan trailed off as Blondie told him to shut up and stay out of the way before she kicked him off the ambulance.

Tegan was grateful for his solid presence and was thankful when he obeyed the woman because she didn't want him kicked off. He grew quiet and moved to the only free seat, right in Tegan's line of sight. Seeing him there gave her strength she knew she was going to need.

Soon enough, she knew the police or a detective would be at the hospital to question her. Which meant all her past secrets were about to come spilling out. Just great. Aaron already seemed to judge her or dislike her for whatever reason—today's behavior was an anomaly. He definitely wouldn't like her once he heard all about her past.

Arms crossed over his chest, Aaron stood next to Tegan's hospital bed as the doctor spoke quietly to her. She hadn't lost consciousness during the explosion so that was a good sign. He'd been worried she had internal injuries but the doctor had more or less determined that she had a very mild concussion. Which wasn't great, but considering the alternative, he was grateful how minor her injuries were. Other than that and the few scrapes on her palms, she was okay. Just shaken up. Not that he could blame her.

When his gaze strayed to her pale face, his gut tightened. She'd pulled her dark auburn hair up into a ponytail since arriving at the hospital, but a few strands had come loose, framing her bright blue eyes and sharp cheekbones. Freckles dotted across her nose and cheeks, making her look younger than he knew her to be.

He still couldn't get the image of that explosion out of his head. Even when he closed his eyes. She could have been in that car. He scrubbed a hand over his face, wishing he could banish the horror that wanted to keep replaying in his head, over and over.

He'd seen his share of death and it wasn't pretty. Some movies liked to romanticize war, but during his four tours in Afghanistan and Iraq he knew there was nothing glamorous about it, especially death. The sight and stench of burning bodies was something no one should have to experience.

"Mr. Fitzpatrick."

His eyes snapped open at the doctor's voice. "Yes?"

Dr. Morales nodded once at him. "I want to keep Miss O'Kelly here for another hour of observation. There's a detective waiting to talk to her anyway so she might be here longer than that. I need to know if you'll be able to drive her home—"

"That's not necessary. I can call someone to get me." Tegan's brow furrowed and Aaron had the most ridiculous urge to smooth out the lines.

Whenever he was around her, he simply wanted to touch her, to see if her ivory skin was as soft as it looked. Nothing would ever come of his fantasies, but that didn't seem to stop them. She was a combination of sassy and sensual. At maybe five foot two, she was petite and curvy with a bottom lip that always seemed to be pouty. He'd had way too many thoughts over the last eight months about what it would be like to take that lip between his teeth, to stroke his tongue between her lips…

Hell, he needed to focus. Tegan wasn't for him. "I'll take you, Tegan. Let me do it. Please." Because he didn't want to leave her side.

He wasn't sure what that was about either, but when he'd seen her fly back after that explosion, out of his line of vision when she tumbled behind that car, he'd lost years of his life as he raced to her. Right now he was feeling protective. Probably irrationally so. But he needed to make sure she was okay.

"Only because you said please," she murmured, a smile ghosting her face.

God, he loved her smile.

"I've written her a prescription for a strong nonsteroidal anti-inflammatory drug. But Tylenol or Advil will work, too. If she wants the prescription, you'll need to pick it up before taking her home. Make sure she takes it." The doctor glanced over at Tegan. "You can't take anything with codeine or any sort of opiate in it. I don't know that it's necessary given the mildness of your concussion, but it wouldn't hurt to have someone wake you up every few hours tonight. We want to make sure you're not too sluggish."

Before she could respond, Aaron cut in. "I'll take care of her."

Out of the corner of his eye, he could see she wanted to protest, but instead crossed her arms over her chest and settled back against the bed. She'd protested putting on the hospital gown, but had done it anyway. Now it gaped at her neckline, showing off all sorts of smooth, kissable skin. He felt like a bastard for even noticing.

"Good. I—"

A sharp knock sounded on the door, then it opened. Detective Carlito Duarte—a man Aaron had called in as a favor—stepped into the room, his expression grim. "You need more time?" he asked the doctor after a nod at Aaron.

"We're done here." He turned back to Tegan, his expression softening. "I'm going to write that prescription but if you need anything, buzz the nurses. You were very lucky."

She nodded and for the first time since everything had happened, tears filled her eyes. "I will, and thanks."

As the doctor left, Carlito stepped farther into the room. "How're you feeling, Miss O'Kelly?"

"Good as can be expected. And just call me Tegan."

"Okay…I need to ask you some questions," he said, looking at Aaron now, his intent clear. He wanted Aaron to clear out.

Aaron took another step closer to her bed so that he was right next to her head. He wasn't going anywhere unless Tegan asked him to. "I'm not leaving—I was a witness, too."

"Can he stay, please?" Tegan's quiet voice pulled both their attention to her.

Carlito nodded, though his expression was annoyed. Aaron didn't care. He wasn't leaving Tegan.

Aaron was a little surprised she'd asked, but thankful. He figured she'd need some support and he wanted to be it. He knew what it was like to be laid up in a hospital room, alone with no one there when he woke up. Not even remotely the same circumstances, but he simply couldn't leave her now. As far as he knew she didn't have any family here. Or any family at all, really. He'd asked his brother, who was friendly with her, and Callan had seemed to think she was alone.

Aaron had already called work to let them know he wouldn't be in today and he'd asked his brother to pick Dillon up from school so there was nothing dragging him away from her bedside.

"He can stay as long as you want him here." Carlito's voice dropped to a softer, speaking-to-a-victim tone, and for that Aaron was grateful.

When he pulled up a chair on Tegan's other side, Aaron did the same with a rolling stool and sat next to her. He had the most irrational urge to take her hand in his, but resisted.

"As you can imagine, I've got some questions for you. I've already spoken to some of the eyewitnesses, but I need to confirm that your vehicle was the one that exploded." Carlito rattled off a license plate number and held out a digital camera. The screen showed a picture of her mottled, ruined car, pieces of it strewn across the street and sidewalk.

She wrapped her arms around herself as she nodded. "Yeah, that's it. It exploded when I pressed my key fob to unlock it. I'd come outside to give Aaron part of his order he forgot, and on my way back to the shop I decided to grab my sweater since a jacket would be too heavy. And…I'm rambling. Yes, that's my car."

"You're not rambling. I want as many details as you can remember. Is it normal for you to go to your car during the day?"

"No. I almost never leave the shop when I'm working. But we don't get our rush until about eight, so…" Her face grew even paler. "I was supposed to leave around noon today during the shift change. That's one of the busiest times downtown." Tegan started to breathe harder, wheezing in and out in a panic, so Aaron slid a hand behind her back and started rubbing up and down in a soothing motion.

Her gown only tied at the neck so all he felt was smooth, soft skin. No bra, something he didn't want to be noticing.

"Do you want a glass of water?" Carlito asked as she started to get herself back under control.

Aaron still didn't remove his hand and she didn't seem to want him to. Touching her was stupid for his sanity, but he didn't care. She needed comfort right now.

"No, I'm good. I want to help you find who did this."

"I'm going to start with the obvious. Do you know of anyone who could have wanted to harm you? Any enemies, ex-boyfriends? From what I heard from some of the eyewitnesses, you've done a lot of design work for the shops downtown, so what about other freelance work? It's a stretch, but any contracts that didn't work out? I want the names of absolutely anyone you can think of."

Chewing on her bottom lip, she flicked a wary glance at Aaron before she looked back at the detective. "There's only one person I can think of who would want to hurt me enough to kill me, but he's dead."

Aaron almost jolted at that, but remained where he was, his palm on her back. Her heartbeat had evened out now. What the hell? The thought of anyone trying to hurt her made all his protective instincts rise up.

Her gaze dropped to her lap. "Have you ever heard of a man named Enzo De Fiore?"

It sounded vaguely familiar to Aaron, but he couldn't place it.

Duarte seemed to be having the same issue. "That sounds familiar."

"He is—was—a gangster in Chicago. Before he died eight months ago, he was convinced that I helped my brother steal a bunch of diamonds from him. Diamonds that *he* already stole from someone else. I didn't take them, but that didn't matter to him. Before I settled here I was on the run for two solid years because he was convinced I knew something." Her cheeks flushed a delicate shade of pink. He couldn't be sure, but she looked almost guilty as she continued.

"I didn't take his diamonds, but…I did steal his dog when I ran."

CHAPTER THREE

Enzo slammed his fist against the steering wheel but it didn't make him feel any better. Nothing would make him better until he got his fucking diamonds. He'd been watching that little bitch Tegan for a few weeks now and her lifestyle wasn't like someone who had a stash of millions of dollars' worth of diamonds at her disposal.

He'd have gone after her sooner but he had other shit to worry about—like the Feds not believing he was really dead. Coming after Tegan and potentially showing his face in Miami eight months ago would have been stupid. Especially with all the CCTVs they had in the city. So he'd done what he had to do. He'd lain low in a backwoods small town in the middle of nowhere until the time was right. He hadn't been in the news lately so he'd sent his partner ahead to get a place ready for him, a place close to Tegan.

Ever since, he'd been watching and waiting for the right opportunity to make a move.

Then she'd almost gotten herself killed in town today. So now he was sitting in the hospital parking lot while she was inside hopefully not fucking dead.

He wasn't sure who would want to kill her—other than him, of course. Maybe she'd double-crossed a partner when she'd taken his damn diamonds. And deep down he knew she had to have had a partner. Probably her brother. Though that fucker was a ghost, long gone. Enzo hadn't even gotten a hint of where he might be. He didn't think her brother would try to blow her up though…no, there had to be someone else involved with her. Or maybe she'd stolen from someone else after him?

It didn't matter. Whoever wanted her dead would just have to wait.

She couldn't die until he got what he wanted—hell, *needed*. Those diamonds were his ticket out of the country, away from the federal charges he'd be facing if the FBI knew he was still alive, his key to escaping his life of crime. He was tired of always looking over his shoulder, wondering who might try to kill him from day to day. He just wanted to retire comfortably. He deserved it after all.

Keeping his ball cap tugged low, he pulled out his cell phone.

His partner answered on the first ring. "Yeah?"

"How is she?"

"Good. From what I hear, she just has a mild concussion. Maybe not even that. Cops are here, though. A detective, I think, and some guy, one of the witnesses. He apparently works for a security company, but I don't know more than that."

Now would be the perfect time to search her place. With her damn dog that she'd stolen from him, and her schedule—*and* her nosy neighbors—it had been impossible to get inside. Even now it was a risk because there was no guarantee a neighbor wouldn't see him. But if she was at the hospital he had to take this chance, since it was clear someone wanted her dead. No one was getting his diamonds. No one. "I'm going to search her place. Call me when she leaves the hospital."

"Okay."

He ended the call without responding further. There was nothing else to say anyway.

The drive to Tegan's place didn't take long even with traffic, but his heart was pounding erratically the entire time.

She could have died today. If it hadn't been for what sounded like dumb luck, she would have. Then where would he be? Fucked, that's where. The last eight months he'd been in hiding, she'd been setting up her pathetic little life. He thought he had plenty of time to go after her, time for her to get comfortable, to put roots down—to start *using* those diamonds.

Now to know that someone else wanted her dead moved his timeline up drastically. It might blow his cover and prove that he wasn't dead, but if pushed, he'd just take her and torture the information out of her. Hell, it was what he should have done back in Chicago. He'd made a mistake with her, had thought she'd be too afraid to cross him. That was one mistake he wouldn't make again.

After driving by her place twice, he parked a few blocks over and made his way to her townhome. Instead of going up to the front door, he kept walking around the side of the place. The townhomes were like little gingerbread houses, all lined up and perfect with clusters of palm trees in every yard. The majority of the people who lived here were in their twenties but there were some older, retirement age people in the neighborhood—including one of Tegan's neighbors.

An old woman who was always looking out her window, clearly worrying what her neighbors were doing.

So he avoided her and walked briskly around the opposite side of Tegan's place. There wasn't much space in between the residences. When he reached the end of the townhouse he peered around and saw her small back porch.

Just a round table, two chairs, and a charcoal grill in front of a sliding glass door. Looked like it always did. He hurried onto the back porch and made quick work of the door. It took longer than he'd have liked to get inside but he didn't want to break the glass and risk drawing attention to himself.

Sweat dripped down his face despite the cool weather as he finally got the latch free and quietly slid inside. No alarm went off. She didn't have a sign outside that she had an alarm system, but not all people did. He let out a sigh of relief when everything remained quiet. He'd been avoiding breaking in in case she had a security system, but now he'd been pushed to his limit.

He shoved the long curtain out of his way and quickly surveyed his surroundings. The place looked normal enough, though certainly not high end. A couch, loveseat, big-screen television, some prints on the wall. Even though it was almost Christmas she didn't have any decorations. None that he could see. Not even a tree. He stepped farther into the room, his pulse accelerating.

If he were in her shoes and wanted to hide diamonds, he'd keep them close. In his bedroom. In a safe.

Deeper into the house, he froze when an alarm beeped, the shrill sound grating against his nerves. That was when he saw the sensor in the corner of the room.

Damn it.

The sliding glass door might not have a security contact, but she still had a system in place. For a long moment he debated his options. It would take the police at least ten minutes to get there. But that old bitch next door might come over. He had no problem killing the woman but that would take time and would slow his escape. Not to mention if he stabbed her he'd end up with blood on him. He couldn't be walking around with blood spattered all over his clothes. Not if he wanted to remain invisible. Plus, he wasn't prepared for a kill today and he'd no doubt leave evidence behind if he killed someone. If his DNA got into any online database the Feds would be all over Miami looking for him. Yeah, time to get the hell out of there.

Jaw clenched, he backtracked toward the sliding glass door. He'd make a quick exit and be long gone before the cops arrived. As he passed one of the side tables, he saw a picture of Tegan smiling widely with her arm slung around a full-grown husky.

Anger surged through him at the sight. Unable to control his rage, he knocked it off the table, watching as it slammed to the ground before hurrying back the way he'd broken in.

Time to disappear. For now. But he'd be back. Next time he was going to get what he wanted.

The handsome detective and Aaron both looked at Tegan with a mix of surprise and possibly horror.

Aaron was the first to speak. "You stole a gangster's dog?"

She lifted a shoulder. "She was a puppy when I took her. Jerk was abusing her." And she felt no guilt over what she'd done. Kali was hers now. "The last time Enzo dragged me into his office I knew—or thought—he was going to kill me because I didn't have what he wanted. After he gave me an ultimatum he stormed out, his thugs trailing behind him. I scooped up the puppy and shoved her into my bag." She'd been so tiny back then, about six pounds soaking wet. "Kali was so scared, probably because the only thing I'd ever seen him do was kick her or yell at her, so…" She shrugged again, feeling defensive at the way they just stared at her. Tegan might have saved Kali's life, but it went both ways. Her sweet dog had saved Tegan right back. Kali had been her only true friend and companion the last two years. The only constant in her life.

"He could have killed you!" Aaron shouted, a red flush creeping up his neck.

She didn't appreciate the anger. "I wasn't just going to leave her to be abused. And that's not the point." She turned back to the detective.

The other man cleared his throat. "Let's start at the beginning. Like what kind of ultimatum De Fiore gave you, and why he dragged you into his office in the first place. And why you were on the run from him for two years."

Taking a deep breath, she kept her focus on the detective, trying to ignore Aaron's intense stare. "My brother was in the Army, but when he got out he was different. Angry, disillusioned…which isn't really the point, I guess."

She rubbed a hand over her face, pushing down all the painful memories of how distant he'd been when he'd come home. The detective didn't need to know all that. "Anyway, he started drinking and gambling. He got in really deep with the wrong people, had some debts he'd never be able to pay off. So he agreed to do some jobs for De Fiore, transporting stuff. One of those transports was a bunch of stolen diamonds. For all his faults, my brother was well trained and, when he wasn't drinking, highly capable. During the transport, my brother and the diamonds went missing. De Fiore thought I knew where my brother was."

"Do you know?" Detective Duarte asked, his expression neutral.

"No, but I imagine he's dead. He wouldn't have run off with a bunch of diamonds when he would know De Fiore would come after me first. He simply wouldn't have done that." She'd bottled up her pain for a long time, knowing her brother was gone for good.

The detective's mouth pulled into a thin line. "People do crazy stuff for money."

That was true enough, but she knew her older brother wouldn't have left her to fend for herself. Colm had certainly had his faults, just like any other freaking person, but he'd been more into self-destruction than anything else. He wouldn't have let her hang for a crime he committed. "Not him."

Even though she saw a flash of doubt in the detective's eyes, he simply nodded. "So your brother went missing and so did the diamonds."

"Yeah. De Fiore had some of his thugs come and get me as soon as my brother went missing. It's actually the only reason I knew Colm was gone at all. De Fiore told me that if I didn't find my brother or get him to come in with all the stolen diamonds, I'd be dead. I looked for my brother, went to all his haunts—even though I didn't think he would be at any of them." Someone had to have stolen them because Colm simply wouldn't have left her to fend for herself. No way. "The next day someone torched my car with a mannequin inside it. The mannequin had a red wig. The message was pretty damn clear. So I ran."

"Did you go to the cops?" Aaron asked, his voice filled with concern.

She glanced at him and found strength in just looking at him. He might be surly sometimes but he was a solid presence right now. Even if he had just shouted at her, the man made her feel safe. Like nothing could get through him. "There was nothing they could have done to help me. I never saw De Fiore torch my car—or more likely one of his thugs did anyway. I didn't have anything against the man. Not actual *evidence* anyway. I had my word against his, but that's nothing in the legal system. I watch the news, I know how the system works. And everyone in the neighborhood knew the Feds had been after him for years. *Years*. If they didn't have enough evidence to convict him, what would the cops be able to do to protect me when I came to them with nothing but a story that he threatened me? Nothing, that's what."

The detective made a sort of grunting sound that almost sounded like he agreed with her. He would know how the justice system worked. It was like restraining orders. For the most part they were absolutely useless. "How'd you avoid him for two years?"

"After college—before coming back to Chicago—I backpacked for a couple years because I wanted to travel. So basically I just used the same principles from my traveling days and stayed off the grid the best I could. I deleted all my social media accounts, lost contact with everyone I knew, and I used cash everywhere. I got jobs that paid under the table and I didn't stay in one place long."

Constantly moving had worn her down emotionally, though. She'd been tired of looking over her shoulder all the time and having no real connections to people. "When I saw on the news that he'd been murdered, I settled in Miami." For the first couple of months she'd still been off the grid for the most part. Kimmy had paid her under the table until a few months ago when Tegan had finally started to feel safe enough to truly put down roots. But she didn't think the detective needed to know that Kimmy had been paying her in cash in the beginning of her employment.

She cleared her throat. "It's sunny here all the time and the people I've met in Florida up to this point have been so nice. For the first time since I was a kid I feel like I belong somewhere…" Her voice broke and, to her horror, the tears she'd been keeping at bay started pouring out in an unexpected wave. Her throat tightened, making it impossible to talk as emotions strangled her.

She didn't want to go on the run again, didn't want to leave the friends and home she'd made. Before she could swipe the tears away, Aaron had pulled her into his arms. She didn't bother pushing back, but buried her face against his chest and blocked out everything else as sobs racked her body.

She'd been strong for a long time, always trying to keep positive even when she'd been on the run and her only friend had been Kali. Now someone had tried to kill her today. She'd almost died. By all accounts she would have if not for dumb luck. Which meant someone was out there who wanted her dead. Someone who wouldn't simply stop because they'd failed.

At that thought, another sob tore through her and she clutched Aaron's shirt. She was sure she'd be embarrassed later for blubbering all over him but right now she didn't care.

She wasn't sure how long they stayed like that, with him rubbing his big, callused hand down her back and murmuring soothing words she couldn't really make out. She didn't care what the words were anyway. They made her feel better, whatever they were.

Eventually she pulled back, sniffling and, yeah, embarrassed when she saw the tear and mascara stains on his white button-down shirt. "I'm sorry," she muttered.

"Don't be sorry," he murmured as he handed her a box of tissues from the built-in nightstand next to the hospital bed. As she took them she realized the detective was gone.

"Where'd he go?" she asked, swiping at her cheeks and under her eyes, hoping she got the smudges she knew were there.

"He got a call." Aaron was watching her carefully, his expression concerned.

Before she could respond, the detective walked back into the room, his expression even grimmer than it had been before. "Your security company called the department about a breach at your home. Someone broke into your place."

Aaron watched as Tegan's face paled.

"Is someone in my house?" The words came out raspy and trembling.

"Not now. Two officers did a sweep of your place. A picture frame is broken and it's clear someone broke in through the sliding glass door, but they can't tell if anything was taken. No visible electronics are missing so you'll have to do an inspection yourself."

Aaron wanted to pull her into his arms again, to comfort her, but held off for now. "What are you guys going to do about this situation?" he demanded. Because someone tried to kill her today and now her place had been broken into. Not a coincidence.

He planned to call his boss as soon as he could and see if Porter Caldwell could look more into Enzo De Fiore. Or more specifically, if Lizzy Caldwell, Porter's wife, could. The woman was a genius when it came to hacking. She was the best security analyst—aka hacker—they had at Red Stone.

"We're going to keep a detail on her house for now. And I'm going to call the Feds about De Fiore, see if they suspect he might not be dead." Carlito shook his head, clearly frustrated.

That wasn't remotely good enough. "She'll be staying with me until this shit is figured out." Because despite what Tegan seemed to think about him not liking her, she couldn't be further from the truth. She was the first woman he'd been interested in since his wife had left him and their young son almost five years ago. And she terrified the hell out of him. Tegan was a sweet, sexy, smartass woman and she brought out all his protective, possessive instincts. Even if he wasn't insanely attracted to her he'd still have to help. He was involved now and it was clear she didn't have anyone else to help her. He couldn't turn his back on her.

"Um, *she* is right here." Tegan shifted against the crinkly sheets, a frown tugging at her pretty mouth. "That's really nice, Aaron, but I can't stay with you. Someone wants me dead and now someone broke into my place? I'm not bringing that kind of danger to your doorstep—especially because of Dillon."

His chest squeezed that she automatically thought of Dillon. "He'll be staying with my parents and you can stay in my guesthouse. I have a little mother-in-law type suite behind my place. It's a one bedroom, one bath apartment, basically. It's small but no one knows there's a connection between us, because we don't have one. There are no phone records between us, nothing. You'll be safe."

Her jaw tightened and it was clear she planned to argue more.

Well, this was an argument she'd be losing. "It's not happening."

"Fine. Then I'll just stay with you."

She blinked, her mouth opening a fraction. "You can't do that. I won't let you."

"I'll just stay outside your house along with the police detail. Which will make me a target if someone is watching your place."

She stared at him as if he'd lost his mind, so he continued. "Look, I work for one of the best security companies in the country. Maybe the best. I've got eight years' worth of the best training in the world thanks to the Marine Corps, as well as experience in combat zones. I'm fucking trained. You'll be safer with me than anyone else." He knew he was being pushy—he just didn't care. After seeing that explosion with her so close, knowing what could have happened to her, he realized he was a moron for ignoring the spark between them. He wasn't going to let anything happen to her.

"He's right," Duarte said, his voice way calmer than Aaron's. "My former partner is one of the owners at Red Stone. The company does exemplary work. I'm still going to put a detail on your house because I want it under surveillance, but they won't be with you twenty-four-seven. And if there's an emergency in your area and they get a call, they'll have to go. If I were in your shoes, Miss O'Kelly, I'd take Aaron's offer. You can lie low at least for a few days while we investigate this. I'm bringing the Feds in and we're going to try our hardest to find out who wants you dead. Until we do, the best thing you can do for yourself, for everyone around you, is to hide out where whoever is after you will have no idea to look."

Aaron could freaking kiss the guy right now. Because he could see that the detective's words had an effect on Tegan. Big time.

She bit her bottom lip in the most adorable way. He'd fantasized more than once about nibbling that very lip. He jolted when she looked at him with wide eyes. "Are you really sure?"

He nodded. "Christmas break is just starting for Dillon. He's already asked to stay with my parents for a few days, so this isn't disrupting anyone's schedule." His parents would be thrilled to keep Dillon longer than a couple of days.

"Can I bring my dog?" Her chin jutted out just a little, as if she expected him to say no.

"Yes, of course."

Sighing, she looked back at Duarte. "Can I get my clothes and other stuff from my house?"

He nodded. "We're going to need you to do an inventory of your place anyway to see what, if anything, was taken."

"Okay." Her expression was unreadable as she looked back at Aaron. "I'll stay with you. And thank you, truly. I…I really appreciate it." She swiped at fresh tears and he resisted the urge to do it for her.

No one was going to hurt her again, not if he had anything to do about it. And he was going to make damn sure no one followed them back to his place. They'd have to take precautions leaving the hospital so that they weren't seen together if anyone was watching. He mentally started making plans for how to do just that.

CHAPTER FOUR

"If you keep giving her treats she'll never leave you alone," Tegan said to Dillon. Callan had just dropped Dillon off and Aaron was somewhere talking to his brother while Tegan and Dillon hung out in the kitchen with Kali.

The adorable five-year-old wasn't doing a very good job of hiding how many treats he was giving to Kali under the kitchen table.

He turned to look at her with dark, amber-flecked eyes so similar to his father's, his expression intent. "I don't want her to leave me alone."

The kid was always so dang serious. "Well, I think she'll play with you whether you give her treats or not. She's always so excited to see you at the shop. And she's not like that with everyone."

Kali thumped her tail against the kitchen floor and actually *nodded*, as if to reiterate Tegan's point. She swore that dog was half human some days. *Most* days.

Dillon grinned widely. "Really?"

"Really."

Kali jumped up onto Dillon's seat, placing one paw on his leg and one on the chair. She kissed Dillon's face, making the boy giggle and wrap his arms around her neck. "Do you think I could have ice cream?" he asked, his voice muffled against Kali's neck.

The sweet husky was soaking up the attention as usual.

Tegan pushed her chair back and was glad she didn't feel nauseous. The doctor had said it might be a possibility but other than a low-grade headache she actually felt okay. "Sure. What kind do you guys have?"

"Vanilla and chocolate swirl is my favorite."

"No ice cream until after dinner." Aaron's deep, sexy voice was only mildly exasperated as he stepped into the kitchen. He'd long since ditched his jacket and was wearing dark slacks and a white button-down shirt with the sleeves rolled up to his elbows—showing off all sorts of sinewy, hard muscles. The man was way too sexy.

"Come on, Dad! Tegan said it was okay."

His eyebrows arched. "Only because she doesn't know the rules."

Tegan inwardly winced, realizing she'd made a mistake. Of course a kid couldn't just have ice cream in the middle of the afternoon. Or she guessed they couldn't. He'd need vegetables and stuff like that. Yeah, she wasn't ready to be a mom anytime soon. Another reminder that Aaron wasn't the guy for her, because he and Dillon were a package deal, no doubt about it. And she didn't know the first thing about kids. Other than they were a little terrifying.

"Sorry," she murmured.

Aaron shrugged, clearly not annoyed if the sexy half smile on his face was any indication. "He still tries it with his uncle Callan and anyone he thinks will give him what he wants."

"Nana always gives me..." Dillon's dark eyes widened. "Hey, can we get a dog, Dad?"

Smooth topic change, Tegan thought, fighting a smile.

"We'll talk about it," Aaron said to him before looking back at Tegan. "Callan's going to hang out at Kimmy's shop the next couple days and keep an eye on the place."

"Thank God." Tegan had been worried about that. Just because she wouldn't be at the shop didn't mean that someone looking for her wouldn't come by ready to finish what they'd started. "Maybe Callan will finally work up the courage to ask her out."

Aaron's mouth lifted into another one of those devastating half smiles. It was like he'd been holding onto all this sexiness for eight months and was now letting her see a softer side to him. It was irresistible. Almost. Because she had to resist the man. "God, I hope so. Put us all out of our misery."

She laughed. Callan and Kimmy pretty much danced around their attraction to each other to the point of being ridiculous. Kimmy was a widow and a single mom, so Tegan could understand her hesitance in being in a relationship, but it was pretty clear Callan would do anything for her. She couldn't understand why he was so gun shy.

"Look, my mom will be here soon. We'll talk when we're alone." Talking about any of this in front of Dillon wasn't a good idea. She wondered if Aaron knew more from the detective.

After leaving the hospital she'd had a police escort to her place where she'd packed up a bag of clothes, her laptop, and then Kali from her neighbor's house. From there she'd thought she'd have another police escort but instead someone from the company Aaron worked for—Red Stone Security—had picked her up with Aaron already inside. They'd driven to Red Stone, changed vehicles, then their driver had driven them around for over an hour before stopping at Aaron's place even though he didn't live very far from her. Their driver had assured her that no one had tried to follow them. She felt a lot better being here with all the precautions they'd taken.

At the sound of a doorbell chime Kali let out a short yip and raced out of the room, her nails clicking against the tile. Dillon wasn't far behind her.

"She can get a little excited." She couldn't help the apologetic note in her voice. Tegan knew dogs weren't for everyone and Kali was excited to be in a new place. So far she'd been pretty well behaved but she was still loud and jumpy. At least soon Tegan would be able to get her settled into the guesthouse, which was way smaller. Once it was just Tegan and Kali, she figured her dog would calm down a little.

Aaron frowned slightly, falling in step with her. "I had a couple dogs growing up. She's not a problem at all. Okay?"

Tegan released a sigh she hadn't realized she'd been holding. She felt weird being here, like she had to watch her step. It wasn't Aaron's doing. If anything he seemed to be going out of his way to make sure she was comfortable. It was a huge change from the closed-off man who'd been coming into Kimmy's shop the last eight months. "Okay, thanks. I just feel weird, I guess. I don't want to get in your way or anything."

He frowned again, but turned away from her as they reached the foyer. Bree Fitzpatrick, his mother and a friend of Tegan's, was scooping Dillon into a giant hug. Dillon was trying to whisper—and failing—about getting ice cream as soon as they left.

Tegan bit back another smile when Aaron let out an exasperated sigh. Seeing him in full-on dad mode was really, really nice. She'd always thought of him as this intimidating, cranky—and ridiculously sexy—man. Now he just seemed like a sexy, take-charge, do-the-right-thing kind of guy. Seriously, he didn't know her that well but was still offering up his house because she was in danger. In her experience, the world didn't work that way. Which made her want him even more. It was stupid, because she wasn't looking for a relationship and definitely not with a ready-made family.

"Tegan! I heard about what happened." Bree moved at her lightning fast, pulling her into a tight hug. The woman was in her sixties with dark hair, petite, fit, and a force of nature.

She hugged Bree back, glad to see her. Tegan's own mother had been lacking in the maternal department, so whenever she was around Bree, she found herself wishing she'd had a mom like her growing up. "I'm okay," she said, stepping back. It wasn't true. She was a hot mess inside but the answer was instinctive. She didn't want to admit that she was filled with terror that someone wanted her dead bad enough to set a bomb in her car right in the middle of a busy street. "Thanks to your son."

Aaron just grunted and gave his mom a hug. Bree was still shaking her head as she stepped back. "I can't believe what happened. No one can. Neither of you have been named, but it's been all over the news about the bombing."

The neighborhood where Kimmy's shop was located was pretty tight knit. Some of the shops had experienced turnovers in the last few years, according to Kimmy, but it was rare. It wasn't a touristy part of Miami, but a friendly local one, where families had been for generations. Kimmy's was one of the newer places but it was doing well. Part of Tegan was sad that she wouldn't get to go into work but she didn't want to bring any danger to the shop. At least she had her website design projects to work on. It would keep her busy and focused—and hopefully keep her mind off the person who had targeted her to die. Though Tegan knew nothing could do that. Not really. She wouldn't be able to focus until the person was caught.

Bree pointed to a big brown bag by the front door. "The Mederos family sent over a bunch of food for you. I told them I'd be seeing you so they fixed up enough food for three days."

The Mederos family owned Montez's Grill and one of their daughters ran a lingerie boutique on the same street as Kimmy's place. Tegan knew all of them. Everyone had been so welcoming when she started working for Kimmy and she'd redone almost all the websites for everyone on the street at a discount. She knew that people cared, but this act of giving was just too much on her emotional state right now.

Tears pricked Tegan's eyes and she inwardly cursed as she swiped at them. She'd barely cried in the last couple of years. There had been no time in her life for feeling sorry for herself, only survival. Now... "Damn it," she muttered as the floodgates stayed open. "I'm normally not a crier."

Bree pulled her into another hug and patted her back gently. "You're holding up better than I would. I'm glad you decided to show some sense and stay here. If you get tired of my son you can stay at my place."

Laughing, she said, "Thank you." Tears finally dried up, Tegan stepped back. God, Aaron probably thought she was a total basket case by now. Which didn't matter anyway, since she didn't care what he thought. Which was a total lie.

"If you want, I can take Kali off your hands," Dillon piped in.

"What?"

"I can take Kali to Nana's tonight." He gave her the sweetest smile that had just a hint of mischievousness.

"That's a great idea, Dillon. Let's give Tegan a chance to rest. We haven't had a dog in the house in years." Bree gently petted Kali's head and Kali, as always, soaked up the attention.

"Oh no, she'll stay here. She's already in a new place and taking her somewhere else might stress her out." And Tegan wasn't sure she wanted to be away from her sweet dog anyway.

Kali whined. Next to Dillon she was practically vibrating with energy as she tried to sit still. She wasn't doing a very good job, her butt and tail wagging, moving her entire body.

Dillon placed his little hand on Kali's head. "Nana's got a fenced-in yard so she can go out and poop anytime she needs. Then tonight she can sleep with me. In my bed." He looked incredibly excited at the thought.

"I don't know..." She looked at Aaron, hoping he'd say something.

He just lifted his eyebrows and shrugged. "I've learned that when the two of them gang up together, it's a good idea to just say yes."

Tegan looked back at Bree. "Bree, Kali can be a lot to handle—"

"If she's too much we'll just bring her back over here. We only live a couple blocks away. We're in the same neighborhood."

"Oh." Well, that made her feel better. "Are you sure?" Kali was a good dog, but Bree and her husband were older. Tegan was worried she might be too much to handle. And she felt weird being away from her dog. Kali was always a comfort.

"Absolutely. I'll just need her leash and food and we'll be fine. I've still got Bandit's old dog bed and toys, so she'll be fine. And my house is all tile and wood so even if she has an accident it's no big deal. I'll bring her back in the morning on my walk. You need some rest. Take advantage of this."

Tegan looked at Kali, torn. "You want to go with Dillon?"

She barked in answer then licked Dillon's face before trotting over to Tegan and jumping up on her to kiss her as well. Yes, that dog was definitely part human.

Okay then, it was settled. Tegan scratched behind her ear. "Just let me get her stuff." Tegan felt lost letting her dog go but she was too emotional to put up much of an argument and it was clear Dillon really wanted to spend time with her. Considering Aaron was giving her a safe place to sleep, she wasn't going to complain.

She headed for the kitchen to grab Kali's stuff.

"You really don't have to let her go," Aaron said quietly behind her.

She nearly jumped as she picked up Kali's bag of food, toys, and leash from one of the kitchen chairs. She hadn't realized he'd followed her. "I know, but it's hard to say no to either of them. And Dillon looks so excited at the thought of getting to play with her."

Aaron's mouth curved up. "Yeah, he's been begging me for a dog for about six months now."

"I don't know how you ever say no to him."

He snorted. "It'll get easier, trust me."

"If you say so." She lifted the bag but he immediately took it from her.

The gesture warmed her from the inside out even as she reminded herself that Aaron was not for her. He had a kid, and even though she adored kids, they were a huge responsibility. Plus, she knew that Aaron had been hurt in the past. She might not know all the details but she'd heard Kimmy say enough that she'd managed to put some of the pieces together. She knew that things hadn't worked out between him and his ex-wife. She wasn't really sure of the why, though.

Not that any of that mattered. Even if Tegan had been looking for a relationship, he wasn't the type of man she wanted. Except maybe in the sexiness department, because in that one he was off the charts.

"I think they made more than three days' worth of food," Aaron said, hefting the takeout bags the Mederos family had sent over. Relief slid through him that Dillon was at his parents' and completely safe. He was also very aware that he was now alone with Tegan. Months ago he would have hated that. Now he could finally admit to himself how much he wanted her.

"Whatever's in there, I could probably eat all of it right now. I didn't even think I was hungry," Tegan murmured, heading into the kitchen with him.

"You've had a lot happen today. Eating and sleeping are the best things you can do." He knew from experience that sometimes sleep was the only damn thing that could help.

"I'll be okay to sleep with the mild concussion, right?"

"Yeah. Enough time's passed and you're not exhibiting any signs of being concussed but…I think you should sleep in my guest room instead of the guesthouse." He didn't look at her as he spoke, just set the food on the counter and pulled out the top two boxes. He was prepared for her to argue so he continued. "It'll be easier for me to keep one house locked down from any potential threat and I'll be able to wake you up easier as well. I don't know that I even need to but I'll feel better waking you up a couple times tonight, just in case."

He looked up as she pulled out one of the chairs at the island. She raised an eyebrow. "Was that your plan all along, to have me stay at the house?"

"Yeah." Why bother to deny it?

She snorted. "You really are like Bree."

His mouth curved up at that. "Why do you say that?" He grabbed a water bottle from the fridge and slid it across to her.

"She plans on things and just expects everyone to go along with her. She's a bulldozer when she wants to be."

"I didn't realize you two had spent much time together." More than anything he was surprised his mother hadn't said anything about spending time with Tegan. He knew her from Kimmy's shop but his mom hadn't mentioned Tegan other than in passing.

"I redesigned a few websites for some of the charities she volunteers at and I've seen her in action. She gets people to agree to stuff and makes them think it was their idea to start with. And she comes into the shop a lot. I think she's just as frustrated with Callan as everyone else. I once heard her on the phone telling someone that Kimmy would be her daughter-in-law if her son could just pull his head out of his butt."

"I have a feeling you're using nicer language than she did," he said dryly.

She let out a short laugh. "I am. Your mom's feisty." She paused. "Can I ask you something personal?"

With his back to her, he pulled out a couple of plates for dinner. Inwardly he braced for the inevitable questions about his ex. "Sure."

"You said you were in the Marines. Did you ever—and if this is too personal, feel free to ignore me—but you must have seen gunfire and explosions and…"

Surprised, he turned to find her staring at him, looking miserable. He wasn't sure where she was going with the conversation but it wasn't what he'd expected. Normally he didn't talk about his time overseas. Not to civilians anyway. They always wanted to ask jackass questions, like had he killed anyone or how many people he had killed. Like it was any of their fucking business. It was clear she wasn't asking him questions out of a morbid sense of curiosity, though.

He set the plates down and went to sit next to her. "What are you trying to ask?" he said, taking one of her hands in his. Her skin was soft. She let out a little shiver and he didn't think it was because she was cold.

"I honestly don't know. I feel like a mess right now. I know you must have seen way worse stuff than a car bomb so I feel stupid even talking about it. I'm just feeling off kilter, I guess. Really off balance. Whenever I close my eyes, all I can see, feel, and hear is the explosion. And if I let myself really think about what could have happened, I break out into a sweat." She pulled her hand free, wrapped her arms around herself, and started to shiver.

Fuck it. He pulled her into his arms, not stopping at a simple hug. Some intrinsic part of him needed to make this better for her, needed to take away all the bullshit. He tugged her right into his lap, much to her surprise if the little yelp she let out was any indication.

Her petite frame fit perfectly against him. She curled up to him, still shaking a little, but not too badly as he tightened his grip. She laid her head on his chest, letting him hold her. "It's scary to think that I could have been in the car or right next to it when it blew."

"It's going to be scary for a while. You might have nightmares about it." He certainly had. Occasionally he still did. That shit never went away. Not truly.

Sighing, she didn't respond.

"I think you'll be okay, though." After everything she'd told Duarte and him about being on the run from a gangster for two years, he had a lot of respect for her. That kind of life was hard, and she'd handled herself well because she was still here. She was a survivor and she hadn't let her life get her down.

The Marines had been tough and he'd spent a lot of years in the worst shitholes, but he'd always had his men, people watching out for him. She'd had no one and he hated that. Even if it was stupid, he was determined to be the one who had her back now. Even though he didn't want to analyze exactly why he was so determined to keep her safe and close to him. Because she was the kind of woman who could destroy him if he let her in.

She sighed again. "I will. I'm just feeling a little sorry for myself right now."

"You're allowed to." Her sweet scent teased him. Whatever shampoo she used was subtle, some sort of vanilla and lavender combination. Holding her close like this was something he'd imagined countless times, though under very different circumstances—naked ones.

Ever since he'd met her all those months ago he'd been drawn to her. She had such a sunny disposition and a lot of sass. She was the opposite of his ex in every way. He hadn't wanted to be attracted to Tegan, hadn't wanted to be attracted to anyone after what he'd gone through. Now he was losing the fight to keep his distance from her.

He cleared his throat. "Listen, the past few months I might have been kinda...grumpy."

She laughed and pulled back to look at him. Only inches separated them and it took all his willpower not to drop his gaze to her mouth and the very kissable, full lips he'd fantasized about far too often. "That's a bit of an understatement. Why are you like that with me? And don't say it's with everyone because you're nice to Kimmy. But you always seemed annoyed with me—until today."

"I'm nice to Kimmy because Callan would kill me if I looked at her the wrong way."

Her lips curved up. "True enough. So what's the deal?"

He wanted to slide her back to her seat because having this conversation with her on his lap was making it hard to think, knowing exactly how close she was to his cock, how easy it would be to shift positions and…nope. He shut that thought right down. Not that it did much since he was still getting hard. How could he not be with her sitting on his lap like this? "You might know that I was married before?"

Tegan nodded, her blue eyes unreadable.

"After Dillon was born, she split. Signed over all parental rights to me and left town. Said she wanted nothing to do with either of us, that she hated my family and hated Miami." He'd had a lot of bitterness about it for a long time. But he'd let it go because he couldn't be a good parent and be angry all the time. Dillon deserved better than that. His son was going to get the best of everything he had to offer, nothing less.

Tegan's eyes widened. "Seriously?"

He nodded.

She blinked once. "I can understand divorce, but leaving your kid like that?"

His jaw tightened. "She was…she had issues." He'd been young and in lust with her when they'd met. He'd been in the Corps and she'd been sexy and all about him. Or so he'd thought. He'd just been young and stupid, seeing what he wanted to see instead of what was really there: a selfish woman who'd only cared about herself. And Dillon had paid the price for it. "She died of a drug overdose about a year after she left. Somewhere out west."

"Wow. I'm sorry."

He was just sorry that he'd one day have to explain to his son what had happened to his mother. He cleared his throat, finally getting to his point. "You're her opposite and…the first woman I've been interested in in about five years." He couldn't believe he was even admitting this to her, but he felt compelled to. Felt as if he needed to explain to her why he'd been so distant because he wanted to start fresh, maybe start something with her.

"I didn't handle being around you well." Mainly because he hadn't trusted his instincts around women. But after seeing Tegan in action with customers, seeing the way she was with his son, and now after hearing all that she'd been through, he knew she was nothing like his ex. And he wasn't the same boy who'd fallen for the wrong kind of woman.

Tegan's eyes widened and her lips parted ever so slightly.

Against his will, his gaze dipped to those lips and all he wanted to do was kiss her, taste what he'd been fantasizing about for so damn long.

She hadn't responded to his admission but when her tongue flicked out against her bottom lip, he groaned, unable to stop the reaction.

The air was suddenly too heavy and she felt way too good in his arms. He started to lean closer when the buzz of his cell phone in his pocket made them both jump.

She blinked as if coming out of a daze then slid off his lap as though she couldn't move fast enough. He wanted to ignore the call, but it could be Duarte or an emergency with Dillon. As a father, he never ignored his phone.

When he saw it was just one of his friends from work, he ignored it. Not that it mattered. Whatever might have happened between him and Tegan clearly wasn't going to now. She'd moved around the island and was looking at the food he'd laid out, clearly avoiding his gaze and putting solid distance between them.

Part of him was relieved nothing had happened. Getting involved with her was a risk he wasn't sure he was willing to take.

CHAPTER FIVE

Tegan stared at the ceiling of the guest room, replaying Aaron's words over in her head. She couldn't believe he was interested in her. Considering his behavior today she actually *could,* but it was hard to reconcile this change with the man who'd seemed perpetually annoyed with her over the last eight months.

After everything he'd admitted about his ex, she hadn't been sure how to respond. Heck, she still wasn't sure. She wanted Aaron, no doubt about that, but talk about some serious baggage. And she had her own issues as well. She'd been a military brat, and then after her dad died, her mom had dragged her and her brother to a place they hated and had barely been present in their lives. Tegan knew absolutely nothing about kids. She wasn't the right type of woman for Aaron. He should want someone sweeter, more nurturing. Someone…not her.

Getting involved would be stupid—

She sat up at the sound of a doorbell downstairs. The two-story house had a simple layout: kitchen, living room, dining room, and family room downstairs, and four bedrooms upstairs. The place was huge, not to mention the guesthouse apartment out back.

Even though she doubted a would-be assassin would take the time to ring the doorbell, a jolt of panic punched through her all the same.

When she peeked out into the hallway she could hear Aaron disarming the alarm system downstairs. That meant he recognized whoever was on the other side of the door. Still, a low-grade panic hummed through her, refusing to settle until she knew who was there.

A moment later she heard the sound of the front door opening and then came Detective Duarte's voice. She was wearing yoga pants and a T-shirt, so she grabbed a sweater and pulled it over her head since she didn't have a bra on, and hurried downstairs. The fact that the detective was here in the middle of the night was *not* good news. She held back the fear and worry because freaking out before knowing exactly why he'd shown up instead of calling wouldn't do anyone any good.

Aaron was talking quietly to the detective in the foyer when she joined them. Duarte was still wearing a suit, though no tie. Even close to midnight the man looked polished and put together. His gray eyes were startling against his bronze skin and she had a feeling he never wanted for female company.

Still, compared to Aaron, the man did nothing for her. Aaron had more of an edge to him. His dark military-style short hair only highlighted all the hard planes of his face, making him all the more interesting to look at. When he'd told her she was the first woman he'd been interested in over the last five years, she wondered if he'd slept with anyone since his ex. It seemed crazy to think he'd been celibate because, come on, look at the man. But she didn't want to think about him getting physical with someone else anyway. It made something annoyingly possessive flare to life. She wasn't used to it and wasn't sure she liked it.

She cleared her throat. "What's wrong?" Because a detective wasn't stopping by at midnight to chat about the weather and she couldn't do any stupid small talk. She simply didn't have it in her.

"I just had a conversation with the FBI agent who was head of the team to bring down De Fiore right before he allegedly died."

Allegedly? Oh, that was *not* good. The word slammed through her, making it hard to breathe for a moment. She looked at Aaron, needing someone to ground her right now. Because all she wanted to do was grab her stuff, her dog, and run.

His expression was hard, but she knew it wasn't directed at her. "Let's take this into the kitchen."

"Do you have decaf coffee?" she asked Aaron as they entered the kitchen.

He looked at her as if she'd lost her mind. "No point in drinking coffee if it doesn't have caffeine."

A slight smile curved her lips. "What about caffeine-free tea?" Because she needed something warm and soothing that wouldn't keep her up all night.

He shook his head. "How about hot chocolate?"

It was hard to imagine a man like Aaron drinking hot chocolate because it seemed so impractical but he did have a five-year-old. There would be a little caffeine in it, but she didn't care. "Sounds perfect, thanks." Feeling shaky as he started moving around the kitchen, she turned to the detective, a heavy ball of stress tangled in her stomach. "So, allegedly dead?" The question left a sour taste in her mouth.

Duarte pulled out a chair at the island so she did the same and sat next to him. "I'll keep this short, but yes, *allegedly* dead. The FBI was looking into him before he 'died.' They have an airtight case against him. Tax fraud and evasion."

She snorted. "Just like Capone?"

"Exactly. They were about to move on him when he suddenly got murdered."

That seemed convenient. "What about the body, though? Wouldn't they have to confirm that it was him?"

"Yes, and that's where it gets a little tricky. The body was burned beyond recognition. The dental records match but that just means the records match whoever's are on file. He could have paid off someone for that. And..." Duarte sighed, his grayish eyes grim. "There was an issue with the DNA sample taken. It got corrupted during testing—which they believe was intentional. Right around the same time there was a snafu that released the body, which was cremated immediately. So they didn't have anything left to test."

Ice slid through her veins, striking at all her nerve endings with sharp pricks. None of this had been public information or she'd have never settled down in Miami. Even then she'd waited to put down roots because she'd been afraid De Fiore had been somehow waiting to trap her. This sounded way too sketchy. "That feels like a bit of a coincidence."

"Exactly. But without more proof, they can't make a case that he's not dead. He hasn't resurfaced anywhere so if he really is alive, he's basically living off the grid. They want him bad, but can't expend a bunch of resources hunting a ghost who may or may not be dead."

She rubbed a hand over her face, feeling about a thousand years old. "So he's back for those stupid diamonds. Well, he's in for a big disappointment."

Duarte nodded as Aaron slid a steaming mug in front of her. He'd even put whipped cream on top. The sight warmed her heart.

"Thank you," she murmured, glad he was here with her. She might not know him very well, but the man was solid. After what she'd recently learned about his military experience, it was clear he was the kind of man you wanted on your side. Not only that, but he'd stepped up and taken over as a single father, and it was clear that he thought his kid hung the moon. He was a good man. She couldn't fight the guilt weighing on her that she'd brought her troubles to his doorstep. It made her wonder if she should cut and run. For the first time in years she wanted to stay in one place. Wanted it so desperately it was a live thing inside her.

"The diamonds..." Duarte said, drawing her attention back to him. "I don't know if this is about them."

"What else could it be about?" She didn't have any other enemies. None that she knew about anyway. And nothing that warranted the kind of violence from yesterday.

"Honestly, I don't know. I just think it would be pretty stupid of him to try to kill you *before* he got what he wanted. And according to my FBI contact, bombs aren't really his style. He likes to get up close and personal."

The iciness spread, wrapping around her insides and chilling her straight to the bone. Why hadn't she thought of that? It didn't actually make sense for De Fiore to want to kill her. Not yet anyway. Not until he got what he wanted—except she didn't have anything to give him.

"The Feds want to talk to you. They know who your brother is but they didn't realize there was a tie to you and De Fiore or they'd have come to you sooner. They wanted to talk to you tonight but I wouldn't tell them where you're staying. Said I'd bring you in tomorrow morning for a sit down with them. If you want."

She didn't particularly want to talk to more law enforcement and she had a feeling Duarte was just being polite and giving her the illusion of a choice. She'd have to talk to the Feds one way or another. "I'll do it. Thanks for not dragging me down to see them tonight." Under other circumstances she figured they would have tracked her down, but she'd turned off her cell phone and taken out the battery at Aaron's insistence. He said no one should be able to track her without access to her phone.

Duarte's mouth curved up slightly and he shrugged. "You should be rested when you talk to them. It'll be in my office, not in an interrogation room. And if they start pushing you, tell them you want to talk to me or a lawyer. Don't let them railroad you into anything. They can't keep you against your will."

She blinked, surprised by his heated tone. "What could they possibly railroad me into?"

"Don't know that they will. But I know how they operate. They're pushy when they want to be, even to victims. If you start to feel uncomfortable about any line of questioning, end the conversation. You're a victim, not a suspect. Sometimes the Feds need a reminder of stuff like that." There was a hint of derision in his voice.

Grateful for the warning, she nodded. "I'll keep that in mind."

He pushed up and nodded at Aaron, who'd been quiet. "Eight o'clock tomorrow work for you?"

"We'll be there." Aaron's expression was unreadable as he tilted his chin toward the front of the house.

She quickly realized he meant for Duarte to follow him to the door. Tegan didn't bother going with them. If Aaron wanted privacy with Duarte, she wouldn't intrude.

She wrapped her hands around the mug but it didn't do much to warm her. Not when chills snaked through her body.

She hadn't thought De Fiore would fake his own death. Sure, the thought had entered her mind that his death wasn't real, but it had been eight months. And she'd come back onto the grid, so to speak, about three months ago—even if she had settled in Miami eight months ago.

De Fiore had been head of his own little criminal empire but seemingly untouchable. Now to learn he was quite possibly alive? She slid off her chair, that familiar fear grasping her in its sharp talons.

She should run. Far, far away. She'd done it before, and she could go off the grid again. Except now it would hurt worse than before. Chicago had never felt like home. Nowhere their mother had dragged them after her dad's death had really felt like home. After college, and then her years of traveling, Tegan had just gone back to Chicago because it had been familiar and her brother had been living there. She'd never planned to settle down there permanently. When she'd gone on the run she hadn't cared about leaving the city. If anything, leaving behind all those painful memories had been easy. Like cutting away a gangrenous part of her life.

Now would be different. She loved Miami and more than that, she loved the people she'd gotten to know. She'd allowed herself to start putting down roots, to make friends.

"You're not going anywhere." Aaron's deep voice pulled her out of her thoughts.

Blinking, she realized he was standing on the other side of the island, watching her. She hadn't even heard him return to the kitchen. "What?"

"I see the look on your face. Your instinct is telling you to run. Well, you're not going to." There was no room for argument in his voice, in those commanding words.

She wanted to deny what she'd been thinking, but lifted a

shoulder. "Maybe it would be better if I did run." Even if it was the last thing she truly wanted to do. Going on the run drained her in ways she hated thinking about. The last couple of years before settling in Miami she'd been a muted version of herself, always worried, always looking over her shoulder. "Because if it's not De Fiore who wants to kill me, then I'm screwed. I mean, I'm screwed either way but at least if he's the one after me I know what he looks like. Now I'm fighting a ghost, because I have no idea who else could want me dead."

And she was making anyone associated with her a target. Sure, she was relatively safe. For the moment. But it wouldn't last. She couldn't hide at Aaron's forever. Even if they'd taken a ridiculous amount of precautions, maybe there was something they hadn't seen, an angle they hadn't thought of. She shut that thought down before she started hyperventilating. Giving in to fear was weak. She had to keep a steady head.

"Let the FBI and the Miami PD do their job. At least let them investigate this before doing something stupid. The bombing just happened. They're putting all their resources into this."

His tone and the word *stupid* rankled her. "I can take care of myself." She'd been doing it for a long time.

"I know. Doesn't mean you should run. Stay here where you're safe. No one could possibly know where you are right now. There's been no leak to the news of the names of the witnesses, no leak that I was there. There's no fucking link between us." His voice was heated, his expression determined. "And if here stops being safe, we'll figure something else out. I work for a powerful company. They'll help you if the cops can't."

"I…don't think I can afford their help." She didn't know much about the company he worked for but he wore expensive suits, drove a nice truck, and lived in a very nice area. Not to mention she'd seen the Red Stone Security building downtown. That place had been intimidating and seriously prime real estate.

He frowned. "They'll likely do it for free. If they don't, I'll pay."

She shook her head. "Why would they do that?" She wasn't going to ask why he'd offered to pay, only because she didn't want to insult him. And she didn't want the answer. She wasn't letting him pay to help her, period. He'd already done too much.

"Because you need help."

She wanted to tell him that the world didn't work that way but his very determined expression said that he meant every word. Something about the look in his eyes was too intense, too…something. She didn't want to analyze it or what it made her feel. Aaron was not the man for her. She had to keep reminding herself of that. "So eight o'clock tomorrow?" Or today, really. It was after midnight after all.

He nodded. "I'll drive you."

"Are you sure you can take off work like this?" They hadn't actually talked about that. He'd pretty much told her that he was helping her and just taken over. She was grateful for that but didn't want to interfere with his life—or put him or anyone else in danger.

"Yep." He was watching her with that unnerving intensity.

"Are you going to expand on that?"

"What's to expand? I've got time and I'm taking it. We're going to get this mess figured out one way or another." As he spoke he rounded the island so that he was a couple of feet from her.

His proximity and the way he said *we* did something strange to her insides. It was like now that he'd decided to admit his attraction and go all protective he'd let down some sort of wall between them. She wasn't sure how she felt about it. "Okay. Well, thank you." She slid off the chair, her hot chocolate mostly untouched. She'd needed the warmth but her stomach was too tied up to handle much—and she needed space from him. Right now she was feeling weak where he was concerned. Getting involved with Aaron would be monumentally stupid for her heart.

His spicy scent teased her as he looked down at her, and she fought the instinct to lean in to him, to touch him. Her nipples pebbled under that intense stare, making her glad she'd put on a sweater.

His closeness wasn't helping her reaction to him either.

"What?" she asked when he just watched her.

"Just wondering if you're ever going to respond to what I told you earlier." His voice was deep, curling around her, pulling her in and making her feel stupidly secure.

Something she couldn't afford to feel. Not now.

She didn't need for him to specify what he meant. In fact, if he said the actual words again, told her that he was attracted to her, she wasn't sure she could handle it. She cleared her throat. "I don't know what to say. Right now isn't really a good time for me to think of…anything related to…stuff."

A hint of amusement danced in his dark eyes. "Stuff?" He took a step closer, minimizing the distance between them. It was subtle but he was crowding her personal space.

Forget being chilled. Heat spilled through her and she felt her cheeks start to warm as she looked up at him. Had he always been so broad, so tall? "Yes. Stuff. Between you and me." Gah, why did her voice have to tremble?

Before she realized what he intended, he was cupping her cheek, his hold so gentle and sweet she had to resist leaning into it. Oh so softly, he rubbed his thumb against her cheek. A shiver rolled through her. "Now's not a good time. I get it, but…I'm interested. And I'm not going anywhere."

His deeply spoken words rolled over her, enveloping her. Since she couldn't find her voice she just nodded. He was simply putting it all out there, telling her he was interested. But that could mean any number of things. He was probably just interested in sex.

The truth was she was, too. More than sex, though. She didn't want something casual, not with a man like Aaron. But…no. She simply didn't have time to think about sex or relationships or anything else. Not tonight. Not when she had a meeting with a federal agent in the morning to talk about the probably not-so-dead gangster or someone else who might be trying to kill her. That thought was enough to douse her with metaphorical cold water.

"I'm going to reset the alarm." Aaron dropped his hand, his gaze still all-consuming as he took a step back from her, giving her the space she desperately needed.

The second he did it was like she could breathe again. She sucked air into her lungs as he strode from the kitchen. Even the way he walked was sexy.

Sighing, she rubbed a hand over her face. She needed sleep. Unfortunately, she had a feeling it wasn't going to come easy. Not tonight.

Sticking to the low speed limit, Alec Rossi drove down Tegan O'Kelly's quiet residential street. Cute little townhomes and bungalows lined the curving road, and most vehicles were in the driveways and out of sight. Some kids' toys had been left in front yards, but for the most part all the yards were neat and tidy. The majority of homes had Christmas lights adorning them or at least a wreath on the front door and festive ribbons on the mailbox. It was late, after midnight, but the neighborhood was big enough that it wasn't strange to see someone driving home.

Of course he wasn't going home. He didn't live here.

When Alec saw an unmarked cop car in Tegan's driveway he kept driving. Hers was one of the few homes without decorations or lights. He cracked his knuckles, frustrated by the extra security. But it was to be expected after the bombing. If there hadn't been anyone outside her place he would have been even more suspicious.

There were two entrances to the neighborhood so he used the other to leave instead of heading back down the street. If he did the latter, just circling back by the cop car, it would draw attention he didn't need. For all the cop knew, he lived here, and Alec didn't want the guy to see him twice.

Not in this vehicle anyway. He'd have to ditch it now and procure another one.

The O'Kelly woman was making things difficult for him by not doing what she was supposed to: die. It wasn't personal and if she wanted to blame anyone it was that stupid prick Enzo De Fiore.

Enzo should have stayed dead. He had enough money to get out of the country. Or he should have had enough if he was smart. All those years as top dog, the man should have been squirreling away funds. But Enzo thought the woman had a bunch of diamonds and wanted them, had refused to leave the country without them.

Too bad for Enzo she didn't have jack.

Unfortunately for the woman, she needed to die because of Enzo's belief. She was a loose end and her death had to be violent and spectacular. To make it look like her nonexistent partner had killed her.

That way Enzo would just walk away. She'd be dead and, without any leads, the fool wouldn't have anyone to hunt anymore. He would leave the country and be out of their hair. Or he'd just keep hunting her imaginary partner until he got caught by the Feds.

Of course, Alec could just kill Enzo and be done with it, but his boss didn't want him to do that. Not unless he had to.

Stupid code of honor or whatever. Alec didn't agree with it, but that was just the way it was with these old school gangsters sometimes. They had rules they liked to follow. At least when it suited them. Because if Enzo got in the way, Alec knew his boss would order him to kill the guy.

Hell, he might kill Enzo regardless. Just because he could. He could make that one look like an accident. Or just kill him and dispose of the body so that no one would find it.

It was certainly something to think about.

Glancing in the rearview mirror, he saw that he wasn't being tailed so he started heading back to his temporary residence.

The good news was, if the woman had a police detail on her place, she was home. Or it was more likely that she was. Nothing could stop Alec when he was on a job, so a little thing like a bodyguard outside wouldn't save her.

He'd just have to break in and kill her. Then set her house on fire, making sure the entire place was razed to the ground. It was one option.

Tomorrow he'd head to where she worked and see if he could get to her there. Unfortunately, if she had a police detail it would make his life more difficult.

Which was just as well. His jobs had started to get boring anyway. Livening things up a little wasn't such a bad thing.

He just wished he knew for certain if the woman was home. He'd tried tracking her phone but couldn't get a ping on it. She'd probably taken out the battery.

Something he found very interesting. Most people wouldn't have thought to do that.

But she *had* been on the run from Enzo for a couple of years so she was adept at hiding. Clearly. Going off grid the way she had would have been difficult for most people. But humans could do amazing things in an effort to stay alive. The survival instinct in some was a powerful thing. Maybe taking out the battery was a habit she'd picked up. Alec just hoped she didn't go on the run again.

Because if she did, Enzo would try to track her and he'd have to track her, too. All he wanted to do was wrap up this job and head home. Not hunt after some bitch who should already be dead.

CHAPTER SIX

Aaron crossed his arms over his chest as he leaned against the wall outside Carlito's office. He couldn't hear anything going on inside other than the murmur of voices. He didn't like that Tegan was in there without him. At least Carlito had insisted on being in there—and he'd been stubborn about it, too—because the Feds had wanted to speak to her alone.

Aaron understood why he'd told Tegan not to let the FBI bulldoze her, because that was exactly their MO. When he'd been in the Corps he hadn't dealt with them, but since working for Red Stone he'd had the occasional interaction with an FBI agent. With the exception of the HRT guys, who were solid, most agents he'd come in contact with were dicks. It was like it was part of the FBI's employment requirement. He'd rather deal with any other agency than them.

They liked to showboat and get their names in the news for closing a big case. Finding out that Enzo De Fiore was alive and then nailing him to the wall with a lengthy prison sentence was just the type of thing that would have the Feds salivating.

Aaron didn't care about any of that shit. He didn't care if De Fiore was dead or alive. He just wanted to make sure Tegan was safe, protected.

This need to take care of her, to look out for her, had taken him off guard. Yeah, he'd been attracted to her since pretty much the day he'd met her. He couldn't deny that to himself. And after seeing the friendly, genuine way she was with customers, he'd started to simply *like* her. But now that he knew what she'd been through, he flat out respected her. Not many people could have gone on the run like she had and come out of it okay.

And stealing a gangster's dog? That just made him adore her more even if he hated that she'd put herself in danger. She'd gotten under his skin and no matter that he told himself to go slow, he wasn't sure he could take his own advice.

There was a steady hum of activity at the precinct but he was tucked down a hallway so he couldn't hear what was going on in the bullpen. Only two detectives had passed him in the hall in the last hour. So when Porter Caldwell stepped into view at the end of the hallway, he straightened, surprised.

Porter was his direct boss, though he'd taken a more hands-on role for many years with Red Stone before taking over one of the security divisions. And the guy was a former Marine, too. *Semper Fi.* Hard not to like the man.

He nodded once as Porter reached him, a small laptop bag in his hand. "Everything okay?"

"Yeah. Carlito called me. Stopped by so I could talk to your girl."

Surprise flickered through him. Tegan might not be his girl, but he wasn't going to correct Porter.

Aaron had planned to tell Porter what was going on with Tegan. When he'd called to let Porter know he was taking time off, the other man had kept things brief because he was on the way to the hospital. His sister-in-law was about to give birth—or maybe she had already—so Aaron was more than a little surprised he was here now. "What's going on with Grant and Belle?"

Porter half smiled. "False alarm but, man, she's close. And they're both ready for that kid to get here."

Aaron snorted. "They'll have their hands full soon enough. How's Maddox?"

"Keeping us busy…" He trailed off as the door to Carlito's office opened.

A man and a woman, both wearing staid dark suits and neutral expressions, stepped out. They barely glanced at Porter or Aaron as they headed down the hallway, murmuring quietly to each other.

Aaron moved into Carlito's office, wanting to make sure Tegan was okay.

Her face lit up when she saw him. His heart squeezed at the sight. Yeah, he'd definitely started to fall for her, no use denying it. For the drive here she'd tucked all her hair into a winter cap, and had worn sunglasses and adorable earmuffs to hide her ears. If whoever was after her had access to any CCTVs or facial recognition software they shouldn't be able to locate her. She'd since taken off the disguise so that her wavy auburn hair was down and around her face.

She stood and he had the strongest urge to pull her into his arms, to comfort her. So he did. He didn't give a shit what anyone else thought either. It had been so damn long since he'd felt this way about anyone. The truth was what he felt for Tegan was more than a case of lust. More than anything he'd experienced in the past. She was so easy to be around.

She leaned into his hold, burying her face against his chest. "They asked a billion questions," she muttered. "And they asked the same question ten different ways. Like they think I'm freaking stupid, or lying."

Both Carlito and Porter snorted quietly, clearly not surprised.

She pulled back and looked at Porter curiously. "I know you from somewhere. You're Lizzy's husband. She was showing off a picture of your son at the shop a while ago and you were in it."

Porter flushed, surprising Aaron. He cleared his throat. "Yeah, she said she'd met you." He looked back at Aaron. "When you told me you needed time off, I didn't realize it had to do with that bombing until Carlito called me."

Carlito leaned against the front of his desk, watching them in silence.

"If you need a safe house we'll set one up," Porter continued.

Tegan's eyes widened slightly as she looked up at Aaron, the question in her blue gaze. Did he want her to go to one?

He quickly weighed the idea. No one knew where she was, and they'd taken all precautions to keep her location quiet so that even the Feds didn't know she was with him. His son was safe and with his parents for the next few days. Since Dillon was on Christmas break he didn't have to worry about school either. Bottom line, if Tegan went to a safe house, she'd be away from him.

Nope, not happening.

He looked at Porter. "She's good with me. If that changes, I'll let you know."

Porter nodded once, as if he'd expected the answer. "I'd like to set up extra security. Something subtle. One agent in front of your place keeping an eye on things."

Yeah, Aaron had thought of the same thing. "I'll pay—"

Porter cut him off with a shake of his head. "This is pro bono. Call it a Christmas present. Anyone could have been hurt in that bombing. Her car was outside a children's boutique." Porter's jaw tightened, rage bleeding into his eyes as he took a breath. "We want to help."

"We?" Tegan asked.

"Me, my brothers—Red Stone. We won't tolerate this kind of shit in our city."

Tegan blinked once but Aaron wasn't surprised. The owners of Red Stone were civic-minded, but if Porter thought Aaron considered Tegan his, then his boss would go out of his way to keep her safe.

Porter held out the laptop bag to Tegan. "This is for you. Carlito said you'd be taking time off work at the coffee shop but would be working on your design business. My wife told me that this laptop is heavily encrypted so if anyone tries to track your movements online, you'll be safe."

Aaron had been with Red Stone Security for five years and, while he'd always been happy with his job and knew the guys he worked with were good men, this went above and beyond anything he'd expected. He'd have never asked for this kind of assistance. Hell, he hadn't even thought about her laptop.

Tegan looked at Porter, wide-eyed, her surprised expression adorable. She seemed to be shocked that anyone was helping her at all, let alone for free.

"Thank you," she finally murmured, looking unsure as she took it.

Porter cleared his throat, flicked a glance at Carlito, and said, "We're looking into De Fiore, too."

Carlito sighed and pushed up from the desk. "Yeah, I'm not hearing this. I'm gonna grab some coffee. I'll be back in a few minutes."

Tegan frowned as the detective closed the door behind him. "What just happened?"

Aaron wrapped an arm around her shoulders and pulled her close. "Carlito doesn't want to hear what we're talking about. Porter has no business looking into De Fiore but Lizzy is...good with computers."

Tegan frowned slightly. "Oh. Okay. So she's researching him?"

"Not exactly." Porter's voice was dry. "More like she's hunting him. If he's alive, there's a good chance she'll find him. Just depends on how far underground he is."

Now Tegan's eyes widened. "You mean she's, like, a hacker?"

Porter didn't answer one way or another but his expression was enough.

"Okay, wow. I...can see that." Tegan's lips curved into a grin. "I started talking code to her about one of the websites I was redesigning and she totally geeked out. She's one of the few people to ever understand me."

Porter just snorted. "If there's anything you think might be pertinent about De Fiore, anything you know, send it to her."

"Ah, I will, but I really don't know much about him. Other than he's a monster who threatened to kill me and maybe tried to kill me yesterday. Also, I don't know how to contact Lizzy."

"I've got her info," Aaron murmured.

"Good, then. I'm heading out." Porter looked between the two of them. "I don't know that I'll even be there if my sister-in-law goes into labor, but either way, bring Tegan to the Christmas party Friday if you guys are going stir crazy. My condo's one of the safest places in the city. We'll arrange a secure pickup so you don't drive your own vehicle and there's no possibility of either of you being seen inside or caught on a CCTV."

"I will." Aaron shook his hand, grateful to have such a good boss. He turned to Tegan as Porter left. "Red Stone has a lot of parties over the holidays. They're having one at Porter's place for the security teams directly under him. It's fun and he's right. His place is locked down tight and if we take the right precautions it'll be okay to take you."

Her brow furrowed slightly. "Don't feel like you have to take me. I'm just grateful you're giving me a place to lie low and that you've helped me with all this. If I go stir crazy it's a small price to pay for safety."

"I *want* to take you." And yeah, he was caveman enough to admit that he'd take pleasure in showing her off. If he thought the place wasn't secure, he'd never consider it but…taking Tegan to a Christmas party with his coworkers and friends? She was the kind of woman he wanted to bring with him. Sure, she was beautiful, but it was more than that. She was fun to be around and wouldn't freak out on him if he left her alone for a few minutes. She had no problem making conversation with other people. Unlike his ex—and he hated that he was even comparing the two of them. There was no comparison. Tegan was one of a kind.

"Yeah?"

"Yes. I would be proud to."

Her cheeks flushed an adorable shade of crimson. With her auburn hair and pale skin, it was impossible for her to hide her reactions, and he loved that he could read her so easily right now.

"We'll see how things go."

He could understand her cautiousness, but that didn't mean he had to like it. And at least it wasn't a no. His gaze dropped to her mouth and all his muscles pulled taut as he ordered his body under control. He was thirty-fucking-one, he'd been in control of his body a long damn time. Except around Tegan apparently. "Just we'll see?" he murmured.

Her eyes went heavy-lidded and whether she was aware of it or not, she leaned into him just a fraction. She inhaled slightly, as if she was smelling him. "I'm still trying to come to terms with this sweeter version of Aaron Fitzpatrick, rather than the man who used to growl at me every time I saw him."

"I never growled."

"Hmm."

"I'm a big teddy bear." He kept his voice low as he slowly reached for her, grasping one of her hips in a purely possessive hold.

When her lips curved up, he groaned. Her mouth had starred in all his fantasies in the past eight months. Every. Single. One. She'd consumed all his thoughts to the point of distraction.

Her bottom lip was just a little fuller so she looked as if she was always pouting. What he wouldn't give to—

The door opened and Carlito stepped in. He looked between them, his expression apologetic. "I've got a couple leads I need to follow up on De Fiore. I'm heading out."

And that was their cue to leave as well. Disappointment washed over Aaron that the kiss was interrupted, but he shelved it.

Sooner or later he was going to finally get a taste of Tegan. Once he did, he was pretty sure he wasn't letting her go.

Moving carefully, Alec scaled the fence to Tegan's backyard and jumped down. The yard was small and lined up perfectly with all the others on the street. He'd just called in multiple bomb threats to a school very close by, giving specific details of where the bombs were located and what he'd used to make them. The details—and the similarity to the bomb he'd used on Tegan O'Kelly's car—were too much for the cops to ignore.

The city was on alert after the car bombing so he knew that her security detail would be called off her house, at least temporarily.

Which was all he needed so he could get inside and kill her. If she was even there. And Alec wasn't sure she was. He'd been by her place of work and he'd heard her boss mention something to another employee about Tegan being away indefinitely.

It was twilight so he used the cover of falling darkness to make quick work of jimmying her sliding glass door open. The security here was shockingly pathetic. Inside he immediately saw the motion sensor so he paused where he was and listened.

It was quiet. The kind of quiet that told him he was alone. There was no dog to greet or attack him, and he knew she had a dog. Still, he had to be certain she wasn't here. Because he wasn't passing up an opportunity to kill her if she was.

Alec lay down on his belly. He was familiar with most security systems, and sensors were usually programed to ignore anything under two or three feet if the owner had a pet. Belly crawling, he made his way down a hallway until he reached the foyer.

When he stood in front of the keypad, the alarm started beeping so he popped the cover off and placed the device on it he'd used many times before. Less than ten seconds later, the beeping stopped.

If you're here, you're dead.

It wasn't personal, something he doubted she'd understand. Pulling out his weapon, he made his way upstairs. Considering no one had come to investigate the alarm going off he was almost positive he didn't need his gun, but being prepared had saved his ass on more than one occasion. It was why he was always armed and, more often than not, wore gloves. No need to leave behind any trace of himself.

He swept the entire upstairs then focused on her bedroom. No laptop, and it was clear some clothes were missing from her closet. Not many, but enough empty hangers indicated she might have packed a bag.

After he finished checking the rest of the house, he saw that her dishwasher was empty, there were no dirty dishes in the sink, and the sink was completely dry, as if it hadn't been used in at least a day. And her heat had been turned off.

His gut told him she was hiding out somewhere. He just hoped she hadn't gone on the run again. Looking around her place, he didn't think she had. There were too many things she owned still here, things she wouldn't leave behind.

In her small office he riffled through what few files she had. Like most people she would pay whatever bills she had online anyway. Still, he needed a clue to where the hell she was.

When he found nothing, he headed out the way he'd come and set the alarm to away mode so it would arm itself. He made sure there was no trace that he'd ever been there.

Though he was frustrated, he kept his annoyance in check. He was a professional and used to setbacks. Hunting people took time. For years he'd done freelance work, just killing for hire. Now he had a boss and, though Alec knew he'd be angry that she wasn't dead yet, the man would just have to deal with it. In his opinion, his boss should have killed her long ago.

But De Fiore hadn't shown an interest in hunting her after he'd 'died.' Not at first anyway. A couple of weeks ago, De Fiore had made contact with Alec, of all people, and told him he might need help with getting a new false ID once he killed the O'Kelly woman. De Fiore hadn't been sure how things would play out here in Miami and wanted a backup ID in case the one he already had in place somehow got flagged.

Alec was simply going to flush pretty Tegan O'Kelly out if he couldn't find her. Make the bitch come to him. Sometimes that was the only way to do things, to make your prey come to you. He couldn't risk De Fiore getting to her first.

Once Alec was in the safety of his newly stolen car, he turned on the voice digitizer app and called her cell phone.

No surprise, it went directly to voice mail. "If you make me hunt you down any longer I'm going to start killing your friends. I'll start with your whore boss and her son. I'll record their deaths so you can watch them both beg and scream. I'll do the kid first." He ended the call and tossed the phone out the window. The phone was a burner but he wouldn't be using it anymore in case the cops tried to track him.

He wasn't actually going to kill a kid—he did have some scruples after all—but he knew the message would freak her out. It might make her scared enough to get sloppy.

He didn't think the message would make her come out of hiding.

Not yet anyway. He was going to leave more messages and make each one worse than the last.

The messages would put her on edge and guarantee she'd call her friends to check on them. From the little he'd watched Tegan he knew she was close with the woman who owned the bakery. A few more messages like that and Tegan O'Kelly would be compelled to call her friends. Once she did, he'd be able to get a location on her—because he was watching her boss's cell phone, waiting for any call from Tegan. Soon enough he'd get a lock on her location. From there, he'd track her down and put a bullet in her head.

CHAPTER SEVEN

Aaron stopped outside the entryway to his living room and eavesdropped on Tegan and Dillon. It had been almost two days since she'd talked to the Feds and so far neither they nor the Miami PD had been able to locate De Fiore. If he was even *in* Miami. Aaron knew they were exploring all leads on the bomber and so far all the cops had been able to find was a few images of a man in a hoodie heading down the street where the bomb had been placed.

They had a time frame for when they thought it had been planted. It had been early in the morning and the man's image had been caught on multiple CCTVs. But the guy had disappeared into the parking garage of a hotel and from there they hadn't been able to trace him anywhere. Without an actual face or fingerprints, they were hunting a ghost. It could be De Fiore or not.

"You don't have to let me win, you know," Dillon said.

"I'm not. I just stink at this game." Tegan's voice was matter of fact.

Dillon giggled, the sound music to Aaron's ears. He might have screwed up by marrying the wrong woman, but he'd gotten Dillon so it was worth it.

"You really are bad. Not as bad as Daddy. We can play something else if you want."

"It's okay, it's still fun. So your dad stinks, too?"

Dillon gave a belly laugh. "He can't even get past level two."

Tegan laughed loudly and Aaron risked peeking around the entryway. The Christmas tree twinkled in the corner, brightening the room. The two of them were sitting on the ground in front of the television, their backs to him. Kali was snoozing next to Tegan, her body stretched out as she lightly snored. Dillon was wearing his Captain America pajamas and Tegan had on a black party dress with a big puffy skirt that had sparkles all over it. It puffed out around her on the ground. Her hair was pulled up in a twist, revealing the smooth, pale skin of her neck and back.

He'd never really thought of backs as sexy, but everything about Tegan was.

Unfortunately, they hadn't had much time alone together since the meeting in Carlito's office. She'd been working on her website designs for the past day and a half, and he was pretty certain she'd been keeping him at a healthy distance after their almost-kiss. Much to his annoyance. He was patient, though. And determined.

"So…are you my dad's girlfriend now?"

Tegan's entire body jolted and he watched as the character on her side of the screen fell off a cliff. She cleared her throat. "Ah, no. We're just friends."

Unfortunately, he thought. He planned to change that soon, though.

"Yeah, that's what he said. I just thought maybe…you guys might not wanna tell me."

"I don't think your dad would ever lie to you."

"I know. But I heard Nana talking to Grandpa about you when they thought I was asleep. She said you were lovely and that it was about time Daddy moved on. I don't really know what she means but I know she likes you. I thought maybe you might be my new mommy."

Aaron winced. Tegan was silent for a long moment and he wasn't sure if he should interrupt the conversation or just let it play out. Dillon had asked about 'getting a new mommy' a couple of times in the last few months so this wasn't exactly out of the blue. He'd even put *mommy* on his Christmas list for Santa. Aaron hated that his son had missed out on a solid, loving, maternal presence.

"I like your dad but we really are just friends. He's helping me out right now by letting me stay here. So how about I be your friend, too?"

"I'd like that. You know, Nana lets me have ice cream whenever I want. Now that we're friends, maybe you can give me ice cream when I want, too."

Tegan snorted. "Your Nana lets you get away with a lot. And the answer is no. You're already killing me in this game. I can't reward that."

"So if I let you win, you'll give me ice cream?"

Tegan barked out a laugh. "No, but nice try."

Aaron quickly moved out of sight as the doorbell chimed. He waited a few beats then stepped into the foyer and in full view of the living room.

"Nana!" Dillon flew past him, moving at light speed before Aaron reached the door.

"Wait." Aaron hurried to the door and looked through the peephole before opening it. He'd tried to explain to Dillon why they had to be extra careful right now but, at five, he just didn't understand the concept of real danger. He barely understood 'stranger danger.'

Aaron pulled open the door and smiled when he saw his mom and dad bundled up in their winter coats. They were earlier than they needed to be, which...was nice. He wondered if his mom had planned that. The Red Stone driver wouldn't be here for another hour. Which would give him much wanted alone time with Tegan.

Dillon jumped into his dad's arms as Aaron hugged his mom. "Thanks for keeping him tonight." They'd agreed to take him so he and Tegan could attend the Christmas party.

Part of him didn't want to go—he'd rather stay here with no one but Tegan for company—but he figured she could use some time away from her voluntary lockdown. She was so positive about everything, never complaining. He wanted to give this to her.

"We should be thanking you," his mom said, kissing him on the cheek. Her gaze strayed past him to Tegan, who he heard entering the foyer. "You look stunning, dear."

"Thank you," she murmured.

Aaron turned around and got the full view of her—and forgot to breathe. He'd only seen her back so far but this…

Her blue eyes seemed bigger, brighter tonight. Her makeup was darker, smoky, and he realized her dress was a dark blue, not black. It shimmered when she moved toward him. She had an almost hesitant smile on her face.

He tried not to stare, but he swept his gaze over her, taking in everything. Her heels were strappy, lacing around her ankles and sexy as fuck. He imagined her wearing nothing but them, digging the spikes into his back as he buried his face between her legs. And the pain would be worth it to taste her, pleasure her. All the tension from the last couple of days coiled tight in his belly as he watched her. He was so damn hungry for her. He was vaguely aware of the others talking but he just stared at Tegan until he felt a sharp nudge against his rib cage from his mom.

"You look beautiful," he rasped out, knowing he needed to say something.

Tegan smiled, her shoulders seeming to lose their tension at his words. As if she could doubt how incredible she was. She was a goddess.

"Well, we're going to get out of your hair," his mother said, already snapping the leash onto Kali's collar. "I don't want you to be late."

Oh yeah, she'd definitely come early for a reason. Aaron could hear it in the tone of her voice.

"And it's hot cocoa time!" Dillon was jumping up and down by the open front door as his dad helped Dillon into his jacket.

Aaron smiled at his son's excitement. "I'll have my phone on me and—"

"I know all that," his mom said, waving a hand in the air. "We've done this a thousand times. We're watching a Christmas movie tonight and having popcorn and hot cocoa. We'll be fine. I'll see you in the morning."

He knew they would be okay, but it was still habit to go over everything with them.

Once Dillon had hugged both him and Tegan and they were gone, he shut the door behind them, glad to be alone with her. Guilt slid through him because he loved his son more than anything, but he craved some alone time with Tegan. Desperately.

If he had anything to say about it, the walls she'd put up between them were coming down tonight. "You really are beautiful." The words came out raspier than before. He couldn't stop staring at her, wanting her. He tried to shove back his impatience that things between them were moving so slow.

Her cheeks flushed pink. "You said cocktail party-type dress so…I thought this would work."

It worked all right. Too well.

He took a step closer to her, wanting to touch her. They'd almost kissed in Carlito's office and it was all he'd been able to think about the past two days. He'd been trying to keep himself on lockdown for her because it had been clear she was keeping a stupid wall between them. For so damn long it had felt as if he was existing in a haze. He'd been living a celibate existence that would have been foreign to him before five years ago. Now all his control and patience were on a wire's edge. "I want to kiss you right now."

Her eyes widened at his blunt statement. "Aaron, you can't…just say that."

"Yes I can." He covered the rest of the short distance between them, his shoes quiet against the wood floor. He didn't reach out and touch her even though his entire body ached with the need to do just that. "I want to taste all of you. Shove that pretty dress up to your waist and bury my face between your legs. I want to make you come so hard you can barely walk afterward."

Her eyes grew even wider, her breathing shaky and erratic as she stared at him, her mouth parting just a fraction. There was a slight gloss to her pink lips.

"Nothing to say to that?" he murmured. His libido revved to life whenever he was around her. He wanted nothing more than to devour Tegan. He wasn't holding back anything now. He'd realized that by playing it passive, by not being more direct with her, he was cheating them both out of something that could be amazing. He knew he could get burned by her, but he was done with living like a monk. She'd woken something up inside him and he wasn't going to run from it. She made him feel alive again in the most primal way.

Her eyes were dilated as she swallowed hard, watching him with a mix of emotions. One of them was fear. He knew she wasn't afraid of him so maybe it was just what was between them.

"Just think about my words all night while we're at the party. It's what I'm going to be thinking about doing to you. What I think about all the damn time—what I thought about this morning while I jerked off in the shower." He knew he was pushing her and didn't care. Those walls had to come down.

Her cheeks were bright crimson now. "Aaron…"

A groan tore from him. "I love it when you say my name." He'd imagined her saying it under very different circumstances.

A shudder racked her and she took a step forward. She lifted a hand as if to touch him, but dropped it just as quickly. "I'm not ready for…a relationship. So much is going on and you're a dad and…I just, I don't think it would work."

Every single thing she said was an excuse. "Do you want me?"

She blinked those pretty blue eyes. "Yes, of course."

The way she said *of course,* as if the need was a given, made his cock even harder. "Then that's all that matters. If you want to keep things between us casual, whatever happens can be just between us." Complete and utter bullshit, but he was going to get through her barriers. Whatever she seemed to think wouldn't work between them, he'd just tear up all her excuses one day at a time until there was nothing keeping them apart. If that meant keeping things between them quiet, that was okay. For now.

She bit her bottom lip. "Really?" The word was a whisper. He could see that she wanted to kiss him, that he was breaking through her defenses.

He advanced on her and she took a step back. He kept moving until her back was against the wall by the staircase and he was pressed against her from chest to groin.

Her breathing was erratic as she looked up at him. His cock pressed hard against her abdomen. There was no way she could doubt he wanted her.

When she placed tentative hands on his chest, he slowly lowered his head, giving her enough time to tell him to stop. If she didn't, absolutely nothing was going to interrupt them this time.

Her eyes started to close and she leaned up to meet him. She let out a little sigh of pleasure as their lips finally touched.

Even though he wanted to slide his fingers through her thick hair, the twist looked complicated and he didn't want to mess it up. He gently gripped the side of her neck and part of her jaw so that he could feel her pulse point.

It was going crazy.

She moaned into his mouth as he kissed her and nipped at his bottom lip. He loved the feel of her tongue and sweet kisses. He wasn't sure how long he lost himself in tasting her, their mouths and tongues teasing each other.

When she arched into him, rubbing against him with her whole body, he pulled back just a fraction so he could kiss a path along her jaw and neck. She sucked in a breath when he reached the juncture of her neck and shoulder.

His control was close to breaking, his cock rock hard, but right now was about her. He wanted to worship her entire body, to spend hours learning all her curves. For now, he was going to taste her as she came against his face. He was going to get her addicted to him and he wanted to stake a claim on her sweet body. She'd be thinking about him all night after this, about how he'd made her feel.

Her hands slid through his short hair, her fingers gripping him as he bent down in front of her. He looked up the length of her body to see her staring down at him, her blue eyes bright with hunger.

Keeping his gaze locked on hers, he reached under the puffy skirt of her dress, his hands skimming up the outside of her smooth thighs until he reached the silky material of her panties. Oh so slowly, he tugged them down her legs, his heart pounded wildly.

Her breath caught in her throat as she stepped out of them. But she spread her legs apart just a little wider, the invitation clear.

This was hotter, more intense than he'd fantasized about. The skirt of her dress had too much material to shove up to her waist and stay in place, so he ducked his head under it. This was sexier anyway. Not being able to see her while he pleasured her, just hearing her moans. He wondered if she'd be loud or restrained. Either choice was a good one but he wanted to hear her go crazy and let go.

She let out a yelp of surprise as he moved between her legs and lifted one over his shoulder, draping it across his back and giving him all the access he needed.

The dim light of the foyer filtered through enough that he could see her sweet pussy. She was completely bare—shaved or waxed, he couldn't tell. Didn't matter. The sight made him groan. Before he tasted her, he dipped a finger between her folds.

She was soaked. The knowledge that she was turned on because of him sent another rush of heat spiraling through him.

Whatever excuses she came up with as for why now wasn't the right time for a relationship, she couldn't deny the chemistry they had together. That would have been impossible to do and be believable. He'd been fighting it from the moment he met the feisty woman.

Her hips rolled as he slid his finger deeper inside her. It was strange not being able to see her face, but incredibly sexy to be solely focused on her pussy and have her literally trembling as she waited to feel what he'd do.

"Aaron." She moaned out his name, as if begging him to do more.

He would gladly oblige. Burying his face between her legs, he flicked his tongue up the length of her wet folds. She groaned, her hips bucking against him as he teased her.

Her taste and scent were sweet perfection against his tongue. Almost as sweet as the little sounds of pleasure she was making. He was surprised by how loud she was, her pleas for him to do more making his cock even harder, something he hadn't thought possible.

"My clit, my clit," she moaned out, the words half begging, half demand.

The demand nearly pushed him over the edge. He hadn't expected that of her, but he probably should have. He'd been intent on teasing her longer, dragging this out, but he was driven with the need to make her come. To taste it. Knowing she was right on the precipice because of him. All the muscles in his body pulled tight, his focus purely on making her come.

Shifting his head slightly, he zeroed in on the little bundle of nerves peeking out from her folds. Her clit was already swollen and just begging for his touch. He rubbed his tongue over it as he slid a finger fully inside her. She was so tight, her inner walls clenching around him as he began stroking her clit.

Her hips moved in rhythm with his tongue, her moans louder and louder, telling him that he was playing her body right. She was absolute perfection.

He added another finger, buried them both deep. She jerked hard, dug her heeled shoe into his back as her inner walls clenched harder around his fingers.

"Oh…Aaron…" Her climax hit, and her body writhed against him as she came.

He continued stroking her clit, not letting up the pressure until she begged him to stop. He swiped his tongue against her one last time before ducking back out from under her skirt.

His entire body trembled with the need to fill her, his cock pressing insistently against his zipper. This had been about her, though.

Her eyes were heavy-lidded as she looked down at him, her breathing erratic and an expression of pure satisfaction on her face. After pressing soft kisses to her inner ankle and thigh, he reached back, gently wrapped his fingers around her ankle, and brought her foot off his back.

When he set her foot on the ground, he wanted nothing more than to strip her dress off completely and bury himself inside her. But he was pretty sure it was too soon for that. Not for him, but he didn't want to push her too fast. Not when he knew she was hesitant to commit to anything. He wanted her to come to him, to have no regrets about them. Because once they crossed that line, he wouldn't let her go. Not without a fight.

She grabbed his shoulders and tugged on him. He obeyed her silent command and stood, his legs shaking. To his surprise, she started unbuckling his pants.

He groaned, letting her take over. Grasping the back of her head, he slid his fingers through her hair. He didn't give a fuck if it got messed up now. He wanted to stamp himself on all of her, so that when she looked in the mirror she saw him there, imprinted on her in the subtlest of ways.

"Fuck, Tegan," he rasped out as she shoved his pants and boxers down.

Her elegant fingers wrapped around his hard length, gripping him at the base. He rocked into her hold, crushing his mouth against hers as she started stroking him. God, it had been so damn long, and knowing it was Tegan touching him…

She pumped him hard, making him lose any train of thought so that all he could do was feel that soft hand bringing him the sweetest pleasure.

His balls pulled up tight as his climax started to build. He wished he was inside her, that her tight sheath was wrapped around him as he came. That would come soon enough, though.

The base of his spine tingled, his orgasm so damn close. Though he hated to pull away from her, at the last minute he pulled back and took over, coming all over his shirt and stomach instead of her dress. She might not care but she looked so fucking gorgeous, and even though he wanted to mark her, he held back. Next time he'd come in her or on her stomach, mark her with himself. Yeah, it was a fucking primitive thought, but she apparently brought out that side of him.

Hunger glittered in her gaze as she watched him, drinking in the sight of him as he finished himself off. Her lips were parted slightly, glossy from their kiss.

As the last of his orgasm ripped through him, he threw his head back, groaning her name. When he opened his eyes, she was still watching him. She looked so damn sexy and just a little vulnerable standing there with wisps of hair tumbling around her face, her lips swollen.

"You're the sexiest woman I've ever fucking met," he rasped out, hating that his words didn't come close to how he felt about her.

She smiled, though, and half her mouth pulled up in a sweet, sensual movement that he felt to his core.

"I didn't let you finish because I didn't want to mess up your dress. Next time though…" He let the words hang in the air, letting her fill in whatever blanks she wanted.

"Next time?" she whispered.

"There will be a next time."

At that she smiled, and something inside him loosened that he hadn't even realized was coiled tight.

He leaned down and brushed his lips across hers, needing to taste her again. "I've gotta get cleaned up," he murmured, hating to pull away from her.

Looking a little dazed, she lifted a hand to her hair and half laughed. "I think I probably need to as well."

After a long moment, she pushed away from the wall, her cheeks still pink as she made her way to the stairs.

He wanted to forget the party and just stay there with her, to take her to bed and spend hours pleasuring each other. But their driver would arrive soon.

And he could be patient. He was pretty sure he'd pushed her enough for right now. At the party he planned to flirt with her, tease her until she couldn't stand it. Then he'd make his move. Afterward he hoped they ended up very naked together. The first time of many to come.

CHAPTER EIGHT

Tegan stepped into Aaron's house and immediately disarmed the security system as Kali raced for the kitchen to get to her food and water bowl. She knew Aaron and Dillon wouldn't be there but a thread of disappointment still wound its way through her that they were gone. She'd thought last night would turn out very differently, that she would get to spend a lot of naked time with Aaron after the party.

But on the way there they'd gotten a call from Bree that Dillon had thrown up so they'd headed back and picked him up. The poor little guy had been puking all night so she'd slept in the living room on the opposite couch to Aaron and Dillon.

Aaron had told her that she hadn't needed to stay with them, but she'd really wanted to. Seeing Dillon's face so pale had scared her. Aaron had taken everything in stride, though, handling it like a boss. The man was amazing to her. She'd been internally panicking, but Aaron had dealt with it so steadily, like he seemed to do everything. Even though Dillon's fever was down and he'd stopped throwing up, Aaron had taken him to a walk-in clinic this morning.

She'd wanted to go, especially since Dillon had asked her to, but it wasn't a possibility. So far no one knew about her connection to Aaron and she wasn't going to make them targets by potentially being seen with them in public. Last night they'd taken protective measures with a driver and an armored vehicle that no one could possibly see inside so she wouldn't be caught on any CCTVs or traffic cameras. It wouldn't be as easy today and it wasn't worth risking. Nothing was worth risking Aaron or Dillon's safety.

After hanging up her coat, scarf, and hat—all of which doubled as her camouflage while out walking her dog—she hooked Kali's leash next to her stuff. Holding onto her gloves, she followed after Kali, who'd collapsed in a heap by her food and water bowls, apparently exhausted from their long walk.

Since Tegan wasn't using her cell phone, she picked up Aaron's landline. It was a little weird using an actual landline since she hadn't in years.

"Hey, you," Kimmy said, picking up on the second ring. She was one of the very few people who knew where Tegan was staying.

"Hey, yourself. How's everything going?"

Kimmy gave a short laugh. "I think I should be asking you that."

"Ah, well enough." Her face heated up as she thought about what she and Aaron had done the night before, how he'd gone down on her right up against the wall—how she'd begged him. Her nipples pebbled just thinking about it. "It's weird being disconnected from everything and not being able to go home. But it is what it is." Eight months ago she would have been used to being disconnected. Now, after settling into a new life, she'd gotten used to being able to call friends when she wanted and do things when she wanted. Not look over her shoulder like a hunted fugitive. It infuriated her that someone had forced her to change all that again.

"I'm sure you're going to have a ton of voice mails. Everyone's been asking about you at the shop."

She inwardly cringed. Crap. She'd been checking her e-mail and staying up to date with her design projects the last few days but she hadn't checked her voice mail since everything happened. *Crap, crap, crap.* She'd been in contact with her insurance company about her car and had given them Aaron's home phone number to contact instead of her cell. "How's everyone else doing? Are all the shops open?"

"Things are kinda tense down here, but all the shops are open and, surprisingly, we're all doing incredible business. I guess people are just morbid or something and want to see where the bomb went off because we're getting a lot of new business. Cops have been down here, too, more than once, questioning and re-questioning everyone."

"I just hope they find whoever did it." A shiver racked through her, chills dotting her arms and the back of her neck. The longer it took for the police or FBI to find any leads, the harder it was for her to stay positive.

"No kidding. Let me know if you need anything. I haven't told anyone where you are. Most people are just glad you're okay but some of the shop owners are freaking nosy." She snorted. "Old Mr. Pritchett was insistent he know where you are. It was ridiculous. I told him if the cops thought he should know, they'd tell him."

Tegan laughed, not at all surprised. Mr. Pritchett ran the hardware store and was grumpy twenty-four-seven. It was his only setting. And not grumpy like Aaron used to be. Mr. Pritchett was a fussy old man who gossiped more than anyone she'd ever met. "I'm just glad everyone's okay and that the businesses weren't affected."

"Me, too."

They talked for a few minutes and once they disconnected she used Aaron's phone to call her voice mail. Kali whined at the back door as she started listening. Twenty-two new messages. Not as bad as she'd expected but still, yikes.

She opened the back door, letting her dog out as she started listening to her voice mail. Leaning against the doorframe, she watched Kali race around the yard. When she got to the tenth message her blood iced over as a digital voice came across the line.

"If you make me hunt you down any longer I'm going to start killing your friends. I'll start with your whore boss and her son. I'll record their deaths so you can watch them both beg and scream. I'll do the kid first."

Her fingers were numb as the call ended. Fumbling, she saved the message then disconnected.

She called Kimmy back, her heart pounding erratically in her chest. *Pick up, pick up –*

"Hey—"

"Where's Brendan? Is he okay?"

"He's fine. He's here today, actually. What's going on?" Kimmy's voice went from calm to worried in a second.

"I just got a creepy message from someone saying they're going to hurt you and Brendan. Their voice was disguised so I don't know who it was, but it could have been the person who planted the bomb." She hated even saying the words out loud. She almost felt as if once she did it would give credence to them, to put the reality out there in the universe.

Kimmy sucked in a sharp breath.

"Is Callan with you?"

"Yeah, he's been helping out all week. He and Brendan are in the back making cookies."

Some of the tension around Tegan's chest eased, but not by much. She needed them to be safe, not out in public for some lunatic to attack. "Okay, good. I'm going to call the detective on the case and tell him about this. I just wanted to make sure you were okay. Are you going to get Brendan out of there?"

"Yeah. Jeez, this is crazy." She let out a shaky sigh. "I'm going to close the shop right now and get out of here." Kimmy's voice was trembling and Tegan couldn't blame her.

The bomb was terrifying enough but this direct threat against people she cared for was worse. She kept playing those words over and over in her head. "Good. I'll call you in an hour." After she got out of there and to a safe house. She had to get away, for Aaron and Dillon's sake. "I've got to call the cops and let them know about this." For all she knew they'd be able to track where the call to her phone had come from. She also needed to call Porter Caldwell and see if he'd been serious about that safe house offer because she wasn't staying there a moment longer.

She knew Aaron would try to convince her to stay but it wasn't happening. Whoever had left that message had no problem threatening kids. So far very few people knew where she was staying or her link to Aaron. She planned to keep it that way.

Getting far away from him as soon as possible was her only option.

Tegan's hands trembled as she pulled out a suitcase from her closet. "You don't have to stay here while I pack." If anything, the uniformed police officer's presence made her even shakier. It was a reminder that she was in danger, that her house wasn't safe right now. This was the place she'd made her own, where she'd added her personal touches, where she'd felt freaking safe when she put her head on her pillow at night. She wondered if she'd ever feel safe again.

After calling Detective Duarte, he'd sent over the uniformed officer who'd been watching her place to pick her up since he'd been the closest to Aaron's home. She'd been ready to call a cab, anything to get away from Aaron's place as fast as possible.

Being there had felt like she was contaminating his home, making him *and* Dillon targets. Aaron was going to be upset that she'd left, but she hadn't been willing to wait. She wasn't sure how long he'd be at the clinic anyway.

The officer nodded politely. "I'll be downstairs if you need me." He was about six feet tall with dark hair and dark eyes, and his solid presence reminded her of Aaron. Which just made her feel crappier.

Before the man had taken two steps back toward her bedroom door, the doorbell rang. "Stay put," he ordered. The officer tensed and placed his hand on the butt of his secured weapon. He didn't draw it, but he hurried out the door and down the stairs.

She figured it was a neighbor or possibly a reporter but still tensed as she followed after him. She stayed at the top of the stairs, mostly following his orders. It wouldn't be Carlito yet—he'd told her that he was in Coconut Grove following up on an anonymous tip about an

Enzo De Fiore sighting. He said it sounded legit so she was hopeful he'd find the bastard.

Knock, knock, knock. "Tegan? I saw you drive up with the police. Is everything okay?" a muted female voice called.

Tension easing from her shoulders, Tegan hurried down the stairs as the officer turned to her, a question in his gaze.

"I know her. Name's Gina. She's a neighbor and a regular at my part-time job." The woman came in every day to get donuts or crepes or some sort of high-carb snack—and never seemed to put on an ounce. She must live at the gym. Or maybe just had ridiculous genes.

The officer nodded after looking through the peephole again and then opened the door.

"Oh..." Gina stepped back, her smile faltering as she came face-to-face with the officer, even though she had to know there was a cop there. His vehicle was in the driveway. Kinda hard to miss.

He seemed speechless, too, but more likely because of her Jessica Rabbit curves.

Gina flicked a glance over at Tegan, who was a few feet behind him. "I just wanted to stop by and see you. I brought homemade cookies." She held them up tentatively and gave a megawatt smile to the officer—who blinked, almost in a daze as he stared at her.

Right about now talking to people and making polite conversation where she pretended to be okay was the last thing Tegan wanted to do, but Gina had been up at the hospital after the bombing. They weren't exactly friends, but she lived a few doors down and always came into Kimmy's place. Tegan would feel like the biggest jerk if she turned her away. "Ah, I'm not going to be here for long, but come in for a few minutes. I appreciate you stopping by."

"Oh, I won't stay long. I just saw you get out of the police car and wanted to come over and make sure you were okay. It's good timing, too. I just finished this batch of cookies."

Tegan smiled, stepping forward as Gina entered. "We'll be fine. I'm just going to finish up packing," she said to the officer.

"Packing?" Gina popped off the lid to the white chocolate chip macadamia nut cookies. "They're fresh," she murmured to the officer. "Want one?"

He nodded, taking one. "Thank you."

"So, packing?" Gina asked again, falling in step with Tegan, who just wanted to get the hell out of her place and to the safe house Porter said he'd have ready for her.

"Ah, yeah. Just heading out of town for a few days." Not exactly true, but after talking to Carlito, she'd called Porter. He'd been adamant that she not tell anyone where she was going—as if she would anyway. She *liked* breathing. Even telling one person where the safe house was could put them and her in danger.

"Have the police found any leads about the bombing? They've been questioning everyone in this neighborhood and down by the shop. I've been questioned *three* times." Gina sat on the edge of Tegan's bed while she returned to her closet.

It was a little weird that Gina was here, but Tegan knew this was what people did. It was human nature. They brought over food and wanted to know what was going on in situations like this. Especially since they were neighbors. Still, Tegan just wanted her gone.

"I think they have a few leads." It wasn't like she could tell her anything anyway. Carlito and the FBI had been careful not to leak any information that Enzo De Fiore might be involved. Publicly they were treating it as a potential terrorist attack, not an attack against her personally. They didn't want to tip their hand that they thought De Fiore might still be alive.

"It's so scary that something like that could happen right here in Miami."

Tegan nodded, pulling a couple of shirts off a hanger. "Yeah."

"You want a cookie? They're still warm."

"I'm okay, but thanks."

"You're sure?"

Tegan turned from her closet at the odd note in Gina's voice. She sat cross-legged on the edge of Tegan's bed, her low-cut sweater showing off an insane amount of cleavage. For the first time since Tegan had met the woman, she noticed she was wearing flat black sneakers instead of her normally spiked high heels. "Yeah, I'm not really hungry. But they look great." She tried to inject some positivity into her voice, but she was mentally exhausted and, yeah, depressed that she wouldn't be staying at Aaron's anymore.

Last night, before the party they'd never made it to, had been wonderful. *Incredible.* It had been so damn long since she'd been intimate with anyone. And Aaron wasn't just *anyone.* She trusted him, adored him, and despite her better judgment had completely fallen for him. Even as she'd told herself not to, to keep her distance, it was impossible to resist him.

Gina pressed the top back onto the cookie container and sealed them in. She sighed as she did it, making Tegan feel guilty. She could force a stupid cookie down if it would make the woman feel better.

Before she could say anything, Gina reached into her clutch purse and pulled out a small gun.

Tegan sucked in a breath and stared at the weapon. "Gina, what—"

"Shut the fuck up," Gina said quietly. "You should have eaten that damn cookie and made things a hell of a lot easier on yourself."

Her body went numb. "You poisoned the cop?"

Gina rolled her eyes and pushed to her feet. Her perfectly manicured hands looked steady as she held the gun on Tegan. "He'll wake up in an hour or two with a headache." She used the gun to motion to the door. "We're leaving now. Stay in front of me and don't try anything stupid. You do, I'll shoot you in the fucking knee."

Tegan dropped the shirt she'd been clutching and somehow made her legs obey her brain. She barely remembered moving but found herself downstairs in the foyer. The cop was slumped against the door, looking almost peaceful. A quarter of the cookie was crumbled on the shiny wood floor next to one of his open hands.

"Move him out of the way," Gina snapped.

Tegan looked back at her. Gina was still holding the gun and had it pointed right at her head. "Why are you doing this?" She was going to have to get out of this on her own. But she needed to know what she was up against.

Gina lifted a shoulder, not answering one way or another. "I'm doing it for Enzo, you stupid bitch. Stop asking questions. Now move that guy. Just roll him over so we can get out the door."

Doing as she said, Tegan grunted as she shifted the man to the side. At least he was breathing. She just hoped that Gina had been telling the truth, that the guy would wake up soon. For a brief moment she contemplated taking the cop's gun, but it was secured in a holster. By the time she unsnapped it, pulled it out, and turned, she'd already be shot in the back.

When they stepped out into the bright sunshine, Tegan had to shield her eyes. Only the cop car sat in the driveway. Gina must have just walked from her place—oh God. Was Enzo there right now?

More ice settled around her chest, making it hard to breathe when she saw two little kids playing across the street as their mom watched. Even if she wanted to scream and make a scene, there was no way she could risk putting anyone else in danger.

Tegan had no idea how dangerous Gina truly was—and that probably wasn't even her real name. As Tegan turned to see how far behind her Gina was, she inwardly cringed.

Gina stepped up right beside her and pressed the gun into her ribs. She was using one of Tegan's jackets to cover it up. Must have grabbed it from the coatrack in the foyer.

"We're just going to walk down to my place and you're going to have a little talk with my Enzo. You'll tell him what he wants and we'll all go our separate ways." Her voice was a low murmur as they walked across the little stone path that led to the sidewalk.

Tegan's instinct told her to simply stop moving, to refuse to go any farther. But she didn't know this woman at all. She had no idea if she would hurt those kids or just shoot Tegan and run. She knew for a fact the woman was lying to her. Tegan wouldn't be walking away from this. There was no way they'd leave her alive once they got what they wanted—or didn't in this case. Once they realized she didn't have what they wanted she'd be useless. Disposable.

As they reached the sidewalk, Aaron's familiar blue truck pulled into the driveway.

Oh God. *No, no, no.* She hadn't even seen him driving down the road, hadn't been able to focus on anything other than Gina and the gun. There was nowhere to go, nowhere to hide from him. "Let me get rid of him. If you hurt him, you'll never get your fucking diamonds," Tegan said through gritted teeth. They would never get them anyway, at least not from Tegan. But she had no problem bluffing to save Aaron's life. She couldn't let him get hurt because of her. It wasn't an option.

The woman's dark eyes narrowed slightly but she nodded. "Do it fast," she murmured.

Aaron's truck shuddered to a halt and the big, sexy man jumped out, slamming the door before he hurried toward her, moving like a lethal predator.

A mix of concern and, yeah, anger played across his features. He flicked a glance at Gina, who was still standing incredibly close to Tegan, and nodded once in a half greeting.

"What the hell are you doing?" he snapped, clearly not caring that they had an audience. He clutched a piece of paper in his hand and she realized it was the note she'd left him.

Bone-numbing fear punched through her. Why the hell had he come? "I…can't stay with you anymore. What we had was nice but I'm not interested in playing mom for your kid." The words were harsh but it was the only thing she could think of to get him to leave. "Don't call me again." She also hoped he realized that she was in danger and called the cops. Regardless, she just needed him to let her *go.* All it would take for Gina to hurt him was to raise that gun and pull the trigger.

A wave of nausea swept through her at the thought. She couldn't let that happen.

"Tegan—"

"Leave me alone!" Heat infused her words before she looked at Gina. "Come on. Let's go."

He stared at her wide-eyed, as if she'd slapped him in the face. As if he had no idea who she truly was.

He had to know better. God, she hoped so.

The whole scene was weird with the cop car in the driveway next to Aaron's truck—with no police escort in sight—and she silently prayed that Aaron realized that.

Gina tightened her fingers around Tegan's arm, hidden by the bulky jacket. The gun stayed pressed against her ribs as they started walking down the sidewalk. Once they reached the corner it wouldn't be long until they reached Gina's place. She couldn't believe Enzo had been so close to her all this time. She'd never been safe. Not truly.

Tegan's legs were stiff as she walked. She resisted the urge to turn around, to look at Aaron. She couldn't risk—

Gina grunted as a huge blur of motion slammed into her from behind.

Aaron tackled Gina, moving like a pro football player as he knocked her to the ground. The gun clattered to the sidewalk.

Without thinking, Tegan lunged for it, grabbing it as Gina screamed out in rage. The sound cut off sharply as Aaron wrenched her arms behind her back.

Gina started whimpering in pain. "Please don't hurt me. He made me do it." Her voice was so different from the demanding, angry woman she'd been inside Tegan's house.

"Shut the fuck up," Aaron snarled.

Tegan held the gun at her side, unsure if she should train it on Gina, she was shaking so badly. It was clear Aaron had everything under control as he secured her wrists together with his huge hands.

"Are you okay?" he asked, looking up at her, fear etched into every line of his face.

She nodded. "Fine." She wasn't fine, but now wasn't the time to have a breakdown. Out of the corner of her eye she saw the woman across the street rushing her kids inside. Hopefully they'd call the cops. "I…oh my God, I need to check on the cop. And call Carlito."

Aaron paused for a moment then nodded. "Let's go."

"I think De Fiore might be at her place. She was taking me there. It's around the corner." Tegan pointed toward the end of the street. "It's not even a block down."

Aaron pulled out a pistol before he stood and yanked the woman to her feet. Keeping her wrists secured, he marched her back to Tegan's, ignoring Gina's protests as he propelled her. He was vigilant, looking over his shoulder and scanning the street like a trained warrior.

She couldn't believe he'd showed up but she was grateful he had. Emotion clogged her throat but she shoved it back down. Now wasn't the time to lose her cool.

"My cell's in my jacket pocket," he said.

She fished it out as they hurried back to her place, and avoided looking at Gina. She immediately called Carlito, her pulse hammering in her throat. If Enzo was truly at Gina's, the cops could arrest him now and her nightmare would finally be over.

CHAPTER NINE

Tegan sat in the cushy chair in front of Carlito's desk, watching Aaron pace back and forth like a caged wolf. After the cavalry had arrived and arrested Gina—and subsequently the SWAT team had stormed the woman's rented house and also arrested the not-so-dead Enzo De Fiore—they'd been taken to the police department. The FBI were currently foaming at the mouth trying to take De Fiore into their custody while Gina—whose real name was apparently Grace Gambino—was being interrogated by Carlito and another detective.

Tegan had answered dozens of questions from a detective and so had Aaron. They'd been separated, of course, but as of a few minutes ago, they'd basically both been dumped in Carlito's office.

Aaron had barely said two words to her. Watching him now felt like watching an angry predator. He wore a beige cable-knit sweater and dark slacks. The sweater sleeves were shoved up to his elbows, showing off all those sinewy muscles and striations. But he wouldn't look at her, as if he couldn't stand to. Instead, he simply paced. The divide between them was shredding her up inside but she wasn't sure what to say.

She'd been held at gunpoint, and had discovered the man she'd thought dead was really alive and after her again. She'd been so certain she would die. Right now she was about to crawl out of her skin at the silence. It was the first time they'd been alone since he'd tackled Gina—gah, Grace.

Finally, she couldn't handle it anymore. "I didn't mean any of those things I said!" She didn't mean to shout, but the words just came out angry and desperate as she surged to her feet. She couldn't take this silent treatment. She was barely keeping it together as it was.

He stopped pacing to turn and look at her. The little flecks of amber in his eyes seemed to be almost glowing, which she knew was ridiculous, but he was angry and it was clear in every line of his body. "You think that's why I'm pissed?"

"I…yes." She faltered because he was looking at her as if she was out of her mind.

He took a few steps toward her, but his movements weren't normal. No, he was stalking her, as if she were a little bunny and he were the big bad wolf that was going to devour her. "You left a fucking note." His voice was eerily calm.

"Well…yeah. I didn't want to just leave." And she couldn't use her stupid cell phone. Gah, she really needed to get a TracFone for emergencies. Or maybe she could even start using her own phone now. It was too soon to know yet what threat was still out there.

"A pathetic fucking note that had me going out of my mind. You should have waited until I'd gotten back and we could have come up with a game plan."

"That's exactly why I didn't wait. I knew you'd try to talk me out of leaving, and likely succeed. If anything happened to you or Dillon because of me…" Her voice cracked on the last word as the memory of that voice mail message played over in her mind. "You didn't hear that message! It was awful. He threatened Brendan and Kimmy. I…" She couldn't continue, couldn't force any more words out as her throat closed up.

"No! Don't fucking cry!" His expression was a mix of anger and horror as he took another step toward her. "Please don't cry, baby."

"I'm not crying," she muttered, wiping away the tears that started to fall down her cheeks. Damn it. What the hell? Until recently she almost never cried. Now it was like her tear ducts were permanently malfunctioning.

Suddenly his arms were around her, his quiet strength soothing her as he pulled her close. "Hell, Tegan, *please* don't cry."

She sniffled against his shirt before turning her cheek against his chest. His heartbeat was solid, steady. "I didn't know what else to do. I just knew I needed to get out of your place. I couldn't make you guys a target." She'd do it again, too, but left that part out, knowing it would just annoy him.

He stroked a gentle hand down her back, up and down, the action soothing and sweet. "I got a call from Carlito right as I got your note. Felt as if my world had imploded. I…thought you might just go on the run again." He stepped back but kept his arms around her, never letting her go. "I thought you might be gone for good," he rasped out.

She looked up at him. "I wouldn't have done that. I called Porter and he said he'd set me up with a safe house. I was going to call you as soon as I settled in."

His expression was tight. "I thought I wouldn't see you again. I panicked."

She knew he'd dropped Dillon off at his parents' place before storming over to hers. Thank God he had, too. "You saved my life. I don't know if I ever thanked you."

He made a sort of growling sound before he kissed her, hard and definitely claiming. At least that's sure how it felt. This man completely owned her when he took her mouth, kissing her until her knees felt weak and she was clutching his shoulders for support.

The sound of a throat clearing made her jerk back. She hadn't even heard the office door opening and clearly neither had Aaron. Somehow, she figured that lack of awareness was out of character for him. Good to know he was just as affected as she was.

Carlito stood there, his face neutral. At least he didn't look like the Grim Reaper. Maybe that meant something good. Like, maybe De Fiore had signed a full confession and apologized for all the pain and suffering he'd caused over the years. She nearly snorted at the ridiculous thought. Yeah, right.

"What've you got?" Aaron demanded.

"Good-ish news. Grace is ready to confess to pretty much everything in exchange for immunity."

Rage surged through Tegan. She started to speak when the detective held up his hand.

"We're not giving her full immunity. She won't do jail time but she'll be under house arrest for a long damn time. I know it's not what you were hoping for, but the Feds want De Fiore and she's serving him up on a silver platter. We're working together on this and"—he spread his hands out apologetically, and by his expression she could tell he truly was sorry—"they're calling the shots on how it plays out." That was anger in his voice.

"So she walks?" Tegan asked. "After holding a gun on me, kidnapping me, and knocking out one of your guys? Isn't that assault on a police officer or something?"

"She's not walking exactly but...yeah, it fucking blows." He rubbed a hand over his face. "But this is the way the system works sometimes. Enzo will go to jail forever. She's got a lot on him—her backup plan in case she ever got arrested. You won't be looking over your shoulder for the rest of your life. Grace doesn't give a shit about you, and all her movements will be monitored by a tracking device. She might not be going to jail but her life will be seriously altered."

Tegan leaned into Aaron, tension curling through her, tearing at her insides. He hadn't said anything about the bombing, and as far as she was concerned, De Fiore might not have been behind it.

As if he'd read her mind, Carlito continued. "Grace has been clear that Enzo never meant to hurt you in that car bombing. It was just a scare tactic."

She blinked in surprise. She hadn't been expecting De Fiore to be behind it.

"What does De Fiore say?" Aaron asked quietly. His hold around her shoulders tightened.

Carlito's lips pulled into a thin line. "Not a damn thing. Won't talk until his lawyer gets here. The guy's flying in from Chicago, so until then he's staying silent."

"We free to go?" Aaron's tone said that they'd be leaving no matter what Carlito said.

The detective nodded. "We might have more questions."

"You know where to find us. Tegan's staying with me tonight." There was no give in his words or body language.

Yeah, she wasn't going to argue with that. She released a breath she hadn't realized she'd been holding. She was tired of being afraid—*tired* being a pathetic word to describe anything. It was as if the weight that had been shoving her down for years had finally been lifted. She could breathe normally again for the first time in what felt like forever.

"You guys need an escort?" Carlito asked.

Aaron shook his head. "Red Stone's sent a security team down here to get us through the media circus. They'll be waiting at one of the back exits. You ready?" he asked her, not even waiting for Carlito to respond.

All she could do was nod. This nightmare was finally over. Now, maybe, she and Aaron might have a chance at something real. She still wasn't certain she was ready for a family, wasn't sure she had the right skills to deal with one, but she didn't want to let Aaron go.

CHAPTER TEN

"How's Dillon?" Tegan asked, after sipping the mug of tea he'd set in front of her. Aaron had bought a variety of teas since she'd been staying with him.

"Good. Sleeping." He wasn't surprised, not with the stomach bug Dillon had. He set his cell phone on the kitchen counter and drank in the sight of her. "I'm going to let him stay at my parents' tonight." It didn't seem like just this morning he'd taken Dillon to the walk-in clinic to get him checked out. So much had happened since then. They'd spent hours at the police station answering stupid questions from both the police and the FBI. He should be exhausted. Instead he was keyed up. He couldn't get a read on Tegan, though. It was frustrating.

Lord, the woman in general frustrated him even as he wanted her more than his next breath. He understood her reason for running. Hell, he respected it. She'd wanted to keep him and his son safe. But he'd thought they were starting something amazing together, and now he couldn't read her at all.

She frowned. "I hate that his schedule has been all messed up because of me."

Aaron lifted a shoulder. "It hasn't. Not really. He's on Christmas break right now and he's at my parents' every other day, it seems. If I'm on an out-of-town security detail, he stays with them. Trust me, he's fine." That was something he'd learned early on as a parent. Kids were adaptable. More so than adults.

"Oh. Good." She tapped her finger against the counter, watching him with an unreadable expression.

"What?" He rounded the island, not wanting any space between them.

She swiveled in her seat as he approached, keeping her mug in her hand. It looked an awful lot like a barrier. "Nothing. Just wondering…where we go from here."

To his bedroom or any flat surface, if she was willing. He kept that thought to himself. For now. It didn't matter that he was dying to strip her, taste and tease all of her before fully claiming her; they clearly weren't on the same page right now.

Almost losing her today drove home the conclusion he'd already come to. He wanted something real with her. And now that the threat from Enzo was over, he didn't want to keep a relationship quiet either. "I'd like to take you on a real date. Then another one and another. And if you don't have plans, I hope you'll join us for Christmas dinner in a couple weeks."

Her bright blue eyes widened. "What will we tell Dillon?"

"What do you want to tell him?" He sat in the chair next to her, even though he wanted to take the mug from her hands and pull her into his lap.

"I don't know yet. I like you…a lot. But I know you two come as a package deal."

"Do you not want…" He tried to think of the right way to ask what needed to be said. "Am I not an option for a relationship because of my son?"

She paused for so long he was sure she wouldn't answer. Dread curled in his stomach. He'd never considered that this was a real issue for her. When she'd thrown out the excuse of him being a dad, he'd thought…hell, it didn't matter.

Finally, she cleared her throat. "Not in the way you think. My mom wasn't exactly present. She dragged my brother and me around everywhere. She was rarely home and when she was, she didn't care about us. She wasn't abusive, not physically anyway. It was clear she'd have been happier if we weren't around, dragging her down."

Aaron took the mug from her hands and set it on the counter.

Though he still wanted to pull her into his arms, he captured her hands in his. "I'm sorry."

"I'm just telling you so you know that I know zero about kids. I'm not the best female role model for a kid is what I'm trying to say. And I don't want to be in his life, then suddenly not be there when we break up."

He stiffened at her words. "When?"

"Okay, *if,* but you know what I mean. I'd hate to cause him any pain."

He nodded because he did. It only made him care for her more. She was concerned about Dillon's welfare in all this. How could he not adore this woman? "I've never brought any women into Dillon's life. I…haven't had any women in my life anyway. Not since…" He cleared his throat. "So I understand your concerns. I have them, too. But what I feel for you isn't casual. I want exclusive. If we need to play the 'we're just friends' game in front of people for a while, then I'll do it. Not because I want to, but I'll do it for you."

She tightened her hands around his. "No, I don't want that. To be just friends, I mean. I really like you. After today I feel like I should hold onto you and never let go." Her cheeks flushed pink. "But maybe around Dillon we don't put a label on you and me. Other than friends. For now, anyway. I just…I never want to hurt that kid."

Aaron scrubbed a hand over his face. She said the absolute perfect thing and he knew she wasn't trying. He wasn't letting her go and as far as he was concerned, they wouldn't be breaking up. She'd woken something up inside him, made him feel alive, and he wasn't stupid enough to let her go.

"Come to bed with me tonight?" It came out more like a plea than anything but he didn't care. He needed this woman like he needed his next breath. He wasn't even sure they were at that point yet—well, *he* was at that point. But she'd been through a hell of a lot recently.

Her eyes went heavy-lidded as she got off the chair and moved to stand between his spread legs. Wordlessly she slid her hands up and around the back of his neck, linking her fingers together.

He settled his hands on her hips and tightened his grip. For a long moment he just stared at her. Her eyes were dilated and her breathing was erratic.

His own heart was beating out of control as he looked into her bright blue eyes. After months of holding back, of denying what she meant to him, he was walking a tightrope of control. Now that he had her within his grasp it was hard to think straight.

He reached down and grabbed her ass. She let out a yelp of surprise as he hoisted her up, but she didn't pause as she wrapped her legs around him.

He crushed his mouth to hers, wordlessly demanding everything from her. After tonight he knew there would be no going back for him. As her tongue teased against his, he walked them out of the kitchen, her lithe body plastered to him.

Very soon they were going to be skin to skin. His body shuddered as he thought of it, of finally having her completely bared to him.

When they reached the foyer, he paused by the bottom of the stairs then veered into the living room. They weren't going to make it to the bedroom.

The Christmas tree lights and the faux fire from the fireplace gave them more than enough illumination. It would let him see her fully, as he needed right now. As they passed the couch, he blindly reached out and grabbed some of the blankets.

Somehow he tore his mouth from hers. "In here okay?" It seemed those were the only words he could force out.

"Oh yeah." The heat in her voice slid through and around him.

He worked quickly to toss the blankets on the floor before tugging her down onto them.

Laughing, she tumbled onto the blankets and cupped his face. "I'm not going anywhere, Aaron," she whispered.

He just nodded. Hearing the words did a little to soothe all his jagged edges, but not much. Almost frantic, he tugged her jeans off to reveal tiny black panties barely covering her mound. The twinkly lights from the tree played off her smooth ivory skin, and her auburn hair seemed brighter.

Part of him wanted to carry her upstairs to his bed but he needed to be in her right this second. Before he could make a move to finish undressing her, she pushed up and stripped off her sweater. Her tiny black bra barely covered breasts he'd been fantasizing about for way too long.

He could see the outline of her hard nipples through the lacy material. When his gaze finally strayed back up to her face, he found her watching him with a sensual half smile.

"You have this look on your face, like you want to..." Even in the dimly lit living room he could see her cheeks flush that sexy shade of pink.

His cock pressed insistently against his pants. Too fucking bad for him. "What?" he murmured. "Like I want to eat you?"

She made a sort of coughing sound as she nodded. There was an innocent quality about her that he adored. Last night when he'd told her what he'd wanted to do to her, how he'd wanted to shove her dress up and eat her pussy, he'd loved getting a reaction out of her, loved seeing that sweet blush on her cheeks. Tonight he wasn't going to stop at just tasting her. He was going to fully claim her, show her how good they could be together.

Tegan watched as Aaron lifted one of her legs and brought her ankle to his mouth. He kept his gaze on hers the entire time as he raked his teeth over a section of skin she'd never thought was sensitive.

But the oh-so-gentle way his teeth grazed her skin sent shivers skating through her. She felt vulnerable, stretched out in just her underwear while he was still fully dressed. She wanted to reach for him, to strip his clothes off so that nothing was between them, but it was clear he was taking charge right now.

And, yeah, it was pretty hot.

Everything about Aaron melted her, right down to the way he listened to her concerns about broadcasting their relationship to his son. She'd met a lot of people during her time on the run and he was truly one of the best men she'd ever known. It was too soon to say the L word, but she knew she was heading that way fast, if she wasn't there already. Because the deepest part of her trusted him, was connected to him in a way she couldn't put into words.

He reached her knee, kissing her slowly, following up with his teeth. He had his other hand on her opposite leg, holding her thighs open for him.

On instinct she spread them wider. Heat flooded her core with each kiss, each nip of his talented, wicked mouth. As she remembered what he'd done to her last night, another rush of need filled her. The man made her feel things she'd hadn't in…ever. He made her feel alive and grounded at the same time.

Everything about him was solid—hers.

She moaned when he crawled higher, reaching her inner thigh. Her legs were trembling as he took his sweet time teasing her.

She slid her fingers through his hair and held onto his head tight, dying for the moment he put his mouth to her folds.

"Tell me what you want, baby," he murmured, his teeth nipping at one of her most sensitive spots. The soft skin of her inner thigh seemed to have a thousand nerve endings as he focused on it—probably because all she wanted him to do was shove her panties to the side and give her what she needed.

He was clearly enjoying teasing her.

"To come," she rasped out. With him. She desperately wanted to feel him inside her, for him to find release, too. She loved what they'd shared last night but she needed more and she knew he did as well.

He chuckled against her skin; the sound a little bit wicked. Instead of responding, he teased her soaked panties to the side and barely skimmed his finger along her folds—and nowhere near her clit. "Do better than that." His words were a bare whisper.

She rolled her hips, needing so much more. "Your mouth on my clit."

He growled softly, the sound reverberating through her. His tongue flicked out, barely grazing her clit.

"Aaron." His name tore from her lips.

That was apparently all the motivation he needed because he

sucked on her clit, making her jerk against his face. She shouldn't be this close yet, but she was already on edge just being around him, thinking about what might have happened, and she wanted everything from him. When he fully slid his finger inside her, she grabbed onto his shoulders. Yes, this was what she needed.

The man had learned her body so quickly and she couldn't wait for him to fill her.

He added another finger and began thrusting inside her, his movements so gentle, so smooth. It was too much and not enough. She didn't want his fingers. She wanted his cock.

She squeezed his shoulders tight, dragging at his sweater. She needed him naked right freaking now. "Aaron."

He paused and looked up at her with the gleam of a predator in his gaze. She shivered at the intensity, more than happy to be his prey.

Her hands stilled at the hem of his sweater. "I want to come with you inside me."

It was like her words set him off. His big body shuddered. Still crouched between her legs, he stripped his sweater off and tossed it behind him.

Her breath caught in her throat as she devoured the sight of him finally bared to her. For months she'd wondered what he had under the dark suit he normally wore to the shop. She wanted to grip his broad shoulders or muscular arms as she rode him. Or hold on tight as he pinned her to the soft blanket by the Christmas tree.

She was surprised to see a tattoo on his left pec, one of an eagle, globe, and anchor, the Marine Corps symbol. The tattoo only made him hotter, something she hadn't thought possible. He was already off the charts making her crazy.

She continued staring as he shifted slightly and finished stripping, losing his pants and boxers in a few fluid moves.

She'd been lucky enough to hold his cock last night, to stroke him to orgasm, but he'd still been mostly dressed and he'd finished himself off. Seeing him on his knees, that thick length jutting forward, and the tree lights highlighting all his perfection was enough to render her speechless.

He didn't seem to mind as he crawled on the blanket toward her, moving with a sleekness that told her exactly how strong and capable he was.

She shuddered as he covered her body with his, caging her in with his arms. His breathing was harsh as he stared down at her. Lust shone in his dark eyes so clearly it stole her breath.

Hungrily, she reached for him, stroking over his chest and arms, desperate to explore every inch of his muscular, toned body.

"This thing I feel for you…I've never felt like this about anyone, Tegan." The words came out guttural.

The truth of his words rocketed through her. She felt the same way but couldn't find her voice, could barely think straight. She didn't trust her voice anyway. Though the truth was part of her was afraid this would all be ripped away from her. That he was too good to be true. She'd been on the run, alone for so long, she was terrified that she wanted him too much. And because she did, she'd lose him. As if the universe were just waiting to kick her one more time. To give her everything she wanted, then take it away.

For now, she shoved that fear aside and focused on the here and now. On him. Reaching between their bodies, she wrapped her fingers around his hard length. He pulsed in her grip, his hips rolling into her hold.

She stroked him slowly, holding tight like she'd discovered he liked last night. That one time with him wasn't enough—it barely counted in her book. She needed all of him so badly she was trembling with the need. It had been over two years for her, something she'd confessed to him last night when they'd been lying on his couches, with Dillon fast asleep. It had just been the two of them awake, talking.

He'd admitted it had been way longer for him. As in, since his ex. So while she was desperate for him, she was also a little nervous. It felt like a big deal to be his first since—

He crushed his mouth to hers, splintering those stupid worries and scattering them to the wind as he took over.

As he flicked his tongue against hers, he reached between their bodies and grasped her wrist, tugging her hand from his cock.

She started to protest until he guided both her hands above her head, stretching her out fully underneath him. She loved the feel of being pinned beneath him as he held her wrists in place.

Arching into him, she moaned into his mouth and wrapped her legs around him. The feel of her breasts against his chest, his cock against her stomach, the skin-to-skin contact, made her feel alive.

"I want to touch you everywhere," he murmured against her lips, his mouth still skating against hers.

She rolled her hips against him in response. How was he even talking, thinking? Her inner walls ached, needing to be filled by him.

He nibbled a slow path along her jaw, reaching between their bodies with his free hand and cupping one of her breasts. "I thought about this so many damn times," he rasped out. "Every time I saw you in the shop, every time you made a smartass comment. All I could think about was this."

"Yeah?" She wanted to know what his fantasies were, but couldn't force the question out.

"I thought about bending you over one of the display cases, pushing into you from behind." He tweaked a nipple, rolling it between his fingers in a sensual move.

Combined with his words, heat flooded between her thighs. "Do it now. Bend me over."

He stilled, lifting his head slightly to look at her. She squeezed her legs once around his waist then let go, letting them fall to the soft blanket.

He shoved up on his arms, still caging her in with that huge, sexy body. He looked a little uncertain, as if he wasn't sure this was what she wanted. How could he ever doubt?

Wordlessly, she rolled over and moved onto her stomach. Before she could push up, he wrapped an arm around her middle and tugged her to her knees and back against him. His cock was hard against her behind.

She clenched her fingers into the blanket as he smoothed a hand over her ass.

"You are fucking perfection," he murmured. He tested her slickness with a finger before pushing inside her so slowly, making her crazy.

His thick length pushed deeper, deeper, until a moan tore free from her throat. "God, Aaron." There were no words left.

She felt consumed by him. For so many years she'd been on the run, moving from place to place, looking over her shoulder and waiting to get a bullet in the head. Now it was as if she'd been running straight for Aaron and hadn't even known it. She was still scared that things wouldn't work out, but she couldn't be a coward any longer and not take a chance on him.

On them.

She knew this kind of connection was rare, that what they could have was special. And she'd be the worst kind of coward if she ran from him.

She arched back as he reached around, cupping one of her breasts, tweaking and teasing her nipple as he thrust over and over. Pleasure poured through her as he took her, battering at her nerve endings.

He was just a little rough, a little on edge, and she loved it. He'd always seemed so rigid, so in control until recently and this was the best surprise of all. That and his dirty talk from last night.

She grew slicker the harder he pushed, turned on by the groaning sounds he made. His other hand tightened once around her hip, his hold hard enough that he'd probably leave a bruise. Some primal part of her she hadn't even known existed was excited at the thought.

When his hand slid around her and cupped her mound, strumming her clit, her entire body jolted in awareness.

"Faster," she moaned. She just needed him to speed up and—she surged into orgasm, her inner walls tightening around him like a vise as the pleasure speared out to all her nerve endings.

He must have been holding back because as soon as she let go, he did the same, her name a rough growl on his lips.

She clutched at the blanket, her fingers tightening into the material as over and over he continued thrusting inside her. Her entire body felt oversensitive, like one big nerve ending as her climax seemed to go on forever.

They both collapsed onto the blanket almost in unison. Thankfully he rolled off her and sidled up next to her. Lying flat on her stomach, she turned her head to look at him since that was all the energy she had at the moment.

He was on his side, his head propped in one hand. Leaning over, he brushed his mouth against her forehead, the action sweetly sensual. She could feel the possessiveness humming through him when he kissed her.

He smoothed a hand down her back, lightly stroking against her spine. She shivered at the contact and he immediately grabbed another blanket draped across the nearby ottoman and pulled it over them.

She finally moved, curling against his chest as he stretched out onto his back. The lights twinkled beside them, casting shadows around the room. For the first time in years she felt safe, whole. All because of the man next to her.

She wasn't sure how long they lay there, and didn't really care. "When I was on the run, it was hard." The words were out before she could think about what she was saying, or how much she was opening up.

His grip tightened ever so slightly around her, but he didn't respond. He was simply silent so she could get the words out.

Tegan was grateful he was letting her open up. "I…sometimes had to do things I wasn't proud of. I pretty much left with the clothes on my back and a few suitcases. A couple times a year I…stole license plates to switch them out with mine so it would be harder to track me." She still felt guilty about that.

"That's smart."

She huffed out a laugh at his words, surprised there was no recrimination there. "In the first six months it was really hard even though I'd done the backpacking thing before. A couple motels I skipped out on paying because I was scared what little money I had wouldn't be enough to cover me until the next town."

His grip tightened again, his lips brushing over the top of her head. "You're incredible, Tegan." Sincerity laced his words.

She'd expected…well, she wasn't sure what she'd expected—him to judge her, maybe. Looking up at him, she met his gaze. "I think we should just lie here all night," she murmured.

"That sounds like a good idea to me." His voice was just as quiet as he watched her, that familiar intense look in place.

She was glad he felt that way because there was nowhere else she wanted to be.

CHAPTER ELEVEN

A thrill shot through Alec to see Tegan O'Kelly leaving the police station on the news. A man was with the redhead and there appeared to be a group of security escorting them...cops off duty, maybe?

It was hard to tell. But he recognized the face of the man from his files. Aaron Fitzpatrick went into Kimmy's Cakes and Coffee occasionally.

From the phone records Alec had acquired, it didn't appear that Tegan had ever had contact with the man so he hadn't even been on the radar as someone important. But the images on screen didn't lie, and that man was very much invested in Tegan's safety. Every movement he made was designed to protect her from harm. It was the way the man carried himself, the way he blocked her from everything. And the expression on his face when he glanced at her...they were definitely in a relationship.

There had been a couple of calls from Fitzpatrick's house directly to the coffee shop recently. Alec had been monitoring the shop's phone but hadn't thought anything of it since that phone number belonged to the brother of the man the shop owner was likely fucking.

This was all very interesting.

Now that Enzo and that bitch Grace had been arrested, Alec knew he'd have to act fast. Because something told him Grace wouldn't keep her mouth shut. No matter how hardcore she liked to act, she'd sell Enzo out—and Enzo might be tempted to sell out someone else higher up the food chain in an effort to reduce his sentence. Which meant Alec's boss would be under the microscope and, subsequently, Alec would be, too. That was unacceptable.

So he still had to kill Tegan. Now that the Feds knew Enzo was alive, this was even better. Alec would kill Tegan and lead an obvious money trail back to Enzo, 'proving' that Enzo had hired someone to kill the woman. It wouldn't matter if Enzo tried to cut a deal with the Feds once that became public knowledge.

If the FBI made a deal with him after a woman like Tegan O'Kelly got murdered on Enzo's orders, a sweet woman who worked in a coffee shop and had already survived a bombing, the public would go crazy for blood. The FBI only liked to be in the news if they were being praised.

Yes, yes, this could work. Alec would even get a bonus for this. He'd been sent to kill the woman so Enzo would never know that she *wasn't* the one who took those diamonds. Now her death would work even more in his favor. It would ensure Enzo went away forever, maybe even got the death penalty.

Pulling up his laptop, he worked fast, typing in commands. Her phone still wasn't turned on, but he'd find her. Now that he had a pretty good idea of who she'd been staying with, or at least had a relationship with, hunting her down would be easy enough.

Then he'd kill her, make it look as if Enzo had ordered it, and leave a trail as wide as the Grand fucking Canyon back to the old fool. It wouldn't even need to be spectacular. Just a clean kill. Sure, the Feds would attempt to hunt Alec down after he killed her, but he wouldn't leave an evidence trail to himself. He never did. He'd just ghost out of town.

So Enzo would go away for the murder and the Feds would just have to be happy with Enzo. Because they'd never catch him. Alec was too good for them, always had been. And taking on one woman would be one of the easiest kills he'd ever done once he caught up to her. She had no training.

After she was finally dead, Alec's boss would be happy. Everyone would win. Everyone except a pretty redhead who should have died years ago.

"Higher!" Dillon squealed as Tegan pushed him on the swing, his excitement infectious.

Aaron, standing with her, leaned over and kissed her cheek. "Gonna hit the head. I'll be back in a few."

She smiled at him, feeling light and free for the first time in years. "We're not going anywhere."

Kali danced around the big swing set, thrilled to be out and playing. The park was mostly empty and for the first time in years she knew she was safe. Well, as safe as anyone could be. No one was hunting her. She was outside, breathing fresh air and free from the worries of the last couple of years. Dillon and Aaron were safe. All her friends were okay. Enzo De Fiore was in custody and not going anywhere.

As Aaron headed down the winding walkway, he turned and half waved before he disappeared behind one of the jungle gyms on his way to the washroom. The park was massive and she was surprised there weren't more people there, especially since it was a Sunday. Maybe people were sleeping in since there had been a cold snap overnight.

Of course, Florida cold compared to some of the places she'd lived wasn't too terrible. To her it was invigorating. There was no snow on the ground but there was an icy nip in the air that made her think of sitting in front of a crackling fire and sipping hot cocoa—with a certain sexy man at her side.

"You want to walk to Kimmy's shop and get some cocoa after this?" Tegan asked Dillon amidst his shouts of "higher, higher." The park they were at was only a few blocks away from the strip of shops where Kimmy's place was located. Tegan wanted to stop by the Mederos family's restaurant and Julieta's shop, too, to see everyone who'd been so concerned about her and thank them for all the food they'd sent.

"Yes!" he shouted. He seemed to be in 'shout mode,' as Aaron had called it earlier this morning when Bree had dropped him off.

Apparently whatever virus he'd had was long gone and the kid was full of energy. Aaron had told her it was normal, that was just how kids were. They bounced back like nothing had ever happened.

Even though all her worries about Enzo were gone, there was still a little niggle at the back of her mind that something was going to go wrong. That this bit of happiness she'd found would disappear. Logically, she knew it was a learned response because she'd lived in fear for so long. She wasn't actually anticipating danger.

"I want to go on the merry-go-round!"

"Okay." Laughing, Tegan stopped pushing and let the swing start to slow.

She glanced around the park again, unable to shake that weird feeling in the pit of her stomach. A mother was on a bench while her two kids raced across monkey bars. Another mom stood next to a small toddler attempting to climb onto the head of a big plastic fish that had been made to look as if it was coming out of the ground. It was in the middle of a big circular section with soft, squishy material instead of concrete where different plastic sea life sprouted from it. When Tegan had asked Dillon if he wanted to play there, he'd looked at her so seriously and told her he was a big boy now and that section was for babies.

Rolling her shoulders once in an attempt to get rid of the residual tension, she reached for the seat of the swing and stilled it completely so Dillon could slide out.

"Daddy said you're coming to Christmas dinner with us this year," Dillon said, tucking his little hand into hers.

The trusting action seemed so natural for him and it warmed her better than any hot chocolate ever could. She still felt like she was navigating foreign terrain where kids were concerned but so far Dillon seemed to like her. "Yes, he asked me to. Is that okay with you?"

Kali fell into place next to them, prancing as only she could as they made their way to the merry-go-round.

He grinned up at her. "Yep. I even got you a present."

She blinked. "You did?" Oh, crap. She needed to get them presents. With everything going on she hadn't even thought about Christmas. Not really. The holiday had been in her face since November with decorations all over the city and on television but it had been an abstract thing for her. She hadn't thought about Christmas because she'd planned to be alone again this year. For her, holidays had never been a particularly fun time of year. Her mom had barely put in a half-ass attempt to celebrate with her and her brother. Forget about lights or a tree. She and her brother had always gotten one present for each other but that had been the extent of their holiday celebration. After her mother had died, Tegan hadn't really cared to put in much effort either. She'd usually just done something with her single friends.

"Yep. It's awesome, too." He continued chattering, telling her about what he'd gotten his daddy for Christmas and how he hoped Santa brought him Thor's hammer. It took her a moment to realize it was a reference to *The Avengers*.

As they headed across a grassy incline, an SUV slowly steered through the parking lot. The windows were tinted dark. On the back she saw one of those little stick family sticker collections, including a dog.

She glanced over her shoulder, looking for Aaron. The place was big but he'd find them. Still, she wished he was with them.

God, she had to get over whatever this weird anxiousness was. After the bombing, the doctor had mentioned she might have some lingering effects, including panic attacks. Maybe she really did need to talk to someone. The thought of opening up to a complete stranger felt weird, though.

As they reached the merry-go-round, she glanced over as the SUV backed into a parking spot. The parking lot spanned around three sides of the park and everyone had parked by the main entrance, their vehicles clustered together. This driver parked about twenty spaces away from the other vehicles.

"Spin me!"

Tegan started spinning Dillon as a man wearing a sweatshirt, jogging pants, and a black knitted cap got out of the SUV. When he started stretching she realized he was going to use the running track that looped through the park. Rolling her eyes at herself, she turned back to the merry-go-round where Dillon was still hanging on and giggling.

A smile broke over her face—until she saw a man jogging across the other side of the parking lot in their direction. He was coming from a nondescript truck parked far away from everyone else. It took all of a second for her to recognize the man. She didn't know his name but she knew that face. A large scar slashed over his left cheek on a ragged angle, almost looking like a sideways V covering most of his cheek. It was very memorable.

Terror jolted through her, the jagged lightning bolt edges making her freeze for a moment.

A sidewalk and fence separated them but he was moving in their direction with purpose.

Everything funneled out as she jerked the merry-go-round to a halt. "Dillon, come here. We've gotta go now."

Next to her Kali whined, maybe because she sensed Tegan's tension. There was still no sign of Aaron.

"We'll get ice cream and whatever you want. Come on—" She stopped talking as the man's gaze connected with hers.

She yanked Dillon into her arms, ready to run. The man broke into a sprint. Without pause, she started running, Dillon wrapped around her like a little monkey.

Her heart was in her throat as she tore over the grass. "That man's bad. We've gotta find your daddy. If I tell you to run and hide, you've got to listen. Okay?" Her words were coming out in gasps, her heart galloping in her chest as she raced toward the two buildings in the middle of the park. That was where Aaron had gone.

"Okay," Dillon whispered, fear flickering across his features.

"Aaron!" she screamed, not caring that she looked like a crazy person. She didn't care about anything other than getting Dillon to safety. "Aaron!" His name tore from her throat. She knew she sounded like a savage animal.

Dillon stared at her wide-eyed but just clutched her tighter. Kali growled low in her throat as she ran next to them. Oh God, where was Aaron?

One of the moms screamed. "He's got a gun!"

Panic exploded inside her as they raced past one of the jungle gyms. She glanced over her shoulder to see the man jumping the fence, a huge pistol in his hand.

Adrenaline rocketed through her as a shot rang out. She braced for pain, for an impact, but felt nothing.

She didn't slow down as she sprinted, but the restrooms were too far. Holding Dillon tight she raced toward a cluster of trees. Clumps of dirt flew up in the air as she veered to the left.

Screaming Aaron's name again, she dove behind a huge oak as wood splintered inches from her head.

Aaron leaned against the brick wall exterior of the multi-bathroom building, his cell phone to his ear as he talked to Porter. "Yeah, I'll be good to go in a week. I still want to take off the next few days—"

"Aaron!" The sound of Tegan's scream made all the hair on the back of his neck stand up. Aaron shoved away from the wall, pocketing his phone as he withdrew his weapon in a fluid, practiced move. Fear gripped his chest. His son and Tegan were out there. Years of training kicked in.

"He's got a gun!" A woman's terrified scream ripped through the air.

Adrenaline poured through him as he raced toward the woman's and Tegan's cries. He had to get to Dillon and Tegan.

When he heard the sound of gunfire, only years of training forced him to slow down as he reached the end of the brick wall. Weapon out and crouching low, he peered around the corner of the building.

For a moment he froze, all the muscles in his body tightening. Tegan and Dillon were huddled behind a tree as a man with a SIG raced toward them.

There was no cover for Aaron, but he was going to take this guy down before he got to Tegan and Dillon. There was no other option.

He'd keep his son and the woman he loved safe.

Suddenly Kali burst out from behind the jungle gym, a rabid, feral warrior that looked nothing like the sweet husky she was. She was racing for the gunman at full speed. The man turned to the left, facing the threat and putting his back to Aaron.

On a burst of speed, Aaron raced for them as Kali lunged at the gunman. Shots rang out as Kali jumped into the air. Everything else around Aaron funneled out as Kali slammed the man to the ground. The SIG went flying so Aaron kicked it out of the way as he reached them.

The man was unmoving under a motionless Kali. *Oh God.*

There was no time to check on the dog. He needed to secure the threat immediately. Keep Tegan and Dillon safe.

Before he could move, the man kicked out with a snarl, knocking Aaron's feet from under him. Aaron fell back as the man jerked up, shoving the dog off him.

Blood soaked the man's hoodie. He lunged at Aaron.

Aaron went on the offensive, slamming his fist against the guy's jaw. It didn't slow the asshole down. With fevered, dark eyes he swung at Aaron.

Aaron ducked his head to the side and rolled to his feet. He didn't want to kill the guy, but he would if he had to. He aimed his weapon at him. "Don't fucking move," he snarled.

The man was on one knee, calculation in his gaze. He had to have another weapon.

Aaron's aim was steady. He would absolutely shoot this son of a bitch if he had to. "Go for it. See who gets off a shot first."

Something like resignation flared in the man's eyes. He lifted his hands in the air and lay flat on his belly. "I've got a gun in my ankle holster and a knife at my back." Breathing heavily, he turned his face to the side against the grass.

Gone was the fighter from moments before but Aaron wasn't going to let himself be lulled into a false sense of security. He didn't bother disarming the guy. He had faith in his abilities to disarm him, but he wasn't risking it right now. With Dillon and Tegan so close, he wasn't going to take the chance that the guy would attack when he got Aaron at closer range. Anything could happen in a split second. He'd wait for the cops to get here and do their job.

With his free hand he started to pull his cell phone out of his pocket when Dillon's scared voice came from behind the tree.

"Dad?"

Another surge of panic pummeled him, but he didn't take his focus off the man on the ground. "Stay where you are! Everything's fine. Just stay put."

"We're okay and we're not moving," Tegan called out, her voice shaky. "Cops are on their way. Should be here in a couple minutes."

Almost as if on cue, sirens wailed in the distance, the sound of them music to his ears. He just hoped this nightmare was finally over—and that Kali would make it. She hadn't moved since she'd been shot, but he could hear her labored breathing and she was softly whining. He hated that he couldn't help her. But he couldn't take his focus off the gunman, not for a second.

CHAPTER TWELVE

"She's going to be okay." Aaron wrapped an arm around Tegan's shoulders as they sat in the waiting room of the vet's office.

Kali was in surgery and Tegan didn't know what she'd do if her sweet dog didn't make it. Kali had been her constant companion through the crappiest moments of her life. She was young and sweet and had fought like hell to protect her and Dillon. To lose her after everything they'd gone through, after the rough start she'd had to her life…

Tegan's throat tightened and she swallowed hard because she didn't trust herself to respond. Not without having a meltdown anyway.

The front door opened and Tegan jumped. Her nerves were frayed and she couldn't take any more surprises.

Aaron straightened and stood when Carlito stepped inside.

Tegan was surprised to see him there. Her heart rate stuttered at his grim expression. She shot to her feet, tensing for the worst. "What's wrong now?"

He blinked. "Nothing. I just…how's your dog?"

"No news." She slumped back in the chair, but Aaron remained standing.

"Why are you here?" he asked quietly.

"Good-ish news. Grace lost her deal with the Feds because she lied to them about who was behind the bombing of your car."

Tegan raised her eyebrows. Now she knew that the man who'd come after them in the park was behind the bombing, not Enzo.

She'd recognized him from Chicago, had seen him once talking to Enzo. While she hadn't known Alec Rossi's name, she'd known he wasn't at that park by chance, and had been there for her. "Really, she lost the deal?"

"Yeah. She'll be doing jail time. Not as much as I'm sure you'd like, but it's something. Enzo will be going away for a very long time, too."

"Why do I feel like there's a *but* in there?"

Carlito flicked a glance at Aaron once before sitting a few chairs down from them. "There is. Sorta. Alec Rossi is in federal custody. He's going to do jail time, but..."

Next to her Aaron tensed and she didn't blame him one bit. That bastard had come after her at a children's park. And he'd shot at her while she'd been running with Dillon, *a five-year-old boy*. All the muscles in Tegan's body went tight. If Carlito said he was getting some cushy deal, she was going to let any reporter who wanted to interview her do one. And she'd tell everyone exactly how screwed up their justice system was, until it was splashed all over every headline she could make.

Carlito held up a hand as he turned back to her, probably seeing the rage on her face. "He's definitely going to jail. He was hired by a man named Stefano De Fiore, Enzo's cousin."

Tegan nodded. "Yeah, I know the name. He was Enzo's second in command. I met him once." *Met* was a bit of a stretch. He'd been in the same room as her once, and when Enzo had wanted to hurt her, the cousin had made it sound like a bad idea—and convinced Enzo that it was his idea to back off. "He seemed...smarter than Enzo."

"According to Rossi, Stefano hired him to kill you when he got word Enzo was hunting you for those diamonds."

It took her a moment to digest why. "Because Stefano took them, didn't he?" Which meant Stefano had killed her brother. Or at the very least, ordered his death. Otherwise why bother coming after her? He'd needed to cover up the fact that he'd taken them in case Enzo figured out Tegan hadn't been behind the theft.

Carlito nodded, a touch of pity flickering in his gray gaze. "Yeah. And—"

"My brother is dead. Is that what you're going to tell me?" She held the tears at bay. Barely. She'd known he was gone, had known it in her heart.

Aaron silently wrapped his arm around her shoulders and held her close.

"Yeah. Rossi killed him on Stefano's orders. He was supposed to completely incinerate the body but he didn't. He kept your brother and a few others as leverage should he ever need it." He cleared his throat, his expression softening. "They're in an industrial freezer, well preserved. He knew this day might come. He's turning evidence against Stefano and giving the location of all the bodies. Those families deserve closure and so do you. And it will bring down that entire criminal empire in Chicago. I'm so sorry, Tegan. Truly."

She clenched her jaw and squeezed her hands together to stop them from shaking. Aaron just pulled her closer, his presence the only thing keeping her from breaking down. "What's he getting in return?"

"They're taking the death penalty off the table. And he gets to choose the prison he wants to go to. It'll be a supermax, high-security prison but he still gets to choose where. He'll be in solitary confinement, though. For his protection."

She and Dillon—and other innocent people at that park—could have been killed by that man. It was a miracle no one had been injured except Kali. Wetness covered her cheeks and she realized she was crying. Deep down she'd known her brother was dead but there had been that stupid, tiny spark of hope that refused to give up.

Aaron's arms were fully around her before she could blink. She buried her face in his chest, unsure how long she remained there, letting the tears come. Eventually she raised her head when she trusted herself to be able to talk again. "Why did Gina—uh, Grace, lie?"

Carlito scrubbed a hand over his handsome face. "I could give you a diplomatic answer but the truth is she's fucking stupid. From what

I gather, she thought with you dead, you wouldn't be around to testify, so things would go easier on her sentencing and on Enzo. Even though she turned evidence against him, she apparently still cared enough about Enzo to try to give him that. I don't know what was going on in her head. Her lawyer's pissed at her. She has no leverage now. The woman is a fucking moron."

Tegan nodded, glad the woman would be going to jail.

She looked up at Aaron, her miracle. She didn't care if it was too soon or if she was assessing her feelings while on emotional steroids, but she loved him. Clearing her throat, she looked back at Carlito. "Glad she won't be able to get out of it. I think I know the answer, but how did Rossi find me?" She hadn't even thought to ask Carlito when the cavalry had arrived, because she'd been too worried about Kali.

He'd had an ambulance race Kali to the vet and, breaking all sorts of protocols, had let Tegan stay with Kali for the first part of her surgery. Once she'd come through the worst of it, Tegan and Aaron had gone back to the police station for a crapload of questioning and paperwork—though Carlito had gotten them out of there as fast as he could. For that she was grateful. If she never saw the inside of a police station again, it would be too soon. She was tired of people trying to kill her and tired of stupid questions.

The detective lifted a shoulder. "Your phone. He'd actually figured out who you were staying with after that clip of you on the news, leaving the station with Aaron. But he just tracked your phone to the park this morning when you turned it on. Illegal as fuck and he'll be charged with that, too. He's being charged with everything we've got. He'll never see the outside of a prison once he goes in. Hell, he's been denied bail completely so he won't have any freedom from this point forward."

Tegan nodded, her throat tight. "Thank you for coming to tell us."

"I'm just sorry for all the hell you've been through." He stood and took a step toward the door before stopping. "Now I get to go deliver the good news to Enzo in person. He'd been planning on turning evidence against his cousin. With all Rossi's information, the Feds don't need Enzo at all. He's not getting a deal. Can't wait to see the look on that fucker's face when I tell him he's going down."

Tegan blinked. "You told us before him?"

Carlito nodded, standing. "Figured you should know in person. That guy will never hurt you or anyone again. And he'll know for a fact that his own cousin betrayed him and took those diamonds. You're not on his radar anymore. You're nothing to him. He's going to spend the rest of his life behind bars, probably plotting how to kill his cousin and Rossi. I'll keep you up to date with everything."

Once Carlito was gone and the door had shut quietly behind him, Tegan's shoulders slumped and she turned toward Aaron once again. She wrapped her arms around him tight. "Thank you for everything you've done." He'd taken her into his home, kept her safe, and saved her life twice in a matter of a few short days. Her chest felt hollowed out. She couldn't take another blow—wasn't sure she could handle it. Aaron was the one bright spot in all this mess.

His grip tightened. "Don't ever thank me for that. I…I'm in love with you, Tegan. I know it's too soon and—"

Her head snapped back and she looked up at him. Emotions flickered in his dark eyes, too many to figure out. "I love you, too. So much it hurts. I love the way you are with your son. You're such a good dad and that's crazy sexy. Something I never imagined thinking. You're kind to everyone and you went out of your way to keep a virtual stranger—me—safe. Ever since then you've been a rock, someone I know I can count on no matter what. I…I just love you."

His mouth curved up in a sweet half smile but it fell as the door to the back opened. The operating room and the other rooms were back there. The vet, not her assistant, was standing there.

For one brief moment Tegan feared the worst until the vet gave her a relieved, bright smile.

"Kali's through the worst and she's going to make it."

EPILOGUE

Six months later

Tegan used her key to Aaron's place to let herself in. He'd given her a key almost immediately after Christmas but she rarely used it. Because she was seldom here when he wasn't.

He'd asked her to stop by his place and pick something up for him before meeting him at his parents' for their weekly Sunday dinner. They'd spent most of the morning together, but she'd gone home for a couple of hours because she'd needed to finish up some design stuff for her growing business. Soon she was going to have to make a decision about staying on at the coffee shop or going full time with her business. And she knew she needed to make some other decisions as well. Aaron wanted her to move in with him and Dillon but she couldn't do it. She was an old-fashioned kind of girl. She couldn't live with him until she had a ring on her finger. It was the way she was wired.

Some people didn't need that piece of paper, but she needed it. Needed the commitment it symbolized. But she hadn't told him that, hadn't wanted to put any pressure on him. She'd just told him she wasn't ready for that yet, that she was happy the way things were. Which was mostly true.

When she stepped inside Aaron's place she frowned as she shut the door behind her. The alarm hadn't gone off and she knew he was vigilant about setting it. Any fear she might have had disappeared when she turned around and saw a piece of paper on the ground with an arrow, clearly drawn and colored in by Dillon. Curiosity replaced concern.

Smiling to herself, she followed the arrow into the kitchen to find a little sign with a painted red heart and a bunch of glitter covering it on a small stand. Underneath it was another arrow pointing toward the back door. The blinds were closed on the door so she couldn't see what was out there. *What are those two up to?*

Heart pounding with excitement, she dropped her purse and keys on the counter and hurried out the back door. Aaron and Dillon stood there, smiles on their faces, and Kali beside them, tongue lolling. The back porch was decorated with a string of red heart lights and more handmade items, all Dillon's art, with drawings of the three of them holding hands—and Kali was in all of them, too.

Kali, who was back to her healthy self, trotted up to Tegan when Aaron patted her head once. A little sign hung from around her neck, attached to a red ribbon. She bent down and rubbed Kali's head as she read the sign: Pull Me. She tugged on the ribbon and a little box fell onto the ground.

She plucked it up and realized it was a jewelry box. Her heart started pounding even wilder in her chest. When she looked up, Aaron was already on one knee in front of her.

The smile was gone as he watched her with that intensity she felt all the way to her core. "I love you more than I ever thought possible. You're the best thing to happen to us. Marry me?"

Throat tight with emotion, she nodded. She tried to get the word *yes* out but tears were pouring down her face.

"I thought you'd be happy!" Dillon's stricken voice and little face made her find her voice.

"I'm so happy." She tugged him and Aaron into a big hug. "This is the best proposal ever. I love you guys!"

"You haven't even seen the ring," Dillon's voice was muffled because she was probably squeezing him too tight.

Laughing, she pulled back and brushed a kiss over Aaron's mouth. "Yes, yes, yes."

He slid the ring on her finger before she'd even had a chance to look at it. When she did glance down, her breath caught. Instead of a traditional diamond it was a cluster of their birthstones. The symbolism that they were truly a family made her chest tighten. "It's beautiful." The word seemed inadequate to describe what she truly thought of the ring. Of what it meant to her. For the first time in her life she felt like she truly was part of a family.

"You're beautiful," he murmured, the heat in his eyes a promise of what was to come later.

"Santa was pretty late, but you're the best Christmas present ever!" Dillon tackled her again in a hug.

She wrapped her arms around him, her tears slowing, and joy suffusing her entire body. Aaron joined him, wrapping his arms around both of them. "She's the most precious gift in the world."

LETHAL GAME

CHAPTER ONE

Isa looked at her phone screen, pretending to check her email as she waited for her partner to make the drop-off. He was five minutes late.

Which wasn't out of the realm of normalcy for him.

But today was the final day of their job and they were already cutting it close. She had to smuggle the necessary information out and they'd be done. Finally. She liked the temp jobs she took, especially since she got to steal all sorts of interesting stuff, but she was ready to get out of this place. Two weeks was longer than normal for a job.

"Marci," a familiar male voice called out, using her fake name, forcing her to look up. She'd already gone through the body scanner and if her freaking partner would hurry up, she could get the flash drive and be gone. She only had eight more minutes until she had to be out of the building and meet her boss.

She pasted on a pleasant smile even though she knew Brent was going to ask her out. Again. Guy needed to learn to take no for an answer. "Hey, you leaving already?"

He nodded, his smile a little too big. "Yeah, about to grab some drinks for happy hour at Instant Replay. What about you?"

The sports bar was a few blocks away so she wouldn't have to worry about running into him, thankfully. "I'm meeting with friends." She kept her answer as neutral as possible. As far as looks went, the man was attractive. About six feet, dark hair, dark eyes, in good shape, maybe seven or eight years older than her. He was successful too, the VP of one of the marketing departments of the agricultural company. But he was pushy and she didn't like that. Who was she kidding? She didn't want to date anyone right now. Not after the way her heart had been broken a year ago.

"If you want to meet up with me when you're done, I'll be out for a couple hours…" As he continued talking she spotted Antoine, her partner, in her peripheral vision.

He was a new member of the security team at the agricultural company so he didn't have to go through the scanners. Technically he was *supposed* to, but the security here was lax and the guys who were watching everyone didn't follow all the rules.

It was definitely a problem the company needed to fix. Lucky for her they hadn't yet. But they would after today, she was certain. The owner had hired Red Stone Security—where she *really* worked—to literally steal from them.

Antoine rolled his eyes at Brent's back. Yeah, he didn't like the guy either. Whenever they worked jobs together he was always protective. Actually he was protective of women in general, something she adored about him.

Since Isa and Antoine weren't supposed to know each other she didn't acknowledge him, just moved to the side ever so slightly, giving Antoine his opening. They'd worked together enough that she knew exactly what he would do to get Brent off her back.

In a seemingly clumsy trip, Antoine shoulder-bumped Brent, dropping his coffee onto the floor. The dark liquid spilled on Brent's shoes, creating a pool. "Sorry, man." Antoine's expression was full of remorse as he turned toward Brent.

At the same moment he slid his hand behind his back, handing off the flash drive to Isa with practiced efficiency. He continued with his apology, practically shoving himself in Brent's face and offering to help clean up—giving Isa her escape.

"Gotta run, Brent," she said, her heels clicking across the tile of the lobby floor as she made a beeline for one of the glass doors. Time was ticking down. She and Antoine only got their bonus if she made it to the meeting by or before the deadline.

She heard Brent call out her name, but ignored him as she pushed open the door. A cool rush of air rolled over her. December in Florida was milder than most places but the change in season was much needed from the sweltering summer they'd had.

The neon sign of the sports bar across the busy four-lane street flashed blue and red, advertising happy hour prices. Once there was an opening in traffic she raced across the street. Jaywalking was the least of her crimes today.

As she reached the other sidewalk she could see Harrison Caldwell through one of the huge windows, sitting at a high top table with Kenneth Fairfax, CEO of the company she'd just stolen from.

Harrison glanced at her and raised his eyebrows. No doubt he'd give her grief later about how close she was cutting it.

She just pursed her lips and hurried through the front door. Ignoring the hostess's attempt to seat her, she made her way through the crowd of loud men and women until she reached the window table.

Fairfax startled in his seat to see her. "Ms. Harper."

She nodded once and set the flash drive on the table. "You need to reevaluate your security, Mr. Fairfax."

Frowning, he looked at the small black flash drive. "What is this?"

"Very sensitive information, including new info for a patent on wheat." She might not understand all of the science behind what she'd stolen, but it had been carefully secured in their system. Which meant it was important.

He still hadn't touched it. "You're scanned every day when you leave," he said, his expression disbelieving.

"I am." She tilted her chin at the drive. "See what I left the building with, then let's talk." She nudged Harrison with her elbow. "Forget your manners?"

He just snorted and moved over so she could sit while Fairfax plugged the flash drive into his tablet.

"Cutting it close," Harrison murmured.

She just smiled sweetly. She was on time. That was all that mattered.

He frowned again and she knew he wanted to ask her if Brent had been bothering her, but he wouldn't say anything in front of Fairfax. Harrison could go all protective male sometimes. Something about the men of Red Stone Security—they were all ridiculously alpha.

Harrison always treated her like a kid sister, something she secretly liked since she didn't have any siblings. Harrison and his wife Mara had pretty much taken her under their wing a year ago when she started working for Red Stone, and she adored both of them. Most people at work were scared of Harrison but she didn't understand why. Especially since Isa had seen the way he was with his wife and his nephew. The guy was a giant teddy bear where they were concerned.

She lifted a shoulder while Fairfax clacked away on his tablet. After a long moment, Fairfax cleared his throat, his face pale as he removed the flash drive and tucked it into his pocket.

"I watched you on the security feed today," he said to her, his voice accusing.

"You hired me—us—to show you your company's security flaws. What did you see when you watched me today?" They didn't always tell their clients the day they'd be stealing the info, but sometimes they did to prove a point. Fairfax had been watching her like a hawk via a video feed on his laptop; had even had the security team on high alert today. Not for her specifically, just a general alert. But security hadn't been watching very diligently after people went through their scans. And too bad for him—he hadn't known about her partner. Something he should have thought of.

"You working like normal. You didn't even take a proper lunch break. You didn't take any company property out of the building and even left your cell phone at the main desk when you started work."

"You're right. However, I had a partner. Once I was free of the security scans, I just had to wait for him in the lobby to drop off what I'd already downloaded and stolen first thing this morning. I got in early so I could hack into one of the assistants' computers. I used a manager's code to access the info. From there it was simply a matter of getting it out of the building. I told my partner where the drive would be so he could pick it up. He avoided security because he is part of your security team." So there was no electronic trail either, no real proof that any info had left the building. They never would have known they'd been robbed.

Fairfax's expression went dark and he looked to Harrison for confirmation. "Partner?"

"You contacted me because you wanted to test your security. Don't act surprised that I didn't tell you all the measures we'd be taking. A real thief certainly wouldn't tell you their plans. Her partner is one of my employees and has been working in your security department two weeks longer than Isa. You need stricter security protocols for the actual security department more than anything." Harrison's words were to the point.

"I've already started a list of measures you'll need to take to lock things down more tightly. What you have now isn't bad," Isa said, softening her voice just a fraction. "You just need to strengthen things, that's all. You did the right thing by hiring us."

Fairfax straightened in his chair, nodding more to himself than them. His expression wasn't as grim as it had been. "Well...I must admit I didn't think you'd be able to steal anything this important, but I'd rather know now. Thank you both. If you'll excuse me, I need to make a call."

Isa turned to Harrison as Fairfax slid out of his chair. Once he was out of range she picked up a beer from the ice bucket and tipped it toward Harrison. "To another success."

Half-smiling, he lifted his own beer. "He was so smug before you showed up, so sure you couldn't steal from him."

She snorted. "You look far too happy that we've disappointed him."

"Heck yeah, I am. We just got a sweet bonus and...I have a new job for you. One I think you'll find challenging."

"Yeah?"

"Yep, but no details until tomorrow. I've assigned Antoine to an actual security detail for the next month so you'll be working with a new partner."

She wanted to grill him but knew better. Harrison could be very tight-lipped when he wanted. Since she knew he'd once been a spook, she figured even torture wouldn't get the details out of him. "Fine. Unless you need me for anything else, I'm ready to get out of here."

Shaking his head, he flicked a glance over her shoulder for the briefest of moments. Something strange flashed in his gaze. He looked almost annoyed. She turned around and saw Fairfax on the phone and a bunch of other random people. Nothing looked out of the ordinary.

"What's up?" she asked, turning back to face him, wondering if she should be alarmed about something.

"Nothing. Just tired. Ready to wrap up with him and get out of here." His espresso-colored eyes didn't give away anything.

She slid off her chair, small purse in hand. "Then I'll leave you to it. See you in the morning."

As she skirted her way through the crowd her breath caught in her throat when she saw a familiar face through the group standing near the bar. When she blinked, however, he was gone.

Heart racing out of control, she inwardly cursed herself. Tall, Dark and Stupidly Handsome had never been there at all. What was the matter with her? He would have no business being in Miami—or anywhere in her vicinity.

She hadn't thought about him in…a couple days. Which was a record for her. She'd been so busy working it had been easy enough to forget about the lying sack of shit who'd broken her heart a year ago.

Good thing for him that he wasn't here. Because if he was, she'd have followed through with the violent impulse to punch him in his perfect face.

"Don't give me that look," Graysen snarled as he slid into the seat across from Harrison. He'd been waiting for that CEO to leave.

Harrison had started to respond when the bartender who'd been serving Graysen earlier approached the table. "You leaving the bar?"

"Yeah, joining a friend." He tried not to snarl at her, since she was just doing her job. "I'll close out my tab." He pulled out a few bills and left them on the table. "Keep the change."

Her eyes widened slightly but she just nodded and pocketed the money—then not so subtly left a piece of paper with her phone number on it in its place. "I get off in an hour."

He didn't respond as she left, but crumpled the paper up once he was sure she wasn't looking and tossed it into the empty ice bucket. He didn't want anyone but Isa.

"What were you thinking, showing up here?" Harrison's voice was razor sharp.

"I had to see her." Graysen knew he'd be meeting with Isa tomorrow, but the urge to get just a glimpse of her again in person was too much. The woman was his obsession. After a year of no contact, no hearing her voice, he was at his breaking point.

Harrison scrubbed a hand over his face, the action out of place on the normally stoic man. "She's going to be pissed tomorrow."

"She'll get over it." Isa had to. She had to forgive him. He couldn't live with anything less. He wouldn't. "And I'm bringing you a huge job." Graysen had gone to Keith Caldwell instead of Harrison, asking Harrison's father—also the founder of Red Stone Security—to hire him now that he'd left the Agency. He was more than qualified, but he didn't just want a *job*. He wanted to specifically work with Isa. So he'd brought an exclusive government contract Red Stone wouldn't want to turn down. It was practically tailored for Isa's expertise. If she was forced to work with Graysen, he could remind her how good they'd been together. And he could work on getting her to forgive him. Which…was the biggest problem.

"Yeah, and you never let me forget it," Harrison muttered.

Graysen lifted a shoulder. He wasn't sorry. He'd do anything to get Isa back. Once she'd left him he'd gone into a downward spiral. After trying to get her to forgive him, apologizing too many times to count only to be shut out, he'd drowned himself in vodka for about a month until he'd realized he was being a giant pussy. He wasn't just going to let her go. So he'd spent the last few months working on getting a huge contract to bring to Red Stone when he left the CIA. It had been a balancing act, getting this contract while still working for the government. But a lot of people owed him favors and he'd cashed in a ton of them. She was that important to him. Hell, she was the most important thing to him.

"If she refuses to work with you—"

"She won't."

Harrison eyed him over the top of his beer, his expression unconvinced. Harrison was a couple years younger than Graysen but he'd been a damn good agent back when they'd been in Black Ops together. They hadn't worked together often, but Harrison was one of the few people Graysen truly respected. The man had a solid code of honor and he was a patriot. Maybe more of a Boy Scout than Graysen, but that wasn't necessarily a bad trait.

Televisions blared inane sports bullshit above them and people were talking and laughing with no concern for anyone around them. Whereas he knew how many people were at the bar right now, the specific layout of the restaurant, how many exits there were—which were closest—and how many people were outside the window. No doubt Harrison could detail all that information as well.

"Mara's pissed about the whole situation," Harrison said.

"You told her?" He snapped out the words louder than he'd planned, but no one around them seemed to notice.

"Yep." No apology from Harrison either.

"Is she going to tell Isa?" Because Harrison had made it clear to Graysen that Isa meant a lot to Mara. And Mara had been a spook too. Graysen wasn't exactly sure which branch but he guessed MI6.

"No, but she wants to."

"After tomorrow it won't matter."

"Look…just don't get your hopes up about this." For the first time since Graysen had known Harrison, the guy actually looked and sounded concerned. For him.

"About what?"

"About Isa. She's never mentioned you, never mentioned an ex, nothing. And what you did was… I don't know if you can come back from that."

Graysen didn't respond, just turned to stare out the window at the passing traffic and the bright lights of downtown Miami. Yeah, he'd screwed up good. That was the understatement of the century.

He'd infiltrated her father's business, lied about who he was, seduced her and broken her heart—and inadvertently gotten her father killed.

If it was the last damn thing he did, he was going to make things right between them.

CHAPTER TWO

Did you do what I told you to?

Isa shook her head as she read Mara's text, a smile tugging at her lips. A man stepped up next to her, joining the crowd of people waiting for the elevator.

Her fingers flew across the screen. *Yes, weirdo. You're the only woman I know who would order me to dress sexy when going to a meeting with said woman's own husband.*

Mara had called her this morning and ordered her to wear something designed to make a man's tongue fall out of his mouth. She hadn't actually done what Mara had said because this was a professional environment, but she'd dressed up a little more than normal.

You'll thank me later, came Mara's responding text.

Is this about who I'm meeting with today? You know I don't mix business and pleasure. So even if her new partner was sexy as sin it wouldn't matter. He might as well be sexless. She didn't have any interest in anyone, anyway. Not since… She swallowed hard, shutting that thought down.

"You look really familiar," the man next to her said.

Since Mara hadn't responded Isa tucked her phone into her purse and gave the man a neutral smile. When she looked at him, however, she realized she had seen him somewhere. The memory of that 'meeting' was disgusting. "I don't think so," she murmured. Yeah, she really didn't want to talk to *this* guy.

"No, I'm really good with faces and I'm certain we've met before."

He watched her carefully, looking at her as if he was trying to decide if he'd seen her naked or not.

The guy's whole demeanor was off-putting and she wondered if he was a new client for Red Stone. She certainly hoped not. "The reason I probably look familiar," she said quietly, dropping her voice so that the others around them couldn't hear, "is because I was at Club Bardot the other night and saw a prostitute give you a blow job right in the VIP section." She'd been there following someone for one of her past jobs—seeing if there was another angle to being able to infiltrate the company. Meaning, potential bribery of an employee. She hadn't had to use that angle, thankfully.

He blinked in clear surprise, but he didn't seem embarrassed. "She wasn't a prostitute."

That was his response? She coughed to cover up an uncomfortable laugh. "Oh, I just assumed."

He straightened, clearly not deterred. "Well, listen—"

She shook her head. "I'm not trying to be rude, but I literally had to see your dick against my will when you whipped it out for the entire VIP section to see. I don't think we have anything to say to each other."

Isa heard a woman snicker behind her and realized she hadn't been as quiet as she'd thought. But seriously, it was too early in the morning for this. She hadn't even had her coffee yet.

The guy shrugged, not even fazed. "Your loss."

She snorted to herself. Yeah, she was sure she'd lose a lot of sleep over this guy. When two elevators' doors opened, she slipped into the opposite one he got into. At thirty she was too young to be out of the dating game, but damn, if this was what was out there, she was fine being single. She hadn't been in any state of mind to start dating again over the last year, and right about now she was glad for that.

As people streamed into the elevator, her phone dinged a few times in a row. Scrolling through her messages, all from work, she started responding as the car whooshed to life. A few people quietly talked amongst themselves but one by one everyone disembarked as the elevator rose higher and higher. Normally she made an effort to talk to people and be polite but this morning she didn't have it in her.

After leaving the restaurant yesterday evening she'd been feeling off. She knew why, too. She'd thought of Graysen West all night. Had even dreamed of him. It was making her edgy, and she hated that—but she didn't hate him. That was what drove her the craziest. She should hate the man after what he'd done, but…some stupid part of her still held on to all those sweet memories.

Lies, she reminded herself. All those memories might be real but everything about them had been a lie. *Ugh, get the freak over it already.* She wished life was that easy, that she could just order herself to forget him and move on. Unfortunately, getting over a man like Graysen was hard. It wasn't just that he was sexy—which he was. He was giving and sweet… *Gah,* and a giant liar. What the hell was wrong with her? He wasn't giving or sweet. He sucked.

As a woman moved off past her, Isa slipped her phone into her jacket pocket and glanced at the shiny chrome keypad on the elevator wall. Only three floors to go. She hadn't dressed as sexy as Mara had said to, but she was wearing a dark green sheath dress with high heels that she could admit showed off her toned calves. She didn't love everything about her body—what woman did?—but she liked her legs.

"You really need better spatial awareness." A familiar, deep voice from behind her made her jump out of her skin.

Feeling almost numb, she turned to find Graysen West standing there—and looking way too sexy for his own good. Or for *her* own good. She'd thought she was completely alone in the elevator now.

She blinked once. Yep, he was still there. Well over six feet of raw masculinity, bright blue eyes she could drown in, and a disapproving frown that somehow made him look sexy.

"When did you get on?" Okay, that was probably the dumbest thing that could have come out of her mouth, but whatever. She was just glad she'd found her voice.

"Same time you did. But you were too busy on your phone to notice." He frowned, looking all judgmental, and she just about snapped.

"Seriously, that's the first thing you say to me? You criticize me about being on my phone?" She'd been working, not that that was remotely the point. He had no say in her life. If she wanted to play games on her phone, she damn well would.

"You've got to pay better attention to your surroundings. Did you even know there was someone else still on the elevator with you?"

Isa felt almost possessed as she lashed out. A year of built-up anger and hurt came bursting to the surface with his obnoxious 'I know better than you' tone. Her arm was moving before she'd processed what she was doing but when her fist connected with his nose, she cursed at the pain that jolted through her hand. Punching someone *hurt*.

He grunted as his head snapped back. But other than that he barely reacted.

She belatedly realized he hadn't even moved to defend himself, and considering his training, he would have with anyone else. Stupid tears stung her eyes because she felt bad for punching him and she hated the insane way she'd just reacted to seeing him. It was completely nuts. She'd literally just assaulted someone in an elevator.

But Graysen apparently brought out the crazy in her. She spun away from him as the elevator doors opened, glad that no one was waiting and thankful for the escape. She didn't care why he was here. She wasn't dealing with him right now. Not now, not ever.

She heard him call her name but she ignored him and ducked in to the nearest women's bathroom before he could see her cry. She'd cried enough over that man and she'd punch him again before she let him see her have an emotional breakdown.

Fuck, fuck, fuck.

Holding a hand to his bleeding nose, Graysen started to follow after Isa but held back. He'd already screwed up by surprising her in the elevator.

He'd been staring at her perfect ass the last couple minutes and she hadn't had a clue he'd been there.

What if some nut had been in the elevator with her? God, how many times had he told her to pay better attention… He inwardly cursed. Yeah, not the point right now. *Not the point at all.*

Turning away from the closed bathroom door, he headed down the quiet hallway. He didn't want to leave her, but he thought he'd seen tears glistening in her eyes before she stormed off. He didn't want to ambush her again. Not when he knew she needed time to compose herself.

As he moved toward Harrison's office he quickly catalogued his surroundings as he always did. Everything was decorated in soft blues and greens, and Van Gogh prints lined the main hallway. Graysen knew that Harrison headed up a few departments, including the new one that Isa had been working with the last year.

When he stepped into Harrison's assistant's space, the dark-haired woman's eyes widened. She started to stand. "Mr. West—"

He shook his head. "I'm fine."

She eyed him warily but nodded. "Okay… Mr. Caldwell is in his office. He said to send you in when you arrived. Ms. Harper isn't here yet but I expect her any moment. She's always on time." As she spoke she was already buzzing Harrison to let him know that Graysen was here.

Graysen only entered when she gave him the go-ahead. Harrison didn't look exactly surprised when he saw Graysen standing there bleeding.

Harrison rounded his desk and headed to the small bar near the big spread of windows that overlooked the city. With efficient movements, he filled a small plastic bag with ice from the minibar and pulled out a pack of wet wipes. He handed them to Graysen before sitting back down.

"Got a call from security," Harrison said mildly as Graysen started cleaning up the blood. There wasn't much, but his nose still hurt.

Crap. Of course security would have seen Isa punch him. "What did you tell them?"

"To let me deal with it. Damn it, Graysen. Isa is normally one of the calmest, most rational people I know. It's why she fits so well with this new venture Red Stone has taken on. We're appreciative of the new contract you've brought us, but did you ever stop to wonder if you're going to screw up her work dynamic?"

Yeah, he'd thought of it. But this was the only way he could get her to talk to him, to interact with him. She'd shut him down every other time he'd tried to reach out to her—not that he blamed her. "Just give me a chance. This one job with her." The job he'd managed to snag was huge. Raptor Aeronautical—an aeronautical engineering company that took on contract government jobs designing military aircraft. The CEO wanted to tighten things up and do an annual check on security, and Graysen had convinced him to hire Red Stone for the check. They'd just been waiting on the final approval. "One week working with her, and if she wants, I'll step back. You can replace me with someone else." Even saying those words made him break out in a cold sweat. He wasn't sure that he could convince Isa after only a week but he was damn sure going to try.

"Is that a promise?" Isa's quiet voice made him turn in his seat.

Emerald green eyes frosty, her expression was just as icy. All her muscles were pulled taut and her shoulders were stiff as she stepped through the open doorway.

Guess she wasn't the only one who needed to increase their spatial awareness.

He met her gaze, aware of the way his heart pounded. "Work with me one week, once this contract starts. And if it's too much I promise never to bother you again." *Liar, liar,* the little voice in his head said. He wasn't sure he could walk away from her.

She didn't say anything to him, just looked at Harrison in confusion and a little hurt.

The hurt clawed at Graysen. Suddenly his big plan seemed stupid.

"Shut the door," Harrison said quietly.

Once Isa did, he motioned to the seat next to Graysen.

She glided toward him and sat ramrod straight. She'd pulled her long, dark hair into a twist at her neck. Not one perfect hair was out of place. Petite with the right amount of curves, Isa was the only woman who'd ever gotten to him. And then he'd broken her trust and her heart and screwed everything up completely.

"I should have told you Mr. West was going to be your new partner." Harrison's voice was sincere as he looked at Isa. "I'm sorry for ambushing you."

"So you know…about our history?"

Harrison nodded once. "I used to work with Graysen and he recently approached me about a new job."

"Oh." She bit her bottom lip, looking vulnerable.

Graysen had the sudden urge to take that bottom lip between his teeth, nibble on it and her. God he missed her. Had missed her every day and night since she'd left him. Even if it was his own fault.

"Graysen is our newest employee."

Those beautiful green eyes widened just a bit as she finally turned to face him. "You're not with the CIA anymore?"

He shook his head, not trusting his voice and not trusting himself not to say something else stupid.

"He brought a big contract with him as part of his hiring, but it's been top secret until this morning. Still is, if you want to get technical," Harrison said. "It's why I couldn't say anything to you. Not until you'd been approved by the CEO for the job. You've got the clearance for it and so does Graysen, but the CEO still had final approval, and he needed to finish reviewing your file and work history. Hands down, I think you're the best fit for this job. It's a huge deal for Red Stone. I just need to know that you'll be able to work with him."

She was quiet for a long moment and Graysen could practically see the gears turning in her sexy head. Before Red Stone she'd worked for a company that had analyzed other companies' work effectiveness. Often for government facilities. She'd always had a high level of clearance and she was one of the most capable women he knew. It was one of the reasons he liked her so much.

Once things had blown up between them, however, she'd quit her job in DC and moved to Miami to start fresh, away from him and her memories.

"I will be a professional," she finally said.

Graysen noticed the way she subtly flexed her fingers, and handed her the small pack of ice.

It seemed as if she wanted to protest but she took it and murmured, "Thank you."

As long as she wasn't punching him, he'd take it.

Standing, Harrison cleared his throat. "I need to grab a few more items for this meeting. I'll be back in a couple minutes."

Graysen knew that was utter bullshit but figured Harrison wanted to give them time alone.

When the door closed behind him Isa turned toward Graysen. "How's your nose?" Her tone was pointed, her expression making it clear she thought he deserved the pain.

"Not broken." He drank in the sight of her, unable to get enough. Looking at a picture of her wasn't the same as seeing her in person. The elegant line of her neck, the sweet curves of her breasts under her dress—which he shouldn't be noticing right now.

"I...should probably apologize, but I'm not exactly sorry." Guilt flickered in her eyes.

Which made him adore her even more. She felt bad for *not* being sorry. "I deserved it."

She rubbed an unsteady hand over her face. "Jeez, Graysen, what the heck are you doing here? Did you..." She cleared her throat. "I thought you loved your job." There was a hint of bitterness in the last few words and he understood it.

She thought he'd chosen his job over her, over his love for her. He loved her a lot more than a job, but he held back. That definitely wasn't the way to get to her and she wouldn't believe him now anyway. "I'd never planned to stay with the Agency forever. Red Stone is a good company."

"I...hope you didn't get this job in a misguided effort to, uh, win me back." Her cheeks flushed slightly. "Because that's never happening. We're done."

He decided to ignore her words for now. Because he didn't want to lie to her. He'd lied to her enough. Telling her the flat-out truth probably wasn't the way to go either. Telling her that hell yeah, he'd gotten this job for her wouldn't do him any favors at the moment. "I go way back with Harrison. Keith Caldwell too. I'd always talked about working here once I retired." Of course he'd been a couple decades away from retiring. "Some stuff happened at work recently and that timeline got moved up."

"Oh." She seemed relieved by that. "Well…it's a shock seeing you." She let out a nervous laugh and gestured to her iced hand. "Obviously. But I promise no more outbursts of violence. Unless provoked."

He'd have given anything to be able to take her hand in his, stroke his thumb over it, try to ease her pain. Pain he'd caused her yet again. "How's your hand?"

"Okay. I've never punched anyone before." She let out another one of those nervous laughs as her cheeks flushed again.

He hated being the cause of her discomfort. "Well, you're good at it."

She gave him a real laugh and rolled her eyes. "That's a strange compliment."

Before he could respond Harrison strode back in, his expression all business. Time to get down to work.

Even if that was the last thing he wanted to do. But he had to play this right, to be professional and show Isa how good things could be between them. Show her that he still loved her—and that he would never hurt her again.

Because in his end game, Isa was the woman he wanted to spend the rest of his life with. Even if he didn't deserve her, he'd damn sure spend the rest of his life making her happy.

CHAPTER THREE

I'm going to kill you Isa texted to Mara as she headed down in the elevator to her office.

I think you mean thank me. Otherwise you wouldn't have gotten all sexy today. How's your hand feel?

How do you even know about that? Isa hadn't left Harrison's office until a few minutes ago.

I have my ways.

I can actually hear you cackling as you say that. Ugh, my hand is fine. I'm a little embarrassed though.

From what I hear, he deserved more than a punch.

Isa had never told Mara about Graysen. Not specifically, anyway. When she'd become friends with Mara, Isa had mentioned an ex who was a liar, but that had been the extent of things. Talking about Graysen had just been too hard and she didn't like people knowing all her business. But if Harrison knew about Isa and Graysen's history, then no doubt Mara knew everything too. Still, Isa didn't feel like talking about it now. She just wanted to hide out in her office and lick her wounds and pretend that when the new contract started in two weeks she wouldn't be working with her ex-boyfriend—for one stupid week.

Probably, she texted back.

She tucked her phone into her purse when she reached her floor. And when she made it to her office and found Lizzy Caldwell sitting in the chair in front of the desk, offering up a cappuccino, she almost burst into tears. "That's for me?"

Lizzy grinned. "Yep, just the way you like it. I added two sugars."

"I freaking love you."

"I know. I'm very loveable." Lizzy kicked her feet out in front of her and Isa saw that she was wearing purple and pink Chuck Taylors. She had on jeans and a T-shirt that said *Nerd? I prefer the term Intellectual Badass*. The shirt made Isa grin. Lizzy didn't care about 'being professional' at the office. Probably because she was head-hunted by government agencies all the time and knew how invaluable she was to the company. It didn't hurt that she was married to one of the owners, either.

"Not that I don't appreciate this," Isa said, holding up her drink as she sat. "Or the company. But what are you doing in my neck of the woods?" Their offices were actually on the same floor, but they didn't work together often.

Lizzy shrugged, a mischievous grin on her face. "Just knew you'd be back in the office today and wanted to say hi. And…I heard you punched a guy and wanted to ask why."

"Oh crap. Does everyone know?" Isa had worked so hard to fit in here. After escaping DC and the hellish stories—truth—of her father being a traitor, she made a point to be a professional at all times. She was sure some people knew about her past, though no one had ever called her on it. Which was fine by her. She didn't want to talk about that with anyone.

Lizzy snorted. "I don't think anyone does, really. I just heard from Porter—who heard from one of the guys in the security room. They let Harrison, Porter and Grant know as standard procedure. Said you have a nice right hook, *chica*."

"It's the first time I've ever punched someone." She took a sip of her cappuccino, grateful for the comfort drink. Her hand was tender but didn't bother her as much as it had a while ago.

"Well why'd you do it?"

"He deserved it."

"Don't be obnoxious."

"I really don't want to talk about it. Not now, anyway. Harrison just gave me a new job and I've got to start prepping for it." Which meant reading over a bunch of files and learning about her 'new colleagues' before she started with them. That was just the tip of the iceberg of what she had to do for her prep.

"Okay, but if you change your mind, just call me. And not because I want gossip—though I always do. And seriously, if you want me to mess up this guy's life, just let me know." She got a wicked glint in her eyes that Isa knew too well. Lizzy really could be scary when she wanted to.

"He's a Red Stone employee."

Lizzy's eyebrows raised. "Porter left that part out."

Isa lifted a shoulder. "He's my new partner for my next job, so please don't screw up his life."

"You're really not making me want to know about him any less, but if you don't want to talk about him, I get it." She stood, pushing the chair back. "I'm here if you need me."

"Thanks, I appreciate it." Once Lizzy was gone Isa set her mug down on her desk and groaned to herself.

She was going to be working a job with sexy, frustrating Graysen West. How the heck had this even happened? Seeing him in that elevator and then in the office had jolted her back to over a year ago, to the first time they'd met. The first time he'd introduced himself and acted as if he had no idea who she was.

As if he hadn't targeted her for a specific reason.

She looked at her cappuccino and frowned, pushing back all sorts of unwanted memories. If she ever had a reason to start day drinking, now was it.

She was too much of a professional to do that though. Or she hoped she was. Because a mimosa—or three—at lunch today sounded like a good freaking idea.

CHAPTER FOUR

Fourteen months ago

"I think this is yours."

The deep, male voice made Isa turn around and look up, up, up into arresting blue eyes.

"What?" She couldn't tear her gaze away from the stranger in front of her. Didn't want to, if she got to look at this eye candy.

"The coffee. I think I grabbed yours by mistake." That deep voice wrapped around her, his mere presence making everything else in the small coffee shop fade away.

Blinking, she looked at the cup he extended then looked at the one in her hand. She turned it and saw the name Michael scribbled in purple ink. She frowned at herself, surprised she'd taken the wrong cup, but held it out to him as he traded with her. "Sorry about that."

"No worries." His smile was easy, those eyes ridiculously gorgeous, and he looked a little out of place in this coffee shop that attracted mostly corporate types.

He had on jeans, a thick Columbia jacket and heavy boots. He topped off the sexy look with a hint of a beard—probably five or so days' worth of dark scruff—and he looked a bit like a lumberjack. Or a ski instructor. Whatever the look was called, he was walking sex appeal.

She smiled again and was starting to leave when he held out a hand. "I'm Michael."

Stopping, she shook with him. "Ah, Isa."

"Nice to meet you." When her fingers touched his she swore she felt an electric spark travel up her arm. Which was stupid, like something out of a clichéd romantic comedy, but she didn't care.

"You too."

"I was about to head across the street to the park to take my dog for a walk." He motioned to the little gray and white fluffy dog secured outside, looking in the window, watching its master patiently and adoringly. "Want to join me?"

Isa needed to get back to work, but... "Okay." She hadn't been on a date in a while. Mainly because work was insane. And fate decided to drop this guy right in front of her? Yeah, she'd be an idiot to say no.

Shaking herself out of the buried memory, Isa glanced up from her temporary desk, expecting to see Hamilton Ridler, the CEO of Raptor Aeronautical, since it was Monday, the first day of her temporary job.

Instead it was Graysen, looking good enough to eat in a charcoal suit and a pale grayish-blue tie. It didn't matter what the man wore—he always looked good. Something he knew and used to the best of his advantage. They hadn't talked much in the last two weeks, and for that she was grateful. Now she only had one week to get through and she could tell Harrison she didn't want to work with Graysen anymore.

He'd been here the whole time, working with Mr. Ridler as a new employee—one Ridler was supposedly personally grooming for a high management position. Graysen had been brought in early, and because of his new "position" he had the highest security clearance.

As did she. But she didn't have to lie to the people she was working with about her temporary job. Not really. She'd been hired as a special analyst to see where the company could make some cuts. So of course everyone was terrified of her reporting to the big boss that their job was unnecessary. It also meant people avoided her, which was a good thing. She could do her work in peace, and mostly avoid Graysen in the process.

"Hi, Mr. Evans," she said, using his alias for this job. For the next couple weeks, he was Garret Evans. She got to keep her first name; they'd just changed her last name.

"Isa." He nodded once, his look smoldering as he leaned against the doorframe, not bothering to hide all that heat and hunger.

Gah, why couldn't he keep that stuff to himself? She didn't want to know how much he still wanted her. "Can I help you with something?"

He blinked, as if coming out of a trance. "Yes. I wanted to see if you'd have lunch with me today. You haven't left your office all day."

Frowning, she looked at the clock on her laptop and was surprised to see it was already one o'clock. "I'm not really hungry." She could get like that when on a job—everything but her work took a back seat.

"I insist," he murmured, stepping into the small office that consisted of a desk and an empty bookcase. At least it had a window, but other than that it was bare. There was something in his tone that made her straighten, however.

She stood and started to pick up her laptop but he gave a subtle shake of his head.

She picked up her purse instead, and even though she had questions, she didn't bother asking. She would wait until they were alone.

Once they were in the hall he placed his hand on the small of her back, the action not exactly intimate but it somehow felt like it. "Thanks for taking this tour with me." When he spoke it was a little too loud.

She quickly realized that it was because he *wanted* people to overhear him. He continued talking about the company and how even though he was new, that he and Mr. Ridler were going to make sure Raptor was running as smoothly as it could.

When they reached the elevators she started to ask him why he'd wanted her to leave her laptop but he shook his head again and casually scratched his ear. *Oh, right, someone might be listening in the elevator.* In past jobs that had never been an issue. She'd usually worked with Antoine, but they almost never had any interaction except right until the last day of a job. And even then their contact was covert.

A couple floors later Graysen steered her into what turned out to be a private, windowless office set up with multiple video feeds—including one of her office.

She turned to him, wide-eyed. "You're watching me?" She couldn't believe he hadn't told her. Or that she hadn't noticed a video camera.

He nodded and motioned to the desk with two takeout boxes. "I got you a spicy tuna roll and an edamame salad for our lunch date."

She shouldn't be surprised he remembered that was her favorite. "Thanks…but what is all this?"

"We're staking out your office for the next hour."

She snorted and took a seat in the surprisingly comfortable chair in front of her takeout box. It was cushioned and had a remote control to adjust the back setting as well as a heater for her butt. It had to be a couple grand, easy. "Where'd you get this seat?" she asked as he sat next to her in a normal-looking chair.

He shrugged as he adjusted one of the screens. "It was already in here… No one should bother us on this floor. It's where we'll set up our base of operations."

But there was something in his tone that said it hadn't been and she couldn't help but wonder if he'd gotten it for her. She didn't ask because she didn't want the answer. "So, we're staking out my office. Why didn't you tell me before you had it wired?"

"I knew you'd act weird if you knew I had a camera on you."

Well, that was true. "Okay, fair enough. So…this is a little different from what Antoine and I normally do for our jobs. I didn't think you and I would have much contact."

"As of this morning, Ridler told me that he's certain someone is stealing from the company. Funds from two accounts have gone missing in the last twelve hours. Both over a hundred grand. He's got one of his tech guys on it too, but because of the nature of this breach no one else knows about this."

She opened her lunch and smiled at the spicy scent. "And you think what, someone's going to try to hack my computer?"

He shrugged again, slanting her a glance that reminded her of how he'd looked at her in bed on more than one occasion. She wasn't sure what it was, but something in his expression triggered naked memories. She swallowed hard and focused on the screens. The other feeds displayed the hallway outside her office and what appeared to be a couple of stairwells.

"Can I say something not related to this job?" His voice was low, almost hesitant.

Which was so very unlike him. He was always confident. She tensed. "Sure." She kept her tone as light as she could, even though she knew he was going to talk about them, their past. Now wasn't the time. But the truth was, there was never going to be a good time.

"I know I've said I'm sorry but I'm going to say it again. Did I target you? Yes. Did I plan to sleep with you? No. Fuck. *No.* I'd just planned to meet you and get an invite to your father's estate. That was it." His tone grew harsher, his voice thicker as he continued.

Against her will she turned to him. She didn't want to see his face, didn't want to see any emotions there. For the last year she'd done a good job of locking up all memories of Graysen West into a tiny box in her head.

He looked…vulnerable, his expression so open her breath caught. "Then why did you fuck me?"

He flinched at her harsh wording. "It was more than that."

"Maybe so, but I just…don't even know you. I feel like the man I slept with, told secrets to, doesn't exist. You even lied about your freaking dog too. I opened myself up to a man named *Michael.* So whatever you think you feel for me, I don't feel for you. I felt all those things for him. And he was a lie. And it freaking hurts, Graysen."

"I'm sorry. I know it's hollow and useless, but I am. I wish I could go back. I want...a second chance, Isa. I know I don't deserve it, but I—"

She shook her head, unable to let him continue. "No. There will be no second chance. No chance between us, ever."

He nodded once, swallowing hard. "Is it because of...your father?"

God, she didn't want to talk about her father. She still hadn't come to terms with the man her father had been, all the lies he'd told everyone. He'd been selling state secrets to *terrorists*. "I understand why you and your people went after him and...I believe he wanted to die in that gunfight."

It had been a 'suicide by cop' type of situation, only in her father's case he'd opened fire on FBI agents who'd been working with Graysen's covert CIA team. The FBI had taken him out with little effort.

"That's not why. I can never trust you now. Simple as that." He looked so damn broken she found herself continuing even though it went against all her self-preservation instincts. She knew from experience that he was a good actor. Still, he'd gone to a lot of trouble to work with her. "We can be civil. If you're working for Red Stone, I don't want to be enemies or anything. So, yeah, we can be friendly. That's it though." It took work to say the words.

His blue eyes went shuttered as he nodded. "Okay. Fair warning. I want more. Always will."

"Graysen—"

He stiffened, his gaze darting to one of the screens. She followed where he looked and her eyes widened.

A woman in her mid-forties wearing a navy blue dress went to the window in Isa's office and leaned against it, looking out at the skyline, her body language casual as she started to slowly do a visual scan of the office. It wasn't overt; her moves were very relaxed. Her gaze skimmed right over where the camera must be.

"You really must have hidden that camera well," Isa murmured, watching as the woman quickly went to the laptop and clicked on the keyboard.

Graysen grunted, his gaze intent on the woman for a second, as if memorizing her face. "Gina Scott."

Isa blinked in surprise. "You know her?"

"Not personally. I just memorized the names and faces of anyone who had access to the funds missing."

"That's like…over a hundred people."

He shrugged, as if memorizing that many names and faces wasn't a big deal. She knew he had a good memory, but that was a lot of information to retain. He slid a laptop in front of him, and, fingers flying across the keyboard, pulled up a program she recognized well. Working quickly, he shadowed what the woman was doing so they saw what she saw, but on their own screen—and Gina Scott was completely unaware of their presence. The spyware program was incredible.

Isa frowned. "It looks like she's pulling up different personnel files."

Graysen's frown matched her own. "She's copying them to a flash drive."

Isa pulled out her cell phone and called Emerson Lincoln, a computer programmer/analyst who worked for Red Stone Security. Emerson had been assigned as their backup to run checks on people and handle various research that would save them valuable time. Isa had been working with the sweet woman for about eight months and she was very good at what she did.

Emerson picked up on the second ring. "Hey, girl. How's the job going?"

"Potentially we might have something good for you. Can you do a detailed run on Gina Scott?"

"No problem. Anything specific I should look for?"

"Just the usual stuff," Isa said, even as she took over one of the other laptops, pulling up a file on Gina Scott. "I'm going to review her employee records, but look up all of her financials." It was usually a good place to start with anyone. If someone had new, offshore bank accounts or unexpectedly large deposits into their current one, that was a pretty good sign they were up to no good. Usually people weren't so sloppy, however—Isa wished her job was that easy. But she never knew. If someone didn't realize they were being watched they could get arrogant and sloppy.

As they disconnected Isa watched the woman pull her flash drive out of the computer and tuck it into a slim pocket of her dress. She couldn't even see a tiny bulge giving away the flash drive.

"What did she take?" she asked Graysen.

"It looks as if she just copied financials of other employees. Basically information pertaining to what their annual salaries are."

Isa lifted an eyebrow. "Could just be nosiness."

"Maybe." But Graysen shook his head. "That was a ballsy move."

"Yeah, she moved like a pro, too. Almost like she's done this before." Isa continued scanning Scott's personnel file, noted that the woman had a high-level position in one of the design departments.

"I'm sure Emerson will have something for us soon," Graysen said, speaking about Emerson as if he knew her.

Which for some reason grated on Isa's nerves. Not because she thought he had a chance with the other woman—no, Emerson was smitten with a local detective—but because she'd come to think of Red Stone Security as her home, her people. It was weird to be working with Graysen, for multiple reasons. Because he'd said that he'd bow out of this job after a week if it became too uncomfortable for her. But he hadn't said he'd stop working for Red Stone.

She wasn't sure how she felt about that. About any of this. Because just being in the same room with him, breathing in his addictive, subtle masculine scent, made her a little bit crazy.

"I kept the dog," he said abruptly. Graysen didn't look at her as he focused on the display of video screens, scanning the various secret feeds he'd set up. She wasn't certain where some of the feeds were coming from.

Isa blinked, taking a second to digest his words. He couldn't mean… "Peaches?"

He nodded. "Yeah. She grew on me. She misses you, so if you ever want to stop by and see her, you're welcome to."

She blinked again. "Seriously? You're stooping to using a dog to get in my good graces?"

Graysen's lips perked up the slightest bit. He was clearly unapologetic. "I'll use anything I can to get into your good graces. Including a sweet, adorable dog who would love nothing more than to see you. But I'm not lying. She's currently with her dog sitter, probably soaking up sun on the beach or at the park."

Isa looked away from him. Why the hell had he told her that? She'd loved that little mutt, Peaches. The little girl was a mix of who knew how many breeds, with gray and white fur, floppy ears, and weighed maybe ten pounds soaking wet. And Graysen had kept her?

She knew that the dog was originally part of his cover. He'd admitted as much after his operation blew up in his face. She couldn't believe he'd kept Peaches. It was so obvious what he was trying to do—getting her to come over to his place and see his dog. A dog that she had dearly loved.

He was being so honest and blatant about what he wanted from her and she wasn't sure how to deal with it. After the way he lied to her, betrayed her, being around him again in a new atmosphere had completely rocked her world on its axis. For all she knew, he was lying to get something else from her. Even as she had the thought, she simply couldn't imagine what it would be, what he could hope to gain. He worked for Red Stone now. Had pulled strings to get this job, from all accounts. Just so he could work with her.

She just wanted to get through this job and put some space between them. Only one week, she reminded herself. Maybe then her life would go back to normal. She nearly snorted at the lie she tried to tell herself. Now that Graysen West was back in her life again, she knew things would never be normal again.

CHAPTER FIVE

Alan Persky watched on the video feed from the company's security room as the pretty, dark-haired woman entered the lobby. It was the end of the day and the woman, Isa Johnson, was here at the behest of Hamilton. Hiring that bitch should have gone through him as well, but no one had mentioned it to Alan.

Hamilton could do what he wanted, he always did, but bringing someone in to "trim the fat," especially someone who had the right kind of security clearance to work at this firm, even temporarily, was something Alan should have been informed about.

But Hamilton had been acting strange lately, almost secretive. Which wasn't out of the realm of normalcy, but Hamilton never acted that way with him. Right now there was too much on the line to question the CEO, however.

Frowning, he watched as she exited the building. Her name was so common—Johnson. There were a billion Johnsons in the world. He'd already downloaded her resume and other necessary hiring files and planned to follow up on her, but he wished she wasn't here at all.

Alan didn't need somebody nosing around in any work files right now. Not when he was so close to finishing what he needed to, cashing out and leaving the country for good with the woman he loved. He'd fake his own death as well, but later, once he was long gone. There was the slimmest of chances that Johnson would find what he'd done and he couldn't risk her stumbling upon it.

He could just kill her or have one of his men kill her, but that wouldn't solve anything. It would only draw more attention to the company and his boss would just hire somebody new anyway. No, Alan would just keep an eye on her and make sure she didn't get into anything she shouldn't.

If she did, then she'd have to die.

The other new hire was the one who had him really worried: Garret Evans. There was something about Evans that bothered him on a bone-deep level, but he wasn't certain what it was. All he knew was that he didn't trust the guy. Hamilton had recently hired Evans as well, without running it by him first.

Alan had contemplated that Hamilton might know what he was up to, but if the old man did, Alan would already be in jail and facing charges of treason. If that ever happened, they'd throw him into a dark hole and never let him out. A dark shiver of fear snaked down his spine at the thought of getting caught.

No, he was just being paranoid because of everything on the line. They were getting close to the end of this job and he was letting his fear get the best of him.

Still, it never hurt to be careful. Not with so much at stake.

When the door behind him opened he half turned and nodded politely at one of the security guys coming back from a smoke break. He'd stopped by under the guise of an impromptu visit—as was typical of him to do. Considering his security clearance, when he offered to watch the feeds for a few minutes so the security guy could smoke, the twenty-something man had jumped at the chance. It was against protocol, but when *he* bent the rules people were usually okay with it. That was one of the benefits of his position with the company.

"Nothing unusual," he murmured to the guy before stepping back out into the hall.

He smiled to himself once he was alone. In just a week he would be out of the country, millions of dollars richer, and away from his bullshit, boring life. He was going to leave everything behind him—his debts, his stupid ex-wife, everything. His new fiancée got him like no one else did. She was beautiful, smart and supported him. She wanted to leave the country too. Was so taken with him that she'd go anywhere with him.

Starting fresh was what he needed. Hell, what he deserved. He'd given everything to this company, and yeah, he made decent money. But he could be making more. He should be making more.

At the thought of all the money he'd have soon, some of the earlier fear faded away.

Only a week to go. He still had a couple more things to finish to complete his mission, and then he was home free.

And he'd be incredibly rich. If anyone got in his way, they would simply have to die. Because failure wasn't an option for this. He'd already committed and would see this through until the end.

CHAPTER SIX

"I'm going to need clearance to get into Red Stone tonight," Carlito said into his phone. His former partner and best friend worked there—was one of the co-owners.

"That's your greeting?" Grant Caldwell's voice was dry.

Carlito scrubbed a hand over his face as he headed down the sidewalk in the now quiet business district of downtown Miami. During the daytime it was bustling, but after five or six o'clock it was a ghost town. Tonight it was ice cold, especially for Florida, but it was close to Christmas and while it wouldn't be a white one, they were getting some serious chill. "Sorry, man. How's Belle?" Grant's wife was nine months pregnant and close to popping. They'd already had a few false alarms and rushed to the hospital but as far as Carlito knew, they were back home now.

"We're doing good, she's just tired and cranky. And I can't blame her." Grant sounded exhausted.

Carlito couldn't actually see Belle being cranky—the woman was like a ray of sunshine. She'd been through hell after being kidnapped by a psychotic serial killer, *and* she'd married his grumpy former partner, so she was a saint as far as he was concerned. "Any more false alarms?"

"No. And I hope after the next trip we take to the hospital, we come home with a healthy baby."

"Her family's going to descend on you guys like locusts." Belle's Greek family was huge and...wonderful. They'd pretty much adopted Carlito because of his close relationship with Grant, and he loved them. And Belle's mom was always hinting that she'd love to set him up with one of her nieces. But Carlito only had eyes for one woman, hence the call to Grant tonight.

Grant let out a short, tired laugh. "They already have. They've been dropping off tons of casseroles. We've frozen most of them. The food has been amazing so I can't complain too much. So what's up? Why do you need to get into the building?"

"You know exactly why," he gritted out.

"I know, I just want to hear you say it."

"Emerson is working late, and I want to bring her dinner." Emerson Lincoln, the woman he planned to marry one day. If only he could ever get her to see him as something other than a friend.

Grant laughed again. "You are so gone over her."

Yeah, no shit. "You really gonna give me grief tonight?" His shoulders tensed as he reached the high-rise building. He loved Grant like a brother, but right now he didn't need to be reminded that the only woman he'd ever truly wanted was still out of reach. Still not his. And she had no clue how he felt about her.

"Nah. I'll call the security team, tell them to buzz you up. You've just gotta ask her out."

"I have." Countless times. They went out all the time. As friends.

When he'd first met Emerson she'd been coming off a bad breakup and definitely hadn't been interested in him. He'd known she was the one, so he hadn't pushed. The truth was, he'd never had a problem with women. They seemed to flock to him. Ever since he was fifteen. When he was a teenager, he'd reveled in it. Then he'd grown the hell up and gotten more discerning. Especially after spending years in war zones. He wasn't a teenager and he didn't want an easy lay.

He wanted Emerson. Forever. So he was playing things right. Unfortunately, around her he turned into a moron. He was suddenly that awkward teenager he'd never been during his actual teen years. It was like karma was punishing his ass for having it so easy with women for so many years.

"You're not trying hard enough… Hold on." There was a faint

rustling in the background, then Grant talking to someone, then he was back on the line. "I just called it in. You're good to go."

"Thanks, man." Once they disconnected, he slipped his Bluetooth out of his ear and slid it into his jacket pocket.

Since he'd just gotten off shift at the police station, he was still in his suit. But his detective's badge was out of sight. His shoes made slight thudding sounds against the lobby floor as he strode across it. Once he reached the main security desk, he nodded at the security man he'd interacted with on many occasions—always when he was coming to see Emerson.

He set the bag of food on the counter. "I've got my service weapon on me." Even though the guy knew him he still wanted to inform him about his weapon.

The man nodded. "Figured you did. Grant said it's okay for you to take it up. How long you plan on being here?"

"Couple hours, maybe." Monday nights Emerson seemed to work late and this had become a standing ritual between them. He hadn't called her today though, had been so caught up with closing a case. But once he'd finished all the paperwork, he'd headed over here.

The need to see her, to be around her, was a live thing inside him. She was it for him and he'd known it pretty much from the moment they'd met. Man, she'd blindsided him too. He'd met her at one of Grant's get-togethers six months ago, and when his former partner had introduced her as "the new girl," he'd been a goner.

Her looks played into it a little, but after getting to know her that night, he hadn't been able to get her out of his head. She was smart, and a blend of sweet and sarcastic. He just liked being around her, plain and simple. Unfortunately, she hadn't seemed as interested. They'd gotten along great, but he knew when women were coming on to him and she never had.

Not once.

No coy looks or subtle flirtations. Nothing. They were just friends. Maybe he was a masochist, because that just seemed to make him want her more.

The elevator ride to her floor was quick as usual. And her floor was empty, again as usual, considering the time he was getting here. The security at Red Stone was tight, however, so the most protective part of him didn't mind how late she worked. Not that she'd asked him, and not like he had the right to an opinion. He also liked that she was working and not out with some douchebag.

He cared about her safety. Some intrinsic part of him simply needed to know she was cared for.

The hallway leading to her office was lined with prints of classic paintings, like most of the building. Everything here was designed to be soothing. Unlike where he worked. The PD was loud no matter the time of day or night, and the color of paint on the walls or type of art wouldn't make a damn difference.

When he reached her office, the door was slightly ajar. He pushed it open to find her in front of her computer screen, the soft glow highlighting her sharp cheekbones. Her long blonde hair was pulled up in a ponytail and her heels were lying haphazardly near the full-length window overlooking downtown.

He watched her for a long moment, taking in the myriad of facial expressions as she clicked away on the keyboard. He was certain she had no idea he was even there. When she got in the zone of working, everything else faded away. She made these adorable little sounds of frustration, then one of triumph before she nodded at the screen victoriously.

God, he adored her.

"You need better awareness," he murmured, stepping into the room.

She let out a squeak and glanced up at him, pinning him with those dark espresso eyes that completely captivated him. "You've got to stop sneaking up on me." Frowning, she looked at her screen and her eyes widened. "Jeez, I didn't realize how late it was."

"I figured," he said dryly, setting the takeout bag on the front of her desk. He'd brought her favorite.

"You're my hero." She smiled, eyeing the big brown bag.

Yeah, he'd love to actually be her hero. Her lover, her…something other than her friend.

"Please tell me that's what I think it is."

He just snorted and started pulling out the utensils and paper plates. Of course it was. She loved a Chinese restaurant a few blocks away, called it a hidden gem in the city. She wasn't wrong. "Have I ever disappointed you?"

"No. I wasn't sure if you were coming today though, when you didn't call."

He flicked a glance at her at the tone in her voice. He couldn't quite pin it down, but something was off. "You can always call me too, you know."

"Yeah I know, but with that case you're working on, I didn't want to bother you. Figured you had a lot going on this week."

He'd never be too busy that he couldn't make time to talk to her. "I've wrapped everything up, for the most part." And thank God for that. Holidays seemed to bring out the crazy in people though—and crime never took a break—so he knew he'd be assigned another case probably tomorrow. Maybe sooner if a call came in tonight.

She turned off her computer screen, dimming it to black. Some of the things she worked on were confidential. Not just anyone could waltz up into the offices on her floor. The only reason he was able to was because of his relationship with Grant and the entire Caldwell family.

"I bet you skipped some paperwork though." Her half-smile was knowing as she rounded the desk, pulling her chair with her so they could eat on the same side. She was wearing a sweater dress that pulled at the soft swell of her breasts. The dress was definitely professional but it didn't hide anything. Her smooth, toned legs drew his eyes as they always did. Without her heels on she was about five feet five inches and he loved seeing her so relaxed around him—loved looking at her curves. Who was he kidding? He loved looking at all of her.

He lifted a shoulder as he pulled out a box of sesame chicken and broccoli. He slid it over to her, loving the way her eyes lit up as she eyed it.

"I seriously love you," she said, laughing. "I only had a protein bar today because of Lizzy. That woman is crazy."

His heart skipped a beat at the casual way she said the "L" word. He knew she didn't mean anything by it, and that was a huge disappointment. Jesus, what was wrong with him? He rolled his shoulders once and pulled out his Mongolian beef and rice.

"Why did she make you skip lunch?" Because a protein bar did not count as food.

Emerson shook her head, still laughing. "She's on this crazy exercise kick where she works out for her entire lunch break, running up and down all the flights of stairs in the entire building. More than once. She decided she needed a buddy and I'm apparently a sucker."

Carlito let out a short laugh and sat in the chair in front of her desk. "How long do you think you'll keep it up?" He knew she preferred yoga or Pilates to running and other cardio.

"Maybe another day or two. I'm working on a new job and know I'll be busy for the next couple weeks so I figured it was good to stretch my legs while I can."

For some reason those benign words made him think of stretching her legs out in a very different scenario. Stretching them around his waist or draping them over his shoulders as he buried his face between her legs. Clearing his throat, he shifted uncomfortably and focused on his food. "So…you headed to see your dad tonight?"

"Yeah." Her voice took on that odd tone again but when he looked at her, she was scooping out chicken onto her plate. "What are you up to after this?" Something about her voice was strained. It was slight, but he knew her well enough by now to pick up on it.

"I…thought I'd go with you." He always went with her to visit her dad in his assisted living facility. Which was more like a posh golf resort. Frowning, he set his fork down. "Unless you'd rather go alone?"

"No, I… I just talked to Camilla earlier and she made it sound like you couldn't go tonight."

"She did?" His oldest sister and Emerson talked all the time. They had ever since his sisters and mom had met Emerson at a Halloween party a month and a half ago.

"Yeah." Again with that weird tone. And he noticed she wouldn't look at him, was way too focused on her food.

"Well, she's wrong. I probably should have stayed late and finished up with that paperwork, but it'll wait until morning. I wouldn't miss seeing your old man." He loved the guy—Emerson Sr.—loved talking to him about his days in the Corps and hearing stories about Emerson when she was a kid. He liked being part of her life, knowing the people most important to her.

Her shoulders eased at that. "Well, good. He loves seeing you."

"What about you?" he asked.

"What about me?"

"Do you love seeing me?" he asked in a teasing tone—even if he did want to know the answer.

She rolled her eyes before giving him one of those heart-stopping grins that made him forget how to function, let alone speak. "You just brought me food. Of course I do."

One day he was going to put that smile on her face because he'd given her the best damn orgasm of her life. Because he loved her more than any other man ever would. He was going to convince her that they were meant to be together.

She was already one of the closest friends he'd ever had, and that was saying something. His family loved her, and hell, even if they didn't, he wouldn't care. He just needed to get his shit together. Christmas was soon and he planned to let her know how he felt then. Planned to give her a present that made it crystal clear how much she meant to him. If she didn't return his feelings…

He'd deal with it.

CHAPTER SEVEN

As Isa steered into her garage she frowned at the sight of headlights in her rearview mirror, pulling into her driveway. They quickly went off, making her frown deepen.

She lived in a quiet neighborhood. She'd rented for about a month when she moved to Miami, but then she'd found this adorable little ranch-style home in a quiet cul-de-sac neighborhood that she loved. It was filled with palm trees and pools in practically every backyard, and she loved everything about it, including her neighbors. Everyone here knew everyone and they looked out for each other.

She pulled out her pepper spray from her purse and quickly exited the vehicle. It wasn't too late for visitors, but no one ever stopped by for a random visit and she didn't recognize the vehicle.

When she saw Graysen's familiar form step out of an SUV, that momentary spike of panic left her body. Maybe there had been an emergency at work?

She tossed the pepper spray onto the driver's seat and hurried out of her garage. "Hey, what's going on?" she asked, her heels clicking on the pavement.

Instead of answering, he opened the door behind the driver's side and a bundle of gray and white fur jumped out. Yipping excitedly, Peaches raced toward her and as she jumped into the air, Isa caught the adorable mutt in her arms. She was inundated with licks and kisses as she buried her face against Peaches' head.

"What are you doing here?" she asked Graysen.

He wore the same suit he'd had on today, sans tie. The top button of his dress shirt was undone and for some insane reason she wished she'd been the one to take off that tie, to unbutton his shirt, to…

Nope, nope, nope. Not going there.

He lifted a shoulder. "Peaches missed you."

"There's no emergency at work?"

He shrugged again, all casual nonchalance. "Not that I know of."

Her eyes widened. "So you just decided to stop by with your dog? Out of the blue?" *Like we're freaking friends?*

"Yep."

She narrowed her gaze at him, tried to keep her annoyance clear, but it was hard to look serious and frustrated when Peaches was licking her face, just begging for attention. "How'd you even know where I liv— Never mind. Don't answer that." He'd probably found out long before he started working for Red Stone.

"Aren't you going to invite us in?"

"I must be out of my mind, but come on." She didn't want to stand outside and have whatever conversation he wanted to have while any of her neighbors might see and come out to check on her. She turned back toward the garage, and, still holding Peaches, grabbed her purse and laptop bag from her car before shutting the door. Once inside her mudroom she disarmed her alarm system, but only after making sure Graysen turned around. Not that it would likely matter. He would probably have no issue breaking into her place if he truly wanted to.

Before they'd taken two steps into her kitchen, Graysen stepped in front of her, his weapon drawn. A little burst of panic set in before she realized what he was doing.

The man was a total freak sometimes. Even when she'd thought of him as Michael, he'd been the same: vigilant about security.

"Sure, go ahead and sweep my house as if you have every right," she muttered more to herself than him as he made his way through the kitchen to one of the attached rooms.

He clearly wasn't listening and didn't care anyway.

"You are in luck," she murmured against Peaches, who'd stopped squirming and was now sitting contently in Isa's arms. "I've got a treat for you."

Peaches knew what the word treat was and started wiggling again, licking Isa's face as if she loved her more than anyone in the world. Unexpected tears stung her eyes. She'd really missed this sweet dog. She'd even contemplated getting one of her own when she moved to Miami, but she'd been a mess a year ago and hadn't been ready.

Now... Yeah, she could get one now. Of course, no dog compared to Peaches.

Reaching into her pantry, she held onto the dog with one arm and opened the plastic bag of fake bacon treats. "One or two, do you think?" she asked.

Peaches let out two little yips, as if she actually understood.

Laughing, Isa gave her the two strips and when she wiggled to be freed, set her down. Peaches scurried away, probably to hide one of the strips, right as Graysen walked back into the kitchen. He was sheathing his weapon as Peaches raced by him.

"So any dangers lurking in my secured house?" He clearly knew the security system had been armed.

"You're good." He frowned slightly at the bag of treats. "Why do you have dog treats?"

"Babysat a neighbor's dog not too long ago."

"Ah."

"So...why the heck are you here?"

"I wanted to see you." Heat flared in his blue eyes as he watched her.

She didn't like that she was affected by that look—and his mere presence. "That's not an answer."

"It's the truth. I told you that if in one week you're done with me, I'll walk away from the job. We have six days left."

"That doesn't give you the right to just show up at my house unannounced." But it was so typical Graysen. He could be incredibly pushy when he wanted. Which...she'd liked about him. *Before.* Back then she'd liked *everything* about him.

Before she'd discovered what a liar he was. Before her father had died.

"I know."

"But you did it anyway?"

He leaned against the island in her kitchen, looking at ease here, as if he belonged. Or more likely that was just wishful thinking on her part. "Two people after Gina infiltrated your computer today. I wanted to make sure you were safe." He said it as if he truly had been concerned about her. Which, okay, wasn't actually a surprise.

"No one there knows who I really am." She always took precautions when she worked on a Miami job. When she was out of town it was easier to maintain anonymity, but when she was in her own city she had to be careful for sensitive jobs. And the one they were on was definitely sensitive. People were afraid they might be losing their jobs because of her. Not only that, someone was stealing from the aeronautical company. Clearly some employees were going to be let go because three employees, including Gina Scott, had copied information from her laptop.

Isa still couldn't believe the three of them thought she'd be stupid enough to just leave her laptop lying around unlocked. But given enough time and what they thought had been an opportunity, three individuals had sneaked into her office in the middle of the day. The only miracle was that they hadn't run into each other while doing it. The video footage Graysen had gotten was pretty damning too.

"And I don't think I was followed home." Well, except by Graysen, but he might have just come to her house since he would have had her address. The man was too skilled at getting information to not know where she lived.

"You weren't followed. Except by me." He sounded positive about that, and if anyone would know, it would be him. She might not know what most of his training had entailed, but he'd worked for the CIA for eight years—and been in the Marine Corps before that. He'd certainly fooled her.

She stared at him for a long moment and tried to bury all the emotions that wanted to push their way to the surface. Emotions she should have buried long ago. He simply watched her right back with those bright blue eyes she could easily drown in. She'd gotten caught up in his gaze more than once in the past. It was like he ensnared her, and once she was hooked he was impossible to escape from.

Right now she had no idea what he was thinking. He had that neutral expression in place. The neutrality did nothing to hide the savage edge to the man. There were handsome men and then there were men like Graysen, who fell into their own category. He was good-looking, all right, and knew it. But there was an intangible edge to him that rolled off him in waves, warning he was trained and lethal. And…she liked that about him.

She cleared her throat, feeling unnerved by her physical reaction to him. "You don't have to make sure I get home safely every night." Because the thought of him coming into her home for the next week was too much to deal with. He was too much to deal with.

"You're my priority." His voice was low and somehow sensual.

"This job is the priority."

"Not to me." He rounded the island, closing the distance so only about four feet stood between them. Definitely not enough space.

Being this close to him had her entire body heating up and her nipples tightening. *Stupid physical reaction!* It was hard to remember to breathe when he was this close. All day she'd managed to maintain a certain distance from Graysen. Even when they'd been watching the video feeds together, she'd been so focused on work that it had been easier to tune out his presence. Obviously not completely, because he was Graysen. But still, easier.

Having him in her personal space, her domain, was jarring and messing with her head. And after what he'd just said? Yep, no response for that.

He took a step closer. "You want to have dinner together?"

Against her will, her gaze briefly strayed to his mouth. She mentally shook herself. "Not tonight."

He took another step, his advances slow and precise. A patient panther, stalking its prey. "But another night?"

She cleared her throat again, willing her voice to work. "What do you think you're doing?" She hated that her voice trembled, hated that he had a sort of power over her.

"I've got a week, Isa. I want to spend time with you when we're not at work. I've missed you, thought about you every damn day." The sincerity in his eyes pierced her. He lifted a hand as if he wanted to touch her, but quickly dropped it.

Yeah, well, she wanted a lot of things, mainly to rewrite the past so they didn't have such a shitty history. And she didn't want to be affected by him. Not only that, she'd never agreed to see him after work hours. "Call or text me, then. Don't just show up at my house." If he did that, she could just blow him off.

He opened his mouth but her cell phone buzzed in her purse, the sound music to her ears. Turning away from him, she grabbed it, glad to see Emerson's name on the screen.

"Hey," she said, answering on the second ring.

"Hey yourself. I'm heading out for the day but just sent updated files to both you and Graysen on the three top suspects."

Isa wasn't surprised Emerson was just now leaving work. The woman always worked late. She also got to work from home sometimes and had leeway with her schedule—and got paid very, very well for her skills. "Thanks for letting me know."

"They've all got interesting financials, but take a good look at Gina Scott."

"Will do."

"I'll be in later tomorrow, probably around ten, but I'll have my phone on me if you need me."

"Okay. Tell your dad hi for me."

She could practically hear Emerson smiling through the phone. "I will. He said thanks for the popcorn tin and wants to know when to expect more."

Isa smiled, glad he'd enjoyed it. "I'll get more in time for Christmas."

They talked a minute longer and when they disconnected she felt more like herself, more in control. Setting the phone on the countertop, she turned to find Graysen leaning against the island, looking all casual and sexy as he watched her.

"Emerson sent us updated info. And…I need you to go, Graysen." She needed space from him. Having him sprung on her for this job wasn't as easy to handle as she'd thought it would be. Yes, she could be professional. "We need boundaries. Showing up here? I'm not okay with that."

His jaw tightened once but he nodded. "Okay. I'm sorry."

She blinked, surprised he'd acquiesced so easily.

"Have dinner with me this week?" he continued. "We can meet somewhere." The slight edge of desperation in his voice took her off guard, almost made her say yes.

But… "I just want to get through this job."

He nodded once, let out a short whistle then Peaches raced back into the kitchen, her nails clicking on the tile. Instead of running to Graysen, she charged Isa again.

Heart melting, Isa picked her up, snuggled her against her chest.

"I'm not giving up on us." His quiet words had the effect of a grenade going off.

There is no us she wanted to shout at him, but the words stuck in her throat. Somewhere, deep down, though she didn't want to acknowledge it, she knew they could have something incredible together.

But she was terrified of all the ugly baggage between them. Worried that she'd never be able to move past his betrayal and would just resent him if she let him back into her life again. If she did that and things spiraled downward…

She just didn't know if it was worth the almost guaranteed heartache. She wasn't a masochist.

She glanced away from him, used Peaches as an excuse for a distraction and grabbed another treat for her. "I'll walk you to your SUV," was all she managed to get out.

Because telling him anything else wasn't an option.

CHAPTER EIGHT

Stepping into her dad's office, Isa leaned against the doorframe as her dad spoke into his phone. Even on a Sunday afternoon he was working; no surprise. Larger than life, her dad smiled at her and held up a finger that she should wait before he continued his conversation.

Isa had to get up early for a meeting tomorrow and her place was in DC. Sometimes she stayed over at her dad's but his estate was in Virginia and while the drive wasn't terrible, her boyfriend Michael had asked her to stay at his place overnight. Had said he wanted to talk to her about something. Whatever that something was had butterflies dancing in her stomach. She was actually running late, but she'd call him as soon as she was on the road.

"You leaving, baby girl?" Her dad's booming voice cut through her train of thought. Everything about him was loud, larger than life.

Shaking herself, she nodded and stepped farther into the room. "Yeah. I've got some work to do before my meeting tomorrow." And okay, she wanted to get plenty of naked time with Michael. Not like she'd be saying that out loud, however.

"Thanks for coming over for lunch," he said, standing and rounding his desk. "I don't see you enough lately."

"I know." They'd always had weekly lunches or dinners, either in the city or at his house. Usually in the city, since he worked for a big defense contractor. "I'm hoping after Christmas things will slow down." Usually January and February were her slowest months, and from what she knew, her dad didn't have a big contract coming up.

"Well, I've got to head out the day after Christmas. Probably going to

sign a new contract soon. Which will mean travel." He winced slightly, looking guilty.

Disappointment filled her but she hid it. "It's okay. I always understand work." And she did. Her mom had died in childbirth, so it had just been the two of them from the beginning. She knew he dated, but he'd never brought anyone home. And he'd worked incredibly hard to send her to the best schools. He'd given her everything she'd ever wanted or needed. When she was younger she hadn't appreciated how much he'd done – what kid did? – but now she understood how much he'd sacrificed for her and how many opportunities she'd been given.

"I know that you do." He looped his arms around her, pulling her into a bear hug before he kissed the top of her head. "Text me when you're home. I want to know you made it safe."

"I will." She was almost thirty but it didn't matter to her dad. She'd always be his baby girl. And she was okay with that.

"So is that man of yours planning on proposing any time soon?" he asked, stepping back and eyeing her.

"Ah, I think it's too soon." Though if Michael asked she would say yes. Which seemed insane to admit, even to herself. The chemistry she had with him was unlike anything she'd ever experienced before, and when they were together Michael had eyes for no one but her. She felt treasured and safe in a way she'd never expected or thought possible. None of her previous boyfriends held a candle to Michael. He could be a little overprotective and worried about her safety, but there were a lot worse qualities she could have in a significant other.

"Four months isn't too soon. I knew your mom was the one after a month." His dark eyebrows pulled together, his brow furrowing.

Shaking her head, she just gave her dad another hug. She'd heard the story a million times, it felt like. Her mom had been waiting tables at a diner and he'd been one of her customers. He'd been smitten from the start, but it had taken a week to convince her mom to go out with him. "I've really got to run, but I promise to let you know when I'm home." She'd told Michael she'd leave a while ago, had even packed up her car – including her cell phone. He'd probably called her, wanting to know where she was.

Stepping out into the hallway, she started to head for the front door but caught herself at the stairwell and headed back up it instead. She made her way to one of the guest rooms where she'd left her laptop. As she picked it up, something caught her eye. She glanced out one of the windows onto her father's huge estate and frowned. The two buttercream curtains were pulled back, revealing acres and acres of rolling green grassland. The front of the property was covered in trees, mainly live oaks. But she'd thought she'd seen a flash of black dart behind one of the trees.

Laptop tucked under her arm, she moved closer to the window, the warmth of the afternoon sun bathing her face as she peered outside. More of the yard and the long, winding driveway that looped out to the west side of the property came into view.

Her breath caught in her throat as she tried to digest what she was seeing.

A line of dark SUVs were rolling down the drive, some with flashing blue lights, and a swarm of men dressed in all black were rushing the house.

Ohmygodohmygodohmygod!

She was racing for the door, ready to shout for her dad, when an explosion sounded downstairs.

"Dad!" she screamed as she spilled out into the hallway. Fear lanced through her, sharp and stinging. What the hell was going on?

At the top of the stairs she saw that the explosion had been someone ramming the front door open. It hung off its hinges and two men in tactical gear with huge freaking guns pointed them up the stairs at her.

"Hands in the air, now!" one of them shouted.

Without thought she dropped the laptop and threw her hands up. Her heart was an erratic, out-of-control beat in her chest as her computer tumbled down the stairs, clacking along the wooden steps.

"Face down on the ground!" the same man shouted.

Even as she was complying, falling to her knees at the top of the stairs, both men were racing up toward her. Seconds later one of them yanked her arms behind her back and slapped handcuffs on her.

"Dad!" she screamed for her father even as the armed man yanked her to her feet. She could see the FBI logo on their vests so she knew they were from the government, but none of this made sense. Why would they be raiding her

father's house when he worked for a defense contractor? He was one of the good guys.

Pop. Pop.

She jumped at the sound of gunfire. Two more sharp pops went off in quick succession. Then glass shattered.

Oh God, her father. Was he injured? Before she could do or say anything…

Crack. Crack. Crack. Crack. Crack.

The sound of staccato gunfire made her flinch even as the armed man spoke to her. She had no idea what he was saying, couldn't comprehend the words. No, she could only focus on the terrifying sounds of gunfire in her childhood home and the people swarming in through the broken front door. They were like roaches, all dressed in black.

"Where's my father? Is he okay?" she shouted, unable to get her voice or her heartbeat under control as the man led her downstairs. She was vaguely aware of the other man having left them and storming into the guest room she'd just been in. Maybe they were looking for more people? Maybe they thought someone else was here?

She struggled to push the fear aside. This had to be a mistake. Whatever was going on they would fix it. But she just needed to find her father, needed to see that he was okay.

The man leading her downstairs didn't respond, just spoke into an earpiece. She wanted to keep shouting at him, to keep screaming, but knew it wouldn't do any good.

As they reached the bottom of the stairs Michael stormed through the front door. She froze, looking at him, not comprehending why her boyfriend was here. There were so many people hustling in and out of her father's home.

She felt as if she was watching this happen to someone else, that this was some nightmare she'd wake up from.

"Get those cuffs off her!" Michael shouted at the man next to her.

Fear for him slid through her veins like slow-moving ice, sharp and burning. She started to tell him to back off or something, worried that this armed man would handcuff him too, but to her surprise she felt the handcuffs being released. The armed man practically shoved her at Michael before hurrying off upstairs, his boots stomping loudly on the treads.

Blinking, she stared up at Michael, trying to find her voice and trying to understand this entire situation. "What are you—"

That was when she realized he was wearing a jacket that had the FBI logo on it. A blue windbreaker that seemed too light for the current weather, not that it mattered one bit.

She blinked again, frozen in place. "You're FBI?" she asked stupidly. He'd told her that he was a security contractor for a private company. Just like her father.

His jaw tightened. "Come on. I need you out of here." He wrapped his fingers around her upper arm.

She pulled back from him, ignoring the strangers moving around them as if they had every right to be here. "My father—"

He didn't let her go even though she tried to yank away. His grip only tightened. "I need you out of here now!"

"I need to see my father!" Her voice rose with every word. Her entire body trembled and all she knew was that she'd heard gunfire.

In her childhood home.

And her father wasn't calling for her.

A sick sensation pervaded her, making her stomach lurch. "My father?" she whispered.

Even though she was certain Michael didn't hear her over the cacophony of noise, he shook his head, his jaw tight and his expression tormented. He turned slightly to the side and she saw an earpiece.

His grip dropped for an instant as one of those armed men stepped up to him, spoke in quiet tones. It was the only opening she needed. Shoving away from him, she sprinted down the hallway. Two steel bands encircled her from behind as she reached the doorway of her dad's office.

But it was too late.

Her father was sprawled on his blue and green Persian rug, the crimson of his blood staining it and him. A gun lay near one of his limp hands. Blood covered the front of what had been a pale cornflower blue shirt, one she'd given him for his last birthday. Two huge holes gaped in his chest and there was a bright red stain in the middle of his forehead.

Oh… God. No, no, no.

"Noooooo!" She realized she was screaming only as Michael lifted her into his arms and tossed her over his shoulder, racing her away from her worst nightmare.

Isa's eyes opened with a start, her heart racing out of control, sweat dotting her upper lip and dripping down her back despite the cool temperature in her bedroom. She hadn't had that particular nightmare—which wasn't a nightmare, but a memory—in months.

Trembling slightly, she slid out of bed and headed to the bathroom. After splashing cold water on her face she stepped into her bedroom and realized it was only ten o'clock. She'd crashed an hour ago, abnormally early for her to go to bed, but she'd just wanted to shut out the real world, and sleep had been the best way to do that.

Picking her phone up off the nightstand, she texted Mara. *You awake?*

Less than ten seconds later her phone rang. When Isa saw Mara's number on the screen, she smiled. "Hey, you didn't have to call."

"I know, but it's late for you to be texting. What's up?"

"I…" Ugh, she felt like an idiot. Why had she texted? She didn't want to say she'd had a bad dream. It made her sound like a five-year-old. Her throat tightened as unexpected tears stung her eyes. Some days she'd be totally fine about everything—or at least able to cope—and then she'd have a nightmare and it was like she was drowning in memories and grief all over again.

"You want some company?" Mara asked softly.

Isa blinked, the question taking her by surprise. "Oh, no, it's too late. I just texted because…" She let out a short laugh. "Because working with Graysen is harder than I imagined. But this can wait until tomorrow."

"Harrison had to go out of town tonight. A quick trip up to Orlando to meet with a potential client."

"Oh, right." She'd actually known that, had talked to him earlier about what they'd discovered so far at Raptor Aeronautical.

"So, I'm alone anyway and I can't sleep without Harrison. I'll be over in a bit with a bottle of wine. Pick out a movie for us. None of those stupid romantic comedies." She hung up before Isa could respond, as was Mara's way.

A very small part of Isa felt bad, wanted to call Mara back and tell her not to come over simply because Isa was feeling emotional and out of sorts.

After losing pretty much her entire social circle after her father's treachery had been splashed all over the news a year ago, she'd been so damn alone when she'd moved to Miami. No one from DC or even her college friends would return her calls. She'd become a leper overnight.

Landing the job with Red Stone Security had been unexpected and a gift in more ways than one. From that first day, Mara had taken her under her wing and made her feel accepted.

Even though it made her feel a little pathetic that her friend was coming over so late because she was feeling weak and needy, she didn't care. Right now she needed a friend.

CHAPTER NINE

Graysen steered into the parking garage of his high-rise condo. He'd stayed at Isa's house, watching as the lights went off one by one. But then he'd started to feel like a stalker so he'd forced himself to leave. Going to her home had been a risk, a stupid one. And the reason he'd given her for showing up—that he'd been worried about her safety—had been equally stupid. She wasn't in danger.

He'd just needed to see her. It had been selfish on his part, but where Isa was concerned he didn't seem to think clearly.

As he got out of his SUV, memories of the day her father died assaulted him. Isa should have been in DC, far away from everything that went down on that fateful day. But because of bullshit timing, she'd seen everything and her life had been ripped apart. His too, because he'd screwed up everything with her that day.

Not that it mattered. The only thing he cared about was her. She'd ripped his world apart simply by being in it. If he could go back in time… *Hell.* He didn't know what he'd do. Her father had been selling state secrets, had betrayed his country to the highest bidder on more than one occasion.

But Isa had been innocent in it all. Not that it had mattered once the media ripped her father's life apart. Hers had been destroyed right along with it. She'd lost her job, her friends, everything. Guilt raked through him at the knowledge that he'd been part of that.

It was why she'd moved to Miami, to escape the bitter scrutiny and judgment. She'd have never been able to get a decent job in DC again anyway. Not after what had happened. She'd always be looked at with suspicion no matter how innocent she was. There'd been another scandal a week after the story of her father's treachery and death broke, something to do with multiple senators being caught up in a prostitution ring. It was the only thing that had allowed her to start over as easily as she had without further media scrutiny. People cared more about sex, and the politicians' story had been salacious.

Instead of walking to the elevator, he took Peaches out of the garage and headed around the big building to the area designated for pets. A bright full moon illuminated the grassy area. As Peaches took care of her business, that gut-wrenching afternoon replayed in his mind.

Maybe because it was close to Christmas, or maybe because he'd spent most of the day with Isa, but that day was all he could think about.

His heart raced a little faster as the phone rang, as he waited for Isa to pick up. He'd just gotten a call from his boss that today they would be infiltrating her father's estate and arresting him. The man had just taken the bait they'd laid out for him, agreeing to meet with a new buyer to potentially sell the identities of five covert agents. As a defense contractor he wouldn't normally have access to that kind of information but they'd discovered he'd been working with multiple hackers and using his access to areas of high-level security in different government buildings to help get those hackers infiltrated into private intranet networks.

"Hey, babe." Isa's voice was light, her tone easy.

He forced his voice to remain steady when all he wanted to do was tell her the truth. But he couldn't. "Hey, are you headed back to the city yet?"

"Soon, I promise. Just spending time with my dad."

He needed to get a time frame from her but didn't want to tip her off that it mattered what time she got back home. The FBI had moved up their infiltration day and time. Isa wasn't supposed to be anywhere near the estate when this happened. That had been one of his main concerns. Shit like this happened all the time, something he understood. But it had never been personal like this before. He'd never expected someone like her—and had never slept with anyone involved in a case before either. She was so sweet, open, and giving. She made a lot of money analyzing work effectiveness for various companies but gave so much back to the community with her free time. It was hard to believe she was her father's daughter, now that he knew how treacherous the man really was.

"Well hurry back. I miss you. And I have something I want to talk to you about." He hated himself even as he said the words. He needed to tell her everything they'd discovered about her father. He wanted to do it in a calm setting where it was just the two of them. Not that it would matter where he told her—the news that her father was a traitor to his country would devastate her. But he still wanted to break the news to her as easy as he could.

"Are you breaking up with me?" she asked jokingly, clearly knowing that he never wanted to do that.

When he was with her he might pretend to be Michael, but he was still able to be himself, to be Graysen. And he hated himself more and more every day for lying to her face. But too many men and women had died because of the information her father had leaked. People who mattered to him. He had a duty to his country and to all the other people out there who could become a target, could be tortured, murdered and worse because their identities were sold to the highest bidder.

"No." But you'll probably never want to see me again.

"Okay, then I won't push you to tell me what it is. I'll be leaving in the next couple minutes."

"You know I love you, right?" The words stuck in his throat even though they were true. Soon she would look at him in a new light, would see him for the liar he was. He just prayed that she could forgive him because a world without Isa in it was not a world he wanted to live in. And if she ended things with him… Hell, he couldn't go there. He just needed to get through this day.

"I love you too…" There was a rustling, then her voice was muffled for a moment. "Hey, I've got to run, but I'll see you soon."

He glanced at his phone even though he already knew the time. If she left soon, she would be away from the estate when everything went down. That was the only thing that made him feel nominally better about this whole screwed up situation.

Graysen scrubbed a hand over his face and tried to mentally shake off the memory, but it was useless. "Come on, girl." He patted his leg and Peaches ran up to him, the most loyal dog. He'd never admitted it to anyone, but if it wasn't for Peaches, the last year would have been even harder.

At least when he came home at night there was someone there happy to see him. Unfortunately, it wasn't Isa. But he wasn't giving up on her, on them. He simply couldn't.

Part of him wanted to give her the file he'd been sitting on. The file that had all the dark truth about her father—what he'd done, how many people he'd gotten killed and in some cases, tortured. But…he didn't want to be the cause of more of Isa's pain. It would go a long way in explaining why Graysen had done what he'd done, but he didn't know that he wanted to be the one to give her all that brutal truth.

Emerson wrapped her arms around herself as she and Carlito stepped outside into the chilly night air. She loved that he came to her father's nursing home with her every week. Everyone loved her dad, and some of her other friends came with her as well when they could, but those were her girlfriends.

Carlito was… Well, she wasn't quite sure what he was. They were friends, had been for the last six months. Lately, however, she was starting to have feelings for him. And definitely not the "friends only" kind.

She nearly jumped when he placed his jacket around her shoulders. He was a lot broader and wider than her. He had a lean, cut physique, something she didn't want to be noticing. They were friends—she shouldn't be so sexually aware of the man.

When they first met she'd been aware of how attractive he was. Obviously—she'd have to be blind not to realize how sexy the man was. He was handsome and polished, not what she pictured when she thought of a detective.

But he was always put together, his suits perfect and pressed. She could never keep herself so impeccable, but it seemed effortless for him. His bronzed skin seemed to glow year-round and his cheekbones would make supermodels envious. There was an edge to him, however. Probably to do with his job, considering how much death and other awful things he saw. So when he looked at her with those piercing gray eyes it was hard to ignore the sex appeal factor.

So yeah, she'd noticed all of that when they'd first met, but she hadn't been thinking about the opposite sex in terms of dating or anything romantic at the time. Not after her last breakup.

"Thanks," she said, pulling the jacket tighter around her. It was way too big and smelled like him, a distinctive spicy cologne that made her want to inhale deeply.

She'd left her thick coat in the car, thinking she wouldn't need it. But it felt as if it had dropped ten degrees since they'd been inside. Or more likely the heat had been turned up so much in there that it just felt colder now. The fact that he was so considerate touched her. Her father had commented on it, because he seemed to think Carlito wanted more than friendship. He always asked her when she and Carlito were going to get married. She nearly snorted at the thought. This sexy detective wasn't going to be settling down anytime soon. She knew what kind of reputation he had.

"So are you still coming over for Christmas?" he asked.

"Of course, unless... Did your plans change or something?" Carlito's sister Camilla had said something to Emerson earlier today about him dating someone new, so she wasn't sure if that was why he was asking. Six months ago the thought of him dating wouldn't have fazed her, but now...

She didn't like that ugly, twisting sensation in the pit of her stomach. It wasn't like he belonged to her. It wasn't like they were anything other than friends. But she found herself feeling oddly possessive of him lately. Okay, maybe more than just lately. It had been a gradual buildup until one day she realized—she wanted more than friendship from Carlito. Way more.

It was part of the reason she hadn't called him earlier today. When Camilla had told her he was seeing someone else she hadn't wanted to hear the truth from him. Emerson wasn't sure she'd be able to act nonchalant about it. She wondered why he hadn't said anything—even as she was happy that he *hadn't*. She didn't want to hear about him and some other woman.

He let out a short laugh. "Never. My mom would kill me if I didn't show up for Christmas. And she'd probably kill me if I didn't bring you."

The sharpest sense of relief slid through her veins. She adored his whole family but especially his mother. Her own mom had died when she'd been young and part of her had always felt as if she was missing something. "You never told me what I should bring."

"Just yourself. And your dad, if you think he's up to it." He gave her a strange look as they reached her car.

They'd driven separately since they lived in opposite directions, and now she wished they'd ridden together in one vehicle because she wanted to spend more time with him. An hour or two at a time was never enough. It didn't matter that they talked on the phone—when they got to spend time together she always wanted more, more, *more*.

"What?" she asked, feeling self-conscious under his scrutiny.

"Is everything okay? You seemed a little distracted today." The concern in his gaze was real and she adored how sincere he was about everything—and not just with her, but with everyone. It was why he was such a good detective.

What she'd heard about him from others was different than the man she'd come to know. One of her coworkers had mentioned that she thought Carlito was a player, but so far Emerson hadn't seen any truth in that. Or he could just keep that stuff on the down-low. The thought of him with another woman, touching her, kissing her… *Nope.* Even thinking about it hurt too much.

"I'm good. Just have a lot going on with this new job." She wished she could tell him about it, but in addition to the standard nondisclosure she'd signed when she'd been hired by Red Stone

Security, she'd also had to sign another nondisclosure specifically for this job.

"Okay." He nodded slightly, those pale gray eyes she could get lost in narrowing as if he didn't believe her.

Some days… *Gah.* Some days she swore she saw hints of heat in his gaze. But that was likely wishful thinking on her part.

"Do you have plans Saturday?" she blurted before she could stop herself. If he was dating someone new, of course he would already have plans.

To her relief, he shook his head. "Unless something comes up at work, then I'm free."

"One of my friends mentioned something about a boat parade. And I've never been so I wanted to know if you wanted to go with me? Since you're the local." She'd moved here from Orlando when she'd gotten the job with Red Stone, and while she'd been to Miami over the years she'd never been here for the holidays.

"I'd love to." He nodded, that delicious mouth of his curving up into a smile that made her think wicked, wicked things. Mainly naked fantasies about him—she'd seen him in swim trunks at one of the get-togethers at Grant and Belle's place, and holy hotness, the man looked incredible without a shirt on. He should go around half naked all the time.

And at the thought, her face heated up. She cursed her fair coloring in that moment and hoped he didn't notice.

Before she could respond he continued. "I'll pick you up at four on Saturday? That way we can be sure to get there early and get a good spot."

"Sounds perfect." If he was going with her, then he wasn't with some other woman. Maybe his sister had been wrong about him dating someone new. The truth was, if Emerson was seeing a man like Carlito, she'd want all his spare time. Who was she kidding? They weren't dating and she still wanted to see him all the time. She hated that she was too much of a coward to ask him if he was currently single.

But she definitely wasn't brave enough to make a move on him.

After getting burned so badly before she still didn't quite trust her taste in men. And if she was really honest with herself, she was more scared of screwing up the friendship they had by asking if he wanted something more with her. She didn't want to risk ruining one of the best relationships she'd ever had with anyone.

With him, she was always herself. Never felt like she had to put on a show or be anything other than who she was. So the thought of losing that? Nope, she wasn't going to risk it.

But if he made a move on her? That was a different story.

CHAPTER TEN

Going about his daily business when he'd be leaving the country soon, leaving his entire life behind and never looking back, was harder than Alan had thought. Excitement and fear hummed through him 24/7.

It was impossible to sleep and he was barely eating. He just wanted to be done with this life, to have his money and get the hell out of this country with the woman he loved. No more ex-wife, no more debt. Nothing but sandy beaches where he'd live like a king. If he could just get through a couple more days without detection.

When a phone buzzed in his jacket pocket it took him a moment to realize it was the disposable phone he'd been using to contact his buyers and other individuals helping him to get out of the country once he had his money.

A quick glance at the screen revealed that it was a private caller—no surprise. Anyone who called this phone had a blocked line. He answered immediately. "Yes?"

"It's me."

He recognized Yuri's voice. The Russian contact who'd first reached out to him about a way for him to make a lot of money.

From the digging Alan had done into his buyers he knew that Yuri himself was an exceptional hacker.

So when Hamilton had brought in two new employees this week, he'd sent their information to Yuri to look into them. At this point, he couldn't take any more risks. Everything had to go off without a hitch.

"What have you found out about the two newest employees?" Because there was no other reason for Yuri to be calling right now—unless something had gone wrong with the current op. Ice slid through his veins at the thought. Everything was good on his end.

"The woman works for a company called Red Stone Security. Her name is Isa Harper, not Johnson. I'm still not certain what she does there, but she doesn't work for the company listed on the resume you sent me."

He felt all the blood drain from his face, his hands going clammy as he listened. He lived in Miami, knew exactly what Red Stone Security was. They were involved in private security for dignitaries and other wealthy individuals, but they had other divisions as well. Top secret ones.

Yuri continued. "The founder is a man named Keith Caldwell. Three sons now run the company full-time. They have ties with various government agencies and it appears as if the father used to work for the CIA."

That only confirmed the rumors he'd heard. He cleared his throat. "And you have no idea why she's here?"

"No, but it can't be good. And there is more. Her father's name was Jeffrey Harper."

Jeffrey Harper? The name sounded familiar—he racked his brain trying to think where he'd heard it before. But Yuri continued again before he could ask who the man was.

"He was killed a little over a year ago by your FBI. He was selling state secrets to the highest bidders all over the world." There was a short pause. "I did business with him once about five years ago. His information was solid."

"What does that mean?" The woman's father had been a traitor to his country? How did that tie in with anything going on here? Why would she be working here now?

"Maybe nothing. It's just information I have, and you wanted to know everything about her. I do not like her involvement with your company this close to the end of our operation."

Yeah, no shit. "I spoke to Hamilton, and she shouldn't be here longer than another week or so. It's possible that she really is here to help him clean house." Hamilton had made it clear Isa was working closely with him to see where they could make cuts. It made sense his boss wouldn't be honest about what company she worked for. Hamilton wouldn't want to give anyone information about her if she was basically targeting jobs.

"I still don't like it."

Neither did he. "What do you want me to do?"

"Keep an eye on her for now. Did you implant the software into her laptop to shadow her?"

"I did." He'd had someone else do it as a safety measure to himself. Someone Alan considered expendable. "So far she's been looking into various employee files but there's been nothing to make it seem as if she's looking for..." He cleared his throat, not about to say the words out loud. His office and this phone might be secure, but some things he didn't need to spell out. "I've also started monitoring the phone in her office." Something Yuri already knew, but he wanted it clear he had this woman under surveillance.

That he was in complete control.

When Yuri just grunted, he continued. "What about the man, Garret Evans?"

"So far he appears to be who he says he is. His resume appears to be legitimate, and if it is, he has a lot of experience in your field. According to the paper trail I followed, he and your boss have been in contact for a while, farther back than when you decided to sell your...product."

He nearly snorted at the word "product." He wasn't selling a tangible item. Not technically. But product was as good a word as any.

"So it seems unlikely that he brought this Evans in because he's suspicious of you. More likely he's been trying to lure him away from his previous job for a while and Evans finally agreed. That is what it looks like on my end."

"Okay, good." At least one of the new hires was a non-issue. The woman, though...

He didn't like her snooping around all their files even if it was her job. From what he'd garnered, she had unlimited access to everything. That alone was terrifying.

When his intercom buzzed, he quickly ended the call with Yuri. "Yes?" he said after a moment.

"Something big is going on," his assistant Cynthia whispered from out in her office.

The excitement in her voice made him stand without answering. Opening the door, he headed into her office area. She had her cell phone pressed up against her ear and was whispering to someone. Seeing her on her cell phone surprised him since she was always the professional. And cell phones were banned at work, for the most part.

After whispering "Hold on" to whoever was on the other line, she covered the receiver of her phone. "I just heard from someone on the fifth floor that Gina Scott is getting arrested." Her blue eyes were wide, almost as if she was asking *him* for confirmation.

Shock reverberated through him. If Scott was being arrested, it was something he *should* be aware of. Instead of responding audibly, Alan just gave Cynthia a nod and headed toward the elevators. As he reached the closed doors his regular cell phone buzzed in his pocket. Because of his position in the company, he was one of the few people permitted to have his cell phone on him. Of course, no one knew about his burner phone.

He answered on the first ring when he saw that it was Hamilton. "Yes?"

"I need to see you in my office, *now*."

"Is this about Gina Scott getting arrested?" He couldn't believe the woman had been arrested, couldn't even imagine what for. She seemed like such a straight arrow. She was bitchy enough, always had a stick up her ass about something. But she'd been good at her job. Or so he'd thought.

"Yes." Hamilton disconnected before he could ask anything else.

That wasn't out of the ordinary for Hamilton, otherwise Alan might be panicking more. Taking a deep breath, he stepped inside the elevator and pressed the button for the floor above him. If Hamilton knew what he was up to, he was totally and utterly screwed. But it was too late to run now.

CHAPTER ELEVEN

Isa took off her coat before sliding into the booth across from Mara, grateful to be out of Raptor Aeronautical while everything was going down. She hadn't seen Mara since Monday night anyway.

In the past few days Isa, Graysen, and Emerson had been very busy. Two people were being arrested today and another was being escorted out of the building for further questioning—and would likely be arrested. She didn't need to be around for that. Hamilton hadn't come out and said it, but she had a feeling a lot of people would put two and two together and realize that she was part of the reason people were getting arrested.

Mara smiled when she saw her. As usual she looked stunning in a simple green three-quarter-sleeve dress that matched her eyes. And her pixie-style haircut showed off her sharp cheekbones. "Hey, glad you made it. I ordered us an appetizer so I hope that's okay?"

"Of course. I'm starving. Today has been stressful." A fallout would follow from the two, potentially three, employees getting arrested, not to mention the fallout for their own families. After having her life ripped apart after her own father's sins, she couldn't help but feel bad for the immediate families of the people involved with stealing from the aeronautical company.

"I bet. How much longer will you be on this job? Or can you tell me that?"

"Another day or two, maybe." Which meant she might have to go in on Monday just to wrap up a few things, but this job had gone much quicker and smoother than predicted—and after Tuesday she didn't have to work with Graysen anymore so it was perfect timing. But there were a few more people she wanted to look into. Just for her peace of mind. She wanted to make sure when she and Graysen were gone that the company was as secure as it could be. At least from this point forward Raptor would be implementing new security measures overall.

"I know you can't tell me specifics, but this job seemed to stress you out more than normal." Concern glittered in her friend's green gaze.

"For more reasons than one." The other night she'd opened up to Mara about everything that had happened with Graysen a year ago. She was pretty sure that Mara already knew everything, considering the vetting process Isa'd had to go through when getting hired at Red Stone. Even if Mara didn't work for Red Stone, Isa thought maybe Harrison had said something. Either way, her friend had been very supportive when Isa had opened up to her.

"Yeah, I can imagine how hard it is to work with Graysen. Can I ask you something personal about him?"

She nodded, then paused to place her drink order with their waitress. When the woman was gone, Isa looked back at Mara. "You can ask anything you want."

"This is a nosy question and maybe I shouldn't even be asking it, so tell me to shut it, if so. You never said if he explained the specifics of his operation—why he did what he did where your…father was concerned." Compassion was clear in Mara's eyes and Isa knew her friend wasn't asking to be malicious.

Familiar pain tightened in Isa's chest. She hadn't talked about what happened with her father with anyone, really. After she lost all of her friends in DC it had been easy to shut everyone out Except for Mara. And she was really glad that she had opened up to the other woman.

"I know the basics of why my father was going to be arrested. But I didn't dig any deeper and…Graysen didn't tell me anything more than what the media reported." And every day since then it was hard for her to come to terms with the contrast between the man the media had portrayed her father as and the man she knew. The man who had sold state secrets was a monster, someone she couldn't imagine knowing.

Mara nodded, her lips pulling into a thin line. "I thought so. Look, I have some information for you. And I know I'm risking hurting our friendship by even bringing this up but I think you need to see it. For yourself, if you're ever going to heal. Some of this is classified, and those parts have been redacted, but everything else you'll be able to read. When you're done with the file you can give it back to me or burn it."

Isa had always wondered what Mara had done before marrying Harrison and getting heavily involved in charity work. Mara had been pretty vague, saying that she'd worked for the British government. Now Isa wondered even more if the woman had managed to get classified information. "You got this information on your own, or from Harrison?"

To her surprise Mara's cheeks flushed slightly. "Neither. I got it from my father-in-law. He pulled some strings. And fair warning, there are some graphic pictures in there. They're not pretty."

Isa could feel the blood drain from her cheeks, but didn't say anything as their waitress brought the appetizer and drinks. She ordered a small salad even though she wasn't remotely hungry anymore, mainly so the waitress would go away. "Will you tell me what's in the file before I open it?"

Mara's expression was grim. "There's information in there about exactly what your father did, and pictures of the people who got hurt because of his treachery."

Isa swallowed hard but nodded. She didn't see any judgment or recrimination on Mara's face. It was still difficult to talk about this with anyone, but if Mara thought she should look at the file, she would. She didn't trust many people anymore and her friend was one of the exceptions. "Okay, I'll read it."

Mara lifted a black and gray wool coat off the bench next to her to reveal a simple black purse that was more a shoulder bag than anything. She unzipped it and pulled out a fairly thick manila file.

She paused for a moment then slid it across the table. "Wait until you're home to read this."

Nodding because her throat was too tight to talk, Isa took the file and slid it into her own purse.

"Is it okay that I brought this up?" Mara asked, concern in her eyes.

Somehow Isa found her voice, and nodded. "It is. It's just hard to talk about." Unless she was mentally prepared for it—which was pretty much never.

She felt as if the file was burning a hole in her purse, and it took all of her self-control not to whip the thing out and see what was inside. But she got through lunch and made it back to her temporary office to find Graysen waiting for her.

Things between them had been awkward since he'd showed up at her place on Monday, and she could admit that she'd been avoiding him most of the week whenever she could.

When she found him leaning against the window of her office, staring out at downtown, she tensed. "Is everything okay?" she asked as he turned to face her.

She'd noticed that there had only been a handful of people in their offices on this floor.

He nodded. "Yes. Hamilton called a company meeting to discuss all of the arrests today. That's why it's like a ghost town."

Nonetheless, she shut the door behind her in case anyone was around and might eavesdrop. "I still plan to go through more employee files this afternoon and tomorrow." She wanted to make sure that they crossed all their t's and dotted their i's. "Was there something specific you wanted to talk about?"

His shoulders were tense, his blue eyes unreadable. For a moment she thought he was going to say yes, but he shook his head. "No."

When he strode for the door she realized he didn't plan to say anything more. Maybe he had just come here to see her.

It pleased her and broke her heart at the same time. She hated this giant divide between them because…she'd never gotten over him. Even if she wanted to deny it, that was a simple truth. Michael or

Graysen, she'd fallen hard for the man. Even with all his lies, they'd shared so many intimate moments that made her feel as if… She sighed, the ache in her chest spreading outward, making it hard to breathe for a moment. It didn't matter. Nothing would ever fix what was broken between them.

It made it harder, knowing he'd jump back into a relationship with her if she said the word. She ached to call out to him, to stop him from leaving, but she had no idea what to say.

Once he was gone she collapsed into her chair and placed her head in her hands. After taking a couple deep breaths she opened her bag and started to pull out her laptop but paused, and plucked the manila file out instead.

She should be working. Probably shouldn't even be looking at this, whatever it was. Mara had told her to wait until she was home and alone, but her curiosity wouldn't let her leave it.

Isa's fingers flew across the keyboard. She was trying to focus on work, but was having a hard time concentrating after reading that file Mara had given her. After seeing the pictures of some of the people who'd been killed because of her father's greed… Nope. Isa swallowed hard and mentally shook herself even as she cursed her trembling fingers.

Taking a deep breath, she stopped typing for a moment. If she allowed herself to dwell on what she'd read earlier she wouldn't be able to do her job. And Red Stone and the clients who hired them deserved better. She should have waited like Mara told her to. Curiosity had gotten the better of her.

Later tonight she would try to digest everything she'd learned. Though she had a feeling it would take a very long time to come to terms with the truth of who her father had been. A year later and she still couldn't quite deal. Now with even more information about the depth of his treachery… She rolled her shoulders once and ordered herself to focus on the present. Soon enough she'd talk to Graysen about what she'd learned today. She couldn't think about that though.

After the busy afternoon they'd had here, she still had more research to do, namely following the trail of emails and other projects Shawn Grady had worked on. Grady was one of the people who'd been escorted out of the building today, but not arrested. Not yet that she knew of, anyway. The other two, Gina Scott and Roy Winston, had been the ones arrested.

But Grady had been one of the people who'd accessed her laptop when he thought no one was around. It turned out that he'd planted tracking software into her laptop so that he could shadow her movements. Graysen had caught the man on video in her office and Isa had quickly figured out what Grady had done to her computer.

But after looking at his financials, it didn't appear as if he was stealing money or information. Which meant she needed to dig deeper into him. If he'd planted that software on her computer it was for a specific reason. Maybe he'd just been better at hiding his trail than the other two. She was determined to find out why he'd wanted to know what she was up to.

Emerson was currently working on the same thing so Isa had no doubt they'd figure out what this guy had been up to soon enough.

As she started looking deeper into Grady's emails, she frowned when she saw a couple from the VP of the company. Looking back through Grady's email history, his communication with the VP was very rare, but then he'd received an email telling him that he was needed for an urgent meeting only an hour before he planted the software on Isa's computer? It could mean nothing—probably did—but she made a note of it. Sometimes the most benign things ended up mattering in her job.

Moving on from there, she did something she hadn't planned to do—she pulled up personnel files on Alan Persky, the VP of Raptor Aeronautical. There were a handful of people Hamilton had said to leave out of their investigation, including Persky.

After everything she'd found to date…yeah, that wasn't happening.

Hamilton had hired Red Stone to investigate the company and that was what she was going to do.

But as soon as she was done today, she was going to ask Graysen to come over to her place tonight. After everything she'd read in that file, they needed to talk. There were some things he hadn't told her—things that would have made her more willing to talk to him a year ago. More open to forgiving him.

She simply couldn't understand why he hadn't given her what Mara had given her today. It certainly would have helped make his case for being forgiven.

For a moment, she stopped what she was doing and rubbed a hand over the back of her neck. She reached for the phone on the desk, tempted to call him. When she'd come back from lunch the security guard had been insistent she leave her cell phone with him.

After the arrests today and all the commotion, she knew Raptor was cracking down on security. And technically the security guard should have been insisting from the beginning that she leave her cell phone every time she entered the building. In her report, she'd already noted the lack of adherence to strict protocol.

Isa clenched her fingers around the phone, picked it up, but immediately put it back in its cradle. Now wasn't the time to talk to Graysen. Not about personal stuff, anyway. And she knew he was with Hamilton right now, going over more of Raptor's security issues. What she wanted to talk about could wait until they had privacy.

Flexing her fingers, she got back to work. But she was determined that tonight she and Graysen were going to have a serious talk. And maybe, just maybe…they had a future after all. She wanted to know the truth of why he'd withheld so much information for so long, was even withholding it now.

If not for Mara, she'd still be in the dark.

CHAPTER TWELVE

Icy fingers of unease danced up Isa's spine as she packed up her laptop. She tried calling Graysen using the landline, but his cell phone went straight to voicemail. Maybe his phone was downstairs too, or maybe he was still in a meeting with Hamilton.

She doubted it, considering how late it was. She'd been in the zone for the last three hours, downloading information to her laptop and a backup flash drive which she'd securely tucked into the pocket of her pencil skirt. It was well past seven and she should have been out of here a couple hours ago. But once she'd started digging into Persky, she hadn't been able to stop. The information she'd found had her edgy and desperate to get it out of the building. But she needed to tell someone what she had first. For all she knew, she was wrong about what she'd found and it was nothing, but...her gut told her otherwise.

Since Graysen hadn't answered her, she peeked out into the hallway. The place was empty so she shut her door and immediately dialed Emerson. Her friend and coworker picked up on the second ring.

"Emerson here."

"Hey, it's me. I'm calling from a landline." She cleared her throat and looked around even though Graysen had personally checked this office for recording devices other than their own and found none. She knew no one was watching her. "Listen, I found some really strange information. I've downloaded everything and I'm heading out of here now. Where are you?"

"At the office still."

"I'm coming over right now. Wait for me, okay?"

"Of course. Is everything okay?"

"Ah, yeah. Have you talked to Graysen lately?"

"No. I tried calling him a while ago and it's going straight to voicemail. Need me to ping his phone, find out where he is?"

"No…ah, yes." Isa needed to talk to him too. She hated that she couldn't just email the files to Emerson but she wasn't able to send such sensitive information over regular email. And she couldn't trust a file hosting service either. It was against Red Stone protocol and Raptor Aeronautical's protocol to send or upload any classified information that way.

Considering the business Raptor did with the government, she understood why they had the security measures in place. And there was a chance the information she wanted to send—specs for military drones—could be seen by the wrong people. Hell, this was the kind of information even *she* didn't want access to. Now that she had it, however, she needed someone with more knowledge than her to look at the files. Since Emerson was part of the team working on this job and was by far the most tech-savvy person Isa knew other than Lizzy Caldwell, it made sense to give her a crack at the files. But she'd be calling her boss on the way to the office to let him know about this as well. She'd be looping everyone necessary into this.

"Give me a sec." There was a flurry of typing in the background, then, "The location of his phone is the lobby of Raptor."

Isa let out a short curse. "So's mine. He's not there." But at least it meant he was in the building. Or she assumed it did. She couldn't imagine him leaving his phone behind.

"What's going on?"

"Ah, I'm not sure. Maybe nothing." Feeling completely paranoid and not caring, she kept her words vague, not wanting to say too much over the phone.

The information she'd found had the VP's digital fingerprints all over the files she'd discovered. As if he'd tried to hide some of the records he'd had access to. He'd done a good job, but she'd been doing this kind of work for a long time, knew exactly what to look for. If she hadn't specifically been looking for anything out of the ordinary, however, she wouldn't have found it.

"I used to work for a tech company that had a strong focus in work effectiveness. I was trained well and I can read code on a basic level and…" She lowered her voice even though her door was shut and she was almost certain she was the only one left on this floor for the day. "There's something wrong with some of the files I came across. Odd-looking code has been input into places it shouldn't be. It's subtle and maybe I'm wrong but…I don't think so. Unfortunately, I don't know what any of it *means*." She just knew it shouldn't be there. She really hoped she was just being paranoid and that it was nothing.

"Okay, head over here now. I won't leave."

"I'll be there in about…ah, fifteen minutes. Maybe twenty. I've got to grab my cell phone downstairs then I'm gone." She wanted to wait to talk to Graysen first, but she needed to get this information out of the building and into the right hands. If anyone could understand this information, it would be Emerson. The woman was brilliant.

"I'll be waiting for you," Emerson said.

Once they disconnected she slid her laptop into her bag. The hallway seemed unusually quiet as she strode down toward the elevators, but she figured that was just her own nerves at what she'd found.

It was weird being so disconnected without her cell phone. Maybe that was why she was feeling so tense. Halfway down the hallway, the lights went off.

Instinctively she froze. Rolling her eyes at her jumpiness, she shook her head. The power going off was weird, but not unheard of. The city lights streamed into the hallway from multiple open doorways, giving her enough illumination to see, but it was so silent. Without the hum of computers, copy machines and everything else, it was beyond eerie.

Still, those icy fingers of unease she experienced earlier intensified as she realized that she could see lights from other buildings. Which meant it wasn't a general blackout. She ducked into the nearest office and strode to the huge window. Every building she could see downtown was brightly lit up. When she picked up the landline of whoever's office this was, there was no dial tone.

So the power in this building went off, as well as access to the phones, and it wasn't storming out? All the alarms in her head went off.

She didn't want to panic and read too much into this, but if it had something to do with what she'd found, she needed to get the hell out of here right now, cell phone or not. For all she knew someone had been listening to her phone conversation. It seemed unlikely, since Graysen had personally checked her office, but...he'd been busy today. They all had. Maybe something had slipped past them.

She inwardly cursed. Maybe she shouldn't have made that call to Emerson at all. But she'd wanted *someone* to know what she'd found before she left the building. As she headed back to the open doorway she paused at the sound of male voices.

Because she was feeling paranoid, she ducked behind the door instead of announcing her presence. She knew she was probably being stupid, but she'd rather laugh at herself later than make a mistake. Breathing unevenly, she looked through the crack of the half-open door.

Muted footsteps strode down the hall at a steady pace.

"She should be up here," a quiet male voice said.

She?

Anxiety slithered through Isa at his words. As far as she knew she was the only person here right now. The floor was very large, however, so maybe—

Her gut tightened as two men holding pistols at their sides slowly moved past the doorway. It took her all of two seconds to realize there were silencers on the end of both of their guns. Otherwise the weapons wouldn't be so long. Beads of sweat rolled down her spine.

What the ever-loving hell was going on?

She didn't allow herself even a breath of relief as they kept going. Hell no, she was in danger and needed to get out of here like ten minutes ago. She slowly reached into her bag, palmed her keys and clutched them tightly so they wouldn't jingle. With a shaking hand, she managed to tuck them into the tight pocket of her skirt. She still had the flash drive in her other pocket. At least the keys wouldn't make any noise. Next she slid her laptop out of her bag and eased her bag to the ground. She didn't need it to weigh her down right now and there was no way she was leaving her laptop behind for someone to find.

Listening to the sound of their soft footfalls, she waited until she thought they were far enough down the hallway away from her to peek out the doorway. When she looked, she saw two shadowy figures stepping into her temporary office.

Heart racing, she knew it was now or never. She slipped out of her heels, tucked them behind the door with her bag and ran down the hallway as fast and as quietly as she could manage. Her pulse was out of control, the sound of her heartbeat thudding in her ears so loudly she was glad she was the only one who could hear it.

She needed to put as much distance between her and them as possible. She didn't care who they were or who had sent them. All she knew was that two men with guns were looking for her.

Just as she was about to reach the end of the hallway where it T-boned into the elevators, she heard a shout behind her.

"Hey!" one of the men yelled.

No way was Isa going to respond or turn around and slow down. Since the elevators wouldn't be working without power, she veered left toward the stairs. Now she didn't bother to mute her movements, and ran as fast as she could.

She slammed her hands into the metal release bar. The door flew open, ricocheting off the wall. At this point it didn't matter how loud she was. She was running for her life.

The sound of her heart pounding in her ears was all she could hear as she entered the dimly lit stairwell. There was an orange glow barely illuminating her way, probably from a generator or something. She wasn't sure if she should try hiding somewhere or just run. In the end she made the decision to run. She didn't have a choice, not when two men wanted to kill her—or maybe they wanted to kidnap and torture her. Either option wasn't good. Because she was pretty sure they didn't just want to talk to her.

The concrete and metal of the stairs was cold against the soles of her bare feet as she made her way down flight after flight. Sweat slicked the back of her neck and down her spine, the fear punching through her, needle-sharp. She alternated between feeling hot and cold. As she made it down another flight, she heard a door slam open from above. It had to be the two men.

Instead of continuing racing downstairs, she stopped at the nearest door and opened it as quietly as she could. She slipped into the hallway of the sixth floor and gently pulled the door shut behind her. She could only hope they wouldn't realize she'd exited the stairwell here.

Her feet were silent along the carpeted hallway and she was grateful for the downtown light helping to illuminate her way. There were so many shadows though, and she was terrified there were more men waiting in them, ready to shoot her. She wished she had a better plan other than to put distance between the two men with guns and find a way to call for help if she couldn't get out of the building. But that was all she could do right now. She also desperately needed to get in contact with Graysen, to make sure he was okay. But she had no idea how the hell to do that, not when his phone was in the lobby. *One step at a time*, she ordered herself. She was going to find a way to call for help no matter what.

Halfway down the hall, she heard a woman talking. On instinct she sidestepped into what turned out to be a copy room.

"Generator…"

"We'll figure it out…" That was definitely a male voice.

Straining, struggling to keep her breathing under control, she tried to listen harder and figure out who the two people were and whether she knew them. For all she knew they were with the men who were running after her.

When the voices got closer, she squeezed behind one of the copy machines. Because there wasn't much light, she was able to use the shadows to help her remain invisible.

She tensed when a woman screamed and a man shouted. What the hell was going on out there? Torn between leaving her hiding space or staying there, her decision was made when she heard a *puff, puff, puff* of air. The screaming and shouting immediately cut off.

Oh, God. Isa bit down on the inside of her lip. They'd shot those people.

Hot tears stung her eyes. Two innocent people were dead. Or dying.

"Damn it… Not the right woman." The man's voice was frustrated and way too close for comfort. She couldn't see but it sounded like he was near the doorway of the copy room or just inside it.

She barely breathed, too afraid to make any noises.

"What should we do with the bodies?" another man asked.

Ohgodohgodohgod. She had no weapon and no way to call anyone for help. All she could hope was that Graysen wasn't in the same situation she was. Of course if he was, he was a heck of a lot more trained than she was to deal with armed men.

"Have someone clean up tonight. Or maybe leave them. I don't know what the plan is but it's not our problem…" His words trailed off and she heard a tapping sound. She couldn't figure out what it was.

"Come on, let's keep sweeping."

"Even if the stupid bitch makes it downstairs she won't get out of here alive." The second man made an obnoxious snorting sound.

She forced herself to stay where she was, and counted to sixty seconds as they moved away from the copy room. Then she counted to sixty again, and again, until ten full minutes had passed.

Even though she was terrified to move from her hiding place, she knew she had to. She couldn't stay here and wait for them to come back. No, she had to get help, find a phone, something. Her knees ached as she pushed up and wiggled out of her hiding spot. Thankfully no one was waiting to attack her. As she stepped into the middle of the room, two legs became visible through the doorway. A three-inch heel dangled from one of the woman's feet and the other shoe was a foot away from her body.

Clutching her laptop tightly to her chest, Isa peered out into the hallway. Now she could see the woman's entire body, and a man not far from her, sprawled on his back. A big stain spread across the man's shirt, and in the dimness it looked black. But she knew what it was. His blood.

Her skin crawled. Just to be sure she tested their pulses, even if there was nothing she could do for them. But both of them were dead. Then, feeling ghoulish, she checked them for cell phones just in case. Nothing.

As one of the killers' words replayed in her mind, she tried to figure out her next move. He'd said if she made it downstairs, she still wouldn't escape. There had to be more of them, or someone else waiting for her.

Think, think, think.

Graysen was well-trained, and if he was in the building would know what to do. She needed to find him somehow, and the only thing she could think to do at this point was to return to her office. She'd already been there so those men likely wouldn't return. At least not right away. Eventually they'd do another full sweep and if they had enough men, they'd find her. She had to get help before that happened.

But maybe Graysen had gone looking for her—she hoped so. If he wasn't there, she would head to the office they'd been using during the week to view the video footage.

If he wasn't in either of those places, she'd figure out what to do then. For now, she would take things one step at a time and just try to stay alive.

Though she hated to use the stairs, there was no other way around it. Instead of using the stairwell on the west side, however, she headed to the east stairwell.

Taking a deep breath, she eased the door open. She couldn't hear any movement and there was just the faintest light illuminating the stairwell. It would have to do.

Her feet were silent once again as she raced up the stairs. And once more all she could hear was the pounding of her heart. This was a nightmare come to life. She'd never felt so vulnerable. Not even the day she'd seen her father's body sprawled on the floor. She just prayed that Graysen was okay.

The thought of something happening to him terrified her. It didn't matter what had happened in their past. In this moment, she desperately wanted him to be alive and well. If anyone could survive, it would be him. And he would help her.

Still holding her laptop in a death grip with one hand, she wiped her free damp palm on her skirt as she reached the tenth floor. Sucking in a quiet breath, she pulled the door open a crack so she could peer into the hallway.

Shadows and muted streams of outside city lights from open doorways greeted her.

When a door from somewhere below her groaned open, she darted into the hallway. As the door shut quietly behind her, a big hand slammed over her mouth.

CHAPTER THIRTEEN

Alan paced back and forth in the lobby. Everything had gone so wrong. Luckily Yuri thought they could still salvage this operation, but too many people were dead to cover this up now.

Which meant they were going to have to make this look like a terrorist attack—and technically it was.

"Stop worrying. We have this under control." The man named Dmitri spoke quietly, not moving from his position by the security desk in the lobby. His dark eyes were like black pools.

Unease crawled up his spine. Alan wouldn't admit it, but the man and everyone else Yuri had sent in tonight scared him. It was probably a good thing Yuri himself wasn't here. "I'm not worried," he snapped.

But...he was. When he'd overheard Isa Harper's phone conversation with a woman named Emerson a half hour ago, he'd gone into panic mode. He'd tapped Isa's phone so he'd know exactly what she was up to. He was worried that he might have overreacted, but something about her tone had bothered him. Not to mention the Emerson woman had mentioned pinging someone named Graysen via the man's phone. And that phone was supposed to be in this lobby. It was too late now to worry about it since everything was set into motion.

Alan had already gone through the phones left with security but all of them had security codes so he couldn't get into them. Not that it mattered. Once Alan had heard that conversation, he'd contacted Yuri—who'd immediately activated his reinforcements: a dozen trained men who'd been waiting in two vans in the parking garage of the building.

Alan had known they were there, of course. The men had been hiding for the past two days. He'd given them security passes to get into the garage and building. No one, not even security, had any idea that armed men had been waiting in those vans.

Alan had only wanted to contain Isa and find out what she knew, if anything, before killing her. He hadn't wanted to kill anyone else in the building. But when she'd said she'd found some files with odd-looking code, he'd had to act fast and get the building contained before she could send anything out or make any more calls. It had to be the files with the specs for the military drones. He wasn't directly involved with the project but he'd modified Raptor's programming. He'd been so damn careful but she must have found something.

Now everything was a giant clusterfuck since too many people were dead. And Alan wanted to know who the hell the man named Graysen was that Isa had referred to. If he had to guess, it was the new hire Hamilton had brought in. Not that he could very well ask Hamilton. The man had gone home for the evening, and as far as Alan was concerned, he was going to come to work tomorrow just like everyone else and find out that their company had been robbed and most of the security guys killed. To cover his bases, Alan had made everyone on the security team who had families call home and tell them they'd be working late so no worried spouse would call the cops. Then Dmitri had killed them. That was one thing he didn't have to worry about.

Yuri had rerouted the alert that should have gone to Hamilton when the power had gone out so he never received it. Another thing taken care of. Still… Sweat beaded at the base of Alan's spine as he thought of everything else that could go wrong.

Yuri had a plan in place to frame it on two of their current single security guys—the two men had been killed but their bodies would never be found. Alan had no idea what was going to happen to the bodies, and he didn't much care as long as they disappeared. Yuri was going to leave a paper trail making it look like they'd fled the country late tonight.

Raptor Aeronautical had many patents, so framing the two men for stealing the information and selling it to the highest bidder wouldn't be hard to believe. Alan just hated that things had gotten so messy. This was supposed to have been controlled, with no one knowing anything out of the ordinary had happened here until long afterward. When he put in his notice with the company, he'd wanted it to be without any cloud hanging above him. He might still be able to pull off this op, but the timing of his leaving the company after an attack wasn't ideal.

Alan frowned at Dmitri when he let out a curse.

"What is it?" he asked as Dmitri shoved his phone into the pocket of his tactical pants.

"Two of my men are dead."

He stiffened. "What? How?" The people who worked here were analysts, techs, and computer types. Even the former military hires they had were all intel people. Not highly trained soldiers. And he'd seen the resume of every single person who'd been hired, so he knew that for a fact. The company's security people were all accounted for. Either dead or currently incapacitated by Yuri's people.

"Broken necks." Dmitri's expression was grim and slightly accusing as he stared at Alan.

"You think I know who did that?" He could feel sweat beading his upper lip and across his forehead. Nothing was going according to plan. And he wouldn't be paid the rest of his money until everything was delivered. His fiancée wouldn't like that. She was so insistent they live a certain lifestyle.

He rolled his shoulders, forced himself to think. He'd already input the last of the special code into the final design for the military drones they were releasing to the American government soon.

It had been woven in so subtly to the onboard computers, it was practically invisible. No one would discover what he'd done. Or they shouldn't have been able to discover it. Unfortunately he was afraid Isa had. That was why he had to make sure she didn't make it out of the building.

Once those drones crossed the border into certain areas, Yuri and the people he worked for would be able to commandeer the drones easily. From there…Alan didn't care what they did with them.

That wasn't his problem. The only thing he cared about was making sure that bitch Isa didn't get out of the building alive. And now apparently they needed to find whoever had killed two of Yuri's men and make sure they didn't get out either—because he somehow doubted Isa had broken the necks of two of Yuri's men. He supposed it was possible, but she didn't look strong enough.

"Has anyone made a call to the police?" Alan asked, since Yuri's people were monitoring local police communication.

Dmitri shook his head. "No. You have no idea who could have killed my men?" His dark eyes were murderous as he stared at Alan.

He blinked at the accusatory tone. "No." He wanted his damn money, wanted to leave the country.

Dmitri just gave him another hard look before turning away from him. He shouted out orders to three of his men who immediately headed for one of the stairwells. Alan wasn't certain what he said since he spoke in Russian, but it was pretty damn clear Dmitri had ordered them to find whoever had done this.

The only reason Alan wasn't completely panicking right now was because the building was locked down and there was no way for Isa to communicate with anyone outside it. That was why they had to make sure she didn't make it out of here alive.

If he could leave, he would. But if tried he knew that Dmitri would kill him. He might have already input all the code but he only got paid once those drones were delivered. So they had to make sure absolutely no one was suspicious of the drone project.

He was tempted to simply run and just try to live on the money he'd already made. He and his fiancée would be able to make do… But for now, he planned to see this through to the end. Once Isa and whoever her partner was were killed, he and Yuri's team would all leave the building.

Then in the morning he'd come to work and act just as shocked as everyone else by the massacre that had occurred here. He'd have to deal with questions from the police, and yeah, probably the Feds, but he'd go through with it, appear shaken and distraught.

Nothing that happened here should be traceable back to him. Most importantly, no one would even know the drone project had been compromised. The authorities would be looking for the terrorists who'd attacked the building and stolen the patent to Project ACAS—an important project for the company, but with no ties to him.

He just had to get through the next few hours alive—and make sure Isa Harper didn't.

CHAPTER FOURTEEN

"It's me," Graysen said quietly as Isa reared her head back, trying to slam it against his face.

Immediately she stilled and he let his hand drop from her mouth. He'd been ready to kill whoever had come through that door, to snap their neck—until he'd realized it was her.

She swiveled, fear clear in her expression even under the dim lighting. She opened her mouth to speak but he just held up a finger and pointed down the hallway.

She nodded and he stepped in front of her, wanting to be between her and any more potential threats. He wasn't certain what was going on yet, but this building was under attack. He'd already killed two armed men with Russian tattoos. If he'd had his cell phone or camera, he'd have snapped some images of the tats.

Moving quickly down the hallway, he was aware of Isa directly behind him. Her scent and heat practically wrapped around him, reminded him she was *alive*. The sheer relief he experienced when he realized it was her stepping out into the hallway, that she was unharmed... There were no words to describe how he felt now. All he knew was that he was going to make sure he got her out of this alive.

Whatever the hell *this* was.

He'd left a meeting with Hamilton an hour ago and had been doing some work in one of the offices when the power went out. When he'd noticed that the building was the only one in the city that appeared to have lost power, he'd gone to find Isa.

Instead he'd found two armed men roaming the halls. Two armed men with *suppressors* on their Gen3 Glocks. He'd quickly taken care of the problem—then divested them of their weapons. But he still wasn't certain what he and Isa were up against.

The building was square-shaped, with the hallways running in a perfect square and offices on the interior and exterior. On the fourth floor there was a walkway that attached to a neighboring parking garage owned and used by Raptor Aeronautical. He had no doubt the main entrance to the parking garage was being guarded. But there was another way into the garage, one exclusively used by Hamilton.

The only reason he knew about it was because of the CEO himself. Unfortunately, there was still a chance it was being guarded as well, but at this point they had very few options for getting out of the building unnoticed. If he could just call in for backup, he had no doubt they'd be able to hole up somewhere until then.

Without knowing more about who had this building under siege or how far they were willing to go to flush out anyone inside, his options were limited.

When they came to an office on the opposite side of the building from the elevators, he ducked inside, Isa right behind him. He shut the door and turned to face her, taking in her appearance fully. No shoes, which he'd already noticed, but she seemed unharmed.

"Have you been hurt?"

"No. But they killed two people, a man and a woman." Her voice trembled slightly, but she was holding up well.

"I saw the bodies." He'd nearly lost his mind when he'd seen the motionless female body. For a moment he'd thought it was Isa and... He couldn't even go there.

She swallowed hard before continuing. "I think I know why this is happening. I found something in the specs for military drones about to be released to the US government in the next week—in the actual computer programming. I know I wasn't even supposed to be looking in those files, but I followed a hunch. I have no idea what the actual code means but it shouldn't *be* there. I called Emerson from a landline because I didn't have my cell... This is all my fault. What I said shouldn't have been enough for all this." She motioned with her hand, her voice low. "But I don't believe in coincidence. This has to be because of that phone conversation. Alan Persky is the man I found linked to the code. He tried to cover his tracks and did a damn good job, but I was digging hard."

Persky, the VP of the company. Yeah, he'd have unlimited access to pretty much *everything*. Still, the man would have left a digital trail no matter how hard he tried to hide it. Graysen could see by the recrimination in Isa's expression that she blamed herself for what was going on, but now wasn't the time to reassure her. "You saved all the information?"

"Yeah, on my laptop." She held it out for him and rattled off what name she'd saved the files as.

He snagged it from her, slid it out from the soft case and turned it on. This was a Red Stone laptop, one she'd used specifically for this op. They'd been monitoring it, and had left a security lock off it so sneaky employees up to no good would be tempted to look at her computer. It was the reason they'd managed to get two people arrested today. And soon, likely a third. Not that it mattered right now.

As soon as the laptop fired up, he tried to hook up to a wireless connection. They might not have any power here, but he was hopeful they could connect to a neighboring building. He knew the chances were slim, but he had to try.

"I also saved the information on a flash drive," Isa whispered as he tried to find an unsecured connection.

"Good," he murmured, typing quickly. If he could get a message out to Harrison, they'd be home free.

She started rummaging through the desk drawers. Without asking, he knew what she was doing: looking for a cell phone. *Smart woman.*

"Damn it." Of course there were no unsecured connections in the business district. But he'd been hoping to find a random coffee shop or something with free Wi-Fi. From their location, however, he couldn't connect to anyone. With enough time he could probably hack into someone's system, but right now they didn't have time.

He shut the laptop and looked up at her. "I set up an email to automatically send to Harrison as soon as this computer connects to the internet."

"So what you're saying is, if we don't make it out of here alive, if we get this laptop somewhere secure, the message will eventually make it to Harrison?"

He nodded. "That's the plan."

"Good. Where do you want to leave it?" she asked.

He scrubbed a hand over the back of his neck. One laptop in a huge building would be difficult to locate no matter how many people they had sweeping the place.

"There's a possibility that Hamilton has a cell phone in his office. I spotted a satellite phone on his desk earlier in the week." And leaving the laptop there would be as good a place as any. Not to mention Hamilton had a private stairwell, one that led to the parking garage. Unfortunately, his office was on the top floor.

"We'll have to get up the rest of the stairs undetected." Isa's voice was grim.

He nodded again. "I know. I've got two weapons I took off two men I killed."

Her eyes widened. "Wait…where are the bodies?"

"I dragged them into an office." He hadn't had time to hide them well, not when his main focus had been finding Isa.

She let out a short curse. "Whoever is working with Persky is going to find out soon enough—if they haven't already."

He nodded. "Exactly. And staying in one spot is stupid. We need to be on the move, trying to find a way out of here. I think Hamilton's office is a good spot to start." At the very least they could hide the laptop there while they tried to find a way out. If not through the parking garage, then they'd find another way. Or if they had to, they could just hole up there as long as they could. He had two weapons, which wasn't a lot against an unknown number of enemies.

She nodded after a long moment. "If he doesn't have a satellite phone, we can keep searching for cell phones in other offices."

"Agreed." His voice was low, and even though now wasn't the time, he gently cupped her cheek, needing the contact with her. "I'm glad you're okay."

"I'm glad you are too." She placed her hand over his in a gentle hold, the action mirroring the surprising tenderness he saw in her gaze.

Though it jarred him, there was no time to dwell on it. He dropped his hand and pulled out one of the pistols. He knew she could shoot well, thanks to the training her father had made sure she had. Isa might not like weapons but he wanted her to have one now.

He handed it to her and though he could see slight distaste in her eyes she nodded and took it. She held it against her body and kept her finger off the trigger.

He pulled out the other weapon, and automatically checked to see how many rounds it held even though he'd checked before. Force of habit. "We're going to head to the eastern stairwell. From there we'll go as far as we can. If we hear someone entering the stairwell, we take the closest exit." Graysen had no doubt of his own skill, but he didn't want to put Isa in any unnecessary danger. If that meant lying low instead of facing some of these threats head on, that was the way it had to be. "We'll avoid using these weapons if at all possible." Because he wanted to save ammunition in case they got trapped somewhere. But he didn't tell her that.

She nodded and reached for the laptop, but he picked it up and tucked it into the back of his pants. It was slim enough that it fit fine against him.

"If I tell you to run, you run. Got it?" He needed to know that she would follow orders. There were too many unknowns, and with such a huge threat, he had to be secure in her reactions.

"I'll do whatever you say. You're the trained one."

His gaze fell to her mouth and he had the most insane urge to kiss her. He wouldn't. The timing was pure shit and she wouldn't welcome him anyway, but the urge was still there. It would probably never go away.

He nodded and turned away from her. Quietly, he opened the door a fraction, listening for any sounds. After ten solid seconds and hearing nothing, he drew his weapon and swept out into the hallway. It was empty in both directions. Turning, he motioned to Isa, who hurried out behind him.

She might be a civilian, but she was holding up incredibly well. After everything she'd been through a year ago, he wasn't surprised. Even if he hated that she was stuck here with him right now. He would do anything to get her to safety.

Their movements were mostly silent as they hurried down the hallway. Her breathing was slightly elevated, the only giveaway that she was stressed. When they neared the end of that first hallway he held up a hand and slowed, motioning for her to do the same.

A slight shuffling made him pause. Then he heard it again. When he turned to Isa, saw her eyes had widened, he knew she'd heard it too. He pointed to a doorway with the door cracked open about a foot.

He waited until she'd slipped inside then put a finger over his lips. She nodded but he saw her surprise when he shut the door, closing her inside. He wanted to know she was somewhere relatively hidden while he did some recon.

Someone was trying to be quiet, which could mean another innocent civilian was trapped in the building, or one of Persky's men was hunting for him and Isa. He was betting on the latter. There weren't that many people in the building around this time of night on a regular basis.

With his back against the wall at the end of the hallway, he kept completely immobile, strained to listen.

He heard the shuffling again. Then again. It was very faint, like the sound of clothing rustling. Maybe someone was sweeping offices. Or some innocent civilian stuck in the building had witnessed some of the bloodshed and was attempting to hide. Didn't matter. He needed to find out if there was a threat coming his and Isa's way.

He ducked into the office next to the one Isa was hiding in. He had to trust that she would stay put. She was smart and wanted to get out of this alive as much as he did.

She sure as hell wouldn't be safe forever, so he had to make sure no one got through him. He would keep her safe, no matter what.

He left the door slightly ajar and hid behind it. Using the shadows as cover, he kept an eye on the corner of the hallway so he'd see when anyone rounded the corner. From the sound of it, someone was definitely coming their way.

Adrenaline pumped through him as he honed his focus. But training and instinct wouldn't allow him to zero in only on that potential entry for a threat. He was very aware that someone could come up on him from behind. Unfortunately, that was a risk he was willing to take. Anything to keep Isa safe.

The tenderness he'd seen in her gaze earlier was still with him. He couldn't get the sight of it out of his head. She'd looked at him the way she had when they'd been a couple. When he'd been lying to her about who he really was.

He might have missed her desperately for the past year, but seeing that expression on her face was like a punch to his solar plexus. A reminder of everything he'd lost.

All the muscles in his body tightened when he saw one man, then another, both armed, round the corner. He'd been right—the slight shuffling he'd heard was their clothing. They were quiet enough, but without any external noise like the hum of lights or computers, every sound seemed over-pronounced right now. Which was why he would have to move hard and fast.

He needed to take both these threats out without any fanfare. He hoped there were only two of them. The two men who Isa had seen earlier had been working as a team. And the two men he'd killed had been working as a team as well.

It stood to reason there were only two men here now if they stuck to pattern. But if there were more, he'd end them too. He'd end anyone who thought they could harm Isa.

He waited one beat, then two. Three, four. They moved farther into the hallway, almost past his line of sight. He didn't see anyone else coming. Had to move now, regardless. They were sweeping offices and his would be one of the first.

He watched from the shadows as one man made a hand motion to his partner, showing that they'd split up—one going into the office across the hall, while this guy would move to the one Graysen was in.

Whisper silent, Graysen stepped out, his weapon already raised. He shot the one closest first, then the next. It took 1.5 seconds to make the head shots. The second guy had started to raise his weapon but he never got the chance to fire. Graysen didn't bother checking their pulses. No one survived a head shot.

Keeping his weapon up, he scanned the hallway behind him before easing around the corner the men had come from. He couldn't afford to get sloppy now.

There were a hell of a lot of shadows but it appeared clear. And it was silent.

Moving quickly, he dragged the two bodies into the office he'd been hiding in. Nothing to do about the blood stains on the carpet or against the wall, but at least it put the men out of sight. He patted them down, found no cell phones.

Of course it couldn't be that easy. But he did take their weapons: two more Glocks, again with suppressors, and three blades between them. He was actually glad for the suppressors since no one would be alerted about the shots he'd just made.

He also stripped them from the waist up when he realized they had on Kevlar vests. Took both of them. Then he snagged both hand-held radios, hooked one onto his belt.

Once he'd taken everything from them he and Isa could possibly use, he gave two gentle knocks on the door of the office she was in. They might not have a signal in place but he hoped she wouldn't shoot someone who took the time to knock.

He stepped inside, found it empty. "It's me, Isa."

She popped up from behind the desk, her eyes wide. In the dimness, her normally bright green eyes appeared to be almost black. "I heard a couple thuds. Are you okay?"

"Fine. I took out two of them. Come on, we need to get moving." As she rounded the desk, he held out one of the vests for her. "It wouldn't hurt to wear this. And this," he said, handing her a pair of socks he'd taken from one of the dead men. Her feet had to be hurting by now.

Wordlessly, she slipped the vest on over her head as he did the same with his, tightening the Velcro in places. It stood to reason that any armed men coming for them would aim for the head once they realized Isa and Graysen had on body armor, but accurate head shots were damn hard to make.

When they were done, he handed her the radio. She hooked it onto her skirt, but it was too heavy and slid off so he took it back. After a quick search of three offices, he found a duffle bag someone used for the gym, emptied the dirty clothes in it and dropped everything he'd taken into it—except the laptop, which he handed off to her. Then he hooked the long strap over his body and wore the bag like a satchel.

"You ready?"

A brisk nod, her expression determined. "Yeah."

After peering out and scanning the hallway again, he stepped out, Isa right with him. Adrenaline punched through him as they reached the next stairwell entrance. He motioned for her to stand flat against the wall as he pushed the release bar.

Weapon up, he eased the door open. No one was waiting to ambush them. He was still tense, all the muscles in his body pulled tight as he moved carefully onto the landing. Isa moved in behind him, held the door until it shut quietly.

He pointed upward even though she knew what they were doing. She just nodded. He could have moved faster, but kept pace with her as they headed up the stairs.

Even with the extra added weight of the Kevlar vest and no shoes she was still moving at an impressive clip. Fear of dying could do that to someone. They made it to the top floor in record time but Graysen was still careful as he opened it using the old-school key he'd received at the beginning of this job. Since he'd been on this floor before he knew the layout well.

Glossy tile gleamed under the city lights streaming in. He paused, listened. No signs of life.

Even so, he moved in first, weapon ready as he scanned the area. Hamilton's assistant's desk was clutter free and because it was glass and chrome it was clear no one was using it as a place to hide. Isa stepped in with him, her own pistol in hand.

She looked so damn fierce with the vest and weapon.

He motioned for her to stand next to a bookshelf on one of the walls of the huge, open space.

Methodically, he checked the visitors' restroom, then Hamilton's private one as well as his office before moving on to the conference rooms and other offices not currently in use. The entire floor had the feel of being empty but he had to be vigilant.

Once he was certain the floor was clear, he hurried back to Isa, gently took her elbow and led her to Hamilton's office. Inside, he shut the door and locked it for good measure as she set the laptop on the oversized desk. He did the same with the bag.

"How'd you get a key to Hamilton's office?" Isa asked, her voice still low even though there was enough insulation where they were that no one would be able to hear them.

Instead of answering, he crushed his mouth to hers, pushing her up against the nearest wall. The timing was shit, but he didn't care. There was a chance they weren't going to make it out of here, and if they didn't—he was going to taste her one more time.

She arched into him, grabbing onto his Kevlar vest and tugging him even closer as her lips clashed with his.

The hunger emanating from her was almost a tangible thing, her need matching his as she nipped at his bottom lip. He cupped the back of her head hard, some part of him afraid she'd pull back, and he simply wasn't done. Couldn't stop tasting, kissing her.

He felt like a man dying of thirst and she was his salvation. He hadn't realized how bland his life had been until she'd come into it a year ago. It had been even worse once she'd left him because he'd had a brief glimpse into what happiness was, only to have it ripped away.

The sane part of his brain knew they couldn't do this for long, that he couldn't be distracted. Using willpower he didn't know he had, he pulled back, breathing as hard as her.

"I'm not sorry for that," he rasped out, staring down at her beautiful face.

Her lips were swollen, her gaze slightly dazed. "I'm not either."

Good, he thought savagely. Very soon, they were going to do more than just kiss. If they made it out of here tonight, he was claiming her forever. After the way she'd reacted to him, she couldn't deny the chemistry that still burned between them.

There would never be anyone else for him. He knew that with a bone-deep certainty. He didn't care how long it took to convince her of the same.

Now he just had to make sure they got out of this alive. First thing on his agenda: finding that damn satellite phone.

CHAPTER FIFTEEN

Emerson stared at her cell phone. She'd already called Harrison, Grant, Porter, and Lizzy. No one was answering their phone. The only reason she could remotely think of for none of them answering was that there had been an emergency on another job. Still…one of them should be available. The only other reason she could think of was that Belle had gone into labor and things weren't going well. That thought made her pause.

She had no reason to call the police simply because Isa hadn't showed up to the Red Stone office like she said she would thirty minutes ago. Now Emerson had no way to get in contact with her. Every time she tried to call Raptor's main building, it went to a recorded voicemail. So her options were limited. But she couldn't let this go. It wasn't like Isa to flake on her. And even though she had been pretty vague when they'd talked last, something about her tone had been off. No, something had to be wrong.

Feeling only a little foolish, she decided to call Carlito. He was the first person she thought of and she knew he wouldn't make her feel stupid for being worried about her friend. The job she was working on with Isa and Graysen—whose phone was also still in the lobby of the Raptor Aeronautical building—was classified. While she couldn't tell Carlito specifics about the job, she could still ask him for an unofficial police escort. She'd feel better having someone go with her anyway and she trusted him.

Emerson tried to convince herself that once she got to Raptor she'd discover that Isa and Graysen had gotten tied up with work.

She couldn't even make herself believe the lie.

No matter what, she needed to see for herself that her friend was okay. And if Isa wasn't... No, she wouldn't think like that.

Carlito answered on the second ring. "Hey, I was just coming to see you."

Her heart stuttered just a little bit at the thought of him dropping by tonight to see her. "Are you nearby?"

"Yeah, about two minutes away."

"Do you feel like giving me a ride somewhere? Isa called me a while ago and was supposed to meet me here. But she hasn't shown up. And that's not like her. I think it might have something to do with the job we're working on. I can't really say more than that."

"No problem. But what did Harrison say?"

She let out a sigh even as she started closing down her computer and cleaning up her desk for the day. "I've tried calling everyone I can think of who has the clearance for this job and no one is answering. Do you know if Belle went into labor?"

"Oh hell, that's definitely a possibility. Last time I talked to Grant he said she was really close. Do you want me to see if I can get in touch with their dad?"

She paused as she closed her office door behind her. "Ah, yes, if you don't mind." Technically Keith Caldwell didn't work for the company anymore. He'd handed everything over to his sons, but he was the founder. She simply hadn't thought about calling him, however. "If you get in contact with him, will you ask him to have Harrison call me back?"

"No problem."

"Thanks. I'll be downstairs in a couple minutes."

"I'll pull right up to the front of the building."

"Okay, see you in a sec." She was already feeling better about going over to Raptor Aeronautical now that Carlito was here. Getting to spend a little extra time with Carlito? Not the worst thing in the world. Not even close.

Minutes later she strode through the lobby of Red Stone Security, waved at two of the security guys she knew, and stepped out into the cool December air.

Carlito was waiting at the curb in his big, dark blue truck. And no surprise to her, he jumped out when he saw her and opened the passenger door. The man certainly had manners. In fact, he was pretty damn perfect. She couldn't believe that it had taken her so long to realize that the sweetest man was right in front of her face and that she wanted way more than friendship with him.

"How serious do you think this thing with Isa is?" he asked, his expression pure cop mode, which she'd only seen a couple times before.

"Honestly, I'm not sure." She slid into the seat, was surprised when he leaned over to strap her in.

He did it so quickly, and there was nothing intimate about it, but having him so close to her made her lightheaded for a moment. That masculine, familiar scent rolled over her, made her want to inhale deeper. But she didn't want to look crazy so she restrained herself.

He didn't respond until he'd slid into the driver's seat. "I turned on the seat warmer so if it gets too hot on your side just let me know." She was touched by his thoughtfulness, but before she could respond, he continued. "I couldn't get hold of Keith. So I think they must all be at the hospital. It's the only thing that makes sense. So when I ask how serious this is, what I'm saying is, should I call in backup right now?" He shot her an intent look as he stared down the quiet road in the business district.

"I don't think it's that serious. But..." She contemplated how much she could tell him without divulging anything classified. Emerson took her job seriously, but she needed to look out for her friends. "Today two people were arrested, thanks to the work we've done on this job—which is great news. And one was brought in for questioning. As far as I know he hasn't been arrested yet. We were planning on wrapping this job up by Monday or Tuesday at the latest. Then Isa called and she sounded a little off." And that was all she was comfortable saying.

"Okay." He nodded, looking thoughtful. "We'll park and head

into the main lobby. I'll show my badge, and say I need to speak to one of their employees. How does that sound?"

Relief slid through Emerson's veins. "That sounds perfect. Oh, you'll need to ask for Isa Johnson, not Harper."

Carlito raised an eyebrow, but didn't comment. He cleared his throat as they reached a red light. "About that parade Saturday."

A sharp sense of disappointment threatened to overwhelm her. There was something foreboding in his tone, as if he was about to cancel on her. Maybe he really was seeing someone new and they had plans. She steeled herself for what he was about to say. "If you can't make it, it's okay."

He shot her a sharp look, his gray eyes piercing. "I'm going. I wanted to know if we were going as friends or as a date. For the record, I'm hoping you say the latter."

Her eyes widened as she digested his words. A brief honk from the vehicle behind them made her jump. He faced forward and pressed on the gas.

She stared at his profile, drinking in the sharp lines of his face as she forced her voice to work. "You want to go with me on a date?"

"Yep. I've wanted to ask you out for about six months."

She continued staring, digesting that as well. Carlito wanted to date her? *Um, yes, please.* "Are you talking casual dating?" Because she couldn't do that. Couldn't just be another woman he was seeing. It would carve her up inside. She was an all or nothing kind of girl.

He snorted, gave her another one of those heated looks that made her toes curl in her boots. "Fuck. No."

She jolted at his use of the F word. She'd never heard him curse at all. If anything, he seemed to go out of his way not to. Considering how many former military types she was around all the time she knew he was tempering his language around her. She liked the forceful way he denied wanting something casual, however. "Your sister Camilla told me you were dating somebody."

By his expression, it was clear she'd surprised him. Just as quickly his eyes narrowed. "Is that why you were being weird Monday night?"

"That's not an answer." And she found that she really, really needed one.

"*No*. I haven't dated anyone or looked at another woman since we met. I haven't wanted to. And…I don't think I'm going to want to look at another woman for a long time. As in, ever." There was a determined set to his jaw, and his expression when he looked at her was filled with a kind of raw hunger she'd never experienced from anyone.

Heat swept through her body like a wildfire, singeing all her nerve endings. She collapsed back against the passenger seat. Emerson wondered why his sister had lied to her but brushed that small hurt aside as she focused on the here and now and the fact that Carlito wanted her. From the sound of it, more than simply wanted to date. He wanted something serious and…so did she. It seemed too easy though, that this incredible man was just putting it all out there and admitting he wanted something real with her.

"I want Saturday to be a date too." Some days she could have pretended they actually were dating, for how much time they spent with each other. But she wanted the right to touch him, to kiss him, to see him completely naked and have her way with him, bringing him all sorts of pleasure… Her cheeks flushed at the thought, as she allowed herself to indulge in that fantasy without pulling back.

"I don't want to date anyone else, Emerson."

The way he said her name sent more delightful shivers down her spine. His tone was so serious, intent, she had no doubt he meant it. "Me neither." The second the words were out she knew she meant them too. She felt as if maybe they'd been building to this for a while and she'd been too blind to see it.

He took her hand as they reached the stoplight a corner away from their destination. When he linked his fingers through hers, it felt like the most natural thing in the world. Arousal punched through her as she imagined his hands gliding all over her naked body, teasing and caressing.

"I don't want to wait until Saturday night for a date." Tomorrow was Friday and if he wasn't working, she wanted to see him then too.

He smiled. "Good. I've already got reservations for us at Montez's Grill tomorrow night."

She blinked. It was one of her favorite restaurants. "What?"

"I came by your office tonight with the sole intent of asking you out, of making it crystal clear that I want more than friendship with you."

She'd completely forgotten to ask him why he'd stopped by the office tonight. Not that she was complaining. "It's…hot when you get all growly like that," she murmured, watching him closely. And she loved that he'd already made the reservations.

His wicked grin made her insides flip-flop again. Oh God, this man was going to wreak complete havoc on her system. She'd been fantasizing about what it would be like to be intimate with him, but it wasn't just a fantasy now. By all accounts, it was going to be a reality very soon. If she thought about it too much right now, however, she was going to combust.

She cleared her throat. "Why…do you think Camilla lied to me?" It hurt more than a little because they were friends. Or she thought they had been.

Carlito just shook his head. "I don't know why. But I can guarantee it wasn't to hurt you. She adores you, and has been after me to man up and ask you out forever. Her lying was probably some misguided attempt to…" He let out a short sigh that was more frustrated laugh than anything. "Honestly, who knows when it comes to my sisters or my mom? Sometimes I can't even try to understand their logic."

"So your family will be okay with us being together?" It wasn't a real fear—she adored his family—but she'd also just been his friend until now. Something else she was still trying to wrap her head around. If he wasn't dating anyone else and she wasn't… It felt weird to say the word *boyfriend* where Carlito was concerned, but that was essentially what he was now. Right? She wanted to crush her lips to his right freaking now and seal the deal, to get a taste of this man she considered hers.

"Oh yeah. They'll be more than happy. My mama's been after me to lock you down since the moment she met you."

Emerson flushed with pleasure at his words. His sisters and mom were important to him so it meant a lot that they approved of her. Not that she would have let that stop a relationship between her and Carlito if they didn't, but it made her incredibly happy. "I had no idea."

He pulled into a parking lot across the street from their destination, turned off the engine and twisted to face her. His fingers tightened around hers and yep, those little butterflies in her stomach took off again.

It was as if she'd been given a pure dose of adrenaline. Being around him, with him holding her hand so intimately and looking at her as if she were the most precious thing in the world, it was hard to keep a thought in her head.

"I kept putting off asking you out because I didn't want to ruin our friendship, but...I couldn't do it any longer. I want the right to hold your hand in public, to call you my own." He cupped the back of her head possessively. "To do this..." His voice was all growly again as he leaned forward.

Just as eager as him, she met him halfway.

The second their mouths met, all her nerve endings flared to life as if she'd been shocked. Energy rolled off him as he teased her mouth open, his kiss demanding and sensual. It was as if he invaded all of her, stripped all her barriers away with this one kiss. Moaning into his mouth, she clutched onto his shoulders as she nipped at his bottom lip. Right now was too much and not enough. And sweet Lord, if just a kiss was turning her into a puddle of sensation, she could only imagine how great it would be once they finally got naked.

When he pulled back, his eyes were full of tempered heat. "Let's go check on your friend." His voice was a soft growl.

A shiver streaked down her spine at the heat in his words. After they checked on Isa she planned to have some very private time with Carlito. Shelving that for now—and only because she absolutely had to—she nodded and fell into step with him. It was always quiet in the business district after dark. No restaurants or clubs were down here, and even though there were high-rise condos a few blocks over, there was no reason for people to be here. No, they'd go to areas like South Beach, Wynwood, Midtown, or even Brickell, which wasn't that far from here and had plenty of chic bars for the business crowd. It was always a little eerie when she left work late, and being near Raptor Aeronautical was no different.

"What are their security protocols?" Carlito asked as they crossed the four-lane road directly across from their destination.

Her hand fit perfectly in his and she savored the feel of holding his hand, his callused palm against hers. "About the same as Red Stone," Emerson said, looking up at the huge building looming in front of them. She frowned as she realized how dark the place was. Everywhere else was lit up sporadically, even though she knew most places were closed for the evening. Still, there should always be a couple lights on for late workers, the security team, and cleaning crews.

He nodded, as if he'd guessed that was the case. "I left my service weapon in the truck."

She lifted an eyebrow at him as they stepped up onto the sidewalk. "You still have another one on you though, don't you?"

He just gave her a sly grin. "If we have to go through security, then I'll bring it back out to my truck. But all we're planning to do is ask to page Isa, right?"

She nodded "Yes. And I really hope I'm just being stupid about all this."

"You're not being stupid." He tightened his fingers around hers as they neared the glass front door.

It was weird how natural it felt, after all this time of just being friends, moving into this new stage of their relationship. She really, really couldn't wait until they moved on to the next stage. He'd said he didn't want casual. And even though she told herself to slow down, she could see, well, everything with him. The whole deal. No white picket fence, because that wasn't her style, but...marriage, kids. *Yep.* She could see it all with Carlito. And it scared her only a little.

When he stopped about fifteen feet down the sidewalk from the main doors, she glanced at him. "What?"

He looked at the mostly dark building, then the neighboring buildings. "Maybe the reason she hasn't been able to call you is there's no power." His frown deepened even as she nodded. "I don't like the look of this." He pulled out his cell phone.

"What are you doing?"

"Gonna call one of my guys, see if there have been any power outage reports before we head in there blind." He didn't drop her hand as he typed in his security code.

"Okay." Fine by her.

He tugged her hand as he scrolled down to someone's name. "Come on, let's go back and wait in my truck."

They turned and Emerson froze at the same time Carlito stiffened, his phone up to his ear.

A man was pointing a gun directly at her face.

CHAPTER SIXTEEN

"Dammit." Graysen wanted to pound his fist against the desk, but took a deep breath instead.

"I haven't found anything either." Isa looked just as frustrated as he felt as she closed the last drawer of the filing cabinet she'd been searching.

They'd covered the entire office thoroughly trying to find the satellite phone—or any phone at this point.

"The last time I saw the satellite phone it was on his desk. The only thing I can think is that he put it in his safe." Which Graysen had found behind a painting. But he couldn't break into it.

"Can't you just open the safe?" Isa asked.

He arched an eyebrow. "Just because I used to work for the CIA doesn't mean I can break into heavily secured safes—not without the right tools, anyway."

"So what do you think we should do now?" Isa asked, frustration clear in her voice.

Before he could respond the radio attached to his belt made a slight static sound before a faintly accented voice came over the line. "If you can hear me, I know you are still here in the building. And we have two of your friends. A pretty blonde who I think could be very entertaining to my men. According to her ID her name is Emerson. If that means anything to you, meet me in the lobby in twenty minutes. I just want the information you have. Give it to me and your friends live."

"Oh my God, they have Emerson." Panic laced Isa's voice.

"Shit." Graysen scrubbed a hand over the back of his head. This changed everything.

"He said two of our friends. I can't imagine who else would be with her, other than maybe Harrison."

Graysen nodded. If Emerson had been worried about Isa, she'd have contacted their boss. "The only way I can see someone getting the drop on *him* is if maybe they had a weapon."

"Should we respond to them?"

"No. I don't want them to know we've received their message. The man might have just been fishing, trying to see if he could bait us into responding. Four of his men are dead so they've got to be getting nervous." And there was no way in hell he or Isa would survive if they went to the lobby.

"Maybe," she said, but didn't sound convinced. "That wasn't Alan Persky. I've talked to him enough the past week to know that."

"I agree." He'd talked to the man too. But even if it wasn't Persky, it didn't mean he wasn't working with whoever had just radioed them.

"What are we going to do? We've got to help her."

"I'm going to find and save Emerson." No way in hell she'd be in the lobby either.

She stepped around the desk, moved closer until inches separated them. "You can't go after her and whoever's with her by yourself. That's suicide."

"I've been up against worse odds." And he sure as hell wasn't leaving a vulnerable woman to fend for herself against armed men who'd threatened to make her their entertainment. There was no possible way he could do that and live with himself.

She blinked once before her lips pulled into a thin line. "Well you're not going alone. We'll figure something out together. And you can't go to the freaking lobby, it's a trap!"

He'd never admit it, but he liked her bossy tone—and the fact that she cared about his well-being. "I know it's going to be a trap. But that doesn't mean I can't go look for Emerson and whoever she's with," he said. He'd have to be a ghost, go floor by floor until he figured out where she was being held. It would take too much damn time, but there was nothing else to do since they hadn't found a sat phone and there was no damn Wi-Fi reachable from Hamilton's office to get a message out. No matter what, Isa wasn't going with him to find Emerson. It wasn't happening.

Isa shook her head. "No. I don't care how trained you are. You're one person against…who knows how many. There's got to be something else we can do."

"The best thing for *you* to do is to hide out in the private stairwell. Either that or directly here in the office, but I think the stairwell is the best place. There are only two entrances to it, so you'll know if someone is coming. And you'll be armed." He couldn't go after Emerson knowing that Isa would be in even more danger. Simply couldn't do it. And if she came with him, he'd be more worried about her than anything else. He couldn't have his attentions divided like that and be effective.

She just gritted her teeth and let out a frustrated sound. "If you're going to go after her, you're going to be prepared. I know how to make some quick and not-so-pretty smoke bombs. You can at least lay down some cover. You'll be blind going in once you discover where Emerson is, but the upside is that whoever these men are will be blind as well."

"You know how to make smoke bombs?" He did too. It was messy but he was fairly certain there were enough of the ingredients in the building to make them. And…it was a damn good idea.

She gave a harsh laugh. "My father actually taught me how to make them. Thought it was a useful skill to know. Among other things." There was a flash of bitterness in her eyes visible even under the muted lights from the city outside, but it faded quickly as she continued. "I think we can find enough of the supplies in Hamilton's private kitchen area, but if not we can find them in other kitchens or janitor closets. We can create enough havoc and distraction to really screw these guys up. If anything, maybe it will set off some alarm not connected to the power."

He nodded, liking this idea. "No matter what, it will create enough of a distraction, especially with the hallways already being darkened. But we're only doing it if the supplies are on this floor. I'm not putting you in any more danger looking for this stuff." If necessary, he'd do that on his own once he knew she was relatively safe.

"Fine." She might not like it, but Isa wasn't arguing with him, at least. Turning on her heel, she headed out of the office.

Her stiff body language made it clear she was annoyed with him.

"You'd rather I take you with me?" he asked as they reached the small kitchen. It wasn't happening.

There wasn't as much light in the smaller room, but there was enough streaming in from the oversized window that they could work.

Isa sighed, gave him an annoyed look. "No. I know I'll slow you down and…I'm definitely not trained enough to take on a bunch of armed guys. I just hate feeling useless."

Her honesty surprised him—and touched him. He liked that she was being real with him. "You're not useless."

She didn't respond as he opened the freezer, looked for cold packs because they contained ammonium nitrate. There were multiple ways to make smoke bombs and he was going for the fastest. If there weren't cold packs, he'd use another, dirtier way.

"I know a couple different ways to make these." Isa opened a cabinet, started pulling out sugar and paper towels.

"Me too. We'll probably have to use different methods to make as many as we can. And it's a good idea." A really good one. He'd simply planned to take out as many men as he could one-on-one with head or body shots, or in hand-to-hand combat, and keep looking for cell phones. Sometimes simplest was best, but using smoke bombs was unexpected and would definitely confuse his targets.

"Thanks. Never thought I'd get to use this particular knowledge."

They worked quickly together, making two different types of crude smoke bombs that would be effective. It took longer than he'd have liked, especially knowing Emerson was at the mercy of those men. If that bastard who'd radioed them really did start hurting Emerson after twenty minutes, Graysen was going to make him pay.

He just hoped she could hold on a little longer. Because he was damn sure going to find her.

"How did you get rid of your badge?" Emerson whispered to Carlito.

He shifted his feet slightly. Only a couple feet separated them in the darkness. They'd been zip-tied to shelves in a supply closet by armed men a few minutes ago. A single battery-powered lantern-style light sat on one of the shelves, casting shadows over her face, her stress clear. More than anything, Carlito wanted to reach out, comfort her—and get her the hell out of here.

He'd seen some tattoos on a couple of the men he guessed were Russian, but he didn't recognize them as gang tats. At least not local gangs.

"Sleight of hand." It had been a risk, but Carlito had tossed his badge and ID right before they'd been shoved through one of the main doors into the building. He was still pissed at himself for letting some asshole get the drop on him. That guy had come out of nowhere, but he should have been more aware. "For now, if they ask, my name is Carlito and I'm a new hire at Red Stone Security. You don't know me well, but asked me to come with you tonight." He knew enough about Red Stone because of Grant that he could bullshit if he needed to. And since he and Emerson weren't dead yet, he figured their captors might need them alive for something. Otherwise they would have just shot them once they'd gotten them into the privacy of the building. Keeping her alive and getting her the hell out of here was his only priority at the moment.

Before he could say anything else, one of the armed men opened the door and stepped inside the dim room. Carlito had overheard someone refer to the man as Dmitri. The man shut the door behind him and leaned against it, crossing his arms over his chest as he stared at the two of them.

"Why did you have a gun on you?" he asked Carlito.

Carlito kept his gaze steady. They'd found his pistol in his ankle holster almost immediately. "I'm in the security business. I always have one on me."

He turned his attention to Emerson. "Why are you here?"

Carlito answered even though the man wasn't looking at him. He wanted to keep all of the man's attention on him and not her. "We just stopped by to check on a friend who works here." It was a stupid answer, but what else was he going to tell the guy? So far these guys had no idea he was a cop, and he planned to keep it that way. He needed to keep things as vague as possible.

The man's eyes narrowed on Carlito. "Don't lie to me or I will start cutting her." To underscore his words, he withdrew a five-inch blade from a sheath. He held it at his side, clearly comfortable with a knife in his hand.

Carlito's blood chilled, but before he could respond, Emerson spoke up. "We're here because one of my coworkers called me. She was supposed to meet me and never showed up. That's it."

"Is this coworker named Isa?"

Emerson didn't respond but her expression gave her away.

The man looked at her thoughtfully for a long moment. "I radioed her, giving her time to meet me. I told her that if she doesn't show up, you're going to be entertainment for my men." The dark look in his eyes made Carlito go still.

The threat was undeniably true. Though he wanted to yank against his bonds, to kill this man for the threat he'd just made against the woman Carlito loved, he contained his rage. For now.

The man's hand-held radio squawked. The words were in Russian, but the tone was clear enough: there was a problem.

Without another word, Dmitri pulled out his radio and stepped out of the closet.

Emerson let out a small sound of distress, the fear on her face cutting at his insides.

"We're going to get out of this," Carlito whispered. He was going to do everything possible to get Emerson out of here. Or die trying. Because no one was hurting her.

Emerson jerked at her zip-tied hands. "How?"

There was no guarantee that once they got out of their bonds they would be able to escape. Not with armed men outside the door. But they had to take the chance.

He stood up straighter. "Tighten the zip ties like this." Using his teeth, he yanked on the tail of the tie. It started to cut off his circulation, but it was necessary for what he had to do.

"*Tighten* it?" she whispered.

He nodded. After she'd done it, he held his hands up slightly and eased his body back, keeping his hands stretched out in front of him. "Stand with your feet shoulder-width apart, like this."

She mirrored his action.

Under other circumstances, he would have slammed the heel of his palms against his pelvic bone, in an effort to snap the zip ties free. But with the metal pole in the way they were too constrained. Still, he was going to try the same tactic he knew worked, and slam his palms against the shelf instead.

A single shout of alarm came from the hallway, making him pause. When he didn't hear anything else, he ignored it. "Do exactly what I do."

Putting force behind the move, he jumped up slightly and slammed his hands down against where the shelf and pole were connected. The thud was loud but the ties snapped free. His palms and wrists ached but he ignored the pain. They had to free themselves fast before Dmitri or one of his men came back.

Emerson did the same but it didn't work.

"Keep trying," he whispered as he began searching for something to cut her free, and for weapons. He let out a growl of frustration when he found nothing but a couple mops. It would have to do for now. And it was better than nothing.

Snap.

He turned in time to find her broken ties falling to the ground. "Are you okay?"

She nodded, rubbing her wrists.

He held out a mop to her. "It isn't much, but you can shove the end into someone's throat or eye—anywhere that will do damage."

She nodded, her eyes widening as she pointed behind him. Thick white smoke was billowing under the doorway.

Fire.

Shit. "Stay close." Heart racing, Carlito eased the door open and peered out into the hallway. Or tried to.

A wall of smoke greeted him but…it didn't have the smell of a fire. It was an acrid stench, one he recognized from his PD training and the Corps. Listening, he didn't hear shouts of alarm either, which was…odd. He'd heard one person cry out earlier, but it had been quiet since then.

Maybe it was Graysen and Isa who'd created the smoke. And the guys who'd taken over this building were obviously professional enough not to shout and act like maniacs so, okay, not odd at all. No, they'd be stealthy as they tried to find the threat—which had to be Graysen.

This was their chance to escape. Would probably be their only one.

Carlito shut the door and scanned the shelves again, using the lantern to search. He reached for a box of cleaning supplies at the same time Emerson did. They both pulled out thin surgical-style masks the cleaning staff must use, and put them on.

"Hold on to the back of my pants. We'll use the darkness and smoke as cover. I'm going to stay close to the wall. If we're stopped, keep going and get somewhere safe. Do not stop for me." He kept his voice whisper quiet, but he knew she heard him.

She nodded but the look in her eyes said she wouldn't leave him.

No time to argue. Turning, he eased the door open again.

The dark-haired man with visible tattoos on his neck who'd originally pulled the gun on them stood there, clearly about to open the door. Surprise flashed over his face.

Carlito struck out, slamming his fist into the guy's throat. The Russian's whole body jerked back, his eyes widening. Before the man could react, Carlito punched him again, breaking his trachea. Then he grabbed him by the shoulders and head-butted him in the face.

As the guy crumpled under the assault, Carlito tugged him back into supply room, tossed him to the ground and stripped him of his hand-held radio and two weapons: a Glock—with a suppressor—and a knife. The guy wasn't dead, but he wouldn't be getting up anytime soon, and now Carlito had something to even the odds.

Emerson didn't make a sound, just stepped over the guy's body as Carlito opened the door again. It was difficult to see through the smoke. Only muted light from office windows created a sliver of illumination.

Staying close to the wall, he began creeping eastward, weapon at the ready. When they'd been brought to the third floor he'd paid attention to the nearest exits, and right now he and Emerson were about three doors down from the nearest stairwell. It was time to get the hell out of here and find somewhere to hole up.

He didn't think exiting through the lobby was an option and he didn't know this building well enough to make any tactical decisions. So his first mission was to get Emerson to safety. They could hunker down in an office far away from here. From there, they'd figure out what to do next.

CHAPTER SEVENTEEN

"What the hell is going on?" Alan demanded of one of the only two men currently in the lobby. Dmitri had taken the blonde woman and her security guy up to the third floor to question them a few minutes ago.

Dmitri had wanted to find out if anyone else knew why they'd come here—but something had happened. He'd heard Dmitri speaking rapid-fire Russian over the radio to one of the men in the lobby, and now Dmitri wasn't answering his calls.

"We're not sure." The man's voice was clipped. "There's some sort of smoke on multiple floors, but it's not a fire. Likely smoke bombs."

Smoke bombs? *Shit, shit, shit.*

This was getting way too out of hand. Hell, it had gotten out of hand hours ago. Too many people were dead and now there was no controlling the fallout. The man with Isa, Graysen whoever, had to be behind this. Unless the dark-haired bitch was doing it. He had a hard time imagining the delicate-looking woman killing Yuri's men and setting off smoke bombs, however.

But what the hell did he know? Considering who her father was, per Yuri's file, maybe she had lethal skills and she was the one behind all this havoc.

This was supposed to have been a way for him to cash out, start over somewhere new without anything hanging over his head. No ex-wife or alimony and no debt.

He was still going to split the country with Katya. But instead of coming in tomorrow then waiting it out a couple weeks like everything was normal, he was going to leave tonight. He'd tried calling his fiancée a couple times but she hadn't responded. That was making him more antsy as well. She always answered his calls or at least called him back in ten minutes.

He wouldn't have as much money as he'd have liked, but he could still start over in a Third World country and live like a king. Faking his own death should be easy enough. And he was certain that Hamilton had cash in the safe in his office. That should appease Katya enough.

Alan wasn't in the CEO's office much, but he had a key to get inside and he knew the combination to the safe. He'd take what was in there and leave.

As the armed Russian started talking into the radio again, Alan headed toward one of the exits. His heart raced out of control as the gravity of what he was doing settled in. Screw all this, he was done.

"Where are you going?" the man's voice called out across the lobby, the sound echoing.

He glanced over his shoulder but didn't bother slowing. "I don't answer to you." He shoved at the release bar, exiting into an enclosed hallway that led to one of the parking garages. From there he'd have to cross over to another parking garage and head up to Hamilton's office through the private stairwell.

Alan sneered at that. Hamilton was all about his privacy, didn't even let him use that exit. As if he didn't work just as hard as that bastard.

In the garage he immediately spotted two armed men, nodded at both of them and acted as if he had every damn right in the world to be doing what he was.

If he moved with purpose, it would look as if he was right where he was supposed to be. Out of the corner of his eye, he noted that neither of them got on their radios to let Dmitri know what he was doing.

Good.

He turned his own radio on as he breached the entrance with his key. He heard Dmitri talking on it in quiet tones, in Russian, and tuned the man out. Then Alan turned on his flashlight since the dim orange glow from the generator didn't provide enough light for him.

Gritting his teeth, he started jogging up the stairs, ignoring the ache in his chest as he kept pushing forward. He was more out of shape than he'd realized. It took a while to reach Hamilton's office because of all the stairs.

Breathing hard, he stopped only when he was at the top. He bent over at the waist, sucked in air.

Move, move, move, he ordered himself. He'd berate himself later for being out of shape. When he tried the door, he stilled when he found it unlocked.

Pulling out a gun Dmitri had given him, he slowly opened the door. There were no signs of life in the wide-open assistant's area. Still, he stepped out carefully. Sweat rolled down his spine as he listened.

Fear and exertion pressed in on him. His heart was pounding too hard for him to hear much but he took a few more steps toward the assistant's desk, scanning everywhere as he moved.

There were a lot of windows on the top floor and light from the city streamed in, giving more than enough illumination to see where he was going. No smoke up here, so that was something.

He doubted Isa or her partner had made it all the way up here.

"Drop your gun or I shoot," a quiet female voice said from his right.

Out of the corner of his eye he saw Isa step out of the kitchen area, a gun in her hand, pointing it directly at him.

He could try to swivel and shoot her, but…he wasn't sure if she was a good shot or not. Considering who her father had been and the fact that four of Dmitri's men were dead… Yeah, he couldn't take the chance that she was the lethal killer who'd taken out men who were supposed to be the best.

He stayed still, watching her every move. It would be better to wait until he was closer to her, try to overpower her. If he tried now he'd just end up getting shot.

"I'm putting it down now." His voice shook as he slowly bent, set it on the floor.

"Turn slowly and kick it over to me." Her voice was deadly calm.

Ice slithered along his veins, but he did as she said. He was afraid not to. If the bitch gave him an opening, he was going to take it. No way was he getting brought down by some woman.

Graysen plastered himself against the wall of one of the offices. The smoke on this floor was starting to thin out and he had only two smoke bombs left. He'd used most of them on floors two through seven, trying to weed out where Emerson was being held. It wasn't the best plan, but he'd been hoping they'd move the prisoners if he smoked them out.

He listened to the low crackle static of a hand-held radio from the only man he'd seen on this floor so far.

A man's voice came over it in Russian, stating in frustrated terms that the two prisoners had escaped. Graysen understood him perfectly.

Yes! Relief punched through him that Emerson was free. He hadn't known her long but she was sweet and innocent. The thought of her at the mercy of these men made him see red.

Waiting another moment, he listened as the man responded in quiet tones. It sounded as if they were running low on men, and the plan was to hunt down the blonde and her security partner. So it must be somebody who worked for Red Stone. Not that it really mattered who was with Emerson, as long as they were capable and kept her safe. Graysen felt better knowing she'd escaped, even if he had no idea where to start searching for her.

Now that he knew she was unharmed, he needed to head back up to Isa. They'd been separated for too long, and he couldn't stand being away from her like this. No matter how safe she might be up in Hamilton's office.

And right now safe was a very relative term. Until they were out of this building and these men were either under arrest or dead, he wouldn't rest.

Soft footfalls sounded in the hallway, leading away from him. Graysen slowly peered out of the office door. The smoke was more of a haze now. He could only see one man in the hallway.

Weapon in hand he stepped out, ready to take down the guy, when the man swiveled. Moving lightning fast, the man dove through an open door up ahead.

Thud. Thud.

Bullets slammed through the wall next to the doorway the man had jumped through, hitting the wall closest to Graysen's head. Graysen crouched and returned fire. He could run or try to finish the guy.

He wasn't the running type.

He heard a soft thud and a cry of pain, but the man could be faking. He continued firing until he emptied his weapon. Then he withdrew his backup weapon.

Thud. Thud. Thud.

Three more bullets slammed into a door across the hall and a few feet away from Graysen. The guy's aim was way off so maybe Graysen had hit him.

Heart racing, he eased back a few steps and slipped into the nearest doorway. For all he knew this guy was calling for backup. In fact, he had to be, unless he was completely stupid. Graysen couldn't hear the guy calling on the radio but these guys could have phones. So far he hadn't found any on the men he'd killed, but no way in hell was he going to get trapped down here.

Keeping his weapon trained on the far doorway, he eased out again, giving up cover as he hurried back down the hall and away from the shooter. He needed to put distance between this floor and himself as soon as possible.

As he neared the end of the hall, only feet from the stairwell door, it flew open.

Graysen barely had time to react.

Turning, he aimed and fired. Crimson bloomed between the

man's eyes before he fell to his knees. Before the body hit the floor, Graysen swiveled, knowing he would be attacked from behind. The man who had fired on him before was in the hallway, staggering. He raised his weapon with one hand, his other hanging limply at his side.

Graysen aimed, fired. The man swayed suddenly and Graysen only grazed his face.

Thud. Thud. Thud.

Bullets embedded in the ceiling, wall and floor as the man fell to the ground, his arm flailing wildly as he stumbled.

Graysen pulled the trigger again. This time his aim was true. Another head shot.

The man's body dropped. Graysen didn't bother watching him hit the ground, just turned and hurried through the open stairwell door. Carefully and quietly, he let it close behind him.

He listened, heard footsteps somewhere above him, and he eased back out into the hallway. There was no movement, so he sprinted back down it, looking for another stairwell entrance. He'd killed eight men by this point.

He wasn't certain how many more were here, but eight meant he'd hurt the crew here. They had to be getting angry, and when people were angry they did stupid things, acted rashly.

He just hoped that by thinning out these killers, it would help them escape more easily. Because he and Isa were getting the hell out of this building sooner rather than later.

It took him another ten minutes to make it back to the top floor because he had to move slowly. He agonized every second he was away from Isa. Not being able to contact her, not knowing if she was okay—it carved him up inside.

As he entered the lobby outside Hamilton's office, he froze when he heard a male voice.

"I can help you get out of here." It sounded like Persky.

Rage filled Graysen at the sound of the man who was responsible for putting Isa in danger. Moving quietly, he hurried toward the open doorway of Hamilton's office.

Weapon up, he couldn't hide his shock when he saw Persky plastered against the huge window overlooking the city. The man's hands were above his head and firmly against the window as he faced the cityscape.

And Isa was holding him at gunpoint.

She pushed out a sigh of relief when she saw Graysen standing there. "I didn't want to get too close to him. So I made him stand like that so I could see his every move."

Smart. He couldn't believe how steady she was. "Did he hurt you?"

"No. He never touched me. I got the drop on him." Her voice was filled with just a hint of pride.

Graysen nodded in approval. Damn, she was something. "Don't take your weapon off him."

"No problem."

Keeping an eye on Persky by the window, Graysen found a tie in the personal armoire Hamilton had filled with extra suits. He wrenched Persky's arms behind his back and secured his wrists together, ignoring the grunt of pain the man made.

"Watch the door," he said softly to Isa, who nodded. He returned his attention to the bastard who was behind all this. "How many of your guys are in the building?"

"Fuck you," Persky snarled.

Graysen grabbed the back of Persky's head, twisting his fingers in the man's hair. Then he slammed his face into the window. The sickening crunch of his nose breaking sounded in time with the window rattling ominously.

The man cried out in pain. "Twelve, twelve!"

Graysen shoved Persky's face against the window, ignoring his continuing cries of agony "Twelve exactly?"

Persky's face was scrunched up in pain, but he shook his head. "Fourteen total. Including me."

Graysen had taken out eight men so five were left, since he had Persky. He really, really liked those odds. He could take out five more guys, no problem.

That was, if Persky was actually telling the truth. Since he didn't have time to question the guy and gauge if he actually was, Graysen was still going to be cautious. He patted Persky down, searching for weapons or a phone. Found nothing. Of course not. Why would life be that damn easy? "Where's your phone?"

"In the lobby," he rasped out, blood trailing over his lips.

"Why don't you have it?"

"Left it in case…they tried to track me."

Well wasn't that interesting. Maybe Persky was bailing on his partners. Graysen didn't care at this point. He just wanted to get the hell out of here with Isa. He wanted to know, in very specific detail, why the hell Persky and his men had attacked this place, but wouldn't waste time questioning him now. They'd get their answers later.

He grabbed Persky's bound wrists, turned and shoved him toward the exit. Graysen looked at Isa. "If this bastard is telling the truth, there are only five guys left. I've already taken out eight. We'll go down through the private stairwell." He yanked Persky to a sudden stop. "How many men are in the parking garage?"

"Only…o…one that I saw." The man was trembling now, the stench of fear rolling off him palpable.

Graysen couldn't afford to believe him. "Stay behind me," he murmured to Isa, who still had her weapon in hand.

She nodded, her expression tight, and quickly moved behind him as they headed for the stairwell. They'd hidden her laptop in Hamilton's office but he knew she still had the flash drive tucked into her skirt pocket. One way or another, this information was getting to the right people.

"How were you planning on getting out of here?" Graysen asked Persky.

He didn't answer right away so Graysen slammed his face against the wall by the stairwell exit door. The drywall cracked under the impact and when he pulled Persky back, a smear of blood stained the pale blue wall.

The man screamed in pain.

"Shut the fuck up." Rage pulsed through Graysen, the urge to kill this son of a bitch right here and now nearly overwhelming. "You put the woman I love in danger, sent men to kill her. I will start putting bullet holes in you if you don't answer me when I ask a question." His tone was calm, which he knew would terrify Persky more than if he'd yelled. *Good.* He wanted the guy pissing-his-pants scared. Because Graysen meant every damn word. He didn't relish torturing people but he'd do whatever it took to get the truth from Persky.

He made a sniffling, gurgling sound and spit out blood onto the floor. "Company car…has keys in the console. Big, white Cadillac. Bullet…resistant." His words came out nasal-sounding.

"You planning on ditching your partners?"

Surprising Graysen, Persky nodded. "This wasn't supposed…to happen. Was supposed to be easy money." He sniffled again, his words almost slurred now.

"What about Raptor's security people?" Graysen already knew something must have happened to the security team unless the guys were in on whatever this thing was.

Persky swallowed hard. "Dead."

Graysen gritted his teeth as he rested his hand on the release bar. He wanted to pummel Persky again for the admission. Who knew how many security guys had been murdered because they'd had the bad luck to be on the wrong shift. He couldn't think about that now.

"You ready?" he murmured to Isa.

"Yeah."

Though he wanted to pull her into his arms, to comfort her somehow, he couldn't. He'd save it for later. For once they got out of here.

It seemed to take forever to get down the seventeen floors since Persky was having a hard time keeping pace. The man was out of shape, but Graysen had messed his nose up and his breath was sawing in and out as if he'd pass out at any moment. If Graysen had to guess, the guy was about to lose it completely. He must have had grand plans to try to rip off his company and now everything had gone to shit for him. If Graysen could just stash him somewhere he would, but he couldn't risk Persky getting free or warning someone that they were attempting an escape from the building. Plus he was making damn sure this guy was delivered to the cops.

At the bottom of the stairwell, he turned to Isa. "If shit goes sideways—"

"I'm not leaving you, so save it." Even in the muted orange light he could see her determined expression.

"You're so stubborn."

"Yeah, I am… Did you mean what you said up there, that you still love me?"

The words had just slipped out when he'd been threatening Persky. Because Persky *had* put the woman he loved in danger. He kept his gaze locked on her. "Yes." He turned away before she could respond because he didn't want to see pity in her eyes. He loved her. Had never stopped.

She might consider everything between them a lie, and he understood it. Didn't mean it had all been a lie to him.

"We're going to use the vehicles as cover to the main exit—which will be to the west. If you try to alert anyone, I'll put a bullet in your head. Got it?" he snarled to Persky, who just nodded.

Once they were out in the garage everything was a hell of a lot darker. And colder. He wished he'd found shoes for Isa, hated that her feet were all torn up. The socks he'd taken from one of the dead men would just have to do for now.

They were on the bottom floor at least and wouldn't have to hike up or down floors in the garage. The only problem was, the actual exit was guaranteed to be guarded.

It didn't sound as if it would be heavily watched, considering how many guys Graysen had taken down. But there was also the possibility that Persky was lying about how many people were here. Considering the guy had no moral code, Graysen was betting there were more armed men.

Icy wind cut through his shirt as he shoved Persky toward a four-door truck to their right. It wasn't the best cover but it would have to do. Once they were all behind it, he lifted his head, scanned the rest of this floor of the garage.

Streams of outside light, probably from a neighboring building, illuminated the exit about fifty yards away. Multiple rows of parking and concrete barriers were in their way—not to mention heavily armed men potentially lurking around.

He pointed to a car three spots away. It would be their next cover. Persky nodded as Isa did the same.

Graysen stepped out first, using Persky as a human shield and making sure Isa was directly behind him. His rubber-soled boots and the rustle of their clothing barely made a sound as they moved but all the hair on the back of his neck rose.

That intrinsic survival instinct kicked in just as a man holding a pistol stepped out from behind a van in the parking row across from them.

"Drop your weapon!" Graysen held his pistol out past Persky's body, but still held Persky close as a human shield and never took his eyes off his target. The man paused. "Get behind that car, Isa," he murmured, loud enough for only her to hear. "I need you safe so I can take care of this."

The car was parked right up against a wall so no one would be able to sneak up on her from behind, at least. Graysen angled his body, nudging Isa to move. He was aware of her doing so, but kept his attention solely on the blond-haired man with a weapon. No silencer on this one.

"You think I care about this sniveling piece of shit?" The man's accent was faint, as with the other men from the building, and it was definitely Russian. His gaze flicked to Isa briefly as she moved, but he didn't seem concerned with her as he looked back at Graysen.

Graysen couldn't hear anyone else converging on them, but that didn't mean they weren't around. *Hell.*

Graysen didn't recognize the man from earlier, but…he knew the face from somewhere. It took all of two seconds for it to sink in. He'd seen the man on multiple Most Wanted lists.

Yuri Mikhailov.

"I think you do, Yuri Mikhailov. Surprised you're in the country when you're wanted for so many crimes."

The man's head tilted slightly to the side. He was too far away for Graysen to know for certain if he'd surprised him, but that change in body language was a giveaway.

"You would be wrong. Persky here was trying to flee the country, weren't you?" Ice coated his words.

Persky didn't respond, just breathed harder in Graysen's hold.

Pop. Pop.

Graysen shoved Persky forward into the bullets' path, while firing in return. Yuri dove behind a nearby Jeep. Graysen did the same, throwing himself toward where Isa was hiding—as a searing, tearing pain ripped through his chest.

CHAPTER EIGHTEEN

Isa crouched down in front of Graysen as he struggled to sit up.

Oh God.

Blood covered his shirt, seemed to be spreading everywhere. He had on a vest, but it didn't cover everything. So much blood was coming from his shoulder area, spreading outward in a hideous circle.

She had pretty much zero medical knowledge but pressed a hand to his shoulder where most of the blood seemed to be coming from. "Were you hit more than once?"

Grimacing, he nodded and tried to sit up again.

"Stay put," she whispered.

She held her hand to his shoulder, trying to fight back her own panic. She'd seen him shoot at the man named Yuri after the guy had shot Persky—who was lying in a pool of his own blood about ten feet away. She assumed Persky was dead, but wasn't going to check his pulse to make sure.

"I'm okay. I'm okay," he murmured, his eyes starting to lose focus. "Gotta make sure he's down." He shoved her hand away with surprising force and managed to sit up fully.

She noticed that he held onto his side as he moved, winced. Panic punched through her when she saw more blood seeping through his fingers against his side.

"Yes, you're fine. You are going to be completely fine. You have to be. Because I still love you." Graysen didn't respond. His eyes drooped, his head falling back against the rear of the trunk.

Shit. Shit. Shit. This was not good. She had to get help, had to get a phone. She'd never realized how much she'd grown to depend on her cell phone. Now not having one, not being able to call for help at the touch of a button when the man she loved was wounded? It was terrifying.

She rolled onto her side and looked under the car. Her throat tightened. Two booted feet were slowly inching their way toward them from across the garage. She couldn't even hear the man's movements. She'd been so focused on Graysen, and stopping the flow of blood. She should have been paying better attention.

No way was this guy going to win, going to take away the man she still loved. They'd fought like hell to make it this far tonight. They were damn well going to escape.

Going on instinct, she grabbed her weapon from the ground and fired at the man's legs and ankles. She might not like using guns, but her father had made sure she knew how to use one.

His grunt of pain rent the air as he fell to the ground, landing with a thud. She had a perfect visual of him under the car. Yuri, the man who'd shot Graysen. He'd fallen on his side and was facing her. Ice cold blue eyes stared back at her, his expression murderous.

His gun was still in his hand. He swung it toward her, his jaw clenched tight.

Time seemed to stretch out as she rolled over onto her belly, fired again at his face.

She pulled the trigger over and over until her gun made a *clicking* sound.

Breathing hard, she stared at the bloody mess of the man's face before she shoved up from her position. Bile rose in her throat but she swallowed it down. She'd freak out later.

"He's down," she said, hunkering next to Graysen, whose eyes were now shut. "Please don't die," she whispered.

She needed to get his vest off, to stanch the bleeding better, but first she had to find a phone. Had to get help.

"I'm going to call for help. I…love you, Graysen. I love you so much. Please live for us. We deserve a second chance."

His eyes fluttered open but he didn't respond. Just stared at her with hazy, blue eyes. Okay, that was good. He was awake, even if he wasn't talking. But his breathing sounded bad and his face was gray.

"Just hang on," she whispered before peering around the car. Her heart pounded erratically in her chest. The man named Yuri was definitely dead. His face and head were pretty much gone. She forced the bile back. *Focus*, she ordered herself.

Just because he was dead didn't mean there weren't others hiding. Steeling herself, she picked up one of Graysen's guns and pushed up slowly to her knees, then feet.

She couldn't see anyone in the darkened garage. Couldn't hear any footsteps. Couldn't hear…anything.

On silent, aching feet she crept toward Yuri's body. He was covered in blood, his face looking more like pulverized meat than human. Her stomach roiled again as she began patting him down.

She nearly cried out in relief when her blood-slicked fingers clasped a phone in his front pants pocket. With trembling fingers, she yanked it out. It had a security lock, of course. But she didn't need to get past that to call the police. She swiped the emergency call icon and made the call, but froze at a faint shuffling sound to her left.

Her throat clenched in horror as she made eye contact with a dark-haired man in tactical gear just like the other men she'd seen tonight.

He lifted a gun.

Her fingers clenched around her own gun but she knew it was too late. Grief speared her at the thought of dying without having another chance with Graysen, knowing that Graysen would now be at this man's mercy.

Puff. Puff.

She jerked, expecting pain as bullets tore through her—but the armed man fell to his knees instead, eyes frozen wide as blood bloomed across his forehead.

She swiveled to see Graysen crouched on his knees behind her, gun in hand, face pale. The weapon clattered to the concrete right before he collapsed.

"9-1-1 operator, how may I assist you?" The sound of the

emergency operator's voice on the other end of the phone made her cry out with relief.

Her entire body shook as she answered. "There's been an attack at Raptor Aeronautical. My friend has been shot. We're in the parking garage and need help now! There might be other armed men here! They've killed a lot of people." She shoved up and hurried back to Graysen. She put the phone on speaker as she skidded to a halt in front of him.

His face was ashen, his breathing harsh and his head lolling to the side. More blood pooled around his torso, glistening darkly in the muted light coming in from outside. At least he was breathing.

She fell to her knees beside him and ripped off the vest before pressing her hands to the wound. Tears gathered in her eyes and a burning lump formed in her throat.

Don't die. You can't die on me. Not now.

He had to make it. She refused to believe they'd come this far only to lose him when she'd finally realized she still loved him.

Emerson jumped next to Carlito as lights suddenly flooded the small utility closet they were hiding in. He held a finger to his mouth, in case she was going to speak. He didn't think she would, but he wanted to be careful. With the lights now back on, they should be able to make a phone call from one of the landlines. But he wasn't sure if this was some sort of trick from the terrorists or whoever these guys were.

He started to motion that he was going to step outside and find a phone to call for help, when a familiar voice came over a central com system.

"Emerson, this is Harrison. I'm with the police right now. We're in the building. Isa and Graysen are on their way to the hospital. We are currently searching the building. Do not come out if you are hiding somewhere. We will find you. If you have access to a phone, call me to confirm. But if you're hiding and safe, stay where you are."

Hell, yeah. Carlito pulled Emerson into his arms, buried his face against her neck as she tightened her grip around him.

"Thank God. Everything is going to be okay." Her voice trembled a little.

Carlito held on tight, knew without a doubt that he was never letting this woman go. He'd known for a while that she was it for him, but tonight had confirmed it. He didn't want to live in a world without Emerson in it.

It couldn't be good that Isa and Graysen were going to the hospital, but he'd worry about that later. He was just thankful this nightmare was over.

Still holding her, he pulled back so he could look at her face. "You're coming to my house tonight. Just so there is no misunderstanding about how tonight will go. I'm not letting you out of my sight, probably for the next couple weeks. So you're just going to have to deal with the fact that you'll be moving into my place. I could lie and say it'll be temporary but…once I've got you under my roof, I'm not letting you go. You're mine and no one's taking you away from me."

Emerson gave him the widest smile, easing the worry that she might argue with him. "I really like this bossy, possessive side of you," she murmured.

"It's always been there, at least where you are concerned. You bring it out in me." And he wasn't going to fight it. She was his, simple as that.

CHAPTER NINETEEN

Graysen struggled to open his eyes. He needed to get to Isa. Needed to stop the shooter…

Beep. Beep. Beep.

He blinked, saw that he was in a bed and Isa was in a chair next to it—holding his hand. She was slouched down on the chair, eyes closed, her head tipped slightly back against a pillow tucked between the chair and her head. She had on a pair of jeans and a long-sleeved black sweater.

"Isa—" The word came out raspy, barely audible. He needed water.

Her eyes flew open. She blinked a few times as she pushed up in the seat. Relief filled her expression as her gaze locked with his. "Thank God you're awake. I'll get the nurse." She jumped up from her seat.

"Water," he rasped out. He didn't want a nurse, he just wanted Isa.

She froze two steps from the bed, nodded and poured water from the beige-colored pitcher on a table in the corner into a plastic cup of the same bland color. Some sloshed over the side in her haste but she hurried back to him and held it up to his lips.

He tried to raise his right hand to take it, realized he couldn't. It was in a sling. He lifted his left hand but ended up letting her tilt the cup for him. The cool, fresh liquid was heaven. After he drank it down in two gulps, she refilled the cup again.

This time he took it, and drank three more cups until he felt somewhat sated. "What…happened after I shot that guy? How are your feet?" They'd been so torn up from her running around without shoes.

She blinked once before setting the pitcher back down. "My feet are fine." Her expression softened as she took his hand between hers. "I should be asking you how you're feeling."

He rolled his left shoulder once. He felt as if he was in a haze, probably from whatever meds he was on. "Good… What happened? Is Emerson—"

"She's okay. She's actually here right now, in the waiting room. I sent her home last night but she's back. There's a lot to explain but right now you don't need to worry about it. You don't need to worry about anything. You saved me from that shooter and then Harrison and the cops came in and took over." She lifted his hand to her lips, kissed it briefly as she closed her eyes. "I almost lost you." Pain reverberated in her words.

His fingers tightened around hers, his heart squeezing. "I'm here and you're here." And…he remembered pain. "Was I shot more than once?"

She opened her eyes at his question, nodded. "Twice. In the shoulder and ribs."

He nearly snorted, but didn't want to cause himself any more pain. That was the problem with tactical vests. They covered a lot, but not nearly enough.

"You lost a lot of blood, but the doctors say you're going to be okay. They'll be able to tell you all the specific medical jargon I barely understand, but the important thing is no organs were hit and you've pulled through the worst. And the man who shot you is dead."

He remembered that, even with the haze of the meds making his brain fuzzy. "You killed him."

Her face tightened. "Yeah."

"Did I imagine… Did you tell me you loved me?" God, he hoped it hadn't been a hallucination. Those words were etched into his brain. He prayed that wasn't just his imagination. Her words were crystal clear in his head when everything else was fuzzy. *Please don't die. I'm going to call for help. I...love you, Graysen. I love you so much. Please live for us. We deserve a second chance.*

"I did."

"Did you mean it?" He needed to know right now. If she'd just said it in the heat of the moment, he needed to know.

She cupped his cheek, her expression soft. "Graysen—"

A doctor strode in then, a compact woman with caramel-colored skin and ink-black hair. She gave him a quick smile. "Glad to see you're awake. I'm Doctor Garcia, head of trauma surgery. Do you remember me?"

He strained, vaguely remembered being in an ambulance, Isa shouting at him to stay alive. He thought Harrison might have been at the hospital too. But he didn't remember this woman. And he hated that he couldn't remember her if he was supposed to. For a former CIA operative, having blackouts in his memory made him edgy. "No," he gritted out.

"That's normal for what you've been through. Your shoulder was grazed and your ribs were hit. Not broken, though. Your lung collapsed under the impact but it wasn't actually hit. Which is *really* good. But you're going to be sore for a few weeks. After two surgeries we got you stabilized and you're in recovery. I'm going to have you start on deep breathing and coughing exercises to minimize the chance of you getting pneumonia, but things are looking really good."

He listened as she went over how long it would take him to recover and how lucky he'd been, but most of his focus was on Isa, who'd moved to one of the windows. It was late afternoon, considering the angle of the sun, and he wondered what day it was if he'd had multiple surgeries. He also wanted an answer to his earlier question. Right now he didn't give a shit what the doctor had to say. He was alive and fine. He wanted to know how Isa felt about him. Whether they still had a chance.

"The police would like to speak to you, but I've let them know that's only happening if you're up to it." The doctor's words made him tear his gaze away from Isa.

"Yeah, I'm fine." He wanted some answers, anyway.

"I'm going to get Carlito," Isa murmured, hurrying out the door before he could stop her.

"Your fiancée has been a rock. She hasn't left the entire time you've been here," Dr. Garcia said to him.

He nearly jolted at the word fiancée, but kept his reaction to himself. If Isa wanted to say she was engaged to him, he was more than okay with that. He wanted her to wear his ring, for the entire world to know she was his. But was she? Was that what she wanted?

The doctor squeezed his hand once before turning at the sound of the door opening.

Carlito Duarte, a detective with the Miami PD walked in—Graysen recognized him because he was friends with Grant Caldwell, but mainly because he'd seen the guy at Red Stone multiple times.

"Hey, Mariana." The detective smiled warmly at the doctor.

"Detective. I'm only allowing this because he's awake and says he's okay—and I trust you. If his condition changes, one of you page me," she said, looking back at Graysen. "Got it? You might be out of the worst of it, but you need a lot of sleep right now."

"I'll let him know if I need a break," he said, when all he wanted to know was where Isa had gone.

She nodded. "Good. Your morphine will be kicking in again soon anyway."

"Mr. West," the detective began as the doctor left. He pulled up a chair next to his bed, his expression serious. "I know we've met, but officially, I'm Detective Duarte. Carlito, if you'd prefer. I'm sorry to do this now but I want to get your statement on the record. Technically I can't tell you this, but I'm doing it anyway. I can pretty much guarantee the State's Attorney won't be bringing charges against you. You're not under arrest, nor does the Miami PD plan to arrest you. If anything, they might give you a medal."

"Okay." He'd known there would be an inquiry after he'd killed so many men. Yes, it had been in self-defense, but that was a hell of a lot of bodies to deal with. Not to mention all the other bodies he hadn't been responsible for. Talk about a clusterfuck.

"I just need to get the facts on the record so we can match up everyone's timelines."

That was fair enough. "Isa said Emerson was okay." He took a shallow breath, struggled against his throbbing shoulder and chest. While he didn't doubt Isa, Graysen was still worried something might have happened to Emerson while she'd been captive. "How'd she fare?"

The man's expression softened. "She's good. Out in the waiting room with Isa right now. I was there Thursday, trapped with her."

He blinked, surprised. "Glad she had you with her."

"I know you came for her, so before I start taking notes I just want to say thank you." Expression serious, Carlito held out a hand.

Graysen took it and nodded. He'd have searched for anyone on his team, but it was clear Emerson meant something to the detective.

Shifting slightly against the starchy sheets, he tried to get comfortable. "What day is it?"

"Saturday."

Okay, so he'd only lost a day and change in his memory. He could deal with that. He leaned back as Carlito started in with the questions.

They were expected, if monotonous, but all he wanted to do was see Isa. Hold her, touch her, remind himself she was real and okay. That they were both alive and not stuck in that building. He also had a ton more questions about what had gone down, but knew the detective wouldn't be answering them. He'd have to get his answers from Harrison and Isa.

Then he wanted to know when they could get the hell out of the hospital and he could finally be alone with her.

Isa stood next to one of the windows in the small waiting room, resisting the urge to pace. She knew Graysen was just answering questions, but she wanted to be with him. Unfortunately, they were already bending the rules by allowing Carlito to question him instead of the lead detective assigned to the case. Harrison had asked for a favor and received it—no surprise.

Graysen—meaning, Red Stone Security—had stopped terrorists on US soil. Right now, the city was grateful, even as the media was going batshit crazy over what had happened. She didn't think they'd ever know the real story, the real reason those men had been at Raptor Aeronautical. And she didn't care.

The only thing that mattered was that Graysen, Emerson, Carlito, and she were okay. She hated that other innocents hadn't been so lucky.

"You want some tea or coffee?" Mara asked from her seat a few feet away. Wearing dark pants, knee-high boots and a cashmere sweater, she looked incredible as always.

"I'm okay, but thanks." Now that Graysen was awake she felt as if she could breathe normally again, but her nerves were still in tatters. She was sure he had a ton of questions and she wanted to answer all of them, especially if they were about *them*. But mainly, she just wanted to see him before he fell asleep again. "How's Belle?" she asked in an effort to talk about anything else.

Mara gave her a serene smile. "Fine. Just like she was the last time you asked an hour ago."

"Gah, sorry." She knew Belle was more than fine. She'd gone into labor Thursday night at a family dinner. Everyone had rushed to the hospital, some forgetting their cell phones and others ignoring calls. There had been complications with the birth and Belle had ended up having an emergency C-section. Which was why they hadn't been able to get hold of anyone when they needed to during the hostage situation. It had been a perfect storm of insanity. "You can go see her if you want. Don't feel like you've got to stick around here." She leaned against the window, trying to tamp down her rampant nerves.

"Trust me, I think she's had enough of family for a while. Last I heard, she and Grant were holed up in her room and not letting anyone else in. I think they needed some alone time with the baby before they leave this evening. My sweet little niece." Mara's expression softened so much it was strange to see.

Isa adored Mara, but the former operative wasn't a mushy or emotional woman. "You getting baby fever?" she asked.

Mara just snorted, shook her head. "Babies are fun to play with, then send home."

Harrison strode in carrying a tray of cups. "Amen to that. I think my brothers have lost their minds when it comes to their kids… Hey Isa, got you a hot chocolate. You need something warm right now. How's our man?"

"He's decent, I think. His color was better and he's talking to Carlito now."

Harrison gave a brisk nod. "Good. I want to see him before he falls asleep again." Guilt flickered in his dark eyes as he focused on her. It disappeared quickly, but she knew it had been there. He seemed to feel responsible for them not being able to get hold of him when they'd needed to. Well, no one could have predicted the shit that went down Thursday night and into Friday morning, so she certainly wasn't angry at him.

Even though she hadn't thought she wanted anything to drink, she gratefully took the cup. It warmed her fingers, taking off some of the edge. She wouldn't feel settled until Graysen was officially discharged from the hospital.

"Where's Emerson?" she asked after taking that first hot sip.

Harrison tilted his chin toward the direction of the exit. "In the cafeteria, grabbing some food. She said she'd be back soon, that she wanted to see Graysen now that he's awake."

Isa nodded, glad Emerson would be coming back. As far as Isa knew, Emerson had gone to the police station to answer questions, then home to change, and then come straight to the hospital. Mara had brought Isa clothes, and she'd showered in an empty room because she hadn't been about to leave the hospital.

It felt like forever, but was probably only twenty minutes before Carlito returned. The detective immediately went to the side of Emerson, who'd only arrived five minutes before, and wrapped his arm around her shoulders. It was clear to anyone watching, the man was smitten. And vice versa; Emerson looked at him as if he hung the moon.

He faced the group with a tired half-smile. "He's still awake, but looking pretty exhausted. Everything he said lines up with your timeline and ours," he said to Isa before looking at the others. "He wants to see everyone, but especially you, Isa. I'm gonna hang back, give you guys some space."

"Me too." Mara nodded. "You three go see him."

"Thanks." Isa was beyond ready to get back to Graysen. She'd been here since he'd been brought in, had refused to let the paramedics look at her feet until they'd gotten him into surgery. She had a few cuts and bruises. So freaking what? He'd been *shot*. If it hadn't been for the vest, he might have died right in front of her.

Something she didn't want to think about.

Isa didn't think Graysen was supposed to have more than one or two visitors at a time, but no one stopped them as the three of them made their way to his room. Maybe Harrison or Carlito had said something to the staff—or maybe Harrison had called in one of his favors. The man seemed to know everyone in the city.

Her heart rate kicked up as she pushed the door to Graysen's room open. She hated being away from him, even for twenty minutes. His face lit up when he saw her. The sight was a punch of awareness to all of her senses. She wasn't sure how she'd thought she could have ever lived without this man. Then to almost lose him—it was simply too much.

She headed straight for his bedside. She'd already told the staff that he was her fiancé so she would be allowed access to his room. And Harrison certainly hadn't corrected the staff.

Graysen took her hand as soon as she reached for him, linking his fingers through hers in a solid grip. Another healthy dose of relief slid through her at his firm hold.

"How are you feeling?" she asked, watching his face for exhaustion. He was the type of man to push himself too hard. Right about now, she wished they were alone so she could tell him how much she loved him, that she wanted to start over with him.

"Tired. But Carlito said you guys would be able to answer all of my questions."

Isa nodded, pulling up a seat next to his bed as Harrison grabbed one for Emerson. As she expected, Harrison stood, ever the intimidating warrior.

Arms crossed over his chest, he gave Graysen's lower calf a surprisingly gentle squeeze. "I'm glad to see you looking so good. And I'm sorry about—"

Graysen gave a sharp shake of his head. "No apologies. Carlito already told me what happened. I'm glad Grant and Belle's baby is healthy."

Harrison nodded, but that guilt still flickered across his expression. Not exactly surprising, since Isa knew he considered the people who worked under him more like his family. He took his job and his responsibility to his employees very seriously—as he should. It was why people rarely left Red Stone Security. Once you got a job with them, you didn't want to leave.

"What do you know so far?" Harrison asked.

Graysen lifted his good shoulder. "Carlito mainly asked questions about how everything went down. Wanted to get a timeline of when I took out each threat and on what floor. Sounds like it's a bit of a clusterfuck at Raptor."

Harrison snorted. "They're having a hell of a time with the crime scene."

"I bet. Listen, just tell me everything. Like how the hell Yuri Mikhailov was in the country, much less the building."

Isa hadn't known who he was, but now she knew that Yuri was a hacker/terrorist who was wanted by Interpol and a whole mess of agencies.

"The Feds are going crazy over the fact that he was in the country." Her boss shook his head, his expression grim. "He approached Persky with a deal—to input code into the computer programming for multiple drones under contract by the US government. The drones would operate like normal until they crossed into specific territories. Yuri, or someone working with him, had them configured it so that once they crossed certain physical coordinates, he would be able to commandeer the drones into his command. He could have started a war—or multiple wars—with them. And it would appear that they were under US control."

Graysen frowned. "How did Persky get involved with them though? He wasn't even on our radar. Or the government's radar. Was he?"

Harrison shook his head. "He wasn't on anyone's radar. The Russians approached him and offered him a lot of money. He has—had—an ex-wife, alimony, and debt. It appears as if he wanted to leave his life behind, and start over somewhere new. Not only that…he had a new girlfriend. A young one, who was pushing him to give her the kind of lifestyle she was accustomed to and to run away with him."

Graysen's frown deepened. "She with the Russians?"

Isa nodded. "Yes. And he was an idiot for thinking a woman like her would ever fall for him." Isa had seen the pictures from the file the police had, and the woman who'd targeted Persky had been beyond stunning. As in 'Angelina Jolie and Megan Fox combined' level of hotness. Whereas Persky was not unattractive, but he was middle-aged and out of shape.

Harrison grunted in agreement.

"Why'd they lock down the building like that?" Graysen asked.

"He overheard my conversation with Emerson. Had the line tapped." Isa gritted her teeth at her own stupidity. She'd been vague in what she'd told Emerson, but clearly not enough so.

"He jumped the gun and called Yuri, from the looks of it," Harrison continued. "Yuri already had men in place on site while they wrapped up their operation. They only had one more bit of code to input and it had to be on site, since the programs weren't linked to any outside sources. Yuri simply shut down the building, blocked the exits and killed anyone who got in their way. The place was supposed to be empty that late, but there were a few stragglers. Not to mention Hamilton's actual security team."

Guilt bubbled up inside Isa at the mention of the innocent people who'd been killed. If she'd never called Emerson, maybe they'd all still be alive. Their families wouldn't be mourning right now.

Harrison's mouth curved up into a hard smile. "What they didn't count on was a highly trained former CIA operative taking them out one by one."

"Hell," Graysen murmured, shaking his head.

"From what the couple remaining men who lived through everything had to tell the police, they planned to kill Persky anyway. *He* obviously didn't know that."

"What was their original plan, before things went sideways?"

"Persky planned to continue working for Raptor for a few weeks before putting in his notice of retirement. After searching his place, the cops found multiple fake identities. Looks as if he planned to leave the country, start over as someone else. No one would have ever known about the embedded code. Later they might have figured it out, but it would have been too late to do anything about it. If not for you guys," Harrison said, looking between the three of them, "they'd have gotten away with it."

Isa was still trying to wrap her mind around everything. After the way her father had betrayed their country, betrayed her, she knew what people were capable of. But it was still hard to swallow what Persky had planned to do. "Oh, and Shawn Grady was working on Persky's authority to add that tracking software to my computer."

The police and Feds were still trying to figure out if Grady was complicit in Persky's whole scheme or just following orders of his VP. So far he was just in custody but hadn't been charged with anything yet.

When she noticed how pale Graysen was, she squeezed his hand once, then stood. "All right guys, it's time for Graysen to get some rest." He didn't protest so she knew she was right.

After the others were gone, she resumed her place next to his bed, still holding his hand.

"What do you need? Are you hungry? I can probably sneak in some food so you don't have to eat what comes out of the hospital kitchen."

He shifted slightly, tried to hide a wince.

"Graysen, don't move. I'll get whatever—"

"I want an answer to my question."

She raised her eyebrows. "What question?"

"Did you mean it when you said you loved me?" The desperation in his gaze took her off guard.

Her heart turned over. "Yes. I truly get why you did what you did. Before everything went crazy on Thursday, Mara gave me a file on my father. One you've apparently been sitting on for a very long time. Why didn't you tell me he got Colby killed?" Tears burned her eyes at the reminder that her father had been behind the execution of one of Graysen's best friends. Graysen had never told her, not even when he'd been trying to get her to forgive him.

He cupped her cheek with his good hand, his grip gentle as he stroked his thumb over her cheek. "I didn't want you to know that. He'd already hurt you so much, but he was still your father. I didn't want to destroy whatever love you still had for him."

She swallowed hard, not bothering to blink back the tears now. "I wasn't ready to listen to you a year ago, wasn't ready to face the truth that my father was a monster. But I love you. I've never stopped loving you, even if I wanted to deny it. And I've missed you so damn much." Her voice cracked on the last word. She could have easily lost him.

His grip tightened slightly and she leaned down, erasing the distance between them. The instant her lips brushed against his, the spark of awareness flared out to all her nerve endings. A simple kiss shouldn't have this much effect on her, but Graysen West was alive and relatively well.

She couldn't let Graysen go. Simply couldn't do it. He'd risked his life to save hers and he was one of the best men she'd ever known. She was going to hold on to him tight and never let go.

CHAPTER TWENTY

Saturday night

"I feel almost guilty having a good time while Graysen is in the hospital." Emerson tightened her fingers around Carlito's.

He hadn't been sure if she'd want to even come out tonight but was glad she had. They'd been in and out of the hospital all day Friday and most of today just waiting for Graysen to be able to take visitors. "Visiting hours were over and Isa was staying with him. There's nothing we could have done but sit in the waiting room overnight." And that wasn't his idea of a good time with Emerson. Not when he was dying to get her back to his place, strip her naked and get inside her. He'd been thinking of doing that since they'd been freed Thursday—okay, for the past six months.

"I know. Still…" She trailed off, smiled as he opened the door to his truck for her.

He planned to put an even bigger smile on her face tonight. As he strapped her in, he brushed his lips over hers, deepened the kiss for just a second before pulling back. Her lips were glossy as she looked up at him. Growling, he shut the door and rounded to the driver's side. They'd be home soon.

"So what did you think of the parade?" The annual Christmas boat parade was something he'd only gone to a couple times and that had been years ago, and never with a date. He hadn't even wanted to go tonight, but after what Emerson had been through, he'd wanted to give her a sense of normalcy in her life again.

"I loved it." She reached over, linked her fingers with his as he steered his way through the packed parking lot.

He loved that she didn't hold back with her affection. Now that they were officially together, she made it clear to everyone that she was his and vice versa. It eased an ache inside him he hadn't realized had been so deep. Still, he was counting down until he had a ring on her finger. Then the whole damn world would know she was his.

"You know, I have a friend who got, uh, intimate with her now-husband at that parade."

He glanced over to see her cheeks flushing that sexy shade of pink he adored. "*At* the parade?"

"Oh yeah. She's actually married to one of the guys at Red Stone. I couldn't believe it when she told me."

"Hmm."

"What?"

"Just thinking about the logistics of that—and wondering if you'd be quiet enough for me to stroke you to climax."

Just as he'd hoped, her cheeks flushed even darker. She cleared her throat. "Hopefully you'll find out if I'm quiet or loud soon enough."

He just grinned as he pulled out onto the main street, leaving the crowded parking lot of the park behind. Green and red lights were strung up around trees and light poles all along this strip. "I plan to tonight."

Her breathing increased ever so slightly and just like that, his cock turned rock hard. Tonight was the first night of many with Emerson. The anticipation of stretching her out naked on his bed, of finally claiming her, of seeing every inch of her curves… He shifted uncomfortably.

When his work phone buzzed in his pocket, he bit back a curse. It might be nothing, but it was late enough that if he was getting a call, he was going to have to go in. With this huge case right now, he had no choice. Hell, he was lucky he'd been able to take a few hours off with her.

"It's work, isn't it?" she asked as he pulled his phone out.

Sighing, he nodded as he glanced at the screen. "Yeah."

He answered the call from his boss. Ten minutes later he ended it, more than frustrated.

"Don't worry about it," Emerson said as he set the phone on the center console. She'd heard enough of his half of the conversation to know he'd been called in. "Why don't you just drop me off at my place—"

"What did I say about that?"

She laughed lightly, the sound pure music. "Okay, okay. I was just giving you the option if you wanted it. I feel a little weird being at your place without you there."

He frowned, not liking that at all. His place was hers, as far as he was concerned. But he knew when to keep his mouth shut. Especially since he'd already pushed her into staying with him. Not that she'd pushed back but... He didn't want to give her a reason to leave.

After getting her settled into his place and double-checking that she would set the alarm, he headed to the station. Apparently the Feds were there and wanted to talk to him. Again. Something told him it was going to be a long night.

Carlito stared at Emerson sleeping on his couch. He'd been gone almost six hours so he hadn't expected her to still be awake. A blanket was tucked around her, but one foot was sticking out, showing her painted red toenails with little white snowmen on her big toes. Everything about her was adorable. *Yep, never letting her go.* It might have only been six months since he first met her, but he felt as if he'd been waiting for this woman for a lifetime. As if she'd been made just for him.

She must have been exhausted since she didn't even hear him come in and disarm the security system. Moving slowly, he lifted the blanket off her—froze when he realized she was just wearing one of his T-shirts, then scooped her up. She was lean and leggy, and he loved the feel of her up against him. Knew he'd never tire of it, of her. Protectiveness like he'd never known surged through him as he held her close. He had the insane urge to keep her close to him all the time after what had happened Thursday. Yeah, he knew it would pass, but right now he was in overprotective mode.

She made a soft moaning sound and shifted against him. Her blue eyes opened, her expression softening. "Hey," she murmured, laying her head on his shoulder as she curled into him. "What time is it?"

"A little after three." He'd done everything in his power to get back to her as soon as he could.

"I tried to wait up."

He nudged his bedroom door open with his foot, his cock hard at just the feel of her in his arms. He'd been restraining himself for six damn months, pretending he just wanted friendship. That was all over now. Now she was going to have no doubt how much he wanted her. He felt almost possessed with the need to have her, claim her. After everything that had happened Thursday, he guessed part of his blinding need was because he kept reminding himself she was safe with him.

The wood slat blinds over the windows let in enough light for him to see, even though he had the layout of his room memorized.

He stretched her out on the middle of his bed before switching on the bathroom light. He'd waited a long time for this and he wasn't going to be cheated out of seeing all of her completely bared to him. Every. Single. Inch.

She made a cute little sound as she arched her back, stretching her hands over her head. "You, naked, now." Her voice was as sleepy as her expression.

He grinned at her words, loving this side of her. It didn't take him long to strip off his service weapon and clothes. The only thing he left on was his boxers. Because once those were off, he'd have no control left.

Crawling onto the bed, he spread her thighs as he moved in between them, gliding his hands over her smooth legs.

She shivered, moaned softly as he reached under her T-shirt and tugged at her panties. He liked not being able to see what she had on under, to just feel. When he pulled away a skimpy black scrap of material that was mostly lace, he knew for certain that very soon he was going to ask her to model for him in various stages of undress.

Now the only thing that mattered was tasting her.

"Been thinking about doing this for so long," he murmured, moving until he had her completely caged in beneath him.

"What kinds of things did you imagine doing?" Her grin was wicked as she smoothed her hands up his chest and over his shoulders.

He shuddered at the feel of her touching him. She hadn't even gotten close to his cock and he was ready to come. Yeah, he needed to slow things down. This woman got him more turned on than he'd ever been, just by existing.

"Burying my face between your legs while you were sitting at your desk at work…when anyone could walk in." The truth was he'd never risk anyone seeing her in that state, but it was something he'd fantasized about more than once.

He crushed his mouth over hers before she could respond, savored the way she arched up against him. He could have lost her this week, less than thirty-six hours ago. If she'd gone without him, hadn't thought to call him… He broke out in a sweat just thinking about that. They both needed this.

She wrapped her legs around his waist as he teased his tongue past her lips. When she dug her fingers into his back and started grinding against him, he pulled back, breathing hard. At this rate, he'd be inside her in seconds.

They'd already had "the talk" and were both clean, so he wasn't using a condom. Something he was eternally grateful for. Getting to be inside Emerson without any barriers was his idea of heaven.

She watched him with heavy-lidded eyes as she trailed her fingers down his chest, over his abdomen—he sucked in a sharp breath, rolled his hips back. *Nope.*

"Not yet, darlin'." He simply didn't trust himself, and she deserved a hell of a lot of foreplay.

She pouted a little until he stripped her T-shirt off—and he sucked in another breath.

Fantasizing about her and seeing her bared to him were two very different things. As if drawn by a magnet, he reached out, cupped one full breast. Shuddering hunger sparked in her gaze.

He wanted more of that from her. Wanted everything from her.

Slowly, he teased a thumb over her nipple, watching the pink bud harden even more.

She squirmed against the bed, tightened her legs around him as he began teasing her other nipple. Her breathing grew even more erratic, her face flushed as he oh so slowly ran his thumbs around her nipples, making her hitch in a breath. He could watch her forever.

"You are perfect," he murmured. His cock was heavy between his legs, but he ignored it.

"And you are a giant tease." Her voice was raspy and uneven.

He could tease her even longer, but that would mean depriving both of them. *Not happening.* Leaning down, he took one of her nipples in his mouth, sucked.

The action seemed to set her off. Groaning, she arched her back, trying to push herself deeper into his mouth as he gently pressed his teeth down.

She slid her fingers through his hair, cupped his head tight. "Touch me between my legs." The words were part demand, part plea.

He slid his hand down her stomach, moving slowly until he cupped her mound. She had the barest amount of fine, blonde hair there. She rolled her hips against his hand, the action sensual.

All the muscles in his body were pulled taut as he traced a finger down her slick folds. She was so wet. For him. *Hell, yeah.*

Feeling how turned on she was made it hard to think straight. "I'm not letting you go, Emerson." The words ripped from him as he slipped a finger inside her. Christ, she was tight. *So damn tight.*

He knew it had been a while for her—as it had been for him. Even before he'd met her. He'd seen what his best friend had with his wife, saw what his sisters had, and he wanted it too. He'd just never thought he'd actually meet someone he wanted forever with until Emerson.

"Good. Not letting you go either." She moaned, rolled her hips as he slid another finger inside her.

Desperate to taste her, to bring her to climax, he leaned down, began feathering kisses along her abdomen. Her inner walls tightened around his fingers the farther down he moved.

His cock jerked once as he thought about what she'd feel like once he slid inside her.

Her clit was swollen, peeking out from her folds. He closed his eyes for a long moment, inhaled her sweet scent. He wanted to remember everything about this moment. The day he made Emerson his forever.

When he flicked his tongue over her sensitive bundle of nerves, she jerked against his face, an excited moan tearing from her.

"Carlito." The sound of her saying his name, all breathy and needy, made him crazy. And determined to have her shout it as she came against his face.

He increased the pressure against her clit, stroking her over and over as she writhed against his face.

"Yes, yes…" She dug her fingers into his scalp as she moved closer to the edge.

He had no doubt she was close, could feel the way her inner walls tightened around his fingers faster and faster. Her hips rolled against his face, wild and erratic.

"About to come," she rasped out.

He laved his tongue against her, harder and harder until her back arched and her inner walls clenched convulsively around his fingers. Her climax seemed to slam through her. He didn't stop until he'd wrenched every bit of pleasure from her, until she was lying boneless against his sheets.

On his bed. Right where she belonged.

He lifted his head, felt pure male satisfaction at her sated expression. She looked down the length of her body at him, her face flushed and her eyes a little dazed.

"I'm going to have a ring on your finger by New Year's." He figured he probably should have kept that to himself a *little* longer, but he'd almost lost her. Could easily lose her at any moment, and he wasn't going to waste a second of the time they had together.

More than most he knew how fragile life was. He saw death and what humans did to other humans every day. And he was locking her down, claiming her as soon as possible. A couple weeks seemed like long enough for her to get used to the idea.

She blinked once, quickly coming out of her daze, and pushed up so that she was sitting. "That better not be your idea of a proposal," she whispered. "Because it sucks." With a grin, she reached for his boxers, shoved them down his hips. By the time he'd gotten them fully off, she had her long fingers wrapped around his hard length.

"Not…a proposal," he managed to get out as she stroked him once, twice. Because he was going to do things right. It was old-fashioned and probably what she'd consider archaic, but he was still going to talk to her father first. But no matter what, his ring was going on her finger. If she'd have him.

"Good." She stared down at his erection as she continued stroking him, seemed pleased by what she saw.

And hell if that didn't make him feel a hundred feet tall. But he needed inside her now. Though he hated to stop her from touching him, even for a second, he lightly grasped her wrist, moved it away.

But he didn't let go. He guided her arm above her head, then the other one, and clasped her wrists together as he covered her body with his.

He could feel every inch of her nakedness underneath his. Her nipples beaded tightly against his chest and though he wanted to capture one in his mouth, he stayed where he was, kept his focus on her face. "I love you, Emerson." After what he'd just admitted he needed to say the damn words that he'd never said to any woman.

He wasn't going to hide how he felt, deny what she was to him.

"I love you too." Even with the muted light streaming in, he could see her face clearly, could see she meant every word.

Her words wrapped around him, soothed the darkest edge of him. *She loves me back.* He crushed his mouth to hers as he repositioned himself at her entrance. He'd felt how slick she was, knew she was ready, but he still thrust inside her slowly. Savoring every second.

She gasped into his mouth, jerking her wrists against his hold. He decided to let go because he wanted to feel her fingers stroking over him.

As soon as he loosened his grip she wrapped her arms around him, dug her fingers into his back. She arched, tightening her grip on him as he began thrusting inside her.

This was what heaven was. Pure heaven. His balls pulled up tight as he drove into her, over and over.

He forced himself not to come yet, to hold off as he savored the feel of her tight walls wrapped around him, the way her pliant body felt beneath him.

When she nipped at his bottom lip and slid her hands down until she was gripping his ass, he let go. A man only had so much control.

And Emerson had shredded the last of his.

Groaning, he tore his mouth from hers as he came. He slid his hand through her hair, cupped her head. He wanted to watch her, for her to see exactly how much she owned him.

Then he reached between their bodies and teased her already sensitive clit. A few gentle strokes, and it pushed her into another orgasm. Her inner walls clenched around his cock just as they'd done around his fingers.

But this was more intense. His own climax still punched through him, slamming against all his nerve endings as she found another release.

Though he wanted to watch her as she came, he buried his face against her neck, breathed in her scent as he emptied himself inside her. Eventually he stopped thrusting, lifted his head to look at her.

She had that sated look again as she cupped his face between her hands. "That was perfect." She brushed her lips against his and sighed in satisfaction as her head fell back against the pillow.

Slowly he pulled out of her, even as his cock protested. She was exactly where he wanted to be. Always. But he wanted to clean her up. First, however, he rolled onto his side and pulled her close.

She immediately curled into him, laying her head against his chest. "I'm pretty sure I could stay like this all night. Or all morning now, I suppose." She let out a little laugh at the last word.

"There's no reason we can't do that. I'm not going in later today." He'd already gotten approval from his boss. The Feds and the lead detective on the case were wrapping things up and they didn't need him. And if they did, his phone would be off. He had priorities.

"You sure you don't need to?"

"I'm sure. We're going to be naked the majority of the day. Just FYI."

She laughed against his chest. "Your bossiness really is going to take some getting used to."

He slid his hand down her spine and kept going until he reached her ass, squeezed once. "I think you like it."

"I definitely do." She nipped lightly at his chest and just like that, his cock started to lengthen again.

Oh yeah, they were in for a lot more naked time before they left this bed.

Emerson pressed mute on the television at the sound of Carlito's front door opening. He'd just left ten minutes ago and said he would be back in about thirty. He was getting them breakfast—well, technically a late lunch by this hour—since he had pretty much no food here. His refrigerator was just as bad as hers.

"You're back early," she called out from the living room. Stretched out on his couch, she hadn't moved since he'd left. The last few hours they'd made love multiple times and she was exhausted.

Happy, but exhausted.

"Emerson?"

She jerked up at the sound of a familiar voice. Two seconds later three very familiar faces came into view as Carlito's mom and two sisters stepped into the living room. Since she was just wearing a T-shirt and panties, and was in his house in the middle of the day on a Sunday, it was pretty clear they were more than just friends.

Camilla, who was thirty-seven years old, beamed then turned to her sister Gabriela and actually high-fived her. "I told you telling her that he was seeing someone would work."

Even though the T-shirt came to mid-thigh, Emerson still pulled the blanket tightly around her and stood. She felt really awkward being half dressed in his living room facing his family, but smiled at them. "Hey, guys. Carlito just went out for food. He didn't say you were stopping by."

His mom hurried over to her and pulled her into a tight hug. "He doesn't know we planned to stop by. But after seeing the news we wanted to come and check on him and he wasn't answering his phone."

Carlito had told her how his family sometimes stopped by unannounced, but he'd left out that they must have keys. "He's doing good. We both are." She narrowed her gaze on Camilla. "You lied to me about Carlito seeing someone?"

Camilla's face flushed a light shade of pink. "It was the only thing I could think of to get you to see him as more than a friend. It was..."

"Totally wrong?"

Her cheeks turned darker as her sister nudged her. "It worked, right?"

Emerson just shook her head. What had worked was Carlito finally just asking her out. But she didn't say that. "So...do you all want coffee or anything?" She was pretty sure that was all Carlito had anyway.

His mother, Ariana, shook her head and sat on the couch Emerson had just been on. She patted it and motioned for Emerson to sit as Carlito's sisters both sat on a loveseat.

Feeling a little like she was under a microscope as the women all watched her almost expectantly, Emerson sat—even if she really wanted to go put on pants. Or real clothes that weren't rumpled and didn't smell like sex.

"So when did this happen?" Gabriela finally spoke. Of the two sisters, she was always the quietest. And that was a relative term. Because his family was pretty loud.

"Ah, well, Thursday night." She wasn't going to go into details about everything that had happened. The news had gotten some of it right, but they had no idea how bad everything had been, what could have happened with those drones. Unfortunately her name had been released to the media today as one of the survivors of the terrorist attack.

"And?" His mother's eyebrows rose.

"And what?" She wasn't sure what they wanted to know. Surely they couldn't want details about their relationship. Emerson had grown up with a father who'd treated her more like a son than a daughter. She'd constantly been surrounded by her father's friends. Which was more than fine with her—she loved the way she'd been raised. But she didn't have many girlfriends, and the ones she did have, well, they didn't really talk about sex and relationships. Most of her friends she talked computers and gaming with.

"When are you two tying the knot?"

Emerson choked on air at his mother's blunt question. "I, ah… I need clothes." She jumped up and hurried from the room, the laughter of the three women trailing after her.

She took her time in Carlito's room, washing her face, brushing her teeth and changing into the clothes she'd worn over here last night. Jeans and a sweater. Better than being half naked. Feeling more prepared to deal with his family, she headed back out there to find the three of them all had mugs of coffee and were sitting in roughly the same place she'd left them.

"We decided to make coffee," Ariana said. "Grab a cup and join us."

Nodding, she did just that and once again found herself under the microscope of three nosy, beautiful women. They might be intimidating but she loved the idea that soon she'd be part of this wonderful family.

"We need babies in our life again," Camilla said abruptly.

Emerson just nodded, hoping the woman wasn't talking about her and Carlito. Thankfully, she heard the front door open and internally sighed. Carlito was back to save her!

Her sister nodded, as if what Camilla had said was normal. "All our kids are pre-teens or teens. So it's up to you and Carlito to give us all babies."

She stared at the three of them in slight horror as Carlito stepped into the room. He gave his mom and sisters each a quick kiss before sliding onto the couch next to her. To her surprise, he pulled her into his lap, wrapped his arm securely around her waist.

"You're ambushing my Emerson about babies already?"

Camilla nodded. "You better believe it. We need cuteness and kids who don't talk back or think they know more than us. Or roll their eyes at us every time they look at us."

"As soon as she lets me, I'll be putting babies in her," Carlito murmured.

Emerson jerked in his hold, turned to stare at his wicked, wicked expression. The man was loving this. And she was going to kill him later.

The three women dissolved into laughter, either from his words or her horrified expression, and started talking amongst themselves about some Christmas party.

"You're insane," she whispered.

"True. But so's my family. Now you see what you're getting into. And it's too late to run now," he murmured, his grip tightening. "I told you. By New Year's."

He'd surprised her last night with that. Sort of. She'd known he was serious, but all the talk of putting a ring on her finger had definitely surprised her—and pleased her. After what they'd survived, she wasn't wasting a second of her life. And the thought of being engaged and eventually married to the sexiest, sweetest man she knew? Why would she run from that? She wanted the world to know he was hers too.

They'd talk about the whole baby thing later when they didn't have an audience. She wanted a few years of just them first, but then… Yeah, the idea of having a mini Carlito made her heart melt.

"I expect a real proposal." Her words were just for his ears.

The heated look he gave her told her he'd do it right. She couldn't wait to see what he came up with. Because she didn't care about the ring or having a flashy proposal. She just wanted something real, that came from the heart. And she knew without a doubt Carlito would do that.

CHAPTER TWENTY-ONE

Three weeks later

Graysen was about to lose his mind. Isa had been taking care of him for the last few weeks and he hated that she seemed to see him as some sort of invalid. He was just fine now. Okay, his ribs ached, but who gave a crap about that? All the important parts were working, especially his cock.

It had been over a year since he'd been inside her. He was done waiting.

Stretched out on her bed, he called her cell phone, knowing he was probably driving her a little crazy by this point. He knew where she was, but was anxious for her to get back home. She'd refused to let him go with her, insisting that he needed rest. Screw rest. He needed to be buried inside her as deep as he could get. Mark her. Brand her as his, forever.

"Hey, babe," she answered on the third ring, breathless.

"Where are you?"

"I…don't want to tell you."

Shoving straight up in bed, he frowned. "What's wrong?"

She sighed. "Nothing. I'm just in the driveway unloading all the groceries. I knew if I told you, you'd want to come help. And I think you need to take it easy."

He gritted his teeth. *Take it easy, my ass.*

He took a deep breath and ordered himself not to get out there and help her bring everything inside. It would just drive her even crazier and put her on edge. And right now, he wanted her in a good mood. Because he had a plan. "I'm actually feeling a little winded." He didn't even feel bad for lying.

"Were you doing something while I was gone?" Her voice was slightly admonishing. He'd never realized how much she could worry.

He liked how much she cared about him, that he finally had her back in his life. But he wasn't a child or an invalid. Very soon he planned to remind her that he was a man. *Her* man.

The last three weeks he'd been mostly laid up at her place. They'd both been forced to take paid vacation from Red Stone—courtesy of Harrison, who'd been insistent that as long as Graysen was home, then Isa was too. *God bless that man.* Graysen might be going crazy on virtual bed rest but at least he got to spend time with the woman he loved.

Now he was past ready for sex. He was dying for it.

Dying to taste her again. They'd made out a lot, but she always put on the brakes, worried she'd hurt him. She was so worried about his ribs that neither of them had had an orgasm in the past few weeks. He was frustrated, and even though she wasn't acting like it, he imagined she was sexually frustrated too.

"I took Peaches for a walk and lifted weights," he lied. He'd walked the dog but there had been no weight lifting. He was saving all his energy for Isa.

There was a tense silence and he guessed she was tempering her response. She cleared her throat. "Where is Peaches, anyway?"

He could hear her moving around the kitchen now, had to resist going in to help her. "I dropped her off for a doggy play date next door after her walk." Because he wanted alone time with Isa with absolutely no interruptions. That included their dog, who didn't understand they needed personal time that didn't include her. And he didn't want Peaches staring at them or clawing at the door trying to get to them.

"Okay. I've got a few more bags to bring in. I'll come see you when I've got everything put up."

"Okay." When she walked in, she'd find him completely naked. He'd planned for her to find him in bed. Now, however… He swung his legs off the bed, twisted back and forth, stretching out. His ribs twinged, but man, he'd definitely been hurt worse. He'd had his femur snapped during a mission that involved jumping out of a plane. This was nothing compared to that.

And nothing was stopping him from being inside Isa in the next half hour. Maybe sooner than that. They didn't have to do acrobatics or anything, but they were both getting off.

At this point he'd settle for just her getting off. Yeah, he wanted to so bad he could taste it. He needed to bring her to climax, to see that sated expression on her face and know he'd put it there. She'd done so much for him, had let him back into her life.

The need was making him too damn edgy.

He made his way to the shower, turned it on and waited until steam billowed out before entering the stone and glass enclosure. Stepping under the hot jets, he savored the way they felt hitting his back. He was getting too damn stiff staying in that bed—and Isa was worse than any drill sergeant he'd ever had. She was so sweet and caring about her desire to make sure he stayed in bed—but there was absolutely no arguing with her. The woman was tough.

"Graysen?" Her sweet voice filled the room as he finished washing his hair.

"In here." He was already hard and aching for her.

"Why didn't you wait for me? I would have helped you." She stepped up to the enclosure, hands on hips.

He drank in the sight of her—wearing far too many clothes. "You got your cell phone on you?"

She blinked. "No."

Moving lightning fast, he opened the door and reached for her, dragged her into the shower with him.

She let out a yelp of protest right before he crushed his mouth over hers. He pushed her back against the slick wall, grinding up against her.

Moaning, she wrapped her arms around his neck, meeting his

tongue stroke for stroke. He noticed she was careful to avoid touching the scarred, tender area on his shoulder. The hunger and need from her was palpable, letting him know she wanted him as badly as he wanted her.

Thank fuck.

"Clothes, off," he growled against her mouth, only pulling back long enough to start stripping her.

"Graysen, are you sure—"

He tugged her soaked sweater over her head, then started on her jeans. Soon she was completely naked, her wet clothes tossed out of the shower. Staring at her, he slid his hands down over her waist, then hips, and back up again. Her light brown nipples were rock hard, her chest falling and rising erratically as she drank in the sight of him.

Even when they'd slept together she'd stayed fully clothed. It was like she was trying to spare him the torture of seeing her but not being able to have her.

No more.

"If you start to feel—"

"I'll let you know." He cupped her cheek with one hand. "My stitches are out and I'm good. I need you, Isa."

Whatever she saw in his eyes must have convinced her because she nodded and for the first time in weeks he saw true, raw hunger. Maybe she'd been keeping it locked down for his sake, but it was all out in the open now. Just like when they'd been together before. She'd always been so sensual with him, so open and free.

"I need you too."

"I haven't been with anyone since you. For the record. And I don't want to know if you have or haven't. I just needed you to know—"

"I haven't either. Couldn't stand the thought of anyone else touching me." She grasped his cock, stroked once, twice before dropping to her knees in a fluid movement.

Elation pumped through him.

Hell, yeah. He hadn't been lying—he hadn't wanted to know either way. But to know she hadn't been with anyone either… Okay, who was he kidding? He was ecstatic.

This was supposed to be about her, but— He groaned as her lips wrapped around his hard length. He shuddered, buried a hand in her wet hair and held on.

Water cascaded down around them, her dark hair slick against her head as she took him fully in her mouth. She gripped the base of his cock hard, held firm as she teased the ultra-sensitive crown.

She knew exactly how to work him, exactly how to tease him until he was begging for more.

Leaning back against the wall he closed his eyes, lost himself in the sensation of her mouth. Deep down in a place he didn't want to acknowledge existed he'd been terrified that they'd never work things out, that he'd never get to experience the sweetness of Isa again.

To be here, at her mercy, with her perfect mouth on him—this was heaven and even better than he remembered. More intense. He rolled his hips as she went deeper. And when she sucked hard again, he knew he was close.

He tangled his hand in her hair, squeezed once before he could get any words out. "Isa, hold off."

She paused, gazed up at him, looking every inch the goddess she was. Her grin was wickedly sensual as she ignored his demand and started to lean back down.

But he tightened his grip. His ribs twinged as his breathing increased, but he didn't care about the discomfort. He was hanging on by a thread, and considering how long it had been since he'd been with anyone—since Isa, over a year ago—he wasn't coming in her mouth. Not this first time.

With a mock pout, she rose to her feet. "I've missed doing that," she murmured, going up on tiptoe and brushing her lips over his. "And I want to finish." Her voice was sexy, sultry.

He had her back against the wall in seconds. Chest to chest, hip to hip—he'd needed this on every level.

Her full, bare breasts pressed against him. The feel of her nipples gliding against him made his brain short-circuit. He cupped one soft mound, shuddered even as she did the same under his touch. He hadn't forgotten how sensitive she was. Had been fantasizing about this for so damn long.

She hitched a leg around his waist, rolling her hips against him. His cock throbbed, the ache flowing through him intense.

His chest was tight, and yeah, he was already feeling a little exhausted, but the adrenaline pumping through him kept him going. Hell, *Isa* kept him going.

Somehow he tore his mouth from hers. "Gotta taste you once." She was his addiction and he'd be damned if he didn't get at least one taste of her before he buried himself inside her.

"Graysen..." She sucked in a breath as he cupped her between her legs, slid a finger against her slick folds.

"Missed your pussy," he murmured, loving the way she blushed crimson. She'd never been a dirty talker and he loved working her up with words.

She dug her fingers into his waist, rolled her hips again, the action jerky. "What else did you miss?" she rasped out.

"Bringing you to climax with my mouth. Bending you over the edge of any surface we could find and fucking you until we were both boneless."

Her eyes closed as she let out a long, breathy moan. "I've missed that dirty mouth."

Smiling, he dipped his head to her throat and feathered kisses along the column of her neck. Her body was slick from the water rushing over them. She slid her hands up his chest and over his shoulders. When she dug her fingers into him, he began a slow path of kisses down her body, stopping at each breast to lavish them with attention.

As he flicked his tongue around her nipple, he continued stroking between her legs. But not enough that she'd climax. Not yet.

Still, he wanted her worked up and ready to combust by the time he got inside her. As he began to kneel down, she started to protest.

He ignored her. He knew his body's limits and nothing was stopping him from putting his mouth on her.

She didn't protest too hard. Once he was kneeling directly in front of her, she lifted a leg, propped her foot on the built-in tile bench—spreading herself wide for him.

When he met her gaze up the length of her body, all he saw was heat and hunger. His cock throbbed, aching to be inside her. But not until she was ready for him.

She slid her fingers through his hair the second before he buried his face between her legs. He'd already felt how slick she was and he wanted her on edge just like he was. So close she could barely take it.

As he teased his tongue along her slick folds, her fingers tightened ever so slightly. She was sweet, just like he remembered. Everything about her was seared into his memory. Including the sounds she made when they were naked and he was anywhere near her pussy.

The memories had haunted him pretty much every night over the last year.

He felt almost drunk on her taste. Focusing on her clit, he applied enough pressure to bring her right to the cusp of climax, but not reach it.

"You're such a tease." Her words were unsteady as she rolled her hips against his face. When she lowered her leg from the bench and tried to squeeze her thighs together he grasped one, held her legs open and continued teasing her. He loved her this way. Desperate. Needy.

She struggled against his hold, trying to find relief, but he kept going, on and on until he knew she was close. And he was going to feel her climax around his cock.

She was his prize for not dying weeks ago.

Eyes slightly dazed, she stared down at him. "You're stopping?"

"We're coming together." His words were a growled promise.

He pushed to his feet and for a second, swayed. *No.* He wasn't going to fail at this. He couldn't. Before he could move, she took over, pushing him onto the bench. Because he needed to sit, he let her move him.

Crawling on top of him, she grasped his cock and pushed up on her knees. He held her hips tight, steadying her as she positioned herself over his hard length. Closing his eyes, he rubbed his cheek between her breasts as she simply hovered over him—teasing him as he'd teased her. It wouldn't take much effort to thrust upward, to completely fill her. But he liked the anticipation. He could spend all damn night touching her everywhere, relearning every inch of her body.

"I'm so close, baby," she murmured. "Not gonna last once you're in me." She eased down on him. Slowly.

He sucked in a breath. Damn, she was as tight as he remembered. His balls pulled up hard and his brain short-circuited with every inch she moved lower until he filled her completely.

"I can't live without you, Isa," he whispered, looking into her eyes, his entire body on fire. Water pounded down around them and for this moment it felt like they were the only two people in the world.

"Good thing you won't have to. I'm not going anywhere."

"Marry me." All his muscles tightened as he held back from coming.

She blinked and he rolled his hips, thrusting upward. She jolted at the sensation, gripped his shoulders tight. "You can't...propose while you're inside me."

"I just did. Marry me next week. I don't want to spend another day without you as my wife." His voice was rough, every muscle tense with the need to drive into her until he came.

"Graysen." She moaned as he thrust again, her inner walls clenching tighter and tighter.

Oh yeah, she was close. And he was going to push her over the edge. But not yet. "I'll do this all night. Say yes and you can come."

Laughing lightly, she nipped at his bottom lip. Now he was the one moaning into her mouth.

"Say yes," he demanded, barely hanging on.

She gently traced the area around his mostly healed chest wound before whispering, "Yes."

He jolted at her simple response. When he looked in her eyes he saw the woman he loved more than anything, the woman he wanted to have kids with, to grow old with. The woman he was never letting go.

Reaching between their bodies, he massaged her clit, adding the right amount of pressure to push her over the edge.

As soon as he started rubbing her, she began riding him. And he was done for. Gritting his teeth, he held off coming until her inner walls started convulsing rapidly around him.

He sought out her mouth as she cried out his name, claiming her as she claimed him right back. She rode him fast and hard as they both found their release.

He had to tear his mouth from hers as his climax crested. Burying his face against her neck, he completely let go of his control.

She was the only woman he'd ever been able to let his walls down around. His sweet Isa, who was crying out his name as she continued riding him.

Eventually they both stilled, and though he was ready to collapse he held her tight to him, his face still buried against her neck. The steam billowed around them, the flowing water providing a soothing sound to the backdrop of their labored breaths. "I'm probably going to say this a lot the next few months, but I love you."

She smiled against his shoulder. "Pretty sure I can live with that. Because I love you too. And we've got a lot of time to make up for," she murmured. "A year's worth of sex, on top of all the regular sex we'll be having."

He laughed, his chest rumbling, and though the tightness and discomfort was there from his wound, it felt good to laugh. To have the woman he loved naked and in his arms.

Next week he was going to make her his wife. Best way he could think of to start the new year—and the rest of their lives together.

EPILOGUE

Valentine's Day

Lizzy Caldwell slid into her husband's lap, wrapped her arm around his broad shoulders as she looked out at the crowd of people in Belle and Grant's backyard. Grant and Belle had decided to throw a last-minute barbeque at their place for the Red Stone crew even though their baby was only two months old. Lizzy wouldn't have been so welcoming to people that early into motherhood, but Belle was taking this whole motherhood thing a heck of a lot better than Lizzy had at first.

The weather was chilly, sunny and perfect for outside relaxing. The grill had tons of food on it and the scent of barbeque filled the air. Someone had strung up red and pink paper hearts so they crisscrossed over the pool and the patio area.

She'd never imagined that when she started working for Red Stone Security, and eventually married one of the owners, her family would grow quite as much as it had.

Porter nuzzled her neck for a moment and she let out a sigh.

"Everyone's having a great time," she murmured. "Apparently we all needed this."

"No kidding." His gaze strayed to their son, Maddox, who was almost two and was toddling around everywhere.

Porter's brother Harrison stood near Maddox, acting like a mother bear whenever he got too close to the pool. Around Maddox or his own wife was the only time Harrison seemed to have a soft side, and it made Lizzy love her brother-in-law all the more for it. "You think Mara and Harrison will ever have kids?"

"Nah. I don't think they want them."

"I don't think so either." Mara was one of Lizzy's closest friends but she'd never talked about wanting kids. Her husband was the same. Lizzy snorted. "Do you remember how terrified she looked when we first handed her Maddox when he was a baby?"

Porter laughed, burying his face against her neck for a long moment that she cherished. His big body shook, the rumble of laughter coming from him music to her ears. "It was like we'd given her a bomb."

"They're good with Maddox though. And Athena." Belle and Grant's new baby. "Well…let's hope they're ready for a new niece or nephew to spoil," she whispered in his ear. Not that it mattered. There were about forty or fifty people milling around the backyard, all drinking, laughing and talking.

Porter stiffened slightly and pulled back to look at her. "Are you saying…"

Grinning, she brushed her lips over his. "Yeah. Got the official yes from the doctor this morning." She'd been feeling nauseous the past couple weeks and had missed her period so she'd gone to see her doctor—even though she'd been pretty certain she was pregnant. Once you'd gone through it, it wasn't a feeling you forgot.

He crushed his mouth to hers hard despite the crowd around them. Porter was the silent type, but he'd never shied away from affection. He looked like he'd just won the lottery when he pulled back from her. "How are you feeling?" Suddenly his face morphed into a mask of concern.

"Really good. No more nausea—for now, at least." Last time it had come and gone throughout her entire pregnancy. This time she hoped it stayed far away.

"How long until we tell everyone?"

"Maybe another four weeks. I want to get through the first trimester."

Still grinning, he simply nodded.

"Hey, you two," Belle said, coming to sit on the cushioned bench next to them, sleeping baby in her arms. "You look like you're up to something." Her gaze narrowed as she glanced between the two of them.

"Just enjoying ourselves," Porter said.

Belle gave him a look that said she wasn't sure she believed him, but continued. "I was worried Athena wouldn't be able to sleep with all these people around but she's been out for three hours."

Lizzy grinned. "I remember those days. Eat, sleep, poop. Repeat."

Laughing, Belle nodded. "Pretty much." When she looked at her little girl, her expression was filled with so much love.

Lizzy was overjoyed that Grant had found Belle. He'd been through so much, only to fall in love with one of the sweetest women ever. "How much does your cousin love that you named your baby after her?"

Now Belle rolled her eyes. "For the record, it wasn't after her. I just love the name, but that doesn't matter to her. She's rubbing it in to pretty much everyone in our family."

Lizzy's gaze strayed to where Athena and Quinn were talking with Travis and Noel—whose little guy was fifteen months old. It was hard to believe how many little ones were running around now. Just three years ago none of her friends had kids. Now it seemed over half of them did. And she loved it.

Loved every second of her crazy life. Going to work for Red Stone Security had changed her world in so many ways. Ways she'd forever be grateful for.

"So guess who I'm pretty sure is pregnant?" Belle whispered conspiratorially. Before either of them could ask who, she said, "Jordan and Vincent. I think, at least." Yawning, she looked across their big yard at said couple.

Vincent had Jordan sitting on his lap on a lounger near the pool, one of his big hands draped protectively over her slightly protruding stomach. The loose sweater she had on probably didn't hide her belly as much as she thought it did.

"Yeah, I kinda figured," Porter murmured. "He's been more growly than normal today to anyone who gets too close to her."

Lizzy just snorted. Vincent was ridiculous when it came to Jordan. Once upon a time Lizzy had thought he was a dog. The man had been such a player. Now that she knew the truth about what had happened between him and Jordan so many years ago—how she'd gone into WITSEC without telling him, breaking his heart—it was good to see him so settled. Even if he was insanely protective. "Sweet Lord, help Jordan if she has a baby girl."

Porter barked out a laugh at that, startling baby Athena, who gurgled and opened those gorgeous blue eyes.

Immediately she tucked her head into Belle's chest, opening her little mouth and making smacking sounds. Lizzy snickered. "Someone's hungry."

"This angel is always eating," Belle murmured, pulling her nursing cover over her chest and Athena's little body. "You guys mind?"

Lizzy shook her head. "Of course not... Did I hear through the grapevine that Carlito proposed to Emerson using the rookies at the PD?"

Laughing, Belle nodded. "Oh yeah. They all held up signs with one letter each and were waiting on the beach where he took her for the proposal. And it took him forever to pick out the ring. Guess who he wanted to drag around with him to stores for his mission—a month after I gave birth? I about killed him." She adjusted Athena slightly under the cover as the baby fed.

"I can't believe he didn't just ask one of his sisters."

"That's what I said. But apparently they've been making him crazy wanting babies. He begged me and I just couldn't say no."

"Sounds about right." Lizzy's gaze strayed for a second as she spotted Isa and Graysen arriving. They were late but it was good to see them. Lizzy loved seeing Isa so dang happy. "Graysen's doing good."

Porter snorted softly. "Yeah, and going crazy on desk duty. I think Harrison's about to send him back out into the field."

"With Isa?"

"Yeah. He thinks they'll make a good team, and after their last job, nothing can be as bad as that."

"I hope not. That was crazy," Belle murmured. As she lifted her nursing cover off, she set Athena on her shoulder and stood. "I need some food but I'll see you guys later."

Lizzy started to stand when Reece, her friend Charlotte's little boy, came racing out of a cluster of people, two cupcakes in his hands and a face covered in yellow and red icing. Kell, his giant of a father, was five steps behind him. He scooped the little guy up—and got a face full of cupcake.

"It feels wrong to laugh," Lizzy said, pushing to her feet even as a chuckle burst out of her. "I'm going to grab something to drink. You want another beer?" she asked Porter.

He shook his head, standing. "Nah. Gotta pick my dad up from the airport in a couple hours. I'll stick to sweet tea for now."

She linked her fingers through Porter's as they headed toward the huge grill. Two big coolers full of drinks were next to it, and tables of more drinks and food were next to that. No one would leave hungry today, that was for sure. "It's been weird not having your dad around the last couple weeks."

"No kidding."

Keith Caldwell had recently gotten married to Lana Gonzalez—a woman they all loved—and they'd decided to take a two-week honeymoon to the mountains.

"Maddox is missing him something fierce," Lizzy murmured.

As if he'd realized he was being talked about, her son locked eyes with her, grinned widely, and raced as fast as his little legs would let him go to her. He didn't care who was in his way either, but thankfully everyone made a path for him.

She scooped him up and kissed his cheeks before lifting his shirt and kissing his tummy, making him belly-laugh. He patted her face. "Mama, mama, mama!"

His favorite word for right now. And she would definitely take it. Her own family was cold, so she'd been determined to raise her son differently than she'd been. Surrounded by love, and people who genuinely cherished and cared about them.

She'd sure found that with Porter and his family. And the family they'd created for themselves in the last three years. Blood didn't make someone family, as far as she was concerned.

When Porter wrapped his arms around her and Maddox, pulling them close, she savored the moment. Their little family of three was soon going to be four. She couldn't wait for what the future held.

Thank you for reading the Red Stone Security Series Box Set: Volume 5. I hope you enjoyed it! If you'd like to stay in touch with me and be the first to learn about new releases you can:

- Sign up for my monthly newsletter at: www.katiereus.com
- Find me on Facebook: facebook.com/katiereusauthor
- Follow me on Twitter: twitter.com/katiereus
- Follow me on Instagram: instagram.com/katiereusauthor/

Also I hope you'll consider leaving a review at one of your favorite online retailers. It's a great way to help other readers discover new books and I appreciate all reviews.

Dear Readers,

I'm so grateful to all of my readers. And I owe a big thank you to those who have been reading this series from the beginning. If it wasn't for your emails wanting more I might not have gone past book one. I'm so glad I did! This has been such a fun ride and it's hard to believe this is the fifteenth story. Now at the final book, it's a lot more bittersweet saying goodbye to my Red Stone crew than I originally expected. There's always the possibility that one day in the future I'll revisit this world, but for now, it feels done. I'm so happy with the way the series has wrapped up—and I hope you are too. And I really hope you enjoyed the epilogue showing a little glimpse into everyone's lives.

To all my Red Stone readers, thank you for reading this series! Thank you for the reviews you leave, the emails you send and the fun posts on social media I see about this world. You guys are the best and I'm forever grateful for your support.

Best wishes,
Katie

Complete Booklist

Red Stone Security Series

No One to Trust
Danger Next Door
Fatal Deception
Miami, Mistletoe & Murder
His to Protect
Breaking Her Rules
Protecting His Witness
Sinful Seduction
Under His Protection
Deadly Fallout
Sworn to Protect
Secret Obsession
Love Thy Enemy
Dangerous Protector
Lethal Game

The Serafina: Sin City Series

First Surrender
Sensual Surrender
Sweetest Surrender
Dangerous Surrender

Deadly Ops Series

Targeted
Bound to Danger
Chasing Danger (novella)
Shattered Duty
Edge of Danger
A Covert Affair

Non-series Romantic Suspense

Running from the Past

Dangerous Secrets

Killer Secrets

Deadly Obsession

Danger in Paradise

His Secret Past

Retribution

O'Connor Family Series

Merry Christmas, Baby

Tease Me, Baby

It's Me Again, Baby

Mistletoe Me, Baby

Paranormal Romance

Destined Mate

Protector's Mate

A Jaguar's Kiss

Tempting the Jaguar

Enemy Mine

Heart of the Jaguar

Moon Shifter Series

Alpha Instinct

Lover's Instinct (novella)

Primal Possession

Mating Instinct

His Untamed Desire (novella)

Avenger's Heat

Hunter Reborn

Protective Instinct (novella)

Dark Protector

A Mate for Christmas (novella)

Darkness Series

Darkness Awakened

Taste of Darkness

Beyond the Darkness

Hunted by Darkness

Into the Darkness

Saved by Darkness

ABOUT THE AUTHOR

Katie Reus is the *New York Times* and *USA Today* bestselling author of the Red Stone Security series, the Darkness series and the Deadly Ops series. She fell in love with romance at a young age thanks to books she pilfered from her mom's stash. Years later she loves reading romance almost as much as she loves writing it.

However, she didn't always know she wanted to be a writer. After changing majors many times, she finally graduated summa cum laude with a degree in psychology. Not long after that she discovered a new love. Writing. She now spends her days writing dark paranormal romance and sexy romantic suspense. For more information on Katie find her on twitter @katiereus or visit her on facebook at: www.facebook.com/katiereusauthor. If you would like to be notified of future releases, please visit her website: www.katiereus.com and join her newsletter.

Made in the USA
Coppell, TX
27 February 2021